PRETENSE

PRETENSE

ELVEN ALLIANCE BOOK FIVE

TARA GRAYCE

Sword & Cross
Publishing

Published by Sword & Cross Publishing

Grand Rapids, MI

Sword & Cross Publishing and the Sword & Cross Publishing logo are trademarks. Absence of ™ in connection with Sword & Cross Publishing does not indicate an absence of trademark protection of those marks.

Cover and Map by Savannah Jezowski of Dragonpen Designs

Dragonpenpress.com

To God, my King and Father. Soli Deo Gloria

LCCN: 2021923412

ISBN: 978-1-943442-26-3

THE WORLD OF
ELVEN ALLIANCE

CHAPTER
ONE

Her elf looked particularly adorable when doing homework.

Essie leaned against the doorframe of Farrendel's new workshop, which his siblings Weylind and Jalissa had grown for him on the forest floor beneath the lift for his birthday a month ago.

Farrendel sat cross-legged on top of the wide workbench that filled the whole back wall. Papers and books spread in neat rows around him, a pen resting neatly next to the nearest stack.

Cabinets filled the wall to Essie's right while, on the left, pegs held gears and tools above the small table with two chairs that stood along the wall. Essie's breakfast waited for her on the table underneath a glass dish, filling the air with the faint scent of bacon and eggs, courtesy of Miss Merrick, their cook and housekeeper. She and her brother had a newly grown cottage set between Farrendel's workshop and Estyra, where Captain Merrick could guard Farrendel while they were here in Estyra.

Essie crossed the space and leaned against the work-bench. "Good morning."

"Morning." Farrendel leaned forward just enough to give her a quick, distracted kiss, his focus never leaving the book spread open before him.

Essie laughed under her breath. Whatever he was reading must be terribly fascinating. She leaned a hand on his knee. "Do you call that a good morning kiss?"

That had him setting aside his book. His mouth tipped in a mischievous smile—the glint in his silver-blue eyes her only warning—before he gripped her waist and pulled her onto his lap.

She couldn't help a shriek that quickly turned into giggling that she couldn't seem to stop, even as he kissed her. Giggling and kissing at the same time wasn't ideal, but she managed.

Farrendel eased back, murmuring as he brushed another kiss across her cheek, "How is that for a good morning kiss?"

Essie leaned into him, still trying to catch her breath and think through the hazy whirl in her head. "I'm going to blush like a tomato the moment your grandmother gives me one of her *looks* when I arrive for tea. And then she's going to tease me about great-grandchildren, and I'm going to blush even *more*."

Farrendel pulled back even more, his gaze searching her face. "Machasheni will stop, if her teasing bothers you."

Now that she thought about it, Leyleira didn't tease Rheva about more great-grandchildren, nor did she tease Jalissa about finding a husband.

"I don't mind." It was Leyleira's way of saying that she shared their hopes and dreams for the future, even if she didn't come right out and say it. Essie trailed her fingers through Farrendel's hair. While it wasn't as long as it had been when she married him, it was nearly there, falling well past his shoulders now. "What are your plans for today?"

"I have magic practice with Weylind and Ryfon while you are at tea." Farrendel gestured at the papers and books spread across the workbench, keeping his other hand on her waist. "And then I am getting my research organized. After the ball, I will have three full days where I can hide here and see no one."

He sounded like he relished the thought of spending so many days alone. As if three days of doing nothing but homework was enjoyable.

It probably was enjoyable for him, compared to spending a single evening at a ball interacting with the elven court.

"No one? Not even me?" Essie tipped her head up to better give him a fake glare.

"Of course I will see you. You do not count as people." He grinned and pressed a light kiss to her temple.

"That would sound insulting if I didn't know it's a compliment coming from you." Essie grinned back. "I, for one, am looking forward to this ball. I can't wait to wear my new dress. It turned out so well with its mix of human and elven design, and I'm so glad the older style of corset is coming back into style. It is actually comfortable and practical, not the torture devices fashion was turning them into. Seriously, fashion should not be more of a concern than the comfort and needs of the person actually wearing the garment."

Essie paused to take a breath, and only then did she notice the tilt to Farrendel's smile. "Right. You've heard my tirade on the evils of modern corsets compared to the apparently far more comfortable ones that were worn in times past."

"I would worry far more if you stopped rambling about random topics."

"Admit it. Nowadays, you ramble about random topics just as often as I do." Essie eyed him, trying to suppress her grin.

"True." Farrendel's gaze flicked back to his book, his mouth pressing into a line as if he was trying hard not to launch into a long spiel about what he had been reading.

From Farrendel, there was no such thing as too much talking. She would willingly listen to whatever technical topic he wanted to wax eloquent about since it would mean she would see his eyes light up and hear his excitement come through his voice in a way she'd never seen and heard when she'd first married him.

She tapped the book he'd been reading earlier. It still rested on the workbench next to the two of them, open to his spot. "What are you researching now?"

The poor professors at Hanford University had no idea what they were getting themselves into when they offered to provide a few correspondence courses for Farrendel for the rest of the winter. They hadn't accounted for an elf who not only had too much time on his hands now that the wars were over but also would rather spend his time doing home-work than socializing with people.

"Theories of magical inheritance." Farrendel reached around her to pick up the book and set it on her knees. "I am writing a paper applying human theories on how magic is inherited to elven magic and how the lack of intermarriage between social classes and between elves, humans, and trolls may have caused magic like mine to become rare."

"Marriage to a human. Oh the horror." Essie found herself watching Farrendel's expressions, far more animated than he had been nearly a year ago when she married him. "Anything interesting?"

He released a long sigh that brushed against her hair. "It just confirms what I always suspected. If I had shared a mother as well as a father with my siblings, then I would have had dark hair, dark eyes, and either healing or plant magic. I am *me* only because I am illegitimate. While magical inheritance is not as straightforward or logical as human magicians attempt to make it, it means I could not have inherited healing or growing magic from either of my parents. And thus, whatever magic our children have, they will not have either healing or growing magic."

"We already suspected that they would most likely inherit your powerful magic." Essie rested a hand on his cheek. As Farrendel had explained in a previous ramble, magic was dominant over no magic. Their children would inherit magic, even though Essie had none of her own. "Your magic is nothing to be ashamed of. I'll be proud to see our children inherit it."

Farrendel's mouth pressed into a thin line as he reached for a stack of paperwork held together in a dark paper file folder. He rested it on top of the book on Essie's lap, though he didn't open the file. "It also means there is a possibility they might not inherit my magic as I have it. Your lack of magic might bring out whatever rare magic I inherited from my mother. Or the combination might present as a unique form of magic. No matter how much I research, there is no scientific way to know for sure."

"Surprises aren't something to be feared." Essie shook her head, gently tipping his face so that he was looking at her. "We will celebrate whatever magic our children have, and they will be taught not to fear it but to love it."

"I know." Farrendel's arm tightened around her waist while he took her hand in his. "And I know I should not worry. I just…"

"You just want to prepare. It gives you a sense of control." Essie squeezed his fingers. With his anxiety, surprises were difficult for Farrendel. And children were the ultimate, uncontrollable surprises. They could not predict what hair color their child would have or what magic he or she would inherit. Not that they were even expecting at this point. But Farrendel's need to be ultra-prepared for everything drove him to research the magical possibilities.

"Yes." He released her hand to fan the pages of the file resting on her lap. "Weylind finally relented and gave me this."

Farrendel's tone was so serious that Essie's stomach dropped. "What is it?"

"All the information my father gathered about my mother." Farrendel reached for another file and added it to the stack on Essie's lap. This file was only marginally thinner than the other one. "And this is everything that your Escarlish Intelligence Office had on my mother."

Essie raised her eyebrows. She hadn't realized Farrendel's mother had garnered such interest from Escarland. Then again, it would only make sense the Intelligence Office would want to learn everything they could about Farrendel, the elves' greatest warrior, including the secrets surrounding his mother.

Not to mention, Farrendel's mother had been killed while trying to blackmail an Escarlish lord who lived just across the border. That would also bring her to the attention of the

Escarlish Intelligence Office, fledgling as it had been a hundred years ago.

"My counselor thought we should talk about *her* in our next session. If I am ready." Farrendel still stared at the two files, his fingers trailing over the edges. "I have not dared to open the files yet. Would you read them?"

There was such pain in his voice. Such fear. This was a part of his past he was still trying to process, though his counselors were encouraging him in that. "Are you sure?"

He gave a small nod, though he didn't look sure.

"Maybe we can read the files together. When you're ready." She kissed his cheek and held him close again. His illegitimate birth was at the heart of who he had become. It was the beginning of his pain and trauma, even if the trolls had caused more later. And it was the source of the tension in his family that was still slowly healing.

"I am not sure I will ever be ready." He buried his face against the crook of her neck and shoulder. His muscles stiffened as he held her. "I know I am supposed to hate her, but—"

Essie pulled away from him as much as she could while sitting on his lap. She cradled his face, searching his eyes. "No. You don't have to hate her. What makes you think that?"

Even though she held his face, his gaze dropped from hers. "My family..."

"Your family is still wrapped up in their own hurt over everything that happened." Essie traced a thumb over the scar on Farrendel's cheek. The one he'd gotten when he was a mere fifteen years old and he'd been bullied for being illegitimate. "It's easier for them to blame your mother than your father."

His gaze didn't lift to hers, but he did place one of his hands over hers on his cheek, leaning into her touch. "My father never blamed her." A wrinkle creased his forehead, as if he was remembering a day long ago. "We rarely talked about her, but I overheard him talking with Weylind once. Dacha said the blame was his. That he was the one who had known better. And that he wished he could have saved her."

"I wish he could have, for your sake." Essie let one of her hands fall to his chest, wrapping her fingers in the warmth of his tunic.

Farrendel's sigh was warm against her wrist. "I do not think even the elf king could have saved her. He gave her enough money to comfortably start a new life, and yet she was still killed while blackmailing an Escarlish lord."

"It's all right to have empathy for her, even if you don't agree with her choices in life." Essie's chest hurt, seeing him in such pain over this.

Farrendel gave a nod against her hand.

Essie withdrew her hand from his cheek to hold his hand instead. "I know it will be hard, but I think it will be good for you to read through these files and figure out for yourself how you feel about your mother."

He drew in a deep breath and let it out with a shudder. "I need to face this. Before I have children of my own, I need to lay my past to rest, if just in my own mind."

"I know." Essie wrapped her arms around him. "And I'll be here every step of the way. You won't have to face this alone."

"Linshi." Farrendel pressed his face into her hair as he seemed to gather himself. Then, he kissed her and drew back, his expression and gaze lighter than it had been a moment ago. "Your breakfast is getting cold. You will be late if you do not eat it soon."

"Your legs are going to sleep, aren't they?" Essie was still sitting in his lap after all. Comfortable enough for her. Probably less so for him.

"Yes." His hands tightened on her waist.

"It's your own fault. You're the one who pulled me onto your lap in the first place." Essie divested herself of the book and stacks of files he'd piled on her and hopped to the floor. "You only have yourself to blame if Ryfon and Weylind defeat you during your practice because your feet are still numb."

Farrendel stretched out his legs, swinging them as if trying to get feeling back in his toes. "I can still defeat both of them even without my feet."

"Don't let Weylind hear you say that, or he will challenge you to try it." Essie crossed the workshop and lifted the lid to her plate of breakfast. She picked up one of the pieces of bacon. It wasn't hot, but it was still warm enough to be edible. As she nibbled, she reached for the fork, pausing when she noticed only a single piece of bacon was left on her plate. "Farrendel, my love, why do I only have two pieces of bacon? I know Miss Merrick always gives us three."

Farrendel gave her that mischievous smile again. "It was getting cold and needed to be eaten."

Essie gave him another fake glare. "It's a good thing you're handsome."

Farrendel's smile turned into a full-blown grin.

With him grinning, Essie couldn't even pretend to be mad.

9

FARRENDEL CROUCHED ON A WIDE BRANCH, a sword in each hand. He stretched his senses, searching for the first sign of attack. The quiet, thick forest of Tarenhiel spread around him, vibrant green with the new spring leaves.

A branch darted out of the thick greenery, headed straight at Farrendel's face.

Farrendel swept it aside with his sword and sliced through it with his magic.

With a burst of magic, a wall of twigs and leaves rushed at him, as if trying to overwhelm him with sheer volume of magic and wood.

Farrendel blasted aside the oncoming magic, incinerating the leaves and twigs. He let his magic crackle out farther, eating the branches and plant growing magic nearly to its source.

Somewhere in another tree, his nephew Ryfon shouted, and a clumsy attempt at a shield shivered against Farrendel's magic.

Farrendel held his magic steady, holding Ryfon at a distance to concentrate on searching for Weylind. Ryfon wielded his magic with clumsy force—much the way Farrendel had before he had gained more control. He was easy to find and counter.

Weylind, however, had more finesse and experience. Fighting him was a lot harder, especially when everything, including the branch Farrendel crouched on, could be a weapon in Weylind's hands.

Ryfon tried another wave of magic against Farrendel's wall of crackling magic. Farrendel did not even have to do anything besides let Ryfon's plants wither to dust.

A slither of Weylind's magic was all the warning Farrendel had before a branch whipped around his ankle and yanked him off his feet. In a heartbeat, Farrendel found himself hanging upside down far above the forest floor.

He could not cut the branch holding his ankle, or he would fall. He twisted, trying to see if there was somewhere he could catch himself.

As he did, another branch whipped at him. Farrendel parried it before it could pin his arms to his sides.

Before he could recover, a tornado of leaves and twigs and branches whirled up at him from below, trying to engulf him before he had a chance to fight back.

Enough of this. Farrendel blasted his magic in all directions, consuming the whirl of Weylind's magic and slicing through the branch holding his ankle.

As he fell, he flipped so that he fell feet first. Catching a slim branch, he used it to swing over to a larger branch, landing lightly in a crouch.

Then Weylind was there, a whirl of flashing steel and magic. Weylind's one sword was longer than Farrendel's two smaller ones, and Farrendel had to leap back to avoid Weylind's longer reach.

As he parried Weylind's strike, he sensed Ryfon's magical attack from behind him. Farrendel flung a wall of crackling magic to protect his back, then swept the magic forward to blast away Weylind's lashing branches.

Weylind spun and launched himself into the air, his sword whipping toward Farrendel.

Farrendel parried and flipped to the next branch over to give himself more space. He kept the wall of magic in place, holding Ryfon back.

As Weylind came in for another attack, Farrendel could feel Ryfon's magic building and growing behind him, until the trees were shuddering with the force of Ryfon's magic bursting from him.

"Dacha!" Ryfon's shout shook with fear, coming from a whirl of his own magic.

Farrendel recognized that fear. He had felt it many times himself when he had lost control.

Weylind immediately halted, sheathed his sword, and hurried toward Ryfon, disappearing into the whirl of Ryfon's green magic.

Farrendel expanded his magic so that he kept Ryfon's power contained, preventing it from exploding into more of the forest. This was not the first time Ryfon had lost control during one of their practices, and it was strangely comforting to see someone else other than himself struggle with magic.

It was a reminder that struggling with control was normal. Farrendel had simply been young and unpracticed, as Ryfon was now. As Farrendel still was, though his increased practice, experience, and faster aging due to the heart bond were helping.

"Take a deep breath, sason." Weylind's calm voice came from within the tangle of Ryfon's out-of-control power. As Weylind spoke, his stronger magic swirled over Ryfon's, easing it under control and guiding Ryfon through controlling it at the same time.

It was training for Ryfon, and yet it was training for Farrendel too. This was a glimpse of what training between a father and son could look like when they shared the same magic.

Farrendel's training had not been like this. His father had tried, but he had never been able to step in close and guide Farrendel's magic with his own.

No, Farrendel's father had stood off to the side, straining until sweat poured down his face and he had nearly exhausted his own reserves as he attempted to prevent Farrendel's overwhelming power from destroying an entire swathe of Tarenhiel's forests—and whoever happened to be standing nearby. Any instructions were shouted over the roar of Farrendel's magic unleashed.

It had been terrifying. Nothing like the calm instruction Weylind could give Ryfon. Even now, Farrendel shuddered to think how many times he must have come close to killing his own father.

Dacha had done his best. There had simply been no one who shared Farrendel's magic and could train him any better than what Dacha had done.

But Farrendel's children would have a different experience. They would have a dacha who could guide them as Weylind did his son.

Farrendel kept his shield of magic steady, though it was unnecessary now as Ryfon regained control and worked through the basic, magical exercises to calm him with the routine and rhythm.

These were the moments when Farrendel could picture himself as a father. He struggled to dream for the future the way Essie did. But when he watched Weylind with Ryfon, he caught a glimpse of what it could be like for him with a future son or daughter.

And he wanted it. Longed for it in a way he had not realized he could desire something that also terrified him to the core.

Not that he had to worry about it for a long, long time. Depending on how long a life his children experienced, it would take them fifty to eighty years to come into their magic. Farrendel would not have to worry about training until he was a hundred and fifty to two hundred, even if he and Essie had a child in the next year or two. Surely by the time he was two hundred, he would feel mature and ready.

"I think that is enough for today." Weylind released his magic, a hint of a smile brightening his usual dour expression.

Ryfon cut off his magic and slumped to the branch. "Good. Is it Uncle Farrendel's turn now? That is always my favorite part."

Weylind turned to Farrendel, eyebrows raised and that smile widening. "Yes, it is."

Farrendel let his shield fizzle out, bracing himself. "I never should have told you about the suggestions for practice that the human professors gave me."

Weylind made a *please proceed* wave of his hand.

Farrendel sighed and strode along the branch until he stood near Weylind and Ryfon. They would be safest if they were right next to him.

Ryfon lounged on the branch, bracing himself with his hands behind him and his legs dangling over the side of the branch. He swung his feet, grinning as if he was waiting for his favorite entertainment to begin.

Farrendel knelt and pressed his hand to the branch. With a deep breath, he unleashed his magic, letting it flow from him in a crackling wave, engulfing the branch, then the tree, then each individual branch and leaf. His power outlined each branch, each twig, each leaf like a blue, sparking layer of frost, yet without incinerating even a single leaf. Only the small section of branch around Weylind, Ryfon, and Farrendel remained free of his magic while the rest of the massive oak was limned with power.

It took concentration, letting his magic run wild and yet keep it from destroying anything. But the exercise in control pushed him to extend his limits beyond what he had thought possible.

Squeezing his eyes shut, Farrendel pushed his magic farther and farther until the entire swathe of forest glowed with his magic. Only when he had a mile of forest in all directions coated in power did he feel the strain of holding so much magic in tight, precise control.

Yet, a few months ago when he had started doing this, he had struggled to even coat the first tree without incinerating something.

"Well done." Weylind's voice remained low, as if he did not want to startle Farrendel. "Now me and my sword."

Farrendel kept his magic in place as he opened his eyes and glanced at his brother. "Shashon, I do not think that is a good idea."

He had practiced this with Essie, but Essie was immune to his magic. Weylind was another story. It was one thing to use his magic on weapons to force opponents to drop them. It was another to safely cover a weapon in the hands of family.

"We live in a changing world, shashon. Our bows, our swords, and our style of fighting cannot compete against the humans' guns." Weylind's expression tightened. "We must change. Your magic can provide a shield against bullets, but our warriors are vulnerable once they step past your shield to fight hand-to-hand. If you could, instead, provide protection for each warrior in the army, they could be shielded all the way to the enemy."

Farrendel could not argue with that logic. Before, he had

attacked sections of the enemy army on his own. He had not dared use his magic around his own army.

But if he could extend his magic so that he could fight alongside others? It would make both him and the entire elven army that much more powerful.

He just had to master wielding that much magic with finesse, not just brute force.

Weylind was still giving him a stern look, waiting and not backing down.

Farrendel pulled back his magic so that he only flooded the forest immediately around their tree. He drew his magic up and, after a pause to make sure he was entirely in control, Farrendel let his magic flow up and over Weylind.

Weylind drew his sword again and lunged into a sword strike at the air, then flipped forward.

Farrendel kept his magic wrapped around Weylind, following his movements.

Ryfon's grin grew, as if he was not afraid in the least that his uncle would accidentally incinerate his father.

After a few more flips, Weylind landed in a crouch.

Farrendel let his magic finally dissipate.

Ryfon let out a cheer, pumping his fist in a way that was almost human in its exuberance. Even Weylind grinned as he sheathed his sword.

A year ago, Farrendel had been so withdrawn from his family. He had been so empty that he had nothing to give. But in his hollowness, he had not realized what he had been missing.

He was functioning again, and that meant he had his family back and they had him back. And he was going to try to never take that for granted.

CHAPTER
TWO

Jalissa, princess of the elves, hurried around a curving end of one of the bookshelves in Ellonahshinel's library, hoping to disappear into her favorite corner before anyone noticed where she had gone. She needed some peace and solace with her favorite book to relieve the endless worry while both of her brothers were gone fighting at the border.

As she darted into another aisle, she nearly smacked into a male elf, dressed in the plain, light green tunic and trousers of a servant. She skidded to a halt, the book falling from her hands.

He knelt, picking up the book she had dropped. For a moment, he stilled, as if reading the cover.

Jalissa stiffened, catching her breath. It was not a good look for an elven princess to be caught reading about the Kingsley Gardens in the Escarlish capital city of Aldon at a time when Tarenhiel was nearly at war with Escarland.

But, after a moment, the servant held the book out to her,

his shoulders hunched and his eyes down. "My apologies, amirah."

"No, the fault is mine." Jalissa did not recognize the elf before her. His long blond hair was darker and more golden than her brother Farrendel's while he stood only an inch or two taller than Jalissa. She could not see the color of his eyes with the way he was subserviently staring at the floor.

"Amirah." The servant bowed one more time to her before he hurried away.

J alissa sipped her blueberry fruit punch as she watched the graceful dancing couples whirl past. The great hall of the treetop palace of Ellonahshinel glowed with golden lights tucked into the twining branches arching over the room. New spring leaves sparkled in the glittering lights, though the nobility of the court outshone it all, dressed in flowing dresses and silken tunics and trousers.

Across the room, Farrendel spun Essie through the steps of the dance, somehow keeping his back to the wall in the corner as he did so. Essie was beaming, her long red hair falling down her back. The strands gleamed against the deep, emerald green of her dress, which had a bodice that was cut in the tight and structured human style, yet paired with a flowing, elven-style skirt. It looked stunning on her, and judging by the way Farrendel could not seem to look away, he had noticed.

Farrendel was even smiling, and Jalissa could not remember the last time she had seen Farrendel smile while attending a court event.

An ache stabbed deep into Jalissa's chest. Yes, she was

thankful to see her brother happy and in love. But right now, it reminded her how lonely her life had become.

She turned her gaze away from Farrendel and Essie to contemplate the dancing couples once again, quickly spotting the young male elves in the court. All winter, Jalissa had been dithering, not picking any of them to attempt a courtship.

She could not keep hesitating. She just needed to pick one. It did not matter which, as long as he was an elf and he was noble. If love was a choice, as her Machasheni Leyleira said, then surely Jalissa just had to pick someone and choose to fall in love with him, and that would be that.

Then why did she feel ready to throw up her punch at the thought of doing that?

It could not be because she had fallen in love with a certain human prince. They had only known each other a little over three weeks. They had been an intense three weeks, from the treaty negotiations in Escarland to Farrendel's capture and the fight across Kostaria.

During those weeks, Jalissa had found herself leaning on Prince Edmund of Escarland. But surely it was nothing more than that. A bonding over a shared, traumatic experience that had brought their two families together.

Jalissa handed her glass of punch to a servant, her stomach roiling too much to take another sip. If the feelings she felt when around Prince Edmund were merely fleeting emotions, then why did her heart ache even five months later?

But it seemed Jalissa was always falling in love with unsuitable options. Her first love, too, had been unsuitable. Elidyr had been a mere servant, working odd jobs around Ellonahshinel.

Now, the court probably would have approved of him, even if he was a lower class. At least he had been an elf, unlike Prince Edmund of Escarland.

Too bad Elidyr had been killed in the war. A war he had only joined as a way to get as far away from her as possible after he had broken her heart.

The dance ended with a final, graceful flourish by the dancing couples.

Jalissa sighed and took a step toward Lord Merellien Halmar, the top candidate on her list of potential suitors. All winter, she had made a point to dance with him at every function and spend time with him when she could.

As was their usual, she would greet them and make it clear she was expecting him to ask for the next dance. Unless he had a prior commitment, he would not turn her away. She was a princess, after all. The only unmarried princess left except for Brina, who was still too young to attend court functions yet.

Still, he never sought her out to ask for a dance. And she had yet to develop more than a detached regard for him.

But more feelings would come, surely. It just took time.

This time—this time for sure—she was going to ask Merellien to walk with her onto the balcony overlooking Estyra. There, she would ask to court him. As a princess, it was her right to make the first move, though he would be free to refuse her. Tonight she would stop being a coward and putting it off.

Before Jalissa could take more than that single step, Essie and Farrendel strode up to her.

"Jalissa, glad we caught you." Essie all but dragged Farrendel the last few steps forward. Though, he kept up with her so well that only someone who knew them well would be able to tell. Despite her exuberance, Essie kept her voice low so that only Jalissa would be able to hear. "Machasheni got caught in a discussion with some of the court members and won't be able to make the next dance with Farrendel. Are you free? I promised Rheva that I'd help her next, otherwise I'd stay with Farrendel."

Farrendel gave a small huff. "I do not need to be passed around like something fragile. I survived these court events before you started organizing them."

"The fact that you call it survival should tell you all you need to know." Essie stepped closer, her teasing smile fading after a moment as she held Farrendel's gaze, a silent communication passing between them. "Admit it. It's much more fun now."

"Yes." His smile widened as he shared another look with Essie. After a moment, he turned to Jalissa. "I would like to dance with you, isciena. If you have no prior engagements."

Jalissa glanced at Merellien, but he already held the hand of another female of the court. She had missed her chance. She probably could track down one of the other ones from her list but putting it off and dancing with Farrendel sounded like the better option. "I have no objections."

As Weylind and Rheva strolled up to them, Essie let go of Farrendel's hand to join Rheva. "Who should we attack next? I noticed that group over there has been particularly stuffy."

Essie did not point—she was still a princess, after all—but she tilted her head in the direction of a group of the more mature ladies of the court. The ones who managed to look haughty and sneering even without letting so much as a wrinkle mar their perfect faces.

Rheva's expression tightened, but she nodded. "Yes, they

are particularly disdainful of humans and of Weylind's choice to make such a close treaty with Escarland."

"Perfect. Let's go inflict my presence on them." Essie set off in that direction, her green skirt swishing around her gracefully, even if her movements were brisker than the way an elf noblewoman would walk.

Still looking mildly terrified beneath her serene mask, Rheva fell into step with Essie.

"Isciena?"

Jalissa shook herself and discovered that Weylind had disappeared into the swirl of people, leaving only Farrendel standing there. He held a hand out to her. "Are you all right?"

"I am fine." Jalissa took his hand and let him sweep her into the languid pattern of the traditional dance.

When was the last time she had danced with him? Farrendel usually avoided these events. Or bolted from them as soon as he possibly could. He had not even danced at the ball to celebrate his wedding.

After he maneuvered them so that they were in a corner with his back to the wall, Farrendel speared her with a searching look. "You are not fine. You have not been yourself for months now."

Jalissa resisted the urge to flee. For months, she had evaded their probing questions and well-meaning inquiries. She could not admit the problem, especially not to Farrendel or Essie. Edmund was Essie's brother, after all. If anything, Essie would feel hurt on her brother's behalf.

Besides, it was not only Jalissa's brief but doomed attraction to Edmund. It was the pressure of having to choose an elf from the court. Her unresolved anger toward Melantha for her betrayal of Farrendel and, by betraying him, hurting their whole family. The loneliness of being the last of her siblings to still be unmarried.

"It is nothing." Jalissa could not hold Farrendel's gaze. If she did, he might see the truth of how miserable she was.

"Isciena…" Farrendel's voice grew even softer. "There is no shame in talking with someone. You saw battle for the first time while fighting your way across Kostaria. You are not weak if you are struggling with that."

Jalissa had to work to keep her movements fluid instead of stiffening up. Of course Farrendel would assume that was her struggle.

Perhaps that was part of it. While she had not fought at the front line, she had seen the gore and blood of the aftermath of battle each day. She and Essie had been caught and nearly killed in a sneak attack one of the nights.

While Essie had been a rock facing all of it—too determined to rescue Farrendel to let herself be shaken by the things she witnessed—Jalissa had needed to lean on someone who made her feel protected and safe.

That person had been Edmund.

Farrendel still studied her, his expression turning even more concerned as if her lack of an answer had confirmed his suspicions.

Jalissa cleared her throat. She had to give him something. He was her brother, and he was truly worried for her. "It is not just the battles. It is…everything."

Farrendel's gaze finally swung away from her as he gave a slight nod. "I understand."

Jalissa swallowed a lump forming in her throat. Melantha's betrayal still hurt so deeply. Perhaps the last few months would have been better, if Jalissa could turn to her older sister for wisdom and support.

But maybe not. Melantha had been prejudiced against humans. She likely would have been haughty about Jalissa's attraction to a human prince. After all, she had been the one who had initially warned Jalissa to choose someone from the elven nobility, even if Melantha had later tried to foist some nonsense about falling in love on Jalissa instead.

As if Melantha had forgotten all about the pressure placed on a princess of the elves. Her family needed her to marry well and, most of all, marry without any whiff of scandal or controversy.

Surely she could do that. Out of all of her family, Jalissa was merely average. Her plant-growing magic was neither remarkably strong like Weylind's, nor was it scandalously weak for a member of the royal family. She was calm, serene, and graceful by nature, not given to the roil of emotions the way Melantha was. Conforming to elven society had never been much of a problem.

Except, it seemed, when it came to falling in love.

But Jalissa was done talking about herself. With a nod, she drew Farrendel's attention toward where Essie and Rheva were still talking with the group of stuffy noble ladies. The elven women were leaning back, as if they desperately wanted to escape. If this conversation was running true to form, then the elven noblewomen had tried to insult Essie, but soon discovered that Essie was so friendly that they could not manage to snub her no matter how hard they tried. "It is a pleasure to watch her flummox the court so completely."

"It helps, knowing that if I panic or need to leave, she will feel it through the heart bond." Farrendel's smile remained, though his silver-blue eyes turned more serious. "I protect her in many places, but here, she protects me."

And now that lump was back in her throat. As if Jalissa needed another reason to feel that lonely pang deep in her chest. She wanted that for herself so desperately.

But she forced herself to smile anyway and curtsy as the dance ended.

Before Jalissa had a chance to return to her husband hunting endeavor, Weylind strolled up to them with Machasheni Leyleira on his arm.

Machasheni nodded at Jalissa. "Thank you for looking after him, senasheni. But I believe it is my turn to claim him. Come, sasonsheni."

Farrendel's eyes widened, and he looked somewhat terrified as Machasheni whisked him away.

Weylind turned to Jalissa. "I believe this is my turn."

Were her brothers conspiring to keep her from throwing herself at the young noblemen of the court?

Jalissa let herself get detoured once more. She had been putting off picking a young nobleman to court for the past five months. Delaying for another dance, another night, would not make much of a difference.

As the new dance began, Weylind made a deep throat-clearing noise in the back of his throat. "Isciena…"

Jalissa gritted her teeth. "Not you too."

Weylind twirled her through the next few steps before he spoke again. "We are all concerned. You have been unhappy. Do not deny it."

Jalissa sighed and pretended to be engrossed in the flourishes of the next few dance steps. When she gathered her courage, she flicked a glance at Weylind's face, his forehead furrowed. "There is nothing you can do, shashon. I will be fine eventually."

"Are you sure?" Weylind paused. "And if you should wish to court your human prince?"

Jalissa staggered, coming close to stepping on Weylind's foot. "Pardon?"

"I have eyes, isciena." Weylind raised one eyebrow, giving her a look that had her squirming.

Jalissa could not meet Weylind's gaze and instead stared at the gold trimming on his tunic. "You know why I cannot. The court—"

"I can handle the court, contrary to what Melantha might have erroneously told you." Weylind's tone took on a huffy note. "Ryfon will make his entrance into court life this year, and their attention will shift to him. He is my heir. His eventual marriage will matter much more than yours, and the court will quickly realize that."

A sour taste filled Jalissa's mouth. "So the pressure to marry well shifts from me to Ryfon. If I marry a human, it will only place more of a burden on him."

How could she justify doing that to her nephew? He was a mere ninety years old. Far too young to carry the weight of the kingdom's expectations.

"He has more than enough time to find someone he loves. He will not have to marry young unless he wishes to do so." Weylind gave a slight shrug. "I believe our kingdom will change a great deal in the next few decades. By the time Ryfon needs to marry, he will not be as pressured to marry among the court—or even marry an elf—as you feel now."

Perhaps Weylind was correct. But that did not solve Jalissa's problem right now. It was one thing to accidentally cause a scandal. But she did not have the courage to purposely set out to do something that would put her under such scrutiny.

"Prince Edmund was merely a...momentary attraction caused by the trauma of those weeks." Jalissa's stomach churned, her face growing hot. That was not a lie. He had not been a fling, exactly. But he had been a weakness. Surely if she could choose to fall in love, then she could choose to fall out of love as well. "I will find someone else. An elf. It will merely take some time."

"Then do not rush, isciena. You do not have to marry now or marry at all."

Jalissa grimaced at the thought of never marrying. Perhaps it was her desperation and loneliness talking, but the thought of being alone forever terrified her. It was a valid choice to remain unmarried, but it was not one she would willingly choose for herself.

Besides, her options were limited and would only become more so if she waited. No, better to pick her husband now from among the elf nobility before all the good ones were taken.

The furrows in Weylind's forehead eased, his expression softer than she was used to seeing from her constantly grumpy older brother. "I know you, isciena. Arranged marriages worked for Farrendel and Melantha. Farrendel, after all, was not going to open himself to love until after he was stuck and forced to do so. The same for Melantha. But you want the whole experience of a courtship and a proper proposal and everything that Farrendel and Melantha skipped."

Brothers could be so annoying when they read her so well. Jalissa sent a glare at Weylind. "I think I preferred you when you were grumpy and harried."

Weylind did not smile as she expected. Instead, he sighed and shook his head, his black hair flowing across his shoulders. "I failed both Melantha and Farrendel. I need to do far better with you."

"Does that mean I shall bear the brunt of your hovering from now on?" Jalissa kept her expression neutral. The last thing she wanted was this overbearing brother turning his full attention on her.

"Only if you need my hovering." A small smile broke across Weylind's face, and Jalissa found herself smiling in return.

Some of the darkness lifted, at least for a moment. She was not sure she dared reach for love. She did not have that much courage.

But, perhaps, she could allow herself a moment to forget about the pressure and dream about a future that was not as lonely and bleak as it seemed.

Edmund crept into the darkened room of Gozat Stronghold where Queen Melantha of the trolls lay sleeping.

He shouldn't approach her. This went against his training and his orders. He was supposed to lurk and watch. Nothing more.

But his feet kept moving forward, steered by that aching part of his heart whispering that Jalissa would want to know her sister was all right.

Jalissa was his weakness yet again. For her, he broke his cover for a second time.

What was a spy supposed to do when he no longer had a job?

Paperwork, apparently.

Prince Edmund of Escarland slumped over his desk deep in the office wing of Winstead Palace. This far away from all the pomp and circumstance, the rooms were filled with basic wooden desks and cabinets of filing drawers. A quiet hum of scratching pencils, shuffling papers, and low voices filled the room designated for use by the Intelligence Office.

A report lay open on the desk in front of him, the words blurring. Reading reports was much less exciting than doing stuff worth reporting.

"Edmund." General Bloam halted in front of Edmund's desk and set down another stack of files. "Have you finished going through the reports from Mongalia—I mean, Mongavaria? Still getting used to their new name."

As were they all.

Edmund blinked up at the general, resisting the urge to sigh. "I'm partially through them. There's something odd, but I can't put my finger on it yet."

General Bloam grimaced. "No kingdom lets themselves be taken over as peacefully as Nevaria has. I don't care that Mongalia agreed to change the name to reflect combining the kingdoms. I don't care that a marriage alliance makes the Mongalian princess the sole remaining heir for Nevaria. Something is up. But no one can quite figure out how they are doing it."

What had once been Mongalia was now expanding to take over the kingdom of Nevaria. The Nevarian king's wife and only child had been killed in an accident nearly a year ago, and a few months ago he had died in his sleep, still a relatively young man. His only sibling had been a sister, who had married the Mongalian crown prince. She was now dead, and her widower was the fifty-year-old prince who had wanted to marry Essie, even though Essie was nearly the same age as his daughter.

30

That daughter, thanks to her mother, was now the heir to the crowns of both Mongalia and Nevaria. Instead of waiting to combine later, the two kingdoms had made the decision it was better to combine now.

Or, at least, that was what the propaganda put out by the Mongalian king was claiming. And, from all reports being sent by Escarland's spies, the process had been a peaceful one. Suspiciously peaceful.

Edmund had to bite his tongue before he asked, yet again, for reassignment to Mongavaria.

General Bloam would only give Edmund the same answer he'd received the past three times he'd asked. The Intelligence Office had decided it was no longer necessary to risk Edmund's life. His gift for elvish made him invaluable for spying on Tarenhiel, but Mongalia—well, Mongavaria— spoke the same language as Escarland, just with a different dialect. Edmund's language skills were not so unique that the Intelligence Office would risk him again.

Besides, the spies stationed in Mongavaria were functioning smoothly. Adding a new spy would only upset the balance and risk their already established network, even if that network now had to expand to cover more territory since Escarland hadn't had a spying operation in Nevaria. It didn't share any borders with Escarland and had been deemed too insignificant to waste resources on.

That left Edmund stuck behind this desk. Going through reports rather than out in the field where he belonged.

"Take a break from studying the Mongavarian reports to go over these." General Bloam tapped the new, much smaller pile he'd set on Edmund's desk. "These are from our people in Kostaria and Tarenhiel. I don't believe there will be any concerns, but you're the expert for those kingdoms."

While Escarland no longer had such an active spying effort in either Tarenhiel or Kostaria these days, passive spying continued to be conducted by carefully placed intelligence officers. They traveled with ambassadors or merchants or those merely visiting. It was the same spying that Weylind and Rharreth did in Escarland, even if it was unacknowledged on both sides.

Edmund nodded and tamped down his relief as he shut the Mongavarian file. Both he and General Bloam knew that giving the Mongavarian reports to Edmund was merely busy work. There were other analysts who had been tasked with monitoring Mongavaria, and they had been doing it for years. They would be far more likely to spot something than Edmund would.

Tarenhiel, on the other hand, had been Edmund's kingdom of operations for years. He had been one of only a handful of Escarlish spies who had established a presence in Tarenhiel since the combination of learning elvish to the point of fluency and disguising oneself as an elf was so difficult.

But now, Edmund's cover had been blown in both Kostaria and Tarenhiel. He couldn't go back.

"I'll have them back to you by tomorrow." Edmund added the files to the stack of papers on his desk.

General Bloam gave a last salute and strode away to the next desk.

Edmund gave another sigh, dug his hands in his hair, and stared at the files. He had become a spy because he didn't want to be stuck at a desk doing paperwork.

He cracked open the first file and quickly perused the contents. A report on the current state of affairs in Kostaria. Nothing had changed. The internal strife had calmed, and most trolls had accepted their new king and queen. A month ago, a few who hadn't been happy with having an elf for a queen had tried to cross into Tarenhiel for a raid. Their bodies had been found at the border, killed by the magic Farrendel had embedded into the ground. That had pretty much ended any thoughts of rebellion.

"Prince Edmund?"

Edmund glanced up to find one of the clerks standing there, a piece of paper in hand. "Yes?"

"We received a message for you at the front gate." The clerk held out a piece of paper.

After taking the note, Edmund unfolded it, recognizing the handwriting even before he read the words.

Finally. Something he could do besides sit at a desk.

EDMUND STROLLED through the narrow streets of Aldon near the bank of the Fyne River that cut through a section of Aldon. Warehouses crowded near the docks while factories filled this part of town. Taverns, small shops, and tall tenement housing packed the alleyways. It was considered one of the seedier neighborhoods in Aldon, and Edmund wouldn't recommend that Essie stroll through the streets alone. But many good, hard-working people lived here, scraping by as best they could.

Dressed in ragged trousers and a sweat-stained shirt, Edmund shuffled along with the rest of the people going about their business at the end of the workday. He had a shapeless cap pulled over his hair and dirt smudged on his face to obscure his features.

No one paid him any mind. Why would they, when he blended into the masses?

Not that he was too worried if they did. The daggers and derringer hidden underneath his clothes would provide plenty of protection should he find himself accosted by anyone intent on mugging him.

In the dusky twilight and flickering glow of the occasional lamp that still functioned in this section of town, Edmund stepped into the Black Dog Tavern. The thick scent of beer and tobacco and sweat assaulted his sense of smell. Raucous laughter came from several of the tables in the center where groups of men—and even a few hard-eyed women—gambled and drank. The bar was crowded with those too focused on downing drinks to move to a table.

Edmund took his time ambling across the room until he reached a table in the corner. One chair at the table was already occupied by a brown-haired man wearing attire similar to Edmund's. The beer mug in his hands remained nearly full while his eyes were clear and sharp. He sat with his back to one wall, leaving the chair with its back to the other wall for Edmund.

Edmund sat in the other chair, his boot sliding in something slimy underneath the table. He grimaced and shifted his boot away from the vomit or spit or congealed beer that was coating the floor. "We really need a better meeting spot."

"Come on. Where else can you find such a lovely atmosphere?" Trent Bourdon grinned and gestured toward the rest of the tavern. Trent had gone to Hanford University at the same time as Edmund, and they had bonded over learning elvish. While Edmund wouldn't necessarily call Trent a friend—princes didn't have the luxury of making close friends outside of the family, and spies even less so—

Trent was more than a mere acquaintance. Even though their jobs of prince and newspaper reporter put them at odds, they had built a give-and-take based on their respect for each other.

"I would take less atmosphere if it meant I didn't have to clean my boots every time I left here." Edmund rested his elbows on the table as a barmaid tentatively approached the table. When she held out a mug and a pitcher, he gave a nod.

Neither he nor Trent spoke until the barmaid finished pouring a mug for Edmund and left.

Edmund took a single sip of the beer. It was warm and watery, and the aftertaste held a suspicious tang of sawdust. Even with the slight alcohol content sanitizing whatever water the barkeep had used in the beer, it still wasn't likely to be healthy to drink the whole thing.

He set the mug on the table but kept his hand on it as if he was just another laborer looking to drown away a day of grueling work. "What's going down?"

Trent wouldn't summon Edmund for one of their secret chats if it wasn't important.

With a sigh, Trent swirled his beer in his mug. "Do you remember that story that I agreed to sit on for a while?"

Edmund's stomach clenched. Trent had been one of the reporters allowed to cover the war with Kostaria. He'd spent a great deal of time with the elves, and he'd had enough knowledge of elvish to understand the things being said about Farrendel.

Newspaper reporter that he was, Trent had followed up the lead and soon uncovered the whole story of Farrendel's illegitimate birth. Shortly after Edmund returned from Kostaria, Trent had come to him.

In exchange for keeping the story quiet for a while

longer, Edmund had given Trent details on politics in Kostaria and the Dulraith that had been fought, something that reporters hadn't been privy to. Trent had been able to publish exclusive stories that had done well for the *Aldon Times* while Edmund had bought time for Farrendel and Essie.

He had hoped the story could be buried forever, but his realistic side had known this day was coming. "What about it?"

"I've heard through my contacts that a reporter at the *Escarlish Sentinel* has been sniffing around your brother-in-law's past." Trent's mouth pressed into a tight line.

Edmund gave in to his own scowl. While the newspapers varied in how they presented the royal family, the *Sentinel* had an anti-monarchy bias, reporting stories that verged on tabloid lies even if the paper stayed just enough on the side of truth to avoid libel charges. Back when Essie had first married Farrendel, the *Sentinel* had been one of the papers stirring up mobs of people and encouraging anti-elven sentiments, like those that had led Lord Bletchly and Mark Hadley to betray Farrendel, Essie, and Escarland.

"Do you think their reporter has learned anything?" Edmund tried to keep his tone and posture casual, in case anyone glanced toward their corner.

"I don't know for sure, but they likely have enough to write a story, even if it isn't well-researched or well-written." Trent's expression darkened even more.

And this was why Edmund maintained his friendly acquaintance with Trent. While Trent was a reporter and the two of them didn't always see eye-to-eye, Trent was at least an honest man who held himself to standards.

Trent pushed aside his beer and leaned forward. "Look. I can't sit on this story any longer."

"The anniversary of our peace treaty with Tarenhiel is in three weeks." Not to mention Essie and Farrendel's anniversary. Edmund kept his voice low, though no one was near enough to eavesdrop. He didn't ask outright if Trent could wait until after that, but the implication hung out there.

"I can't wait longer than a week or two. I wish I could, but I can't." Trent heaved a sigh. "If the *Sentinel* breaks this story before the *Times* and my boss learns that I sat on this for months, it would be my job on the line. Nor do you want whatever twisted version of the story that the *Sentinel* puts together to be told first."

No, he didn't. Edmund stared down at his beer for long moments. Essie and Farrendel deserved to celebrate their first anniversary in peace, not spend it dealing with all the mud-slinging and temporary scandal of this revelation.

But it seemed they would have no choice.

Edmund huffed his own sigh. "What do you want in exchange for waiting a week to give the palace time to do damage control?"

A week wasn't long, but it would let them prepare, at least. Hopefully the first heat of the scandal would pass before the treaty celebrations began.

"An exclusive interview with Prince Farrendel and Princess Elspeth." Trent shrugged, a wry tilt to his mouth replacing the scowl. "I'm not asking for much. You're going to want to schedule an interview with at least one of the papers to tell your side of the story. It might as well be me."

Trent was correct, and Edmund likely would have gone to Trent asking for an interview anyway.

"Deal. If you give us a week, then I'll talk my sister and

brother-in-law into giving you an exclusive." Essie would be fine with it, but Farrendel would be harder to convince.

Trent gave a nod in return. "Done. Though, if it looks like the *Sentinel* is going to release the story early, I'm going to have to do so as well."

"Understood. You'll let me know if that looks likely?" Edmund sat back in his chair.

"Of course." Trent picked up his beer, sipped at it, then set it down with a grimace. "Believe me, I don't like this any more than you do. I'm all right with giving your brother grief on his policies, but your sister doesn't deserve the flack that's coming her way, even if she married an elf."

"He's a rather good elf. As you'll find out when you interview him." Edmund swirled his own beer, sloshing some of it over the rim of his mug. Better on the grimy table than in his belly.

A good elf who was going to be in a rather bad place when he had this dumped on his shoulders.

Perhaps sitting at that desk stuck with paperwork was preferable after all.

Essie held Farrendel's hand in the elven style of clasping their first two fingers with the backs of their hands pressed together as they navigated the branches of Ellonahshinel. "What do you think your brother wants?"

"I do not know." Farrendel's shoulders grew more tense with each step they took toward Weylind and Rheva's set of rooms. Most of the royal family—everyone except Farrendel—had rooms on a large branch near the heart of the elven treetop palace. "But he would not have summoned us to come right away if it was something that could wait until the family gathered for dinner tonight."

That was a good point, and it set her own stomach to roiling.

Essie and Farrendel strolled onto the branch with the royal family's rooms, including the sprawling complex of treehouses that were the king's apartments. The main sitting room had a large porch surrounded by columns formed of twining sapling trees grown with swirling designs and edged in gold. The new spring leaves provided a bright green decoration arching around the airy windows.

With a deep breath, Essie climbed onto the porch, then knocked on the door. Farrendel crowded next to her, tension wound so tightly through him that she felt it through the heart bond.

A moment later, the door swung open, revealing Queen Rheva, Weylind's wife. Her long brown hair was down, and her usual soft smile rested on her face, though it didn't reach her eyes. "Elspetha, Farrendel. Please come in."

Essie stepped inside, her smile dying on her face.

Jalissa, Farrendel's sister, sat in the curving, cushioned seating grown into the walls, focused on her hands folded primly in her lap rather than looking at anyone else. Weylind stood near a chair, as if he had paused in pacing.

But what halted Essie in her tracks was the sight of her brothers Averett and Edmund sitting across from Farrendel's family, both wearing grim expressions. Edmund's frown deepened as he sneaked a glance at Jalissa.

"Avie? Edmund? What are you doing here?" Essie gripped Farrendel's arm with her free hand, needing his warmth and strength to steady her.

Her brothers had come here with no warning. That meant whatever they had to say was something that they couldn't send over the telegraph wires.

Weylind gestured at one of the empty cushioned seats. "Please. Have a seat."

Essie forced her legs to move, and she tottered the few steps across the room before she sank onto a couch grown into the wall. Farrendel took the seat next to her, sitting close enough that she could lean into him. She faced Averett. "Mother? Paige? The boys? Julien? Are they all right?"

Averett let out a long breath. "Yes, yes, they're fine."

Essie deflated in relief, letting her forehead drop onto Farrendel's shoulder. "You had me worried."

"Sorry. I should have realized what this looked like." Averett glanced first at Edmund before focusing on Farrendel. "We're here for a public relations matter."

Edmund stared at his hands rather than looking at either Essie or Farrendel. "One of my contacts reported to me that the Escarlish newspapers have gotten wind of the...circumstances surrounding Farrendel's birth."

Essie caught her breath. Underneath her hand, Farrendel went rigid.

Edmund still didn't look at them. "I bought us a week to prepare, but that's it. In a week, the story of Farrendel's illegitimate birth—both the true version and highly lurid versions written to sell the scandal sheets—will be splashed all over Escarland's newspapers."

It wasn't the death of a family member, but it was a death all the same. The death of Farrendel's reputation. The death of the freedom he'd gained from his illegitimacy in Escarland. The death of what little respect he'd earned.

It had been only a matter of time before this story became public. But this was sooner rather than later.

Her stomach sank, and she glanced at Averett. "I guess you know, now. Edmund had to tell you."

Averett rubbed a thumb over his palm. "I've actually known for a while now. Edmund told me even before he mentioned the file to you when you returned to Escarland the first time."

"But you told me you weren't going to tell Avie." Essie glared at Edmund. She frantically searched her memories, but she couldn't think of any time Averett had ever given an indication of knowing the truth in how he treated Farrendel.

"I said I would quietly bury the file. I didn't tell you from whom I was burying it." Edmund shrugged. "I'm sorry I had to leave you with that impression, but keeping secrets like this is my job."

A valid point, even if Essie didn't like it. Of course Edmund would have reported something like this to Averett as soon as he'd learned it.

Next to her, Farrendel hunched, as if curling in on himself in preparation for another blow. Farrendel's family remained quiet and grim, simply listening. This was a scandal they had dealt with for over a hundred years. Absorbing it yet again was nothing new.

"Does the rest of the family know?" Essie could barely whisper the words past her tight throat. What would Mother think? Paige? Julien? Surely none of them would treat Farrendel differently once they knew. They all loved Farrendel as part of the family.

"I took them aside and explained everything once Edmund told me it was going to be outed in the papers." Averett sounded weary, the lines creasing his forehead making him look older than he was.

Farrendel had both arms wrapped tightly around himself, as if he was trying to hold himself together. His breathing was rapid and shallow, the white look to his face telling her just how close he was to full-blown panic.

Essie wrapped an arm around his waist and leaned against him, trying to hold him together with her warmth and presence. "Thank you for that."

"It was a surprise, understandably. But don't worry, Farrendel," Averett paused, waiting until Farrendel stirred enough to peek up at him. "You're family. That hasn't changed. Not one whit. The entire Escarlish royal family will stand by you through this."

That was quite the promise Averett was making. The reputation of the entire Escarlish royal family would get dragged through the mud over this, and yet they had all agreed to endure this together.

"Thank you." Essie wanted to hug all of them.

"The Tarenhieli royal family will also stand behind you." Weylind didn't so much as hesitate.

Even with both families rallying around him, Farrendel's tension didn't ease, and his breathing had gone from nearly hyperventilating to far too measured.

"Good. Not that I expected anything less." Averett met and held Weylind's gaze. "I hate to ask, but we're going to need to know to get ahead of this. What is Farrendel's status in the Tarenhieli line of succession, given his parentage? Would he actually be eligible to inherit the throne?"

"Yes." Weylind's answer was quick and firm, the lines in his face going hard. "It is so unexpected that an elf king should find himself in this situation that there is no law barring illegitimate children from inheriting. The council tried to badger both my father and I into passing such a law, but we refused. Farrendel is just as much the son of the elf king as I am. My father acknowledged him, claimed him, and gave him all the rights, privileges, and status due him. He is fourth in line to the throne of Tarenhiel."

Farrendel stiffened. "It does not matter. I will never inherit. I do not want to inherit."

Of course he didn't. It would mean Weylind, Ryfon, Brina, and Jalissa had all been tragically killed somehow. If it ever happened, Farrendel would be such a wreck, he wouldn't be in much shape to take the throne.

"I know." Essie kept her voice soft as she kept that steadying arm around him. "I don't want to inherit the Escarlish throne either, but it is still something that needs to be discussed." She glanced up at Averett. "I don't think Farrendel's illegitimacy affects anything there, will it?"

Averett shook his head. "No. When you married Farrendel, it was written into the treaty that he could never be more than your prince consort. That was a concession to ease any fears about an elf gaining the Escarlish throne, but it will also aid our argument now. There are laws preventing someone of illegitimate birth from becoming king, but there are no laws stating that he can't be a consort. Not that either kingdom will ever have to worry about such things."

"But Parliament and the people like to be absolutely sure about their line of succession." Essie grimaced. It was *so* enjoyable, having the court breathing down their necks.

Averett rubbed at his palm, not looking at Weylind or Farrendel. "And you are certain there are no other surprises? No half-siblings of Farrendel's that might show up?"

Farrendel mutely shook his head.

Weylind also shook his head, shifting as if the topic made him rather uncomfortable. "My father made numerous inquiries. Farrendel has no other half-siblings. If anyone steps forward to claim such, we can prove through our healing magic if they are telling the truth."

"Good. That is one concern we won't have to worry about." Averett glanced toward Edmund, and Edmund gave a nod. As if confirming that he had ascertained the same thing during his research into Farrendel while doing his intelligence work in Tarenhiel.

Essie glanced around the circle of them sitting there. "Do you think that Parliament will use this to undermine the treaty? I thought most of the disapproval for the treaty had died down months ago?"

"It has, but it never went away entirely." Averett glanced from her to Farrendel. "There will be those who will claim that Tarenhiel pawned off a second-rate prince on Escarland. While I know that isn't the case, it will help that Farrendel's status is so secure."

"The timing does seem suspicious." Weylind's mouth pressed into an even tighter line.

"I agree it's suspect, and I'm looking into it." Edmund's jaw worked before he shrugged. "But as much as I hate coincidences, it could be just that. Farrendel's illegitimacy is an open secret here in Tarenhiel. It isn't too surprising that word made its way to Escarland as our kingdoms have become closer."

It might have been inevitable, but Essie still hated it. Farrendel had found a freedom in Escarland that he'd never had in Tarenhiel. That was about to change. The same disdain for his tainted birth that he experienced in the Tarenhieli court would now follow him to Escarland.

"What's the plan now?" Essie glanced around at the members of their families gathered there. "You have a plan, right? I assume that's why you're here."

Edmund's posture was only a little less rigid than Farrendel's. "Yes, but you aren't going to like it."

FARRENDEL WAS GOING to be sick right there in front of their family. His head was light and buzzing, the tips of his fingers tingling. As quickly as he dragged in breaths, he could not seem to fill his lungs. He could feel the weight of the gazes fixed on him, but he could not raise his head to meet any of them.

Only Essie's grip on his hand and her arm around his waist kept him on this side of flying apart.

"For the next week, we need you to make public appearances." Averett's tone somehow managed to be compassionate and firm all at the same time. "Both of you."

The one thing Farrendel was incapable of doing.

But he was too frozen to do so much as shake his head in protest.

"I think I see what you're getting at." Essie almost sounded excited, though her hand rubbed up and down his back. "Farrendel and I make three or four appearances that week. It would probably be best if we visit some of the places I would have anyway so it doesn't seem so unusual. The orphanage or the hospital or things like that. We'll get good press that will help mitigate the bad when the news breaks."

"Exactly."

Three or four appearances. Farrendel's stomach churned.

He managed to lift his head enough to peek up at Averett and Edmund sitting across the way. To his right, Weylind's hard face was even more lined and worn.

Averett met Farrendel's gaze across the way. "When the story is released, you and Essie will need to stick around for a few days. Just so it doesn't look like you are fleeing the kingdom."

"And I had to promise a reporter that you would give an exclusive interview." Edmund shifted, staring down at his hands. "It was the only way I could get him to delay the release of the story, at least for his paper."

An interview. On top of going out in public. Farrendel rested his head in his hands. Was there any way he could get out of this?

"All right. So we work on public relations in Escarland for about a week and a half, then we head back here until the furor dies down, and we hope that my popularity with the people is enough to outweigh Farrendel's illegitimate birth in everyone's minds." Essie gave a nod, still running her fingers up and down his back in a way that kept him present instead of falling apart. "What about the planned treaty celebrations?"

Averett shrugged. "We'll make the celebrations more about the treaty itself and less about celebrating you and Farrendel. You'll actually be able to celebrate your anniversary in peace and quiet here like you wanted all along."

As Farrendel had wanted. He was pretty sure Essie had been looking forward to all the events.

Yet, she grinned at him, no hint of her disappointment in her voice or expression. "Which anniversary were we planning to celebrate anyway? Our Escarlish wedding or our Tarenhieli one?"

With so many members of both of their families staring at them, Farrendel could not give her the answer he would have said if it was just the two of them. Instead, he simply squeezed her hand. "Both."

A week and a half of torturous public appearances, then peace and quiet here in Tarenhiel with Essie. If he could only survive, then it would get better.

"The next weeks will not be pleasant." Averett grimaced. "Aspersions will be cast about your family, and your late father. His honor will be dragged through the mud while all the sordid details of Farrendel's mother's life will be splashed across the papers for everyone to read."

Farrendel's stomach churned even worse at that. He had yet to gather the courage to read through the files. Soon, that information would be there for all of Escarland to condemn.

Weylind's jaw worked, his eyes flinty. "There will be much for the papers to report, I am afraid. Though, I doubt your papers will report how she abandoned her child for money."

"Weylind." Rheva's voice had a sharp note to it that Farrendel had rarely heard. Rheva sat straight, giving Weylind a stern look worthy of Machasheni Leyleira. "You forget that I was one of the few who met her that day. Yes, she abandoned Farrendel, and I do not deny that he was in poor shape when she did. But what else was she supposed to do? If she had kept him, he would have grown up in poverty. Instead, by giving him to your dacha, she ensured that he was raised a prince, never lacking for anything. It was a sacrifice of a mother's love."

Farrendel caught his breath. He had never heard Rheva talk about his mother this way. Then again, he had never been in a place to wish to hear and process before.

Had his mother loved him? Even a little bit?

Because even though he had never met her and every-thing was a mix of pain and longing and abandonment, he still loved her. She had been his mother, even if she had been a hole inside of him for his entire life.

"Perhaps." Weylind crossed his arms. "Though she was eager enough to take the money when Dacha offered it. If she had lived, she likely would have tried to work her way into Farrendel's life, manipulating him into giving her more."

"I do not deny that she likely would have manipulated him and called it love." Rheva's gaze held firm. "But as we have seen, our own family is not free of that kind of twisted love either."

Farrendel felt Essie stiffen beside him. Melantha was still a touchy subject. He had forgiven her for what she had done, and they had come a long way in repairing their relationship. But that did not mean that the past pain was easy to forget.

Weylind sighed and tilted his head in a weary acknowledgment.

That same weariness settled over Farrendel. How was he ever going to survive the next two weeks?

Averett made a throat-clearing noise. "We only have a week until the story breaks. I suggest we return to Escarland as soon as possible—today even—and put this plan into motion. If we could schedule an appearance for Farrendel and Essie tomorrow morning, that would be ideal."

The churning filling his chest returned full force. Farrendel tried to breathe through it this time. Tried to stave off the swirling in his head and the way the blackness crowded the edge of his vision.

But some things could not be willed away.

Stomach heaving, Farrendel lunged to his feet and blindly ran for the door. His fumbling fingers found the latch, then he was stumbling onto the porch surrounding the sitting room. He managed to get around the corner before he sank to the floor, head resting on his knees as he tried not to pass out.

This was too much. Far too much. His throat ached with

pressure, his lungs burning as he gasped for breath. His head felt light, as if it would float away from his shoulders.

Footsteps, light and soft, brushed the porch floor before a light touch rested on his arm. Essie did not crowd him as she sat next to him. "You don't have to do this. If you can't handle this, then I'll go back in there and tell my brother to figure something else out. He'll understand."

Farrendel dug his fingers into his knees, focusing on that point of pain. He shuddered through one deep breath, then two. The scent of Essie's shampoo wafted on a breeze that carried the warm, growing scents of Ellonahshinel in spring.

A part of him bristled at that word. *Cannot.* It might be true, but it would be humiliating to admit that out loud to their families.

Even then, he still wanted the relief that admitting *cannot* would bring. He and Essie could go to Lethorel and hide for however many weeks, months, or years it took for the scandal to disappear. Safe and alone.

He released a long exhale, loosening his grip on his knees as his head and stomach settled. Hiding would be best for him, but it would not be best for Essie. She would not last a month before she was miserable. Whenever she returned from a public appearance, she was just about glowing, talking nonstop as she told him about every minute of her day.

She had never asked him to go with her, even though he could see the edge of disappointment that she tried to hide. She wanted to share this part of herself with him, even if she accepted that he could not handle it.

He would have to handle it now. For her sake, he needed to fight for whatever shred of their reputation he could salvage.

"No." He shook his head against his arms, still gripped tightly around his knees. "No. I can do this. I *have* to do this."

Even if it broke him again, he would survive it. After all, he had survived two weeks of torture at the hands of King Charvod of the trolls. This was shorter than that, at least, even if the mental anguish was no less real than the physical anguish had been.

Essie eased closer, her head against his shoulder. "You aren't going to be forced to do you don't want to do. It's your choice, in the end."

Then it would be his choice to force himself through it. Farrendel lifted his head from his arms, forcing his body to uncurl so that he could lean against the wall behind him. He wrapped an arm around Essie, and she tucked closer against him, her red hair spilling across his shoulder and his chest.

He would have Essie at his side every moment. Her presence would make the public appearances, the crowds, all of it bearable. There, she would be his shield. His protector. If the panic overcame him, she would rescue him.

"I know." He rested his cheek against the top of her head.

"Then we'll make this work." Essie's arms tightened around him, as if she was trying to hold him together. "We'll meticulously talk through every appearance until you're comfortable and prepared. Captain Merrick and Iyrinder will be there to watch your back. You'll be able to take your swords nearly everywhere we go. And, thanks to the magic in the heart bond, both of us can use your magic to protect ourselves."

That did not sound so horrible. He would not feel so vulnerable if he had his swords strapped across his back.

And he did have his magic, a magic he could use with much more control and confidence than he had in the past.

Essie tilted her head to look up at him. "Then we can return to Tarenhiel to wait out the initial scandal. Maybe we can go to Lethorel for a few weeks like I know you want to do."

He released a long breath, the tightness in his chest loosening rather than twisting again. "It would be nice to spend our anniversary at Lethorel."

Just him. Essie. A few guards who could be convinced to give them lots of space. It was his idea of the perfect holiday.

If he focused on the coming trip to Lethorel, perhaps he could survive the next week. One week or so of near panic, then he could escape with Essie for a while.

"Yes." Essie sat up, pushing off him and brushing her hair out of her face. "Now go on. I know you're just itching to get in a little alone time before we set out for Escarland. The train won't leave until you're ready."

"Linshi, shynafir." Farrendel kissed her before he stood, his muscles tensed with the need to disappear into the vastness of Ellonahshinel and lose himself in movement and solitude until his tension bled away.

Perhaps, by the time he boarded the train for Escarland, he might even be tired enough that he would not panic when Averett and Edmund inevitably wanted to rehash the plan yet again.

CHAPTER
FIVE

Edmund's heart pounded as he faced Jalissa, the cold Kostarian wind whipping around them. This wasn't the right time. She was leaving for home while he would stay here in Kostaria, spying for both Escarland and Tarenhiel.

But despite his secrets, he found himself tugging Jalissa aside, looking into her eyes, and saying, "Jalissa, I would like to court you, when I return."

Jalissa's face had already been strangely cold, but now her whole body stiffened. When she met his gaze, it was with the same icy, detached expression she had given him when she'd arrived in Escarland on her diplomatic mission. "I am sorry if I have given you the wrong impression these past weeks, but I could never court a human."

With that, she spun on her heels and marched to the train, her head held high as if she had not just chilled him more than the icy wind scouring the Kostarian mountainside.

It was for the best. He had too many secrets he could

never tell her. Those secrets had, after all, broken both their hearts once already.

E dmund followed Jalissa as the meeting broke apart. She kept her head down, her glossy dark brown hair flowing across her back, as she hurried from the sitting room at a pace only slightly more dignified than Farrendel's when he'd fled the room a moment ago.

She hurried onto a branch that led to her room, and Edmund quickened his pace to catch up with her before she could disappear within. His heart pounded, and every bit of common sense screamed that this plan was foolhardy. Hadn't he toyed with Jalissa's heart more than enough already? He had too many secrets, too many reasons why things could never work between him and Jalissa.

But his heart wasn't listening, and he was willing to let himself be convinced that this plan was a good idea.

"Jalissa." He had nearly reached her. The rest of her family had dispersed, giving them a semblance of privacy here on the branch pathway of Ellonahshinel. "Could I speak with you a moment?"

Her back stiffened as she halted. When she turned to face him, her deep brown eyes twisted something deep inside his chest, making his breath catch. But her expression, from her slim nose to her delicate chin, was smooth as porcelain, the picture of a perfect elven princess. "I have nothing to discuss with you."

"This isn't about me. It's about Farrendel and Essie." Edmund held her gaze, willing sincerity to his voice. Yes, this was about Farrendel and Essie. He wasn't foolish enough to think he had a third chance with Jalissa. Not at all.

It wasn't like he wanted to reach for her and hold her close. Nor would he allow his gaze to focus on her mouth as he thought about how much he wanted to kiss her.

She had said no to his courtship. He would respect that, even if it tore him in two.

Her blank mask fractured a bit, reflecting the wariness that also flowed into her posture. "What about Farrendel and Essie?"

"Averett's plan is a good one, and it will shore up Essie and Farrendel's reputation in the eyes of the Escarlish people well enough, but..." Edmund drew in a deep breath. One last chance for him to walk away. One last chance to avoid what was sure to break his own heart before this was over.

If he'd been the type to avoid such risks, he never would have become a spy.

Jalissa raised an eyebrow. "But?"

"I think there is a way to take some of the pressure off them. A way to reassure the Escarlish people about the intentions of the Tarenhieli crown." Edmund struggled to keep his words even instead of blurting them out in a rush. "We can create a news story that would take the focus off Farrendel and Essie so that the scandal can die quicker."

"And what would that be, and what does it have to do with me?" Jalissa eyed him with even more wariness now. For good reason.

"We fake a courtship." His heart choked his throat. Too much of his emotion had come out in his voice. He was supposed to present this as a cold, business arrangement.

"No." Jalissa spun on her heel and started to march away.

"Wait!" Edmund stopped himself from reaching for her, and instead curled and uncurled his fingers at his sides. "It would be for just a few weeks. Long enough to make the Escarlish people think there will be a second marriage of alliance to secure the treaty. It would not take much to re-start the rumors of a romance between us that were flying the last time we were both in Escarland. Then we can quietly break it off. I know you can't...that we can't...that this can't go anywhere."

How those words *hurt*. But he would make them the truth, no matter how painful.

She spun to face him, her expression hard once again. "That would just bring your Escarlish scandal here to Taren-hiel to trouble my brother's court as well. He has dealt with enough trouble after my brother married a human and my sister married a troll. I cannot be seen to even entertain the possibility of marrying a human when I have to marry an elf to regain the reputation of the royal family in my own court."

"I know." He did. Truly. And even if she was free to marry a human, he would be the worst choice. He had spied on her kingdom. If his secrets ever got out, the scandal in her kingdom would be just as bad as what Essie and Farrendel were facing now. "Then use a fake courtship to your advan-tage. When we break it off, you can pick an elf of your choice, and your court will be so relieved that he isn't a human that they won't care if he isn't high in the nobility, or even noble at all. They will simply be glad that he is an elf and isn't me."

Her jaw worked, her eyes still flinty and a touch sad. "That still does not change the fact that it will cause an addi-tional scandal here in Tarenhiel. Nor does it buy me any more time to find a suitable elf since I will be locked in a fake courtship with you."

He could hear what she wasn't saying, even if he wasn't supposed to know. She believed that the only elf she had ever loved was dead.

If he could give her a way to fall in love with someone else, he would. It was the least he could do, after everything he had done to her.

But he could not give away the heart he had so accidentally stolen. Any more than he could take his back.

"I understand, especially since much of our fake courtship would have to be spent in Escarland." Edmund told himself that he didn't stumble over the word *fake*. "But it would buy you a little more time before you had to make a choice."

"This courtship would be *fake*, right?" Her beautifully dark eyes scoured his face. "This is not an attempt to get close to me again, is it? Because I am not going to budge. I told you that I cannot accept a real courtship with you."

"I know, and this isn't." Edmund swallowed. That had to be the truth. Because he would not allow himself to be the kind of man who would do anything so dishonorable as pressure a woman after she had told him no. "You have made your choice clear, and I respect that."

"Do you?" Jalissa gave him that one-eyebrow look again. She knew him too well to be fooled, even if she didn't know why she knew him so well.

Edmund forced the ache away. He had only himself to blame if he'd gotten hurt. All along, she had been the innocent casualty of his own foolishness.

"We are members of royal families who will be working closely together in the future. This tension between us can't continue." He gestured between the two of them, glad that his voice had returned to a business-like tone that matched her expression. "Maybe this can be our chance to end things better than we did. We can use this fake courtship to figure out how to be just friends."

"I hope you realize how ridiculous that sounds." Jalissa's mouth curved into a hint of a smile, the trace of her humor breaking through.

There was the Jalissa he knew, buried beneath the layers of her heartache.

"Yes." He gave in to his own smile for a moment before he turned serious again. "But I'm willing to try it, for Essie and Farrendel's sake. Any little bit of pressure we can take off them—off Farrendel especially—could be the difference between him taking a week or two to recover or facing months of recovery before he's functioning again."

He hadn't seen the worst of it last time, as he had been spying in Kostaria. But he was enough of a spy to figure out just how bad it had gotten while he had been gone.

But considering just the mention of the coming week had sent Farrendel into a panic, how much worse would experiencing it be for him? If Edmund could do something to spare both Farrendel and Essie even a little, then he was willing to do it, no matter the cost to himself.

Yet this plan wouldn't just cost himself, but Jalissa as well.

For the first time, Jalissa looked away from him, delicately biting her bottom lip as she always did when she was considering something, too deep in thought to remember that a poised, elven princess did not bite her lip in front of others.

He understood why she would stop and consider. His plan to become just friends sounded good, but it could just as easily go wrong, and they'd find themselves falling in love yet again.

He was willing to try it. If the choice was between his pain or Essie and Farrendel's, then the choice was easy. Farrendel didn't need anything more to shatter him while Edmund wouldn't break from this. He would be fine, eventually.

Jalissa drew in a shaky breath. "All right. I agree." She lifted her chin. "I am willing to do whatever it takes to protect Farrendel."

Unlike her sister Melantha. She didn't say it, but Edmund could hear the note of anger anyway.

"So am I." Edmund let those words steady him.

This wasn't about him. It was about Farrendel and doing whatever it took to prevent the pressure of public opinion from breaking him. It was about Essie, who would stand at Farrendel's side and suffer alongside him.

And, perhaps, it was about Jalissa. She was so hurt right now. Hurt by her sister's betrayal. Hurt by how their romance had ended. Alone in trying to pick up the pieces of her life.

If he could be there for her right now, maybe he could leave her a little less broken and hurt when they ended things than she was right now. He had played a role in her pain. Perhaps it was only right that he helped her put herself back together before he let her go once and for all.

JALISSA CURLED on the bench in the seating train car and stared out the window as the Tarenhieli forest flashed by in a blur of vibrant green.

What had she been thinking, saying yes to a fake courtship with Edmund? Did she *want* to get her heart broken again?

But he had sounded so certain that this would help Farrendel and Elspetha. Weylind seemed to think so as well, even if he did not know the entire plan. He had not argued when Jalissa had shown up at the train with her luggage and her faithful guard Sarya in tow and stated that she was going to Escarland with Farrendel and Elspetha. All Jalissa had to say was that Farrendel could use all the support he could get, and Weylind waved her onto the train without another word.

Was Edmund right? Would this fake relationship help them end the real one that had come so close to starting?

If that were the case, why did her heart insist on beating harder, her breathing going shallow, whenever she caught sight of him? When he had looked at her with those swirling blue eyes of his, the morning sunlight glinting on the slight curl to his brown hair and turning the strands a hint red, she had been helpless to refuse his fake courtship plan.

She was supposed to be choosing not to love him, not letting her heart have free rein once again. But it seemed she was just as weak as before when it came to Edmund.

At the other end of the train car, King Averett, Edmund, and Elspetha talked quietly. Jalissa probably should join them, but she did not feel up to it at the moment.

Farrendel had disappeared into his and Elspetha's private sleeping car as soon as they boarded the train. Jalissa could not blame him for wanting to soak up what little solitude he could find before they reached Escarland. She was tempted to seek the comfort of a private car herself, except that huddling there sounded even more lonely.

Jalissa sighed and leaned her head against the window, not caring who saw her slumped in such an undignified fashion.

She heard his footsteps crossing the train car before she saw him sit on the bench across from her. The vibrant blue shirt he wore paired well with his deep blue eyes and emphasized the muscular curve of his shoulders. His belt hugged his trim waist while black trousers and black boots completed his look, a mix between rogue and prince. She wanted to snap at him to go away—to stop distracting her with that heart-fluttering smile—but that would not be a good start to their fake courtship.

"I was thinking…" Edmund spoke in a lowered tone, glancing at Averett and Elspetha as if checking that they were still ignoring him and Jalissa. "What if, once Farrendel and Essie retreat, we invite some of the elven nobility to Escarland? We could disguise it as part of the treaty celebrations, to host some select members of Tarenhiel's court in Aldon."

"What good would that do?" Jalissa was too tired to deal with more planning right now.

Then again, she had suffered this lethargy for months now. She should be used to functioning while emotionally weary.

Edmund gave her a small smile, though something of the clever glint had returned to his gaze. "We could make sure to include those elves whom you have been considering. It would be a good chance to really see their character. It's important to you to find an elf who won't scorn Farrendel. If he's willing to travel for the treaty celebrations and face the scandal of Farrendel's birth in the Escarlish court, that will tell you he's at least still in the running while you can eliminate any who refuse to even come."

He had a point. It would be a good test to winnow her options down some. She had resigned herself to a loveless marriage, but she could not marry someone who hated her brother. That was a line she would not cross.

Jalissa blinked, then sat up straighter to better face Edmund. "Are you offering to help me..." She trailed off, not even sure what to call it. Was he truly offering to help her move on and find the elf she would eventually marry?

"Yes." Both his voice and his gaze were steady as he continued to face her across the train car's small aisle. "You're right. Despite this attraction between us, we aren't right for each other. But I still care enough about you to want to see you happy. If I can help make that happen, I will."

It brought a lump to her throat, and she had to turn back to the window for a moment while she blinked back the emotion.

For the past few months, she had felt so alone. And here Edmund was, offering to help her even though she was the one who had rejected him.

She should not lean on him yet again. It would make it that much harder when they ended their fake courtship, the final nail in the coffin of their rather doomed relationship.

Yet, was that not what friends were for? If she and Edmund were going to remain just friends, then they would need to have a good working relationship. After all, the odds were high that she could find herself stationed in Escarland as an ambassador once again, this time with her elf husband at her side.

It would not be fair to her husband if she still had feelings for Edmund at that point. It would be far better if she and Edmund had gotten that little matter behind them and built a good friendship and nothing more in its stead. The kind where they could laugh at what could have been, joke about how wrong they had been for each other, and turn loving gazes onto their spouses instead.

"Linshi." Jalissa had to speak softly, hoping that would disguise the lingering emotion.

Edmund ducked his head a moment, his shoulders rising and falling. When he faced her again, gone were any traces of attraction or pain. Instead, he wore a bright smile that even seemed to reach his eyes. "You'll have a chance to observe them while you still have me for a buffer. They won't be putting on as much of a show, trying to impress you."

He was offering to be her shield, even knowing that it would mean she would walk away with someone else in the end.

She should not let him do this. He was risking too much, giving her too much.

But she found herself nodding, something in her chest easing for the first time in months. As much as she did not like it, she was not the type of person who could face things alone. She needed to lean on someone.

She had tried to deal with this on her own. Weylind, Rheva, Farrendel, and Elspetha had already carried too many burdens for Jalissa to wish to worry them with hers.

Perhaps it was selfish, letting Prince Edmund take that burden when she knew she could never give him anything more than friendship in return. But she was weary enough that she no longer cared.

Hopefully this was not another decision she would come to regret. She had more than enough regrets as it was.

Jalissa curled in her favorite chair in the library, only the stub of a candle lighting the corner. She had not wanted to use the main, magical lights in the library and risk alerting someone to her presence. Instead, she had resorted to a candle, keeping a careful eye on it.

The scuff of footsteps was the only warning before a male elf servant, dressed in plain green, came around the corner. Above the stack of books he was carrying, she could see he was the same elf she had bumped into the other day, his blond hair gliding across his hunched shoulders.

He stopped short and bobbed as much of a bow as he could without dropping the books, his face down and shadowed in the faint light of the candle. "Pardon, amirah. I did not mean to disturb you. I was concerned someone had left a candle lit."

A dangerous thing in a library, and even more so in the treetop library of Ellonahshinel.

Jalissa waved away his apology. "I appreciate your concern. I hope I am not in your way. You must have a great deal of work to do if you are here so late. I can leave."

She did not want to return to her empty room. There, the worries gnawed at her, as they always did when Weylind and Farrendel left to fight the trolls. She had already lost both her macha and her dacha to the trolls. On nights like this, it seemed almost inevitable that she would lose her brothers too.

The slightest curve of a smile crossed the elf's face. "You are not in my way, amirah. I will return to shelving books and leave you to your solitude."

As he turned to go, Jalissa straightened. "Wait."

When he turned, not quite meeting her gaze, she swallowed. Why had she called him back? It was as if a part of her did not want him to go. As if his mere presence was more comfort than her solitude.

"What is your name?" That was a safe question, right? It would not be so odd for her to wish to know a servant's name.

"Elidyr Ruven, amirah." He gave another bow, then left her alone once again with her thoughts.

F arrendel woke in the familiar bed of Buckmore
Cottage, his and Essie's home in Escarland. Essie
lay beside him, her red hair flowing over the pillow
and onto his. Leaving Essie still sleeping, Farrendel dressed
in Escarlish clothing—one of the nicer sets rather than the
worker's clothing—and tiptoed down the stairs to the
kitchen.

Voices greeted him even before he stepped through the
doorway. Miss Merrick stood at the stove stirring an omelet
while Iyrinder leaned against the wall by the door, most
likely waiting for Farrendel. As Farrendel strode inside, Miss
Merrick and Iyrinder halted their conversation, turning
toward him.

"Good morning, amir." Iyrinder bobbed his head in
Farrendel's direction. Even though the plan had been for
Iyrinder to rotate off Farrendel's guard detail to be replaced
with another of Weylind's guards who wished to be trained
to work with the human guards under Captain Merrick's
command, somehow Iyrinder had stuck around.

Farrendel was thankful Iyrinder had stayed with him. It was easier getting used to the rest of the guards changing as long as Captain Merrick and Iyrinder remained the same.

Miss Merrick flipped the omelet one last time before she placed it on a clean plate. She held it out to Farrendel. "Your breakfast, Your Highness."

Farrendel took the plate, his stomach twisting so much that he was not sure how much he would manage to eat. He did not particularly enjoy omelets, even if he had learned to like most Escarlish breakfast foods. But omelets involved mixing meat, cheese, veggies, and eggs, and there was just something about foods mixing that made him anxious.

He did not like to admit that, though. People found it strange.

After sitting at the table, Farrendel forced himself to eat as much of his breakfast as he could stomach.

As he finished, Captain Eugene Merrick, the head of Farrendel's guards and Miss Merrick's older brother, strode into the kitchen. Today he wore his Escarlish uniform, complete with a pistol at his hip. His brown hair was neat, his blue eyes sharp.

Captain Merrick gave a respectful nod in Farrendel's direction. "I was informed that you intend to go into Aldon without your disguise."

Farrendel swallowed one last bite of egg, nearly gagging on it, before he pushed his plate aside. "Yes."

How would the Escarlish people react to seeing him and Iyrinder strolling through the streets with their long hair and pointed ears visible for all to see? Would they throw stones? Would someone try to shoot at them as they had the first time Farrendel and Essie rode through the streets of Aldon?

He touched the straps of his swords. They bunched his

shirt and vest a bit, the Escarlish cut of the clothing not designed to be worn underneath swords like this. Farrendel would simply have to be ready for whatever might happen.

"I was also told that we need to be back by noon." Captain Merrick gestured in the direction of Winstead Palace. "There is a newspaper reporter coming this afternoon."

Captain Merrick did not ask what it was about. Farrendel probably should tell him what was going on, before he heard it from someone else. Though, Captain Merrick might already know most of it. He had spent a great deal of time in Tarenhiel over the past few months and had even begun to learn passable elvish. It was likely he had picked up on a few of Farrendel's secrets.

Farrendel sighed and pushed away from the table. He had hoped Edmund would not be able to schedule that interview right away. Though, it might be better to get it over with as soon as possible.

Almost too soon, Farrendel, Captain Merrick, Iyrinder, and an assortment of human and elven guards strode the main street of Aldon headed in the direction of Lance's workshop. Most people they passed simply stopped and stared. A few even waved in greeting. It was a better reaction than what Farrendel had expected, and he managed a tentative smile back in a few cases.

There was still some grumbling, but nothing of the angry shouting there had been on that first trip to Escarland. In the nearly nine months since then, the war with Kostaria had brought Escarland and Tarenhiel together. Maybe someday, it would no longer be an odd thing to see elves strolling the streets of Aldon.

That was the kind of thing Essie would dream about, and

Farrendel was beginning to catch glimpses of that vision as well.

Would this growing peace between elves and humans survive the shock of his illegitimacy? How angry would the Escarlish people become when they learned their favorite princess had been matched with such a flawed elven prince?

As they passed the intersection with one of the main shopping districts of Aldon, Farrendel halted, glancing up the street to the bustle of men in trousers and coats and women in long dresses and hats covering their hair.

"Your Highness?" Captain Merrick had stopped as well, and he turned to glance back at Farrendel. "Is there a problem?"

Farrendel shook his head, then gestured toward the street of shops. He could not believe he was about to suggest this, especially while his swords, long hair, and pointed ears were on full display despite his otherwise Escarlish dress. "I would like to find a present for my wife. Something for our anniversary."

Their anniversary was not for another three weeks, but Farrendel had a feeling that their schedule would be too busy, and he would be too anxious, to think of this later. Besides, if he wanted something custom, then three weeks was already cutting it close.

Captain Merrick nodded. "Do you wish to proceed to the Aldon Market, then?"

That was the place where Farrendel felt most comfortable here in Aldon, besides Lance's workshop. The market, while noisy and closed in, was self-contained and familiar.

Farrendel forced himself to shake his head again. "No. I wish to visit the larger shops on the main streets."

His stomach twisted, but he could handle this. The

streets were not that busy yet. And this was just the sort of thing Averett had been talking about. Surely it would look good for the public to see him visiting the shops in the center of Aldon to purchase a gift for Essie.

It was strange, to be politically minded enough to use his anniversary gift for Essie to bolster public opinion. But stranger still, Essie—princess that she was—would find such a gift even more sweet.

Besides, Lance would not notice if Farrendel arrived first thing in the morning or did not show up for a few hours. Farrendel had plenty of time to wander Aldon before heading to Lance's workshop.

Captain Merrick led the way in the new direction. Iyrinder and the other guards fell into place around Farrendel, their eyes searching the crowds, the buildings, the rooftops for potential threats.

As they walked, Captain Merrick nodded toward the shops around them. "Is there something in particular you are looking for?"

"Something small." He and Essie had gone a little extravagant for their birthdays recently. They had agreed to keep their anniversary small. "Do you have any suggestions?"

Captain Merrick's eyebrows shot up, and he shared a look with Iyrinder.

Farrendel suppressed a groan. Right. Neither Captain Merrick nor Iyrinder were married. Why was Farrendel asking them? Of the three of them, he was the one who should be the expert on this marriage thing.

Captain Merrick gave a slight cough. "I have heard jewelry is always appreciated."

Farrendel opened his mouth to say that Essie was a princess. She had plenty of jewelry already.

But it was Iyrinder who spoke up first. "Is that what Escarlish women appreciate?"

Captain Merrick shot Iyrinder a look that was somehow both knowing and searching all at once. "They do. Something small and tasteful, I should think."

Was Captain Merrick talking to Farrendel or Iyrinder at this point?

Farrendel would have to ask Essie later because there was something he was missing here, and Essie would know what it was.

"Very well. We will start with the jewelers." Farrendel glanced around the street. He could manage a few stores, at least. If he did not find anything, he would simply get something in Estyra when they returned there.

ESSIE RESTED her hand on Farrendel's arm, the familiar brick and stone buildings of Hanford University spreading around them. Brick walkways wound between the buildings with fountains set in the squares and benches set beneath trees. At the far side of the rows of buildings, the Fyne River rippled and gurgled. Students sat in clusters on the grassy bank that extended down to the muddy river.

A few of the students stopped and gaped, though Essie wasn't sure whether the gaping was due to their princess in their midst or the elf prince walking at her side.

Farrendel shifted closer to her, and she could sense his unease. He wasn't wearing his swords—weapons were banned for students, though Captain Merrick and Iyrinder had gotten exemptions as guards and still wore theirs.

At least the interview the night before had gone as well

as could have been expected. It had been tense, but Trent Bourdon had been polite and professional.

Professor Harrington bustled up to them, bowing first to Farrendel, then to her almost as an afterthought. His brown, gray-flecked hair was a little longer than was fashionable in Escarland while he stood shorter than either Farrendel or Essie. "Prince Farrendel, Princess Elspeth. It's a pleasure to have you here today."

Farrendel managed a stiff nod, but Essie smiled. "It is our pleasure to be here. Where would you like to start this tour?"

Professor Harrington gestured at the campus. "I will give you a proper tour. Not that you need it, Princess Elspeth, but there have been a few changes since you took classes here. We will wrap up the tour by sitting in on the advanced magical theory class that you have been taking by correspondence, Prince Farrendel."

Farrendel nodded again, and Essie stepped as close as she dared in a public setting like this. Through the heart bond, she could feel just how stomach-churningly nervous he was. He was going to make her nauseous if he kept this up.

Professor Harrington led the way, waving at each building in turn and expounding on its history and which classes were held in each. Though, he looked a little flummoxed when he spoke about an ancient building that had been built seven hundred years ago and then Farrendel mentioned that Leyleira had already been over a hundred years old at that point and courting Farrendel's grandfather.

Essie understood the feeling. It boggled her mind at times when she realized how much history even Farrendel had seen in his mere one hundred and six years, much less Weylind or Leyleira.

When the tour was over, the professor led them inside one of the buildings, halting in the hallway outside of an oak door. From inside, the voice of another professor echoed, even if it was too faint to understand through the oak.

Professor Harrington faced Captain Merrick and Iyrinder. "I will have to ask the guards to wait outside. It is university policy that any personal guards must wait outside the room to avoid any disruption of class or distraction to the other students."

Farrendel's face whitened a bit, glancing between Captain Merrick and Iyrinder as if he didn't dare walk into the room without them watching his back.

Essie winced. She had forgotten about this rule. "I'm afraid he is correct. The Escarlish royalty has always complied, and there has never been an incident."

"What if I were a prospective student thinking about enrolling?" Iyrinder shifted as everyone swung to look at him. "Would I be able to sit in the class today?"

The professor shrugged. "You would have to leave your weapons behind, as is required of all students, but it is allowed for prospective students to sit in on classes with approval."

Iyrinder still wasn't looking at any of them. "And if I wished to attend the classes with the amir in the fall?"

"There is no rule against guards taking classes, but you would have to be officially enrolled yourself, going for the same degree." The professor almost looked giddy at the thought. "We would welcome you, of course. Any elves who wish to attend are very welcome to do so."

"Iyrinder?" Beneath Essie's hand, Farrendel's muscles had gone even more stiff. "Is this what you wish?"

"It would be better if one of us were in the room with

you to watch your back." Iyrinder shared a glance with Captain Merrick.

"I will appear less conspicuous standing outside the door since I am Escarlish." Captain Merrick grimaced, though it had a touch of humor to it. "And I certainly don't want to get a degree in magical engineering. I became a guard because I didn't want to spend my days sitting in a class-room. But if Iyrinder wants to do it, I'm not going to stand in his way."

"I am glad to hear it." Iyrinder shared another glance with Captain Merrick that had an undercurrent to it.

Did it have something to do with the way Captain Merrick's sister—who also worked for Farrendel and Essie—and Iyrinder had been spending more time together lately? Essie had noticed, but she wasn't going to say anything. Of course she was hoping for another elf-human romance to blossom, but something like this could cause tension between the two heads of Farrendel's security if they weren't careful.

Essie smiled at Iyrinder. "If you wish to get a degree, Farrendel and I will definitely support you any way we can. We can help pay your tuition, since you'll be taking classes as part of your job to keep Farrendel safe."

A hint of a smile twitched on Iyrinder's face. "Linshi, amirah, but you already pay me well enough that I can afford my own tuition. I am also thinking of my future. In a hundred years, you will no longer be in line for the Escarlish throne. You will be so far down the Tarenhieli line of succession that you will no longer require such tight security. Unless I want to return to guarding Weylind Daresheni, it seems prudent to create more options for myself in the future."

Options that would include an Escarlish magical engineering degree. Which would only be useful in Escarland. Interesting.

Essie studied the expressions that both Iyrinder and Captain Merrick wore, but neither of them gave anything away. Still, it was telling that Iyrinder was taking steps to give himself more ties to Escarland. Almost as if he were thinking that he might marry a human and have reason to live in Escarland for a long time to come.

Farrendel nodded to Iyrinder. "Linshi. I would appreciate having someone guarding my back."

And being his emotional support guard. Essie might have to figure out how to conveniently give both Iyrinder and Miss Merrick a night off at the same time as a subtle way to thank Iyrinder for this.

Farrendel had been nervous about taking classes in person at the university in the fall, and Essie had begun to worry if the anxiety would be too much. She wasn't sure Farrendel would be able to walk all by himself into those classrooms filled with strangers. Iyrinder's presence could be the difference between Farrendel getting through the anxiety or having it crush him.

Professor Harrington cleared his throat. "If that is settled, would you care to proceed, Prince Farrendel?"

Iyrinder quickly divested himself of his weapons, handing them to Captain Merrick. Then, while Captain Merrick took up a station with his back to the wall next to the door, the rest of them filed inside as quietly as possible.

The professor at the front of the room kept lecturing without missing a beat, even though his gaze took them in briefly. Several of the students turned around in their seats to gape. This room was one of the smaller rooms with rows of wooden desks instead of a larger lecture hall.

Essie picked one of the desks in the back row and sat in it. Farrendel glanced between the seat in front of her and the seat across the aisle next to her before finally choosing the one across the aisle. His nose wrinkled a bit, as if he found the desk's sanitary condition rather suspect.

Iyrinder took the seat immediately in front of Farrendel while Professor Harrington remained standing at the back.

After spending a few more minutes of lecturing—some magical theory that Essie didn't understand but had Farrendel leaning forward in fascination—the professor gestured toward them in the back of the room. "Class, as you have noticed, we have guests today. Princess Elspeth is gracing us with her presence, along with her husband Prince Farrendel of Tarenhiel. Prince Farrendel is enrolled here at Hanford University and has been taking this class via correspondence. Let's welcome them today."

Most of the students swiveled in their seats and clapped. A few remained where they were, arms crossed, in protest.

Essie smiled and waved, but Farrendel gripped the desk in front of him with a white-knuckled grip that had Essie worried. If Farrendel had a bad experience today, it would be that much harder for him to step into a class as a student in the fall.

"Prince Farrendel." The professor turned to Farrendel, a broad grin on his face.

Essie stiffened. No, no, no. Was there any way to signal the professor not to call on Farrendel? He was just going to make things worse. Yes, getting called on was a part of taking classes. But Farrendel was not ready for that yet. He needed to ease into this university thing slowly.

But the professor didn't catch Essie's unspoken message. Instead, he kept beaming at Farrendel. "Would you be willing to give us a demonstration of your magic?"

Uh-oh. Essie glanced between the professor and Farrendel. Farrendel remained frozen in the desk, white-faced and white-knuckled. How was she going to salvage this situation?

Essie pushed to her feet, focusing on the professor while holding a hand out to Farrendel. "Actually, why don't both of us give a demonstration of Prince Farrendel's magic? I'm sure you've seen the stories in the papers about our elven heart bond and how I can now use the prince's magic."

The professor looked about ready to swoon in excitement. "Oh, yes, Your Highness. Quite the fascinating magical phenomenon!"

She got the feeling the professor would have loved to study the whole heart bond thing but couldn't because they were royalty. As soon as human professors were allowed to study with the elves in Tarenhiel, heart bonds were going to be one of the first things they attempted to study.

She wished them all the best with that, since the elves considered elishinas to be deeply personal and not something to be discussed, except in the rare cases like an elishina between an elf and a human.

Farrendel's fingers slipped into hers, and he eased to his feet. His magic crackled in the heart bond, but through it, Essie sensed his churning nausea, so intense she had to swallow bile rising in the back of her throat.

She kept a smile plastered on her face as she tugged Farrendel up the aisle between the desks until they reached the front. She faced the students, who stared back with everything from hostility to eagerness to a dead-eyed boredom. "Hello, everyone. I am Princess Elspeth of Escarland. No one in my family has magic, as is well-documented."

A few of the students nodded. Several remained glowering. Others were still so bored they didn't bat so much as an eye. And…was that young man asleep there in the front row?

"Farrendel, dear?" Essie glanced at him, squeezing his hand.

He had gone all hard and cold in full elf warrior mode. It had been a while since she had seen him look so much like the Laesornysh she had met nearly a year ago. With barely a flicker of change in his expression, Farrendel raised his hand and drew on his magic. It crackled to life around his hand, growing into a column of blue lightning that nearly touched the ceiling.

The sleeping boy jerked awake so quickly that he nearly toppled from his desk. He righted himself, gaping at Farrendel as if he had gone to sleep in a boring class and woken up in the middle of the apocalypse.

Essie struggled to keep her smile tempered into a practiced princess smile rather than a smirk. She lifted her own hand, drew on the magic in the heart bond, and let a few bolts of magic curl around her fingers. It was still strange, to see magic coming from her hand, even after all the months of practice she'd done with Farrendel.

After a few minutes of demonstration, Essie wrapped things up and orchestrated a graceful retreat.

When she and Farrendel were finally in the closed carriage, Farrendel slumped onto one of the benches, leaning his elbows on his knees, resting his head in his hands. "I do not think I can do this."

Essie sat next to him, rubbing his back as the carriage started forward. "The public appearances?"

He shook his head, still not looking at her. "Taking classes. I like the correspondence courses, but in person..." His breathing turned ragged, a pitch of panic twisting his voice. "And after the truth of my birth comes out..."

"It will get more difficult, I know." Essie wrapped her arm around his shoulders. "But fall classes don't start for another five months. The scandal will be old news by then."

"I still...I still cannot..." Farrendel's breathing hitched, switching back and forth between ragged and too measured. "Could you come? To the classes?"

Essie grimaced. She didn't want to copy Iyrinder's route and take classes, especially not for a degree in magical engineering. She had taken a few classes—enough to appear to be an educated princess—but she had never managed to get an official degree in anything. It was always a fine line between being there for Farrendel when he simply could not manage on his own and gently pushing him.

"If it helps, I can visit Hanford University on your first few days of classes." Essie reached with her free hand to clasp his fingers. "But you'll have Iyrinder with you. You won't be walking into those classes alone. And you'll have your magic to protect you."

Farrendel rubbed at his temples. "The stone buildings are going to cause an issue as well."

Essie winced. All elves had an intolerance to stone, but Farrendel was especially susceptible. "Right. I'll make a note to make sure we are stocked up on jars of elven healing medicine."

Farrendel nodded against his hands, but he still didn't seem too convinced that this could work.

Essie didn't press him. If she pressed for a decision now, then Farrendel would unenroll before the night was out. No, better to give him silence and space until he was calmer and not in such a panic.

Whenever that would be. Likely not for a while, with all their public appearances and the scandal about to break.

CHAPTER
SEVEN

Jalissa sat on the floor of the library, paging through the book about Escarland's Kingsley Gardens. Elidyr bustled along the shelves, pulling out books, taking notes, then putting them back.

"I'd like to go there someday." Jalissa sighed and stared down at the book in her lap. It was a foolish dream. With the tensions between Tarenhiel and Escarland, they were more likely to end up at war than inviting an elven princess to visit.

"Go where, amirah?" Elidyr glanced over his shoulder at her.

"Escarland. The Kingsley Gardens." Jalissa turned another page, staring at the painting of the rose garden. "I would love to see so many plants in one place."

"Perhaps you will, someday." Elidyr shrugged and turned back to the shelves. "You never know what can happen."

J alissa swiped her sweaty hands on her skirts as she waited in the garden outside the back door of Buckmore Cottage. Why had she ever agreed to this? What had she been thinking?

Footsteps crunched on the gravel of the path between Buckmore Cottage and Winstead Palace a moment before Edmund ducked under a tree branch and stepped into the garden.

As he straightened, that lopsided smile of his crossed his face. "You aren't going to fool anyone if you look that glum to see me."

Jalissa tried to mask her expression, but she did not think she succeeded. Perhaps a blank mask was not much better than appearing glum.

Edmund's smile widened. "Yes, that's perfect. We wouldn't want to make this fake relationship look too romantic. It will be that much harder to call it off later."

Jalissa huffed a sigh and could not help the twitch of a smile. Why did Edmund have to make it so hard to stay icy and aloof around him? "You said we were going into Aldon today. I suppose we are visiting the Market again?"

She resisted the urge to grimace. The Aldon Market was nice enough, especially the artists' section on the upper level. But browsing among so many people in such a noisy place was not something with which she was comfortable.

Edmund's grin remained in place. "No, the Market is more Essie's thing than mine or yours. We're going somewhere that I know you'll like much better."

"And you aren't going to tell me?" Jalissa raised an eyebrow at him as she took his arm. Her guard, Sarya, fell into step behind them.

His expression turned a touch wry. Regretful, even. "You know me and my secrets."

His secrets, yes. After how he had helped the Tarenhieli scouts both during the war with Kostaria and afterwards in Kostaria itself, she suspected much about his past and his skills.

They strolled up the path past Winstead Palace to the main circle drive, where a carriage pulled by matching black horses waited for them.

An Escarlish footman handed Jalissa up into the white, open carriage with its bright red velvet seats facing each other. Edmund took the seat across from Jalissa while Jalissa's guard climbed up to sit beside her. Both elven and human guards surrounded the carriage on horseback.

An open carriage. The better to be seen. It did not take much for Jalissa to relax her face into her serene expression. This was what she was good at, after all. Being the image of the perfect elven princess.

As they drove through the streets of Aldon, Edmund smiled and waved occasionally at the people they passed. Jalissa gave a few graceful waves as well.

Instead of heading into the familiar shopping district, the carriage turned down a street lined with large, stately homes that turned into a square formed of opulent buildings that, based on the signs, were several museums and a large library. The center of the square was dominated by a statue of some long-dead Escarlish warrior brandishing a sword while seated on his rearing steed.

At the far side of the square, an archway was covered in climbing roses, though it was too early in the year for the roses to bloom yet. Past the archway, hedges and manicured gardens stretched for a full city block, all the way to what appeared to be a gleaming, glass structure in the distance.

Jalissa could not tear her gaze away, catching her breath. She had forgotten—or wanted to forget—that these gardens were here in Aldon. She had dreamed about visiting, but that was from a time three and a half years ago filled with late nights and books and a mild-mannered servant.

Edmund should not know these gardens would draw her. It was the gesture of someone truly courting her, not merely for show.

The carriage halted next to the entrance, and in a blink one of the footmen was at the footwell, a hand out to Jalissa.

Jalissa gripped the silken fabric of her blue skirts and climbed down from the carriage. As she stepped to the ground, Edmund hopped down from the other side of the carriage and strolled around to join her.

He held out his arm. "Would you join me for a stroll through the Kingsley Gardens? They are world-renowned. Well, renowned through all the human kingdoms. I don't know if you've heard of them in Tarenhiel."

There was a note in his voice. As if he knew very well that she had heard of them but was pretending ignorance.

"Yes, I have." Jalissa swallowed. She could not force herself to tell him that she had once dreamed about visiting these gardens. Those dreams were a part of a secret she had told no one.

Jalissa started as Edmund strolled toward the entrance. Sarya and the other guards fell into step behind them.

At the archway, they were met by two attendants in green livery and top hats. Edmund paid the small admission fee, though it was not so small by the time he paid for all of them. Then, with several of the guards leading the way, Jalissa strolled at Edmund's side into the Kingsley Gardens.

A maze of hedges outlined the walking paths and opened into small, private gardens. Each garden was meticulously manicured with curving pathways, bubbling fountains, and beautiful statues set among glorious bowers of flowers from all over the world. The early spring flowers bloomed in a profusion of purples and yellows and pinks.

Jalissa trailed her fingers over the plants, resisting the way they called to her magic. This was a place she could visit again and again, each season bringing a different majesty of blooms.

For a long while, Jalissa and Edmund strolled in silence, only breaking it to greet those they passed. She did not mind the quiet. It was peaceful to lose herself among the flowers. If she had been born a commoner instead of a princess, she likely would have gotten a job tending the trees of Estyra or the gardens surrounding the home of one of the elven courtiers.

"Are they everything you imagined?" Edmund glanced down at her for a moment before he steered them into another small garden. This one was a rose garden, though it was less impressive now than it would be in mid-summer when the roses bloomed.

"Yes." Jalissa trailed her fingers over a rose branch, avoiding the thorns. Giving in to temptation, she let her magic flow into the plant. A bud appeared at the end of the branch, then burst into a delicate white bloom.

"Why did you never ask to visit on your other trips to Escarland?" Edmund reached around her and plucked the rose, handing it to Jalissa. His eyes—blue with a few hints of other colors swirling in their depths—focused on her in a way that made her heart beat harder. "For you, milady."

Jalissa looked away, twirling the rose between her fingers. "I thought about it, but…"

She could not tell Edmund this secret. It had only been three years since Elidyr's death, a pain far too recent for an elf. How could she explain about Elidyr and her dream about visiting Escarland and the Kingsley Gardens? Before, it had been too painful to dredge up those memories.

Edmund was still looking at her, studying her face.

Jalissa shrugged and turned away. "It was always too busy whenever I visited. We were trying to stave off a war, then we really were at war. There was not an opportunity for frivolous things like visiting gardens."

"No, there wasn't." Edmund stepped back, holding out his arm again. "Would you like to see the glass house? The gardens in there are filled with exotic plants from places across the world."

Jalissa nodded, and she was thankful when Edmund set a quick pace. She kept up easily without resorting to an ungraceful trotting.

The glass greenhouse glittered before them in the mid-morning sunlight. Arching, deep green plants could be seen through the wavering glass, but it wasn't clear enough for Jalissa to make out their exact shapes.

Edmund held open the door for Jalissa, and she stepped inside. Instead of the damp, chilly air of the Escarlish spring day, the hot and dry air washed over her. It was so hot that Jalissa shed her light blue cloak, handing it to Sarya, her guard.

She stood on a gravel path that wound through gardens of

sand, filled with prickly plants and stalky grasses. She did not wait for Edmund, but instead wandered down the path, stopping to read the labels on the cacti and other desert plants. "These are amazing! I never thought to see desert plants."

"They are vastly different from the trees of Tarenhiel, aren't they?" Edmund grinned as he caught up with her.

"Yes." Jalissa could have stayed in that room forever, but as she and Edmund followed the gravel path, they stepped from room to glass room, following a loop around the outside ring of the hothouse.

Each section of the giant greenhouse held new wonders. There was a room containing a miniature swamp with plants and fungi that would be found in the ogre lands to the south of Escarland. Another room held a small forest of strange trees from the other side of the world.

After several more rooms, they entered the largest, central room. Jalissa gasped and stared.

Large trees filled the space all the way to the glass ceiling, spreading broad leaves overhead. Jungle vines and flowers draped down while either side of the pathway was lined with orchids and other rainforest flowers growing alongside a burbling creek.

Among the plants, butterflies in all colors flitted about, landing on flowers then gliding to the next one.

"Oh, good. I had hoped the butterflies would be here." Edmund stood next to her, sounding supremely satisfied. "The caretakers release hundreds of butterflies in here every spring."

"It is lovely." Jalissa was sure she was gaping in a most undignified fashion, but she could not help it. With her growing magic feeling almost giddy inside her at being surrounded by so many plants, it was all she could do not to race around like a child to see everything.

This was even better than what she had imagined. Jalissa turned to Edmund, a genuine smile twitching her lips. "Lin-shi, Prince Edmund."

When he smiled back, her heart gave another, rapid thump.

This was supposed to be a fake relationship. Not real. She was not allowed to let her heart get involved.

Why was it so hard to remind herself of that when Edmund was looking at her with such an adorable smile on his face?

F arrendel pressed his hands to his knees, trying to stop his legs from bouncing with his nervousness. The closed carriage rumbled over the cobblestones of Aldon's streets, accompanied by the clop of the guards' horses as they rode on either side.

Essie leaned forward to wave out the window, but Farrendel kept his back pressed to the seat, staying out of sight. He needed every moment to gather his wits before he faced the people of Escarland.

After another wave, Essie turned to him, her grin beaming and bright in her green eyes. "I know you aren't excited about this, but I'm glad you're coming with me today."

Even if he felt nearly ready to vomit out the window, Farrendel gave a slight nod. He was glad to be seeing this side of Essie. She wore a green, Escarlish-style dress, though a simple one without ornamentation or the yards of skirts of a ball gown. Yet nestled on her red hair was her Tarenhieli crown formed of twining leaves, the one that matched the one he wore.

"We're almost there." She peeked out the window once again. "Looks like there is a crowd already gathered."

A crowd. Farrendel tried to draw in a deep breath, but it felt stuck in his tightening throat.

"It will be all right." Essie reached for his hand. "I'll stop to talk to several people, but all you have to do is stay by my side and give me an adoring look now and then. I think you can manage that."

Despite the tightness in his chest, he found himself smiling. "Yes."

When she put it that way, it did not sound so hard.

"If you were to talk to one or two people, that would not be amiss." Essie's expression sobered. "But you don't have to. Save your people tolerance for once we get inside the orphanage."

He nodded, staring down at their clasped hands.

Essie squeezed his fingers. "It won't be so scary. They're just children."

When she paused, Farrendel managed to raise his head to meet her gaze.

She smiled at him, though her smile was more sad than warm. "Many of the children at the orphanage are illegitimate sons and daughters of the Escarlish nobility." The smile left Essie's face entirely. "And many of their mothers were not willing participants like your mother was."

Farrendel swallowed and looked away. That was one comfort he had. His parents had made mistakes, but at least he knew those decisions had been mutual. Neither had been forced.

The carriage halted, and Farrendel found himself

following Essie out of the carriage. The gathered crowd started cheering and calling Essie's name, held back by a line of Escarlish guards.

Farrendel trailed behind Essie as she waved and walked past the first few people. Then, she halted and crouched before a woman and a little girl. Farrendel halted as well, standing behind Essie and trying not to look scary.

The little girl held out a bouquet of a few semi-wilted flowers. "For you, Prin'ess Essie."

"Thank you." Essie took the flowers and straightened. For a moment, she glanced between the flowers and their clasped hands, as if she was considering which she would have to drop to regain a free hand.

Farrendel took the flowers from her, earning him a smile from Essie.

Strolling along the line of people, Essie stopped to talk to a few more people. Others gave her flowers, and Farrendel added them to the growing bouquet he was carrying. If he focused on Essie, the gnawing panic remained at the edges.

Finally, the doors opened for them, then shut behind him, blocking out the clamor of too many people crowded in the street.

Several women wearing neat, professional looking dresses waited for them in the entry. They introduced themselves, but Farrendel's head was still in too much of a whirl for him to remember their names or their roles here at the women's and children's shelter.

A servant woman hurried to him, giving a curtsy. "I can put those in water, Your Highness."

Farrendel just blinked at her, then at Essie.

"The flowers?" The servant woman bobbed another

curtsy and pointed at the flowers he still gripped in his hand.

Oh, right. The flowers. Farrendel stiffly handed them over, flexing his fingers to loosen the tension. The poor stems looked a bit worse for the wear after he had been gripping them so tightly.

One of the women gestured toward a door leading off to the right. "The children are doing finger painting, if you would like to join them, Your Highnesses."

Essie grinned, her fingers squeezing his as if to try to bring him back to her from the buzzing, whirling panic that threatened to steal him away.

He just had to get through this. A few more days, then he and Essie could retreat to Lethorel.

ESSIE KNELT on the floor in a cluster of children, her fingers and arms covered in paint as she worked on a finger painting. It was supposed to be Ellonahshinel, but apparently trying to capture the beauty of the elven treetop city was a little much for finger paint, especially with Essie's lack of artistic skills.

One of the little girls held up her picture, featuring a badly proportioned stick figure with red hair that looked more like flames shooting out of the top of her head. "This is for you, Princess Essie."

"Thank you. It is beautiful." Essie carefully took the picture, trying not to get too many smears of paint on it from her fingers.

"And this is Prince Farren...Farrdel..." One of the little boys held up his painting, his forehead scrunched as he tried to pronounce Farrendel's name. The picture had another stick figure, with massive, pointed ears and swords across his back.

"Oh, that is a lovely drawing of Prince Farrendel." Essie grinned, glancing from the painting to Farrendel. Would their children draw pictures like this someday? Family portraits of stick figures with giant ears for him and a disaster of red hair for her?

Farther down the table, Farrendel sat in his own group of children. Only the tip of one pointer finger had paint on it, and Farrendel carefully washed his finger each time he changed colors. Given how he was about cleanliness, Essie was surprised he had even been willing to participate, much less had put up with it so well.

As if sensing that she was looking at him, Farrendel glanced up at her. His mouth tipped in a smile, and he gestured at her. "You have a smear of paint on your cheek."

Essie frowned and reached for her face, then halted when she realized that she would only smear more paint on herself. "It isn't the first time." She lowered her hand and smiled first at him, then at the children sitting around her. "Did you know that in an elven wedding ceremony, they paint runes on each other's faces? The trolls paint runes on each other before battles."

No need to mention that those battles were fights to the death.

Farrendel leaned over the children and touched her cheek. Essie held still as he gently traced something over the smear of paint. When he was finished, he straightened. "That means *Speak kindness*."

The children gazed at the two of them with wide eyes.

93

Essie smiled to reassure them. "Yes. For the elves, such runes are more than a mere wish. It is a blessing."

"Whoa." One of the boys gaped first at Essie, then at Farrendel. "Can I have one?"

Farrendel glanced at Essie, as if asking permission. Essie gave a slight nod. The *Speak kindness* blessing seemed like a simplified version of what they'd spoken during their elven wedding. Like the *Speak honor* she had painted on him before the Dulraith in Kostaria.

Farrendel dipped his finger in the blue paint, then traced a rune on the boy's face. "This one means *Live bravely*. It is the blessing for a warrior."

The boy straightened his shoulders, standing a little taller.

The other boys jumped to their feet, clamoring to have their own faces painted with warrior runes.

While many of the boys flocked to Farrendel, the girls turned to Essie. She didn't know quite as many runes as Farrendel, but she could copy the warrior one that some of the girls asked for and she could do the ones for kindness and honor that the other girls wanted. Soon, they had an entire room full of children running around with elven runes painted on their cheeks and foreheads and hands. Packs of them were running around the room, waving imaginary swords.

Time to take their leave. The children were at the end of their best behavior, and they would want to be given the freedom to go play. Essie stood and gathered the paintings the children gave her while leaving the paintings she and Farrendel had done with the children. Essie said goodbye to the women who ran the orphanage, took the bouquet that a servant produced, then she held out her hand to Farrendel. "Ready to return to Buckmore Cottage?"

Farrendel eyed her paint-smeared fingers for a long moment before he sighed and took her hand. The children were split between giggling and making "ew" noises.

Some of the crowd still lingered outside, and Essie smiled and waved, though she didn't stop to talk to any of them. Her paint-smeared appearance would be reported in the papers, but it would likely be just as much good press as bad.

As soon as they were in the carriage, Farrendel slumped back against the seat and let out a sigh. "I survived."

"Yes. You survived admirably well." Essie smiled and traced the scar on his cheek, leaving a smudge of paint.

Farrendel huffed and started to raise his arm to scrub his face. But he halted as she sat on the seat next to him. "Finger painting creates a mess."

"Yes, but aren't the results adorable?" As the carriage started moving, Essie showed him the painting the child had done of him.

Farrendel's eyebrows shot up. "Is that how my ears look to you humans?"

"Don't fret. They aren't that big. This is a child's finger painting, after all." Essie grinned and waved back the way they'd come. "Did you see my attempt at Ellonahshinel? I think the children were more accurate."

"True." Farrendel's mouth quirked into a broader smile than she'd seen since Averett had come to fetch them from Tarenhiel. He wrapped an arm around her waist and tugged her closer. "That was not as bad as I feared."

"But you're glad it's over." Essie snuggled closer to Farrendel's side. It had been fun spending time with the children at the orphanage again, and it had been nicer doing it with Farrendel.

Yet, there was something about seeing Farrendel interacting with children that sent her thoughts spinning to those someday dreams. The dreams of little red-haired children with pointed ears running around with far too much energy.

Ugh. Essie buried her face against Farrendel's shoulder. She had baby fever big time, and she didn't dare admit it to Farrendel just yet. Especially not with all this stuff going on right now, with his parentage coming to light here in Escarland and him working with the counselors about his own feelings regarding his illegitimate birth. Then there was his magical engineering degree, and that would keep him rather busy for the next few years.

They had plenty of time, most likely, given that the heart bond would cause her to live somewhere between four and five hundred years.

But that didn't stop her from thinking about it every time she saw a baby or a child. And although Essie would live for several hundred years, the rest of her family would have normal, human lifespans. If she wanted her children to have a chance to know her family, then children would need to come along sooner rather than later.

Farrendel remained quiet during the trip back to the palace, and Essie didn't break his reverie, knowing that he was gathering himself back together after the busyness of the morning.

When they arrived, Essie and Farrendel disembarked in front of Winstead Palace, since the carriage house was closer to the main palace than their cottage.

Another carriage filled the drive, this one white and

open. Jalissa and Edmund were climbing down, Edmund reaching for Jalissa's hand.

Essie leaned closer to Farrendel and spoke in a lowered voice. "I wonder what is going on with them. You didn't see them during the war, but they had gotten close. Then they went frosty toward each other overnight. And now they're suddenly all cozy again. It seems strange."

Farrendel eyed Jalissa and Edmund, his forehead wrinkling. "I do not know. I had not noticed."

"And they were in an open carriage. It will be all over the papers that they were seen together, right alongside stories of our visit." Essie studied the way that Edmund and Jalissa were strolling close together. "Edmund would know that. And he never does anything without a reason. It is almost as if…"

As if Edmund had *wanted* the papers to get all distracted over a possible elf-human romance between Edmund and Jalissa.

No, Edmund wouldn't start something with Jalissa to take the heat off Essie and Farrendel, would he? He wouldn't add to the plan without telling any of them.

Except, this was Edmund. He always had his own schemes going, and Essie rarely learned about them unless they involved her. Sometimes she didn't find out even then. Edmund was layers of secrets underneath his easy-going demeanor.

Surely Edmund would have told Jalissa, at least, if he was using her in some plot. He wouldn't toy with her.

"Almost as if, what?" Farrendel turned his gaze onto Essie. "Should we worry?"

"Edmund can take care of himself, whatever he has going on." Essie pasted on a smile, since Jalissa and Edmund were headed in their direction. She still had just enough time to answer Farrendel in a low tone. "But it is Jalissa I'm worried about."

Farrendel frowned, and he was still frowning when Jalissa and Edmund reached them.

Jalissa was smiling, her eyes brighter than Essie had seen since they'd returned from the war in Kostaria. "Edmund brought me to the Kingsley Gardens. I would gladly live there forever."

"Forever?" Farrendel raised his eyebrows.

"Maybe not forever, but I will have to visit more frequently whenever I am in Escarland." Jalissa twirled a white rose in her fingers, smiling down at it with a soft, almost sappy expression.

"I should have mentioned the gardens before." Essie smiled at Jalissa. Of course someone with plant growing magic like Jalissa's would appreciate the Kingsley Gardens.

Edmund had known. And he had taken Jalissa.

Perhaps it was merely that. Maybe Essie was reading more into it than what Edmund intended.

But there was something suspicious going on with her brother. Well, more suspicious than usual.

CHAPTER
NINE

Still dripping river water onto the plush carpet of the royal train car, Edmund stood in front of his brother Averett. "You married Essie off? To Laesornysh? What were you thinking?"

Averett groaned, his head in his hands, his elbows on his knees. "I don't know, all right? It wasn't the plan, but then Essie seemed to take it in her head that it was a good idea, and the elves were pushing for it. We need peace with them. I had to agree to a marriage alliance."

"Then you should have married me off, not Essie." Edmund clenched his fists and spun away to face the wall before Averett read the truth in his eyes.

Edmund would have gladly agreed to a marriage of alliance. Most likely, King Weylind would have arranged it with Jalissa. Surely Edmund could have gotten her to fall in love with him all over again, this time as himself.

Except that Edmund had secrets he couldn't tell her. There was a reason he'd walked away a little over two years ago. His secrets wouldn't be erased, even if a marriage alliance made it possible for a human to marry an elven princess.

"King Weylind wouldn't hear of it." Averett gave another moan. "It was Essie or no alliance at all."

Probably just as well. A relationship shouldn't be built on lies.

"Fine." Edmund turned back to Averett. "I'll go back to Tarenhiel and keep an eye on Essie."

"Thanks." Averett lifted his head, giving Edmund a glimpse of his tortured expression. "I might be able to live with myself if I know you're looking after her."

For four days, Edmund spent nearly every minute with Jalissa. In any other circumstances, it would have been wonderful. Instead, it was torment, pretending he was not falling in love with her all over again.

As Edmund walked into the family dining room in Winstead Palace, he could sense the tension, even before he saw the look on Averett's face.

Averett and Julien sat at the table, their plates set aside and a newspaper spread in front of them. Either Mother and Paige had already eaten, or they had taken their plates elsewhere.

Averett glanced up as Edmund took a seat next to Julien. "We have a problem."

Julien scratched at his thick, red-brown beard. "The *Sentinel* published their story of Farrendel's illegitimate birth even earlier than we expected. Before the *Times* got their article out."

"And it's just as bad as we feared." Averett's frown deepened, and he pushed the paper toward Edmund. "Take a look. There's something about it that's striking me as odd."

Edmund took the paper, and quickly scanned the article. The words had clearly been chosen to be as lurid and shocking as possible. "Well, for one, the *Sentinel* clearly has no fear of our lawyers suing them for libel."

"Yes, though they confined the worst of their vulgar descriptions to the elves involved. I guess they have less fear of the elves suing them." Averett sighed and rubbed a hand over his face. "Though they did cast a few aspersions at Essie and on me for agreeing to the marriage alliance. They seem to assume that I knew Farrendel was illegitimate from the beginning."

"Well, you did. Kind of." Edmund scanned the rest of the article, trying to put his finger on his own uneasy feeling about it.

Farrendel's illegitimacy had been in one of Edmund's reports to Averett, but it had been a footnote, irrelevant for Escarland's national security at the time compared to Farrendel's reputation and skills as Laesornysh. It had slipped Averett's mind until Edmund had reminded him of it after Essie had married Farrendel.

"It is beside the point when I remembered." Averett shook his head. "I might have resisted the marriage alliance more, but I'm rather glad I didn't."

Edmund couldn't help but agree. It was hard to imagine Farrendel and Essie not being, well, Farrendel and Essie.

Julien leaned back in his chair, staring at the paper and grimacing. "What's the plan now?"

"The castle staff will hate it, but we'll have to move up the ball, if possible. Then Essie and Farrendel can make their graceful exit." Averett's frown eased a touch. "I'm sure

Farrendel won't mind retreating to Tarenhiel earlier than expected."

Julien pushed away from the table. "I'll warn Essie and Farrendel. I don't think they'll want to postpone their trip to the veteran's hospital, but they need to be warned what kind of situation they'll be walking into."

Edmund nodded absently, still perusing the paper. Averett was right. There was just something about this piece... "Wait. I got it."

Julien paused, then strode back to the table. Averett leaned forward again.

Edmund pointed at the paper. "Here. And here. The wording is nearly identical to the draft of the article that Trent showed me." His mind swirled as he took in the implications. "The *Times* has a mole who is feeding information to the *Sentinel*. That's how they found out about Farrendel's illegitimate birth."

Julien dragged his hand over his beard.

Averett muttered under his breath, then glanced up at Edmund. "You know what this means, don't you? That exclusive interview could also be in the hands of the *Sentinel*."

Now Edmund had to bite back a few curses in elvish. That exclusive interview had been entrusted to Trent. The *Sentinel* would twist it beyond recognition.

Edmund pushed away from the table. "I need to talk to Trent. I'll be back as soon as I can."

It took a stop at the safe house the Intelligence Office maintained in Aldon to dress down, but by the time

Edmund showed up at the brick building that housed the *Times*, he wore grubby brown trousers, an off-white shirt, and a cap pulled over his hair. Smudges of dirt obscured his features.

He knocked loudly, hoping someone would be able to hear the noise over the incessant clacking clamor of the printing presses.

After a long moment, a boy of no more than twelve opened the door. His gaze swept over Edmund. "What do you want?"

"I got information for Trent Bourdon." Edmund stuck his hands in his pockets, shoulders slumping. "Said he'd have a coin for me if I brought him talk of the elf prince."

"I'll go and see if he has time to talk." The boy shut the door in Edmund's face.

Edmund rocked back and forth on his heels as he waited, keeping an eye on the few men that passed by. None of them looked like they would mug him, but it paid to be wary when walking the streets.

Finally, the door opened, and Trent stepped out. As soon as he saw Edmund, his eyes widened. "What are you...never mind. You saw the *Sentinel* this morning, I suppose."

Edmund nodded.

Trent glanced around, then started off toward the side alley. Edmund followed, neither of them speaking as they trekked around the corner of the large brick building and halted in the dimly lit, refuse-filled alley. A few alley cats lurked in the corners, but no people.

"You have a mole." Edmund started to lean toward the wall, then halted when he saw that it was covered with a mossy slime.

"Don't you think I know that now?" Trent muttered

something under his breath, dragging his hand through his hair. "I have to re-write my entire article. After I just spent an hour with my chief editor trying to prove that the *Sentinel* plagiarized an article that I wrote months ago, not the other way around as it appears."

"Did you turn in the interview already?" Edmund clenched his fists.

Trent faced Edmund. "Yes. I submitted it to my editor last night."

"Then run it. Run it today. Make it a special edition if you have to." Edmund wanted to grab Trent and shake him, if that would make him see how urgent this was. "Surely your editor will agree. The *Times* needs to run your version of the interview before the *Sentinel* manages to steal that as well."

Trent nodded and sighed. "We need to get on top of this story. I doubt they will be so bold as to make it obvious that they stole the interview—nothing the *Times* or the crown could go after them for—but they will make use of it."

"Do you have any idea who the mole might be?" Edmund glanced over his shoulder, checking that they were still alone.

"No." Trent grimaced and paced across the alley again. "And that's what worries me. This business is always a little cutthroat. We all spy on each other a bit. But actually stealing an article isn't done. If the *Times* could prove it, we could get the *Sentinel* shut down. No story, not even something this huge, is worth risking that."

It didn't make sense. The *Sentinel* hadn't had to steal Trent's article and twist it.

Unless the *Sentinel* didn't realize the source of the article. The mole must have stolen the articles and given them to the

Sentinel—a paper known to disparage the royal family—as another way to hurt them.

"I agree." Edmund gestured back toward the front door. "Let me know if you hear anything, and I'll do the same if I find out anything during my own investigation."

Though Edmund wasn't going to tell Trent that he was going to put a stakeout on the *Times* to try to find the perpetrator.

Trent nodded and took a step back the way they'd come.

Edmund drew in a deep breath. "Wait. There's one more thing."

Trent turned back to Edmund, eyebrows scrunched. "Yes?"

"I have another story for you to run." Edmund looked away, staring down at the squishy layer of filth covering the alley's cobbles. "Write that a palace insider told you that Prince Edmund of Escarland and Princess Jalissa of Tarenhiel have confirmed that they are courting. They have been falling in love since the war with Kostaria, and this crisis with Prince Farrendel and Princess Elspeth brought them closer."

Trent's eyebrows shot up. "What game are you playing? Is this the kind of story that I'm going to regret running?"

"Probably." Edmund couldn't hold Trent's gaze for more than a moment. "Don't worry. You'll be the first reporter I tell about any breakup."

"I see." Trent crossed his arms.

He probably did see all too much. He was too canny not to see right through Edmund.

"Just don't tell anyone about this story." Edmund managed to meet Trent's gaze again. "We can't risk the mole getting a hold of this one as well. This is your paper's chance to get the edge back over the *Sentinel*."

"I won't tell a soul about this article even if I have to typeset it myself." Trent's jaw worked. "Sometimes, it just doesn't pay to be an honest reporter."

Or an honest spy, but Edmund couldn't say that out loud.

Instead, he nodded, then strode past Trent back into the larger street, its cobbles shadowed by the large warehouses, tenant buildings, and other brick edifices looming high overhead.

Now he just had to break the news to Jalissa that their pretend courtship was going to be splashed all over the papers tomorrow.

EDMUND WAITED, his words still hanging on the slight afternoon breeze. He and Jalissa stood in a corner of Winstead Palace's manicured gardens, their nook protected by several hedges and a statue.

Jalissa's flowing blue-and white-dress draped around her slim form as she hugged her arms over her stomach. The breeze tossed her glossy brown hair.

It was all Edmund could do to stop himself from pulling her into his arms. She looked so forlorn, and he wanted to comfort her.

But it wasn't his place. He was supposed to be figuring out how to let her go. He was responsible for the mess in her life right now, and he felt burdened to fix it. But, perhaps, it wasn't his place to fix it—to fix her—any more than it was his place to hold her right now.

Jalissa's shoulders straightened and, when she spun to

face him, her face was unlined and frozen in a serene expression. "Very well. This is the reason you proposed this pretense in the first place."

"Yes." Edmund shouldn't let it hurt that she had gone all cold again.

"In that case, I will plan on a carriage ride through the streets of Aldon tomorrow." Jalissa raised her chin slightly. "We need to get people talking about us as much as possible."

Edmund nodded, unable to meet her gaze. This was not at all like what he had envisioned when he'd proposed this farce of a courtship. He'd thought a fake courtship would at least feel warm. Not as cold and calculating as one of his spying missions.

Then again, what else had he expected? He was playing a role, as was she. Roles never had the warmth of the real thing.

"The servants are scrambling, but the ball will be held tomorrow night." Edmund flicked a glance at Jalissa before looking away. "When we attend together, that will cement our courtship in the minds of everyone there."

"I see your plan is working perfectly." Jalissa's tone remained as stiff and cold as her expression.

"Our plan. I couldn't do this without you." Edmund turned back to her, working to put a lighter tone into his voice. "You have quite the knack for this. You're going to turn into quite the spy."

Jalissa raised her eyebrows. "Do you really wish to encourage me to pursue such an endeavor? I may end up spying on Escarland down the road, you know."

"Then you would provide a very lovely challenge." Edmund grinned, wishing he had the freedom to cup her chin and lean closer to savor this moment. "Just wait until the ball. It is the perfect place to practice observation skills. How do you think I got so good at it?"

Jalissa huffed and looked like she wanted to roll her eyes. But at least she no longer had that tight expression marring her features.

E ssie adjusted the bodice of her dress to make sure it lay right. "Farrendel, can you tie the laces for me?"

She glanced over her shoulder as Farrendel stepped behind her, his Escarlish shirt still unbuttoned and hanging loose, giving her a glimpse of his chest.

He gathered her hair, then held it out over her shoulder. "I do not want to tie your hair into the knot by accident."

Holding her dress to her with one arm, she took her hair with the other. "Remember, make sure it's snug."

Farrendel's deft fingers worked on the laces, and Essie took shallow breaths so that he could get her dress tight enough to stay in place. The last thing she needed was a wardrobe malfunction. That would not help them in public opinion.

He tied a knot and tucked the laces into the top of the dress. "How is that?"

Essie let go of her dress and took a few experimental breaths. "Perfect."

She was wearing the same dark green dress with an

Escarlish, structured bodice and a flowing, Tarenhieli skirt that she had worn to the recent ball in Tarenhiel. That was the advantage of attending events in two different kingdoms. She could re-wear dresses in the same year without causing all kinds of gossip about it.

As she turned, Farrendel finished buttoning his shirt. He reached behind him and picked up two Escarlish neckcloths. "Which one?"

Essie studied them as he held up first one, then the other. The one neckcloth was a pure white while the other was a light gray. Against his gray shirt and dark gray-blue Escarlish coat, the light gray one was too subtle. "The white one."

Draping the light gray neckcloth over the chair's back once again, he set to work tying the neckcloth just as quickly as he did the laces on her bodice.

As Essie returned to her dressing table to pick out her jewelry for the evening, a knock came at their door.

Essie halted and glanced over her shoulder as Farrendel reached for the door. They weren't expecting anyone before they left for the ball tonight.

When Farrendel swung the door open, Jalissa was standing there, wearing her gown for the evening. The white bodice had light blue embroidery while the skirt was overlaid with a light blue, sheer fabric that floated as Jalissa moved. A light blue cape edged in gold flowed down from Jalissa's shoulders, lending her an even more regal, elven air.

Jalissa clasped and unclasped her hands in front of her. "Elspetha, would you give my hair an Escarlish style for tonight? It likely would be best, given…the courtship."

Essie grimaced. Jalissa and Edmund claimed they were courting, but there was something off about the way they spoke about it. They weren't acting like two people falling in love. Essie should know, after all, what that looked like.

Still, Essie smiled and steered Jalissa to her dressing table. "Here, sit. I'm not skilled enough with a curling tong to get your hair to curl the way it should for most hairstyles. But I think I can manage a few braids and pinning it up."

Jalissa's shoulders remained tense as Essie gently brushed her hair, avoiding touching Jalissa's scalp with the brush. Essie set to work braiding sections of Jalissa's hair. Once she had a bunch braided, she gathered the rest of Jalissa's hair into a chignon at the back of her head, then pinned the ends of the braids into the chignon. It wasn't as fancy as a maid with training would be able to do, but it looked nice. And, as per Jalissa's request, it was clearly an Escarlish style.

"You'll definitely turn my brother's head tonight." Essie lifted the lid of her jewelry chest set to the side of the dressing table. It took a moment, but she found the slim tiara set with tiny, sparkling diamonds and a few sapphires that would work perfectly with Jalissa's hairstyle. "Here, you can borrow my tiara. I think I have some brown thread to sew it into your hair."

"Sew it into my hair?" Jalissa turned in her chair, eyes widening.

"Yes, that's how we keep tiaras from falling off." Essie located some brown thread in the sewing kit for gown emergencies. It took her a little longer than it would have a maid, but she soon had the tiara securely attached to Jalissa's hair. "An Escarlish tiara completes the look."

Jalissa nodded, then she reached up to touch the tiara. It must feel strange, since elves tended to wear circlets, crowns, and diadems that went around the forehead rather than tiaras.

"While you're here, you can help sew my tiara in place." Essie picked out the tiara she had planned on wearing. This one was set with diamonds as well, though a few emeralds accented the piece. She held out the tiara and the red thread that matched her hair to Jalissa. "I was going to ask Farrendel to do it."

"That would have been a disaster." Farrendel shrugged into his Escarlish coat, adjusting how it fell across his shoulders.

"You would have managed. Or I would have tracked down Miss Merrick." Essie swapped seats with Jalissa, then held still as Jalissa set to work.

Farrendel picked up his swords. "Once you are finished, I need you to clip my swords in place."

"You'll have to take a look, Jalissa." Essie kept her head perfectly still. "The Escarlish tailor did a masterful job with Farrendel's coat. The straps for his swords are underneath the coat, and it is tailored to hide them. But there are four places in the back for the sheaths to clip to the straps, and they entirely disappear once the swords are in place. It looks very smart and dashing."

Jalissa made a *hmm* noise in her throat. Then, she tied off and cut the thread. "I believe your tiara should stay in place."

"Thank you." Essie stood, smiled at Jalissa, then she walked over to Farrendel. He held out his swords, then turned. Essie quickly attached first one, then the other sword in place. "All done."

Farrendel shrugged his shoulders, as if testing how the swords felt. "Linshi. Do you have your gun?"

"Yes." Essie had her derringer strapped to her ankle. It had saved her life when she and Farrendel had been captured, even if it hadn't been enough to save Farrendel from the trolls.

Jalissa glided to the door. "Linshi, isciena. I will see you at the ball shortly."

Essie waited until the door shut before she wrapped her arms around Farrendel's waist. "Are you all right? Given what happened last time we were at a ball like this in Escarland…"

Farrendel heaved a deep breath, but he embraced her, his hands warm against her back. "I am all right. We both have access to my magic now. Iyrinder and Captain Merrick plan to wait outside the ballroom, so we will be guarded on our walk back to Buckmore Cottage."

Perhaps it was an overabundance of caution, but Essie wouldn't argue with it. Last time had turned into a nightmare. She, too, needed this night to end well. She needed to erase the fear that still lingered from those moments of being kidnapped right out of her childhood home.

Essie leaned closer to him, careful not to smudge her cosmetics or knock her tiara askew. In the heart bond, his magic crackled in a comforting way, at her fingertips in case she needed it. "Thank you for taking extra care with our security tonight."

His sigh washed warm against her hair. "I will still likely be jumpy tonight."

"So will I." Essie straightened and touched her hair to make sure her curls and the tiara were still in place. "We might as well get going. We don't have to make a grand entrance."

Instead of holding out his arm, Farrendel took her hand, clasping it in the Escarlish way of holding hands.

Essie didn't let go, and she didn't care if anyone gossiped

about their show of affection in public once they reached Winstead Palace and its ballroom. Right now, she needed the warmth of Farrendel's hand clasping hers and the assurance that this time he wasn't going to get ripped away from her.

JALISSA GLIDED into the ballroom of Winstead Palace with her hand on Edmund's arm. She had done so at the last Escarlish ball she had attended, but this felt even more…real. Back then, she had merely been slightly attracted to the Escarlish prince. That was before the two weeks of fighting across Kostaria when she had turned to him so completely during those dark weeks when one of her greatest fears—that of losing her brothers—had been coming true.

Edmund leaned closer to her, his breath tickling her ear. "You look especially beautiful tonight."

Jalissa felt her ears heat, but she forced herself to glare at Edmund. She refused to be warmed by his compliment. "This is a ruse, remember? You should not be whispering compliments in my ear."

"Perhaps not, but you're too tense." Edmund's chuckle was far too close, weakening her knees.

"And you are faking this courtship far too well." Jalissa could not keep the breathy note from her voice.

When she glanced at Edmund, he had a small quirk to his mouth. "We've drawn attention, whispering like this. By now, half the court is talking about our growing romance."

Jalissa wanted to smack him. Instead, she tried to sharpen her glare. "Perhaps I should stomp off. That would ruin your plans."

"You won't." Edmund started walking again, gently

steering her with him. "Instead, we are going to dance far too many dances together, and we'll spend so much time with each other that no one will question that I've lost my head over the ethereal elven princess."

Jalissa sighed, trying to regain her composure. "And I suppose you'll keep whispering sweet nothings in my ear the entire time?"

"Actually, I was thinking we would play a game." Edmund's smile widened to a grin that glinted in his eyes. He tilted his head toward the gathered groups of Escarlish men in top hats and tailcoats and Escarlish women in large, poofy dresses. "We'll pick out details of those around us and try to make educated guesses about what those details tell us. It will be good practice for judging the character of your elf lords when they arrive."

As he spoke, he swept two glasses off the tray of a passing servant, holding one out to her.

Jalissa took the punch and sipped it to give herself a moment to study Edmund. Her stomach flipflopped at the mention of those elf lords. She was doing her best not to think about having to pick one. "I still do not understand why you wish to teach me how to be a spy."

"You would make a good spy." Edmund gave a hint of a shrug that seemed more an elven gesture than a human one. "I am your friend, whatever else has gone between us. If I can help you find more of a purpose, I will."

Purpose. Jalissa stilled. Edmund knew her far too well. Probably those annoying spy skills of his that gave him uncanny powers of observation.

Because she had only told one person about her longing for purpose. And that person had been dead for three years now.

Trying not to show how shaken she felt, Jalissa sipped her punch again and turned to face the rest of the ballroom just as a stir spread through the couples.

King Averett entered with his wife Queen Paige on his arm. Behind him, Prince Julien entered, followed by Farrendel and Essie. A group of Parliament members waylaid them, causing Farrendel's set expression to turn into that hard, Laesornysh look of his.

Edmund raised his glass in that direction. "We might as well start the game now. Can you tell what each of those Parliament members thinks of Farrendel?"

Jalissa studied them, taking in their stance. "Two of them are attentive. They must be in the coalition that supports closer ties with elves. The one in the green coat is shifting away, his lip curling whenever he glances at Farrendel."

"And the one in the dark blue coat?" Edmund raised his eyebrows as he took a sip of his punch.

Jalissa studied the fourth man talking with Farrendel, Essie, King Averett, and Queen Paige. "He keeps glancing away toward the crowd. I think he is bored with the conversation."

"That's my assessment too." Edmund shared a smile with her. "Good work, spy-in-training."

His words should not warm a place inside her. She did not truly want to be a spy. Nor were there any kingdoms left upon which Tarenhiel needed to spy, now that they had made peace with both Escarland and Kostaria. Sure, Mongavaria had given them some trouble over the Hydalla River and the ocean trade, but that was a minor scuffle compared to the tension and wars that had been fought with the other kingdoms.

The orchestra launched into the first song, and across the

room, King Averett bowed out of the conversation to open the dancing with Queen Paige.

Edmund set aside his glass and held out his hand. "May I have this dance?"

Jalissa set her own glass on the empty side table where it would be cleared by one of the servants bustling around the edges of the room. She took Edmund's hand and glided onto the dancing floor with him.

Yet, as much as she had been dreading this night, she found herself relaxing in Edmund's arms as they danced. Occasionally, he leaned close and whispered some observation. A dessert stain on someone's shirt. A lipstick smudge that indicated a couple had been kissing in the garden before joining the dance. A lord with mismatched socks that could be glimpsed when he walked.

Somehow, Jalissa found herself smiling. Laughing, even. Her heart was lighter than it had been in a long time.

For one night, she let herself pretend that she could allow her heart to fall for this human prince. What was one more pretense, after all?

"Do you feel like you have a purpose?" Jalissa looked up from her book, watching Elidyr as he bustled about with his duties. Even when he happened across her in the library, he never seemed to stop moving, as if he did not dare appear less than the most dutiful servant.

Elidyr halted, then gestured to the bookshelves. "Yes. I am serving my kingdom. It may appear insignificant to shelve books and run errands, but someone needs to do the small, invisible things. Not everyone can be a warrior."

Jalissa wished she had his conviction. Weylind and

Farrendel were both great warriors. Farrendel, especially, had single-handedly turned the tide of war. Melantha had power that made her valuable, even though Tarenhiel had many healers already.

But Jalissa had an average strength of magic and the most common form of it. What purpose could she serve?

E ssie climbed into the open carriage, taking her seat as Jalissa and Edmund claimed the velvet-covered bench across from her. "I'm glad you were able to come with me today. After the ball yesterday, Farrendel isn't up for going out and about again."

Instead, he, Julien, Iyrinder, and the other guards were spending a few hours in practice bouts. And that was after Farrendel had already spent most of the morning by himself in the treetops. How he had enough energy for fighting after getting up far too early and exercising was beyond Essie. Even after sleeping in, she was still tired after the late night.

Actually, she had been tired all week. Apparently she was out of practice handling such a busy schedule.

Captain Merrick rode before them while the rest of their guard detail fell into place around the carriage.

Edmund relaxed against the bench as the carriage exited the palace gates. "It has been far too long since I've spent a morning wandering Aldon with my sister. Not that I would have argued if Farrendel had wanted to come."

"You could have stayed behind and joined the sword practice." Jalissa smoothed her skirt, her words holding a bite underneath her smooth expression.

"And miss this chance to show Aldon just how in love we are?" Edmund's eyes twinkled as he draped an arm along the back of the seat, though he didn't touch Jalissa.

"Of course." Jalissa looked like she wanted to roll her eyes. Instead, she pasted on a smile and waved at some of the people they passed. "We do seem to be the darlings of the press at the moment."

Essie couldn't dispute that. She hadn't thought anything could push aside the scandal of Farrendel's birth, but it seemed that a romance between Edmund and Jalissa, the beautiful elven princess, could do exactly that. The people seemed to be eating it up, and the papers that morning had been filled with such a lengthy report on how attentive Edmund had been to Jalissa throughout the ball that even Farrendel and Essie had been little more than a footnote.

Not that Essie minded, but it was strange how suddenly popular Edmund and Jalissa had become.

Instead of asking Jalissa and Edmund what was going on, Essie turned and waved to the people they passed. She would have to trust that Edmund and Jalissa knew what they were doing. They didn't need her interfering.

"Was there somewhere you wanted to go?" Essie glanced at Edmund and Jalissa. At least the cheers had returned rather than the disapproval. "I have a few errands I'd like to run, but then I'm free."

Since Farrendel wasn't with them, she would take the opportunity to get his anniversary gift. Farrendel had been telling her all about this new model of safety goggles Lance had gotten. The goggles had all kinds of built-in gadgets and stuff, and Farrendel hadn't been able to stop talking about it.

"We could go to the Gardens again." Edmund met Jalissa's gaze, the two of them exchanging a speaking look. "Or we could take a trip to the edge of Aldon. There are some ancient elven ruins that you might find fascinating. They are from the time before the mountain elves and forest elves became two people, because the ruins are stone rather than only wood."

Essie resisted the urge to sag against the back of the bench. She wasn't sure she was up for a trip all the way to the edge of Aldon and back. But, if that was what Jalissa and Edmund wanted to do, then she would go along.

"That does sound interesting, but maybe another day." Jalissa shot a glance toward Essie, as if sensing her weariness. "I would appreciate another tour of the Gardens, and I think the ruins would make a good trip for all of us. Farrendel might enjoy seeing them as well."

Essie sent Jalissa a grateful smile. "Yes, he would."

As the carriage reached the city center, Essie directed the driver to halt. The footman handed her down, and she waited for a moment for Jalissa and Edmund to join her. As the carriage pulled out of the way, Essie turned to Edmund and Jalissa. "I have—"

Something slammed into her. Hard. A gunshot echoed in the tight confines of Aldon.

She was falling, pain bursting across her body.

Screams. People running. Jalissa and Edmund crouching over her. Captain Merrick standing with his back to her, shouting orders.

Essie tried to gasp in a breath, but agony tore through her

chest. The metallic, sour taste of blood filled her mouth. Her ears rang, her eyes blurry.

She fumbled to draw on the crackle of Farrendel's magic, reaching past the searing pain to the heart bond deep in her chest. A weak shield of shivering bolts sprang up around Essie, Jalissa, and Edmund.

But even as she got the shield in place, blackness clawed at the edge of her vision. The pain and darkness were taking her, and she couldn't protect Jalissa and Edmund from more gunshots. She couldn't...

She flailed for the heart bond, reaching, straining.

Farrendel...

FARRENDEL PARRIED IYRINDER'S SWORD, then side-stepped and spun to deflect a guard's thrust. At his back, Julien held off two of the other elven guards who had come along on this trip.

As Iyrinder lunged, Farrendel went to raise his sword. Sudden pain stabbed into his chest, so sharp that he had dropped one of his swords and fallen to his knees before he could draw in a breath.

He pressed a hand to his chest. But there was no wound, no blood on his fingers.

Then he registered the source of the pain, the frantic fear coursing through the heart bond.

Essie.

Iyrinder and Julien were before him. Distantly, their voices blended together, asking if Farrendel was all right.

There was no time to explain. He pushed to his feet, shoved past them, and ran for the gate. He had to get to

Essie. She was slipping away. Too much darkness. Too much pain.

He dragged in a breath, reaching for her through the heart bond and holding tight. Still, he could sense her fading. Whatever had happened, she was gravely injured.

No, she was dying. Too quickly for him to keep her alive through the heart bond while they were apart. He needed to get to her. He had to hold her hand and deepen the connection of the heart bond if he was to keep her alive.

He raced for the iron gate, blindly fumbling to throw himself up and over since there was no time to properly open it.

Hands grasped his shoulders, yanking him backwards.

"Amir, get down." Iyrinder's voice, loud in Farrendel's ear as he bodily hauled him down from the gate and swung him to the side.

Iyrinder staggered, the crack of a gunshot splitting the air.

More shouting. Julien was gripping Farrendel now, dragging him behind the protection of the stone wall. Guards surrounded them.

Farrendel clawed at Julien. "Essie. I need to get to Essie."

She was fading. Too fast. He was losing her, and no one seemed to understand that.

"Stay down." Julien's arms tightened around Farrendel, holding him in place. "You need to shield us. Use your magic."

Farrendel reached for his magic, and he nearly cast it at Julien to make him release his hold. But through the hazy whirl, he could make out Iyrinder lying there, blood soaking the front of his shirt. One of the other guards had dragged him into the shelter of the wall and pressed his hands to the wound.

That was a gunshot. Someone was shooting at the palace.

Someone had shot Essie.

Farrendel shuddered, his chest tearing apart. He drew on his magic, placing a shield across the gate and wall to keep more shots from hitting anyone else.

Gripping Julien's arm, Farrendel struggled to put words in order. "Essie. Shot. I have to get to her." Farrendel gasped in a breath past the agony from the heart bond.

Julien nodded and opened his mouth, then his gaze swung back to the gate.

Now Farrendel could hear more shouting, and he could sense Essie getting closer. He opened a gap in the shield of his magic as the guards swung the gate open.

A carriage raced inside, and Farrendel leapt for it, not even waiting for it to halt before he clambered up and over the side, tumbling to the carriage floor.

Essie lay across one of the benches, her face white, blood soaking the front of her green dress. So much blood.

Too much blood.

Edmund knelt on the floor next to her, pressing his hands to her wound, dark blood covering his fingers. Jalissa held Essie's head on her lap, her own dress bloody.

Farrendel lunged and clasped Essie's hand.

Another, deeper stab of pain lanced through his chest. He dragged in a breath past it, even though it now felt like his own chest, his own lungs, were tearing apart.

The carriage rumbled up the drive until it halted in front of Winstead Palace.

Farrendel only vaguely registered someone shouting for

the doctor. Averett, Paige, and Essie's mother ran down the steps of the palace. Voices babbled in an indistinct tumult.

But his world had narrowed down to Essie and their heart bond. Each breath shuddered through him. As he breathed, so did Essie, trembling with wet, bloody gasps.

This was a wound too deep for Escarlish medicine to heal. Farrendel could tell that already.

He forced himself to raise his head, his gaze so tunneled he could barely see those around him. He focused on Averett and Julien standing on the step of the carriage. "I need to get her to Tarenhiel."

Averett nodded, but he stared down at Essie with puckered lines across his brow. "It would take too long to go all the way to Estyra. I'll send word to Weylind. A healer can meet you at the border."

Farrendel could barely force his own nod. Of course. That would cut the trip nearly in half.

It would still take twelve hours to reach the border.

Even with the heart bond, Essie would not last that long, he did not think.

Averett and Julien disappeared, replaced by an Escarlish surgeon. He climbed into the carriage, Edmund and Jalissa making room for him. He promptly opened his medical bag.

Farrendel took Jalissa's place by Essie's head, kneeling beside the bench. He could not bring himself to watch the surgeon work.

Essie cried out, stirring, her eyes fluttering. Her head tilted toward him. "Farren…"

"I am here, Essie." Farrendel brushed her hair from her face, cradling her head. Her eyes blinked as she tried to focus on him. He brushed a kiss to her forehead. "Do not let go, shynafir. Hold tight to the heart bond, and do not let go."

She might have nodded, but her eyes closed. Her body went even more limp in his arms.

Somewhere, Edmund and the surgeon were talking. Farrendel's mind was buzzing far too much for him to understand.

Averett returned, resting a hand on Farrendel's shoulder. "The tracks are being cleared to Tarenhiel as we speak, and a message has been sent to Weylind."

Then Julien was there as well. "Charles Hadley has agreed to lend us his magically powered locomotive."

That snapped Farrendel's head up. It had been that train —or one of the ones like it—that had taken him and Essie to be handed over to the trolls. "No. Not…" He could not choke out the words past the panic.

"I know you had a bad experience with his locomotives before." Julien's expression was grave, his jaw tight beneath his beard. "But he owes the crown for what his son did to you and Essie. Your guards will be in the locomotive with the engineer to ensure your safety, and it will cut four or more hours from the trip to the border, since you won't have to stop for water and coal. Can you deny that those four hours could make all the difference?"

Farrendel glanced down at Essie's drawn face. Julien was right. Four hours could be the difference between life and death. For Essie…and for himself.

Because he had no intention of letting go. If that meant he died along with her, then so be it.

It was not what Essie would want. She would tell him to let her go when the time came. It was the same thing he had told her, after all.

Back then, she had not let him go. She had done it out of

126

her unflagging optimism, believing that if she held on just a moment longer, then everything would be all right.

He did not have that same conviction. No, he was clinging to her out of despair instead of hope. He was not strong enough to contemplate living without her. Not the best mindset. But he did not care. All that mattered was Essie.

The surgeon sat back on his heels, looking at Averett. "I have stabilized her as best I can. She ought to be brought to surgery."

"What would her chances be for survival?" Averett's tone remained far too calm.

Farrendel was shaking with the need to do something. What, he did not know. A part of him wanted to pick up Essie and simply start running for the border, even if logic told him that such an attempt would be futile.

The surgeon hesitated, looking away.

"That's what I thought." Averett's voice did not waver. "Then we'll send her to Tarenhiel. It's her best chance."

"I will keep her alive." Farrendel bit out the words past the pain. He drew in another, agonizing breath. Whatever the surgeon had done, breathing was a bit easier. Not much, but enough that Farrendel could think more clearly. "I am an elf. I am strong enough. Our elishina is strong enough."

The surgeon just regarded him. He did not seem puzzled, exactly. Perhaps he had been one of the surgeons who had worked with elves during the war, though Farrendel did not recognize him.

"I know you will." Averett met Farrendel's gaze a moment before he turned back to the surgeon. "Would you be willing to go along to keep her stable on the trip?"

The surgeon nodded. "Yes, Your Majesty. I will do my best." He hesitated, reaching for his bag and glancing between Averett and Farrendel. "Would it be all right if I give her a painkiller? Or would that interfere with this...heart bond?"

Farrendel managed a shake of his head. "No. If it will help her, then please give it to her."

"Do *you* need a painkiller?" The surgeon was studying Farrendel now.

Farrendel gave a larger shake of his head. "I must be alert."

He could not risk letting her go. He must consciously choose to hold on tight, giving her of himself to keep her alive.

While the surgeon administered the painkiller, Farrendel kept his gaze on Essie's face, unable to watch the needle as it was inserted in her arm.

Then the carriage was moving again, taking them straight to the small train station that was enclosed inside of the outer palace walls. A locomotive waited there, vibrating with the power of its engines even though no smoke poured from its smokestack. Only two train cars were hooked to it.

As the carriage drew to a halt, Farrendel gathered Essie into his arms, careful not to jostle her. Ahead of him, guards carried Iyrinder on a stretcher, heading for the second train car. Miss Merrick trailed after them, following them into the train.

Farrendel's knees shook as he climbed down from the carriage, Julien and Averett reaching to steady him.

Edmund and Jalissa waited next to the carriage, dark blood drying on their clothes. Edmund had one blood-stained hand gripping Jalissa's shoulder, his arm around her.

Edmund gave Farrendel a nod, his gaze dropping to Essie.

Jalissa reached out and gripped Farrendel's shoulder in an elven hug. She held his gaze for a long moment, her eyes far too knowing. "Keep her alive, shashon."

She did not say it out loud, but he could see in her eyes what she was really saying, *Do not die.*

Farrendel gave a nod, then strode toward the train as steadily as he could.

At the train, Essie's mother met him, then climbed onto the train in front of him.

He did not question her presence. Of course she would come. A mother would want to be with her daughter. Would want to be there if…

He shook his head and forced himself to climb the steps and enter the Escarlish royal seating car.

Essie's mother was already there, arranging the pillows on the bench-like couch that filled one side of the seating area beneath the paned windows.

Farrendel stumbled his way around one of the chairs and the low table in the center before he sank onto the couch, cradling Essie to him.

Essie's mother adjusted the pillow behind him, helped him situate Essie so that her legs were propped on the couch and her upper body was supported against Farrendel, her head on his chest. Finally, her mother spread a blanket over them.

"Linshi, Macha." Farrendel leaned his head against the pillows propped behind him, trying to catch his breath after the short walk to the train.

"If you need anything, I'm here." She took a seat across from them, her face drawn, her gaze focused on Essie.

The surgeon climbed on board, strode over to them, and checked Essie's pulse. After a moment, he nodded. "She still seems stable. I must attend to the elf that was injured."

Iyrinder. Farrendel had barely given him a thought. But he managed a nod now, even as the surgeon turned and left the car for the next one.

The train gave a lurch, then slowly eased into motion.

Farrendel squeezed his eyes shut, gripping Essie's hand and holding her to him.

Eight hours. He had to keep her alive for eight hours.

His breathing hitched, panic clawing at his chest, whirling in his head.

In his arms, Essie's muscles seized, her breathing growing fast and fluttering in time with his.

No. He could not give in to the panic. Essie needed him to take deep, steady breaths. He could panic later.

He forced himself to drag in a deep breath, letting it out slowly. Essie's chest rose and fell in time with his, her heart beating with his. The bandage over her shoulder showed hints of red, and he shifted to press their joined hands over the wound.

Pain scraped his chest with every breath, but Farrendel breathed through it. After all, this agony was nothing new. He had endured worse at the hands of the trolls. That pain had continued for two weeks. Eight hours was nothing compared to that.

It was still far too long. He rested his cheek lightly against the top of Essie's hair, drawing in a breath, drawing in her pain, and releasing his breath and releasing his strength to her.

He was going to get her to the elf healer. Or die trying.

CHAPTER
TWELVE

Jalissa wandered the library, her heart beating a little faster in her chest. Would Elidyr be working late again? She had seen a light gleaming through the windows and hoped it was him. This would be awkward if she found herself face-to-face with one of the other librarians and clerks who worked in the library here at Ellonahshinel.

But as she rounded the corner of one of the shelves, she found Elidyr, placing books back on a shelf. As soon as he spotted her, Elidyr dropped into a bow, his eyes respectfully turned toward the floor. "Amirah."

Jalissa smiled and took one of the books from him. "Would you mind some company?"

"No, of course not, amirah." He remained stiff, but he held out half the stack of books.

They did not speak as they shelved the books, but there was something comfortable—and comforting—about it. For a few hours, at least, this quiet servant's companionship banished her gnawing worry for her brothers.

J alissa stared as the train pulled away from Winstead Palace, wheels clacking against the iron rails in a raucous rhythm so unlike the smooth, nearly silent elven trains.

As the train disappeared out of sight and the guards swung closed the large, wooden gates where the tracks passed through the palace wall, something inside her snapped. She spun on Edmund, hands clenched. "They were supposed to be safe!"

She was not sure why she was all but shouting. She swung her fists at Edmund's chest, tears blurring his blue shirt.

He gripped her hands, pressing her fists against the warmth of his chest. "I know. I know, Jalissa."

The tears were coming too hard for shouting. She did not resist as Edmund drew her to him. Instead, she pressed her face into his shoulder and let herself sob, held secure in his strong arms, his shirt warm against her face.

Right now, she did not care that she was not supposed to allow her heart to fall for him again. She desperately needed his strength, as she had during the war.

She was not sure how long she stood there, sobbing in Edmund's arms. When she finally hiccupped her way to some semblance of silence, she reached to swipe her tears from her cheeks.

Edmund caught her hand. "You'll smear blood on your face."

Jalissa froze, staring at her blood-stained fingers held in his equally bloody hand. That was Essie's blood, crusting on Jalissa's skin. She had only hazy memories of those frantic moments of pressing her hands to Essie's wound, her human sister gasping.

Her skin crawled, and Jalissa shoved away from Edmund to scrub her hands on her dress. But her dress, too, was covered in blood.

All that blood. How was Essie still alive?

Jalissa shook, scrubbing her hands, her breathing growing ragged. She had to get her hands clean.

"Come on." Edmund gently took her by the shoulders, turning her toward Buckmore Cottage. "Let's get you back to the cottage where you can clean up."

He should not sound so calm and controlled. His sister was the one hurt, after all.

But Jalissa had seen the wild light in Farrendel's eyes. Either both of them survived, or neither of them would. Jalissa would lose both her little brother and the sister who had become very close to her, closer than her own sister was at the moment.

Jalissa leaned into Edmund as he walked with her down the path to the cottage. Guards fell into place around them, even more alert and wary than before. Jalissa's personal guard Sarya stuck close, as if prepared to throw herself in front of Jalissa to take a bullet for her at any moment.

When they reached Buckmore Cottage, Edmund handed Jalissa over to Sarya's care, and her guard hustled Jalissa to her room, then left to start the bath running.

Jalissa mechanically gathered fresh clothes, then washed in the large tub with its shower spigot. Farrendel did not like the Escarlish baths, but Jalissa was growing to love them. Perhaps she would have to install one in her suite of rooms in Ellonahshinel, like the one Farrendel had installed for Essie for her birthday.

Thoughts of Essie and Farrendel brought a lump to her throat, and Jalissa forced her mind away from memories of gunshots and blood.

When she was clean, Jalissa dressed in a worn, comfortable dress that probably should have been consigned to the rag bin a while ago. She only wore it when she knew she was not going to be around other people.

For a few minutes, she drifted through Buckmore Cottage, not sure what to do now. It seemed wrong to simply curl up on the couch with a good book while Essie was fighting for her life and Farrendel was fighting to keep her alive.

But what else was Jalissa supposed to do? Once again, she was helpless and left behind with nothing to do but fret.

Perhaps she should walk back to Winstead Palace and wait there with the rest of Essie's family. That was where the message would be sent once Essie and Farrendel reached the border.

Taking a deep breath, Jalissa swung the door open.

Edmund stood there, hand raised as if preparing to knock. His gaze flashed up to hers. "I was just coming to see if you were all right."

"I am fine." Jalissa bit her lower lip before she could ask if there had been any word. There would not. It had not even been an hour since the train left.

Edmund rocked back on his heels, his gaze shifting away from her. "Good. Well, good. If you need anything, Avie and Paige are remaining at Winstead Palace to wait for word. I need to start investigating what happened."

Jalissa caught her breath and straightened. This was something she could do. "I will help."

Edmund considered her for a long moment. "All right."

"Really?" For some reason, Jalissa had expected him to say no.

"You probably want something to do rather than sitting here, waiting." Edmund's gaze swept over her, and he frowned. "You'll need a different outfit."

Jalissa frowned down at her dress. "I agree that this one is a little worn…"

"No, actually, it isn't worn enough." Edmund motioned her to step back into the cottage. "An elf princess wandering the streets of Aldon is a little conspicuous."

She had not thought of that; she was not a spy like Edmund.

He led her back through Buckmore Cottage, then into one of the spare rooms. They managed to find a few trunks filled with discarded servants' clothing. Edmund sorted through the clothing, setting aside one pile for her, one for himself. He left, and Jalissa quickly changed into the scratchy, Escarlish dress, though she kept her own boots with her dagger hidden in its sheath strapped to her ankle.

It took some doing, but she managed to twist her hair into a bun. She then tied a kerchief over her hair the way she had seen some Escarlish women wear it, covering her pointed ears.

When she stepped out of the small room, Edmund was waiting, leaning against the wall. He straightened and gave a nod. "Well done. No one will recognize you in that."

Nor did he look anything like himself, in a slightly oversized shirt and worn trousers with stains at the knees.

Together, Jalissa and Edmund strolled out the gate by Buckmore Cottage. The guards did not even spare them a second glance, since they were likely less concerned about people leaving the palace than those entering. Especially after Essie had been shot.

Jalissa still glanced around warily. She would not think twice about strolling on her own back home in Estyra. But here in Aldon, she had never walked its streets without a squad of guards watching over her. The space around her felt strangely empty with only Edmund strolling at her side.

Edmund looked up, as if scanning the rooftops.

"What are you looking for?" Jalissa swept a glance over the rooftops of the nearby buildings.

"Not sure yet." Edmund kept walking, heading in the direction of the main gate of the palace where Iyrinder had been shot. "I heard the second gunshot as we were racing back to the palace. The gunshots sounded similar, perhaps identical. It was hard to tell over the rattling carriage wheels."

How had Edmund managed the presence of mind to observe all that? Jalissa had been too busy trying not to panic at the sight of Essie's blood gushing between her and Edmund's fingers.

But instead of saying that, Jalissa gave a little shrug. "A gunshot sounds like any other gunshot, does it not?"

"Yes and no." Edmund halted and regarded something, though Jalissa could not tell what had captured his attention. "In this case, we're dealing with a rifle, based on the wounds, the precision of the shots, and the way the sound of the gunshots had the sharp crack of a rifle rather than the boom of a shotgun or depth of a musket."

"A rifle?" Jalissa frowned at Edmund. "Essie and Iyrinder were shot in two different locations. Would that not take two different rifles and, thus, two assassins?"

"Not necessarily." Edmund pointed at a building that

stood a story taller than the others around it. "There. That one. With a good rifle, I think it would be possible for someone to target both the market street and the main gate."

Jalissa turned that over in her head. "That would indicate a level of planning. Are you suggesting this was a premeditated attack, rather than a crime of opportunity? Do you think Farrendel and I were the targets?"

She had to swallow several times at the bile rising in her throat. She had been a target during the war, but that had been in a more general way. Having someone target her specifically would be something unpleasant and new.

"Yes, I think this was meticulously planned. But I don't think you were a target." Edmund grimaced. "Word of the heart bond between Farrendel and Essie is no secret, not after it was discussed frequently during the war and now again thanks to the scandal. Farrendel has proven to be too indestructible thanks to his magic. The only way to distract Farrendel enough to shoot him would be to shoot Essie."

"And therefore trigger the heart bond." Jalissa hugged her arms across her stomach. "But, why? I thought the Escarlish people were coming to terms with having elves for allies? And why target Farrendel? He is a powerful ally to have on your side. Escarland is fortunate to have him."

"All excellent questions." Edmund set off walking once again. "But we don't have enough information yet to answer any of them. Let's see if we can talk our way into getting a tour of the upper floor of that building."

Jalissa hurried to keep up with him. Even with her longer strides, he set a deceptively fast pace that had her trotting to keep up, even though he looked like he was merely ambling along the street.

When they reached the building, Jalissa glanced up at the name above the door. "This appears to be a boarding house."

"Not too surprising. It's in a safe neighborhood, close to the palace and close to the city center." Edmund gestured farther down the street. "Hanford University isn't that far away either."

Before Jalissa had a chance to respond, Edmund lifted the brass knocker and rapped it sharply.

Only a few moments passed before the door swung open to show a thin woman with frizzy brown hair streaked with gray. "Can I help you?"

Edmund flashed that charming and innocent smile of his. "My sister and I are looking to rent a suite of rooms. Do you have any available?"

Jalissa barely kept from starting at the slick lies that poured from Edmund's mouth so easily. Elves could lie. There was no magic preventing them from doing so. But it was not done. It just was not.

The woman's gaze swept over the two of them. "I don't think you can afford rooms here. I run a respectable establishment."

Edmund didn't so much as stiffen. He simply glanced down at himself, his smile turning wry. "Sorry about our appearance. We work at the palace, and just got off our shifts. The rooms aren't for us. Our mother and younger siblings are moving here, and we need a place to rent while we look for a more permanent place for them to lease. We would not need the rooms for another week or so, if you don't have an immediate vacancy."

"Both of you will be pitching in your salaries?" The woman's frank gaze raked over Jalissa.

Jalissa forced herself to nod. She could not make herself verbally affirm Edmund's lies.

The woman didn't soften, exactly. But she gave a little nod. "As it so happens, I had a tenant leave less than an hour ago. I haven't had a chance to clean his rooms, however. If you can come back tomorrow, I can show you the rooms then."

Edmund made a wincing expression. "This is the only day my sister and I have a morning off at the same time. Is there any way we can tour the rooms now? We won't hold their state against you in any way. Your boarding house is so conveniently situated near the palace, after all."

"My family has been running a boarding house here for five generations, due to its convenient location." For some reason, the woman's sharp features broke into a self-satisfied smile. "Let me show you up."

The woman spun and marched back into the house. Edmund motioned for Jalissa to go first, and Jalissa walked into the boarding house. As Edmund entered after her, he leaned close, whispering, "Stay sharp. Note everything."

Then the woman was ascending the stairs with abrupt, firm steps, and Jalissa followed, running her hand up the banister. They climbed flight after flight, though it was nothing compared to all the stairs in Ellonahshinel.

"This is it." The landlady pushed the door open. As soon as she stepped inside the room, her nose wrinkled. "I'm afraid it's in a sorry state."

"I can assure you that my mother will keep up the place in a much more respectable fashion than your last tenant." Edmund spoke from behind Jalissa. How was he thinking of these answers so quickly?

"She would be an improvement. This morning, he let off

fireworks. Inside the room. That I was the last straw. I hustled him out of here promptly, I can assure you." The woman sniffed, sending a glare in the direction of the small fireplace next to the door. "Feel free to look around. I will have it neat as a pin by the time your family is ready to move in."

Jalissa pushed into the room. A wave of scents slammed into her, and it took all her princess practice to keep moving.

The place reeked of human occupation. A mix of body odor and a musty stench, despite the open window in the parlor. And something just a little bit floral that Jalissa could not identify.

But over that was the sulfuric tang of gunpowder. There were the remnants of something in the fireplace next to the door that could have been fireworks. The reek of gunpowder emanated strongly from that direction. Though, there was a hint of a deeper, different whiff of gunpowder that hung over the rest of the room.

The landlady glanced around again, then gave a huff. "He even left the window open, the blighter." She bustled across the room and slammed the window shut.

A window, Jalissa noted, that faced the market street where Essie had been shot.

The woman gave another, louder huff and rubbed her fingers together, black smudges showing on her fingertips. "And he left it terribly filthy. I can assure you, I run a respectable establishment."

"I'm sure." Edmund started strolling around the room. He paused for a moment by the now closed window, swiping his handkerchief over the window before he slipped it into his pocket.

He meandered over to the kitchen, going through it

while striking up a conversation with the landlady. Now that Edmund had seemingly gained her trust, she started up a rant on her previous tenant and the female company he used to bring up there, impugning the reputation of her "decent establishment."

Jalissa shook herself, headed across the room, and entered the bedroom. The blankets on the bed remained rumpled, but she did not find any clothes strewn about or personal items left behind. Whoever this assassin was, he was careful. Besides the faint whiff of a floral scent, no doubt the lingering perfume of one of the assassin's female visitors, there was nothing of interest here.

Here, too, the window was open. Jalissa peered out, taking in the view of the palace gates. From here, a screening line of trees protected the front of the palace while the wall guarded the rest of it. There were only the narrow openings between the wrought iron bars of the gate for the assassin to sight his target.

With a shiver, Jalissa turned away and returned to the main parlor. Edmund was nodding as he peered around the kitchen. The landlady seemed to be giving him a description of the last tenant. How Edmund had worked that into a natural conversation, Jalissa did not know.

"Sha—" No, she could not call him *brother* in elvish. Nor could she call him Edmund. "Eddie." She hoped the trace of her elvish accent was less noticeable to the landlady than it was to her. "There is a lovely view of the palace gate from the bedroom."

From across the room in the small kitchen area, Edmund flashed her a grin, then winked where the landlady would not see. "Mother will love it. And she will be able to watch the girls go into town from the window in the parlor. Yes, this will do nicely, I think."

While Edmund and the landlady discussed rent and the terms, Jalissa wandered around the room one last time, trying to fix every detail in her memory. She was not sure what she was supposed to be looking for. Besides the gunpowder residue on the windows, nothing struck her as a sign that a skilled assassin had been here.

When Edmund finished up, Jalissa trailed him down the stairs, the now smiling landlady in their wake. Neither of them spoke until the landlady shut the door behind them and they had strolled around the corner, headed in the direction of the palace.

Edmund frowned at her. "Eddie? Really?"

"It was all I could think to call you." Jalissa shrugged, then glanced up at him. "You do not like it? Essie prefers her nickname. You do not?"

Edmund shook his head. "No. I was called Eddie growing up, but I never liked it. Nor do I like Ed. Perhaps I have a bit of elf in me, that I prefer my full name."

Nicknames were rather strange, and Jalissa could not really see Edmund as an Ed or Eddie either. He was Edmund, the rather sneaky Escarlish spy prince.

All the lies had soured her stomach, especially the part that would hurt that woman's business. The landlady, after all, did not appear to know she had harbored an assassin.

Jalissa turned to Edmund, frowning. "That poor woman now expects tenants that will never show."

Edmund waved that away. "Don't worry, I'll make sure she has tenants. I'm sure there's at least one servant at the palace with family outside of Aldon who would love to come to visit for a week or two at the expense of the crown."

"Why all the secrecy?" Jalissa hugged her arms over her stomach, grimacing at the feel of the stiff, Escarlish fabric against her skin. "Why not simply tell the truth?"

After all, he was a prince. It was not like the landlady would be less cooperative if a prince showed up to investigate her tenant. If anything, she would have bent over backwards. Perhaps even left them alone in the room where they could have done a more thorough search.

"I want to keep this as quiet as possible." The twinkle to Edmund's eyes faded as his mouth pressed into a thin line. "I don't know where the assassin is getting his information, but based on how well he planned and executed this attack, he is well informed. I don't want him knowing every step of our investigation, as he surely would if I marched in there as a prince and started investigating. What landlady wouldn't noise it about that a prince toured her establishment?"

"Her very respectable establishment." Jalissa could not believe that she was making a light-hearted comment right now. But Edmund made it very easy to forget, if only for a moment, the weight in her chest.

Edmund grinned back at her. "Exactly. But normal, prospective tenants are nothing to gossip about. Sure, we showed up a little too soon after her last tenant left, but she is currently too glad that she already has that floor rented to care that the timing was suspicious. Now, what did you notice?"

Jalissa worried her lower lip, thinking. "The assassin used fireworks to mask the sound of the gunshots. It was subtle, but the gunpowder from the fireworks smelled different than the whiffs of gunpowder by the window."

Edmund nodded, then patted his pocket where he had placed the handkerchief. "That was my thought as well.

There was more residue on the windows than I was expecting. I think he used a muzzle-loading rifle. I've heard a few of the army sharpshooters swear by the older model rifles for accuracy. Better for controlling the amount of powder and the load instead of the newer, cartridge models."

"So…" Jalissa was not sure what to make of that. The Escarlish guns were all the same to her.

"It means we're dealing with a professional." Edmund's jaw worked. He halted alongside one of the brick buildings. "He planned meticulously. Based on the trash left in the kitchen, he was there for over a week, waiting for his chance. And he is a professional sharpshooter. All in all, this points to a coldly planned assassination, not a crime of opportunity."

"One to two weeks?" Jalissa bit her lip. "You received word that the story about Farrendel would be released in your press a week ago. Is that a coincidence?"

Edmund heaved a sigh. "I doubt it. The assassin had to know Essie and Farrendel would be coming back to Escarland. He guessed they would make numerous public appearances in order to salvage public opinion. He would simply have to bide his time for the right moment."

"How much do you trust your friend, Trent Bourdon?" Jalissa glanced around at the peaceful street.

"Two weeks ago, I would have said he was trustworthy." Edmund frowned. "But he was the one to give me the information about the story breaking soon. It was his story that leaked even earlier than expected. Though, when I trusted him with the story of our courtship, he released it exactly as we had agreed upon."

"That does not prove his innocence." Jalissa felt steadier as she glared up at Edmund. "For the assassin, that story did nothing one way or another. If anything, more scandal would have made us retreat to Tarenhiel faster."

"I'll investigate him." Edmund sounded weary, as he had during the war. "Did you notice anything else?"

"Just a faint floral scent." Jalissa shrugged, peeking up at him. "It was so faint that I am not sure I could identify it if I smelled it again. Perhaps it was a perfume or a shampoo?"

"Probably from one of his *visitors*." Edmund grimaced, glancing away from her as if uncomfortable bringing up this topic with a proper elf princess.

"But other than that, no, I did not find anything." She shook her head. "The assassin took all of his personal items when he left."

"He was careful. He left a mess, but nothing that could point to his identity." Edmund started walking back toward the palace. "I saw paper wrapping from the local restaurants. It looks like he frequented many of them, spreading out his appearances so that he would not show up at one place more than once or twice. I'll send someone from the Intelligence Office to ask about a customer with his description, but I doubt they will remember him. I'll also send someone to inquire about fireworks."

Jalissa fell into step with him, shoulders hunching under the weight of her worries once again. "I am sorry I was not more help."

Edmund halted, turned toward her. "You helped more than you realize. Do you think the landlady would have been so accommodating if I had shown up there alone, dressed as a grubby castle servant? No, your presence caused her to relax. You helped her believe my story about having family coming to the city. After all, people tend to trust a pretty, innocent face. In this game, beauty is not merely decorative. It can be an asset."

A weapon, he did not say. But Jalissa heard and understood. Had not she, after all, used her beauty and innocent look to navigate the elven court?

As they started walking again, nearing the castle gate, Jalissa peeked up at Edmund. "So what now?"

"Now, I'm going to set a watch over the *Times* building and see what turns up." Edmund plastered on a smile for the gate guards.

Jalissa did not want to return to the palace and the mind-numbing waiting for word. But what could she do to help him on his stakeout of the *Times*? She was simply a useless, beautiful princess.

Farrendel struggled to draw in another breath, pain tearing through his chest. In his arms, Essie remained still, her face gray and pale.

She was fading. He could feel it in every breath, every heartbeat.

Essie's mother strode from the other car, closing the door quietly against the rushing noise of the train from the passage between cars.

Farrendel spoke quickly before she could ask about Essie. "How is Iyrinder?"

"Stable and comfortable." Macha bustled to the sideboard, picked up the pitcher of water, and poured a glass. She returned to Farrendel's side, holding out the glass. "You need to keep your strength up."

Farrendel rested Essie's hand on his chest, then reached for the glass. His hand trembled so much that Essie's mother didn't fully let go of the glass, steadying it for him as he sipped the water.

He managed three sips before his stomach threatened to rebel. He pushed the glass away. "Linshi, Macha."

"You're welcome." Macha set the glass on the coffee table, then frowned. She pressed her surprisingly cold hand against Farrendel's forehead. "You're feverish."

That would explain why the room felt far too warm, yet chills shivered down his back. He shrugged and rested his head on the pillows behind him. "I am fine. It is simply the strain."

Her forehead scrunched, her eyes filled with concern. "Is there anything I can do to help?"

Farrendel shook his head, then regretted it when the movement caused the train car to spin. "Do not worry. I will keep her alive."

Macha perched on the chair across from him, holding his gaze. "I know you will. But I am not only worried about her."

"You do not have to worry about me." He would be all right, as long as Essie was. Farrendel drew in another breath. A thick, liquid feeling filled his lungs, and he resisted the urge to cough, knowing Essie would cough as well.

Macha frowned, as if she did not believe him. "We have another hour or so to the border."

Farrendel pressed his cheek against Essie's hair. Another hour. Surely he could keep breathing—and keep Essie alive—for another hour. "Could you...please keep talking?"

He needed to keep his mind focused and awake. He could not allow himself to drift into a stupor. That could prove deadly to Essie, if he did not consciously hold tight to her through the heart bond.

"Did Essie ever tell you about the time she smuggled one

of the stable cats into her bedroom and it had kittens under her bed?" Essie's macha smiled and launched into the story.

Farrendel held Essie close as he listened to Macha talk. He drew in a deep breath, taking as much of Essie's pain as he could. He exhaled, giving Essie his strength.

Time bled into the rhythm of the wheels against the tracks, the gentle swaying of the train, Macha's voice rising and falling in pitch as she became more animated in her storytelling.

His fingertips were growing tingly, his head light, stomach woozy.

Was that the train stopping? His chest squeezed, his breath catching. It took him several tries to draw in his next breath.

Then the door to the train car was opening, and Weylind was there. He did not say anything. He simply helped Farrendel to his feet and kept him upright as they disembarked from the train. Farrendel hugged Essie's limp form to him, her head lolling against his shoulder. If not for Weylind's steadying hand, his legs would have buckled.

Farrendel barely registered anything from the walk up the slight rise from the train station to the army outpost beside the Hydalla River. The same outpost where he and Essie had been married in a human ceremony nearly a year ago now.

The next thing he knew, he was ushered into the infirmary. He laid Essie on the surgical table, bracing himself against it as his knees gave out.

Weylind's grip on his shoulders tightened, keeping Farrendel from collapsing entirely.

Something in him broke, seeing Essie laid out on the

table like that. It should be him, bloody and unconscious on the table. He could handle that.

He could not handle this.

An elf healer and a human surgeon approached, with assistants carrying trays of supplies. Rheva was there as well, joining Essie's mother and directing those carrying Iyrinder's stretcher to a second table.

"Amir." The elf healer's hand hoovered just above Essie's wound. "This will hurt you through the heart bond. Do you—"

"Just heal her." Farrendel spat the words between gritted teeth. All this talking was delaying help for Essie. "I can take it. Just do what you need to do to save her."

The healer gave a nod, then he and the surgeon started a discussion in a low tone, their hands moving quickly.

Farrendel turned away, focusing on Essie's face. He still gripped her hand, keeping them linked deep in the heart bond. With his other hand, he brushed the flyaway strands of her red hair from her pale face. She was so wan, so still, so unresponsive even as he could sense the healer filling her with healing magic.

Farrendel pressed his forehead against Essie's, squeezed his eyes shut, and simply breathed.

"She will be fine, shashon." Weylind held Farrendel upright, his voice soft.

A not-quite-laugh choked out of him. He did not straighten from cradling Essie's head. "Last time, you told Essie to let me go."

Weylind gave his own wry chuckle, though it also lacked mirth. "I would not be so foolish now. I have learned better when it comes to you and Elspetha."

Farrendel would have replied, but his breath caught, pain

flaring through him. He dug his fingers into Essie's hair and clung to the heart bond with all the strength left in him. It did not matter if his own lungs shredded, or he gave every bit of strength inside his body. He was going to keep Essie alive through this no matter what it took.

He was not sure how much time passed. Everything was a blur of pain and elven magic and the heart bond that consumed all of him.

Weylind's voice broke through the haze, his grip tugging Farrendel away from the table, away from Essie. "She is all right, shashon. Let the healers finish up."

Essie's hand slipped out of his, and the snapping of the deep connection in the heart bond had Farrendel doubling over, even if he could still feel Essie, alive and breathing.

He was gasping. His head so light it was about ready to float away. His fingers had gone past tingling into numb. He could not see, everything tunneled, black and whirling. His knees hit the floor as shudders wracked his body. He was gagging, choking.

Weylind was saying something, then shouting. His grip on Farrendel's shoulders was tight enough to be painful.

Farrendel should concentrate on that point of pain to keep himself grounded. He was supposed to breathe deeply and bring himself back to reality.

But he was flying apart, scattering into nothing.

"Rheva!" Weylind shouted again.

A flood of soothing magic blasted into Farrendel with such force that he choked, then coughed.

The cough turned into a heave, and a bucket was pressed into his hands. He vomited, heaving until nothing more would come. He gasped and gagged his way to control, hunching over the bucket.

When he was sure he was not about to cast up his accounts yet again, he shoved the bucket away. When he swiped his sleeve across his mouth, he felt a dampness on his face, as if tears had been streaming down his cheeks. Perhaps they had. He had been a little outside himself for a few moments there.

More of Rheva's soothing magic flowed into him, softer and gentler than before. Only then did he register that she knelt next to him, holding Farrendel's hair from his face.

Farrendel could have gladly sunk to the floor and never moved from that spot. Panicking was bad enough. Breaking down in front of people was humiliating.

Weylind slumped into a sitting position, swiping a shaking hand over his face.

Rheva let go of Farrendel's hair, then rested a hand on his shoulder. "If you are all right, I am going to help them get Essie settled."

Farrendel's head shot up. The table was empty. By the time he thought to call out to her, Rheva was already leaving, crossing the room.

His chest squeezing, Farrendel staggered to his feet. "Where is Essie?"

Weylind gripped Farrendel's arm. "She is already on the boat. Come. Let us get you home to Estyra."

Farrendel did not resist as Weylind steered him from the room, then from the outpost. When they boarded the elven boat that would take them across the Hydalla River, Farrendel took a step in the direction of the door that would take him below.

Weylind shook his head. "Essie will be all right for a few minutes. You need to take a moment and breathe."

"But...Essie..." Farrendel did not have the strength to resist as Weylind guided him to the rail.

"You will be able to feel through the heart bond if she needs you." Weylind's tone was stern. "And, yes, this is the same thing we told Essie back when you were recovering. It is good to step away to clear your head."

Farrendel slumped against the rail. As the boat shivered into motion and pulled away from the dock, a cool breeze wafted along the river, carrying with it a wet, murky smell.

With his eyes closed, Farrendel drew in several deep breaths, exhaling slowly. He let the gentle rocking of the boat ease through his muscles while the comforting smell of river and spring forest wrapped around him.

Weylind had been right. This was helping. For the first time in hours, he could piece together some semblance of order inside his head. And, when they docked on the Tarenhieli side of the river, his legs were steady enough that he could walk on his own without Weylind steadying him.

When Farrendel climbed into his private car on the Tarenhieli royal train, Essie already lay on the large bed in the center of the car's spacious bedroom. The warm, pink light of the sunset beamed through large windows on both sides of the car and gave Essie's skin a warmer cast than it had before.

Rheva stood next to Essie, adjusting the pillow, while Essie's macha smoothed the blanket.

As soon as Farrendel entered, Essie's mother crossed the train car to him. "Essie will be all right, sason." She opened her arms, as if prepared to give Farrendel a hug, before she halted, eyeing something on Farrendel's shirt.

Farrendel glanced down at himself. His shirt was soaked with blood.

Essie's blood.

Essie's blood on his clothes. On his skin.

He had to get it off. He had to get clean.

His breathing came rasping and fast again. With shaking hands, he tore his shirt over his head and chucked it as far from him as he could. Vaguely, he heard Weylind behind him, offering to show Essie's macha to her own train car to rest. The door clicked shut.

"I will stay with her, if you would like to clean up first." Rheva gracefully slid onto the chair next to the bed.

Farrendel raced across the train car and all but flung himself into the train car's small water closet. He lunged for the spigot, taking three tries to turn it on.

As the scalding water pounded onto his head, streaming down his face, he slid to the floor, hugging his knees to his chest. Water soaked his trousers. His boots would likely be ruined, but he did not have the motivation to remove them.

How long he curled on the floor of the shower, he did not know.

But Essie needed him. He had to be strong for her.

Somehow, he got up, washed, and changed into the set of spare clothes he always kept in here. Finally, barefoot, he padded from the water closet.

Rheva glanced up as he entered, giving him a soft smile.

Farrendel crawled onto the other side of the bed, sitting next to Essie and taking her hand. Light and shadow flashed across her face, cast from the trees blurring past outside the windows.

Rheva slid to her feet. "I will let you both rest."

"Wait." Farrendel stared down at Essie, watching her chest rise and fall. Through the heart bond, he could feel that she was still weak. He deepened the heart bond, letting her body draw strength from his. He forced himself to glance up at Rheva where she stood, waiting. "Can you check on her one more time?"

He was not sure he could rest either way, but a gnawing deep in his chest needed the extra reassurance that she was, indeed, all right.

"She will be fine, shashon." Rheva returned to Essie's side and rested her hand on Essie's forehead. A green glow surrounded her fingers. After a moment, a wrinkle puckered Rheva's forehead, and more magic flared around her fingers.

That was not good. "What is it? What is wrong?" Farrendel tightened his grip on Essie's hand.

Rheva gave Farrendel a soft smile before she lifted her hand from Essie. "She is fine. It would be better if I told both of you at the same time."

What did that mean? Everything was tunneling again, his head buzzing. "Do not lie to me. What is it? Did you find something wrong? Is she dying?"

There were things even the elves could not heal. Farrendel's grandfather had died of one of those diseases. What if Rheva had discovered something like that?

"Farrendel, shashon." Rheva rested a hand on his shoulder, drawing his attention to her. "She will be *fine*."

"Rheva…please…" Farrendel could not take anything else today. He was empty, his control slipping through his fingers. He had to know before the terror of not knowing destroyed him from the inside out.

The wrinkle to Rheva's forehead returned, and she touched Farrendel's cheek, easing her magic into him. "Perhaps it would be best if I told you now. Then you can work through your panic so that you will be there with Essie later."

What was Rheva talking about? His head was too muddled for all these riddles.

"She is not dying." Rheva's gentle smile lifted into something brighter. "She is expecting."

Farrendel blinked, his head still muddy. "Expecting what?"

Rheva made a sound between a laugh and a sigh. "She is not expecting kittens, shashon. A baby."

For a long moment, Farrendel could only stare at Rheva, his brain and body frozen. "What…how…no, do not answer that. I know how. But…" He squeezed his eyes shut. He needed his mind to function. To process. He gripped his knees with his free arm, Essie's hand still clutched in the other, and tried to breathe. "Are you sure?"

Rheva looked like she would have rolled her eyes, if she was not too dignified for that. "I did specialize in this, you know."

Right. His brain was still trying to catch up. But that would be why Rheva would realize Essie was pregnant while the healer specializing in war wounds would not.

A baby. Their baby. Their dreams and someday and…and…

He snapped his attention back to Rheva. "Is the baby all right? Essie nearly died." He did not know a lot about babies, but somehow that seemed like it would be a bad thing.

The smile left Rheva's face in a blink, replaced with that gentle concern once again. "It is too soon to know for certain. Everything seems fine as far as I can tell right now. We will know for sure if there are no complications in a day or two."

Rheva kept talking, but Farrendel could not seem to

make the words sort themselves out inside his head. It was too much, on top of everything else.

"But you cannot say for certain?" Farrendel interrupted her, searching her expression desperately, almost hoping that she would lie to him, and lie well enough that he could believe it without question.

"No. But, shashon." Rheva paused until he met her gaze. "You kept both of them alive by giving of yourself so sacrificially that, of the two of you, your body shows far more sign of strain than hers does. There is nothing more you could have done."

That still did not banish the terror choking his throat. In the span of a few words, he had gone from worrying about one life to two.

"Now, you need to rest." Rheva's smile returned to her face. "Essie will need you to be there for her when she wakes."

Farrendel nodded, though he did not think he could sleep. Not without a little help getting there. He gestured from himself to Rheva. "Could you?"

"All right." Rheva brushed the back of her hand against Farrendel's cheek, sending another dose of her magic into him. This one slowed his mind, eased his body into relaxing. Rheva pressed her forehead to his for just a moment. "I am happy for you."

Then, she was leaving, and Farrendel lifted the blanket with a heavy hand. He curled next to Essie, close but not touching her besides his grip on her hand.

Closing his eyes and listening to the steady sound of Essie's breathing, Farrendel let Rheva's magic lull him to sleep.

Edmund held Jalissa as she curled against him. They sat on the floor of the hospital tent, surrounded by the smells of antiseptic and blood.

His brother-in-law Farrendel lay dying on the surgical table. Edmund could barely see glimpses of him past the human surgeon, the elf healer, Weylind, Averett, and Essie.

Perhaps Edmund shouldn't let Jalissa lean on him so entirely. But he had no strength to push her away. He needed to hold someone close, and she was the only person he wanted in this moment.

E dmund paced across his mother's sitting room where the family had gathered while they waited for word. As much as he wanted to rush out and continue his investigation, he could not bring himself to leave again until he received word about Essie.

Jalissa sat on one of the couches, worrying a section of

her skirt. Next to her, Paige stabbed at her embroidery, and she would likely have to take out whatever progress she made, given the muddle she was making of the thread.

Averett and Julien also paced across the room, and the three of them had divided up the room by some unspoken agreement so that they could pace their own routes without running into each other.

A knock came on the door before the castle butler himself opened the door. He held out a telegram. "For you, Your Majesty."

Averett hurried across the room and snatched the paper from the butler's hand.

Julien froze where he was in the corner while Edmund halted next to Jalissa, holding his breath.

Averett unfolded the note, his hands trembling. It took so long that Edmund had to clench his fists to resist the urge to take the telegram and open it himself.

After reading the note quickly, Averett's shoulders slumped, and he sank onto the couch next to Paige. "She's fine. Essie is fine."

Edmund braced himself against the couch as Jalissa hunched, her head in her hands while her shoulders shook. Paige dropped her embroidery, reaching for Averett and pressing her face against his shoulder.

Julien braced himself against the wall, swiping a hand over his face.

"They…" Averett had to clear his throat, his voice a little choked. "They healed her, and they are on their way to Estyra where Essie can rest and recover."

And where Farrendel and Essie could stay safe while Edmund investigated what had happened. After all, the assassin failed. He was still out there, and he would try again.

Edmund pushed away from the couch. "Good. Then I need to get back to work."

Averett gave a nod. "Let me know if you need anything. Any resources, any help."

"I will. The Intelligence Office is working round the clock on this, searching for anything that was missed in the reports." At least Edmund had managed to wiggle his way into the investigation so that he wasn't stuck behind a desk with everyone else. He would probably join them at some point, but for now, his place was out in the field.

With one last glance at Jalissa, Edmund left the sitting room and returned to his own room. He dressed in plain, serviceable clothes that would blend in until he could change into the disguise he would use on the stakeout. It took a few moments to stash all of his hidden weapons, then he was ready.

He left Winstead Palace by the back garden door, the guards in the hallways and at the door paying him little attention.

As he headed for the gate, he found a figure pacing across the drive in the gloom, her back straight. Another figure lingered in the shadows.

Edmund sighed and strolled up to Jalissa.

Before he had a chance to speak, Jalissa spun to face him. He had never seen her face so set and hard, except perhaps during the war. Her chin lifted. "I am going with you."

"I'm going on a stakeout of the *Times*. I might be out there for days." Edmund scratched at the back of his neck. "And it's a sketchy part of town. I can't keep you safe."

"That is what Sarya is for." Jalissa pointed to her guard where she lingered in the shadows.

"A single guard won't guarantee your safety in this part of town." Edmund's stomach churned at the thought of placing her in that kind of danger. It had been fun spending time investigating with her, but it wasn't something that would last.

"I am not helpless." Jalissa raised her hand, green magic dripping from her fingers. She touched a nearby tree branch, and it whipped around, coming to life and growing. "I do not have the strength of my brothers, but I am not without magic. I can defend myself if need be."

Edmund sighed. She was right. Besides, this was her choice. He had told her the risks, and she had made the decision that she wanted to come anyway. He would respect that and accept the help she was offering.

In this kind of stakeout, she likely wouldn't be a liability. Jalissa could sit and be patient. If anything, having more people would allow them to catch some sleep.

"All right." Edmund gestured toward the gate. He would have to leave word with the guards that Jalissa was with him, and Averett was likely going to pitch a fit that Edmund let Jalissa come along. But, right now, Edmund wanted Jalissa at his side too much to care about the consequences. "I'll appreciate not being the only one sitting in refuse and vomit all night."

Jalissa released her magic, staring at Edmund. "That is what we will be doing?"

"Being a spy isn't as glamorous as it seems." Edmund grinned, then led the way out of the palace.

He didn't go straight to the *Times*. Instead, he led Jalissa and her guard to the safe house run by the Intelligence

Office, located in one of the nicer row of apartments on the outskirts of the market.

He let himself in, then climbed the staircase to the top floor. At the last set of rooms on the floor, he halted, eased up the corner of a floorboard, and pulled out the key. With Jalissa and her guard looking on with raised eyebrows, Edmund unlocked the door and let them in.

After fumbling in the darkness for a moment, he lit and turned up the gas lamps to light the space. He pointed to the door on the right. "There should be female disguises in that room. Jalissa, pick out something with a ragged cloak and tattered clothing. If it already smells slightly rank, all the better. Put on the gray wig."

Jalissa nodded, then glanced at her guard. "What about Sarya?"

Edmund gestured to the chairs by the table. "Please wait here. I'm going to pick out a variety of male and female outfits. You'll be our eyes ranging about on the streets."

The guard nodded and took a seat.

Edmund walked into the room on the left. Instead of a normal bedroom, this had two narrow bunk beds sticking into the room while every available wall space was covered in racks upon racks of clothes. Trunks held other items, and wigs hung on stands on the tables.

After going to the rack of disreputable clothing, he picked out one, then shrugged into it, grimacing at the gritty feel of the rough cloth. He added a dingy gray wig for good measure and smeared some grease paint across his face to give himself a more haggard appearance. Over everything, he added a ragged cloak. A cane completed his outfit.

He then picked out a few items for Jalissa's guard before he returned to the main room.

Jalissa was already there, dressed in rags reeking of rotting vegetables. She wrinkled her nose as her guard helped her pin her hair up, then situate the wig. "Does this smell terrible enough?"

"Definitely." Edmund grinned, then entered the other room to pick out a few more costumes. He stuffed all of them in a bag as he returned to the kitchen. He held it out to Sarya. "I trust you can figure out how to interchange these to make the most of them."

The guard nodded. "Yes."

"Good. On our way, I'll show you a place where you can change. That will also be our meeting place." Edmund motioned, and the three of them set off. On the walk through the street, he gave his instructions in a low tone that wouldn't carry. Sarya would keep moving on the surrounding streets, changing out her costume on every circuit. Edmund and Jalissa would find a place across from the *Times* to huddle on the street, pretending to be an old, homeless couple.

Sarya would occasionally give them food on her rounds, as if she were a passerby helping a hungry couple. In the morning, one of his colleagues at the Intelligence Office would relieve them.

Assuming Edmund and Jalissa weren't called on to tail anyone. If that happened, the plan was out the window, and they'd have to adapt.

When they reached the street in front of the *Times* building, the large brick building glowed. The clatter of printing presses filled the air, running through the night to get the morning edition of the paper out first thing.

Edmund settled along the wall of a building, pulled the hood of his cloak over his head, and settled into as comfortable of a position as he could.

Jalissa settled in next to him, her hood also over her head. "What happens now?"

"Now we watch and wait." Edmund leaned his head against the brick wall behind him. Something damp and squishy was oozing through his clothes from the wall and the street. The stench of something rancid wafted from all around him.

Jalissa glanced at the slimy brick wall behind them, then at his shoulder. She sighed, her eyes even darker in the shadows. "I suppose it would be best if I leaned against you. For our disguise."

"Yes. Our disguise. That's the only reason." He let himself relax with a chuckle and lifted his arm. Inviting her but waiting for her to make the first move. "So glad my shoulder is preferable over grime-covered bricks."

"Do not flatter yourself. Your shoulder is the lesser of two unpalatable options." She held his gaze with a pretend frosty look for a moment before a hint of a smile played around her mouth.

"Ouch. Right in the ego." Edmund couldn't help but grin, even as an ache settled into his chest. This was what he loved about Jalissa. Beneath that serene princess mask, she had a wit sharp enough to match his.

But this moment couldn't last. Once they caught the assassin and the scandal of Farrendel's parentage died down, he and Jalissa would quietly go their separate ways. Worse, he would watch as she moved on and married someone else. When that day came, he would lie through his teeth and tell her that he was happy for her, if that was what it took.

Tentatively, Jalissa eased her head onto his shoulder. He

adjusted to get her more comfortably situated against him, trying not to think about how right she felt against him.

For several long moments, they sat in silence. The street in front of them remained dark and empty, but farther away the distant sound of a horse's hooves clopping on stone and the murmur of voices filled the night air. Even at this late hour, Aldon was never quiet.

"Is this what it is always like? Spying?" Jalissa's voice was soft, her head heavy against his shoulder.

He had never been able to talk frankly about this part of himself except with his family. Often, not even then. Only Averett knew most of what he'd done over the years.

But his cover had been well and truly blown in Tarenhiel. There was no sense hiding everything, though he could not give her specifics.

"Tarenhiel was much cleaner." Edmund also kept his voice low, testing out her reaction to his words.

Jalissa stiffened against him, but she did not pull away. After a long moment, she gave a tiny sigh. "Of course our forests are much cleaner. And smell better." She gave a little shiver. "I guess Kostaria was colder."

"Yes, it was." Pressed as they were against the damp brick and cobblestones, tonight would be chilly, even huddled together as they were.

They lapsed into silence for another long moment before Jalissa spoke even quieter than before. "This is why this courtship can never be anything but fake."

Edmund breathed through the stab of her words, all the more painful because they were the truth. "I know."

He had spied on her kingdom. He had a secret past that would damage the deepening alliance between Tarenhiel and Escarland if it came to light. Not to mention, the truth was even worse than Jalissa knew.

"But I do wish…" Jalissa trailed off, shaking her head against his shoulder.

He knew exactly what she meant, but he didn't say so. Instead, he wrapped an arm around her shoulders and hugged her closer. "Don't worry. We'll invite all those young elven noblemen here to Escarland and find you the perfect one. You'll fall head over heels for him and forget all about me."

"I doubt that." Jalissa gave a little sniff.

Edmund swallowed, not sure what to say. He wanted to tell her that she was a beautiful person. Clever and dedicated and loyal. The picture of the perfect elven princess, and yet she was here, sitting in the filth of an Escarlish street because she was that determined to catch the person who had shot her sister-in-law and tried to assassinate her brother.

But if he said all that, the depth of his feelings would come through in his voice, destroying the lightness of the moment.

Jalissa yawned, her muscles relaxing against him. "I think I might fall asleep."

"Go ahead. Even if you don't sleep, resting your eyes will be helpful." Edmund fixed his gaze on the building in front of him. "You can spell me later."

Jalissa murmured something, but he could tell she was already fading into sleep. It had been an exhausting day.

Edmund, too, was so weary his bones ached. But exhaustion was nothing new. He had shivered in Kostaria for days without food and sleep. He had crossed half of Tarenhiel on foot, fought a border guard, and swam across the Hydalla while bleeding from a knife wound, all to make it to Essie's eighteenth birthday party on time. Conducting a stakeout while lacking sleep was nothing too difficult, even if having Jalissa slumped against him was new.

If only he could savor this moment forever. She was the woman he'd always dreamed of having at his side. She was the kind of person who could either make a statement or blend into the background as she saw fit. She was clever enough to know how to use her serene nature to her advantage. The perfect complement for a prince or a spy, one who would make her own mark on his worlds—both shadowy and glittering—if given the chance.

He'd had his chance three times over now. And yet, they were still as doomed as they had been at the beginning.

FIFTEEN

F arrendel sat next to his and Essie's bed, grown into the wall of their quiet bedroom in Ellonahshinel. She was still sleeping, her hair flowing across the pillows and the color returning to her cheeks. Even though Rheva had assured him it would be hours yet before Essie fully woke, he could not leave her side just in case.

He had laid out his homework on the bedside table with good intentions of working on it while he waited. But all he had managed was staring at the papers and rearranging them occasionally. It felt so pointless to work on homework while Essie was recovering from being shot and their child might not survive all the stress and he could do nothing to help either of them.

There was a light rap on the door before Essie's macha stepped inside. She crossed the room and touched Farrendel's shoulder. "You should take a break. Get some food. Take a few deep breaths. I'll stay with her for a while."

Farrendel shook his head. "I cannot leave her."

Macha squeezed his shoulder. "I know. I understand. But

you can't take care of her if you don't take care of yourself first. Essie understands that."

Yes, she did. When he was recovering in that tent in Kostaria, she had taken breaks to eat and sleep. She had not kept an unending vigil at his bedside, and he had not thought any less of her for it.

He glanced up at Macha, taking in the lines etched into her face and the strength in her stance. "How did you do it?"

"Do what?" She studied him in return with that soft gaze that felt like a hug.

"Survive losing Essie's dacha." Farrendel stared down at his hands. "My dacha did not. Losing his spouse broke him."

"I can't speak for your dacha." Essie's macha perched at the edge of the bed facing Farrendel. "But I survived because I focused on what I had to live for instead of what I had lost. I had my children who still needed me to be there for them. I had a kingdom to run as regent until Averett was old enough to take the throne."

Then why had that not been enough for his dacha? Dacha had a kingdom to run as well, but he had all but abdicated and handed everything to Weylind. Dacha had three children, and yet he had gone seeking comfort elsewhere, resulting in a fourth, illegitimate child.

Perhaps it was because Weylind, Melantha, and Jalissa were old enough that they did not need Dacha the way that Averett, Julien, Edmund, and Essie had needed Essie's macha, though Jalissa had been about the same age as Ryfon was now.

Or maybe Essie's macha was just that strong of a woman that she had been able to carry on when his dacha had not.

Right now, Farrendel felt more like his dacha than Essie's

macha. While keeping Essie alive in the heart bond, he had not been thinking about their families or everything he had to live for. He had been ready to cause them more grief in order to die alongside Essie if he could not save her.

But that was not necessarily a healthy way of looking at things, especially not now. Not when he would soon have more than just Essie depending on him.

He could not explain to Macha why he was asking these questions. Essie should know before her mother.

Then again, Essie should have been the first to know, even before Farrendel. But things had not worked out the way they were supposed to.

"Now, go on. Get something to eat." Macha gestured toward the door. "Essie will still be sleeping when you get back."

Even if she was not, he would feel through the heart bond when she started to wake up. He could be back by the time she was awake.

Gathering his shreds of motivation, Farrendel pushed to his feet. His legs felt wobbly as he crossed the room and left, so much so that he ran his hand along the new handrail he had installed for Essie as part of her birthday present.

When he entered the main room, he stopped short.

Weylind sat at the table, bent over a piece of paper with several neat stacks set on the table around him. He glanced up as Farrendel entered, then gestured with his quill toward the wooden kitchen countertop. "There is food set out for you, if you want it."

Farrendel's stomach had not stopped churning from the moment Essie had been shot. He had not yet eaten, despite leaving the contents of his stomach back in Escarland. Food did not sound appealing.

Yet, when he turned to the countertop, he found a bowl of a creamy soup, still hot enough to waft steam, and two large slices of bread that sent up such a yeasty, warm smell that his stomach grumbled.

This had to be Miss Merrick's doing, though how she had found the time and energy since their arrival was beyond him.

After claiming the bowl and plate of bread, Farrendel slid onto the chair across from Weylind and set his meal on the one open spot on the table.

He did not have to ask what Weylind was doing there. He was hovering, of course.

For some reason, Farrendel did not resent this hovering as much as he used to. Perhaps Weylind had gotten better, more unobtrusive at it. Or maybe, Farrendel was now able to accept the help Weylind was offering.

Before, Farrendel had been so strained, trying to hold his shattered pieces together that he had been unable to handle his family's help, even when they offered it. It had been too much, even if it had been well meant.

Weylind gestured to his paperwork. "I can leave, if you would like."

"No, stay." Farrendel blew on a bite of soup. It was strangely nice, having Weylind here right now.

"Good." Weylind turned back to his paperwork, flourishing his signature on the paper before adding it to a stack near Farrendel's bowl. "I am enjoying the quiet to accomplish paperwork in peace. The courtiers have discovered my usual hiding places. Perhaps I should have thought to come here before. It will take them a while to find me."

Farrendel had a mental image of his dignified brother crammed into some corner underneath a stairwell or a nook underneath a table. Despite his weariness, his mouth twitched in an attempt at a smile.

His and Essie's rooms would make a superior hiding spot compared to a tiny corner somewhere. None of the courtiers wandered toward this part of Ellonahshinel. None of them would want to associate with the illegitimate prince that they were trying so hard to scorn.

Farrendel popped the bite of cheesy, potato soup in his mouth. It was warm and settled the churning in the pit of his stomach. He swallowed, hardly believing that he was about to make this offer. "Perhaps you could join me in my work-shop sometimes."

Farrendel would probably work on homework, if that were the case. Weylind would want quiet to concentrate, and Farrendel would be too embarrassed to fiddle with magical engineering projects with someone else other than Lance watching.

To hide his nerves, Farrendel stuffed a large bite of bread into his mouth.

Weylind's head shot up, his dark brown eyes studying Farrendel. "I would like that, if it is truly what you wish."

Farrendel nodded, his mouth full.

"Then, I will not presume upon your hospitality too often. Or impose on you too long when I do." Weylind smiled, gesturing at his paperwork.

When Farrendel smiled back, something indefinable shifted. He had spent so long as the much younger sibling, as much a child to Weylind and Melantha as he was a sibling.

But now Weylind was treating him as an equal.

Weylind turned back to his paperwork. "Iyrinder is recovering as well."

Farrendel winced. He should have thought to ask about his guard. Yes, he had been focused on Essie. But Iyrinder had taken a bullet saving Farrendel's life. And, by saving Farrendel, he had saved Essie as well. Farrendel stirred his soup with his spoon. "Once Essie wakes, we will both have to thank him for his quick thinking."

"I already offered to reward him with a promotion." Weylind did not raise his head, but his gaze flicked up to Farrendel for a moment before he drew a large line across his piece of paper, adding it to the stack of items he had not signed. "He refused it. He informed me that he intends to remain on your guard detail for as long as you will have him."

Farrendel was not sure what to say to that. Iyrinder had been incredibly loyal to Weylind before being assigned to Farrendel. What had changed?

Farrendel cleared his throat. "I am glad to have him. He is very skilled, and he handles the travel back and forth between Tarenhiel and Escarland very well."

"Yes, he does." Weylind gave an almost secretive smile, as if he knew something Farrendel did not.

Farrendel was too weary to try to figure out what it might be. Instead, he turned back to his bowl of soup.

They lapsed into silence, punctuated by the scratch of Weylind's pen and the clink of Farrendel's spoon.

When his bowl was empty, both slices of bread gone, and his stomach full, Farrendel stared down at the crumbs left on his plate. He opened his mouth, closed it, then drew in a deep breath, trying to gather the words and the courage.

"I know what Dacha felt, in those moments before your macha died. There were a few moments when I did not know if I could get to Essie before...and I could feel her slipping away and…" Farrendel met Weylind's gaze. "I understand why it broke him. I know why he made the mistakes that he did."

He would not make the same mistakes as his dacha, if the worst had happened and Essie had died. But he surely would have made his own mistakes.

Weylind set aside his pen with a long sigh. "I was there with Dacha, when my macha was killed. I saw the way it broke him. The severing of a heart bond like that is a dreadful thing. I am thankful that it did not happen to you. But if it had, we would have been here for you, whatever it took."

Farrendel could not hold Weylind's gaze. He had already put his family through so much. Thankfully he would not have to ask Weylind to drag him from that particular mire.

When he managed to glance at Weylind, his brother held his gaze, his dark eyes filled with warmth. "One of us will stay here with you. In case you need anything. If that is all right."

"Linshi." Despite his worry for Essie, Farrendel's tension eased. This was the kind of care he could have experienced, if he had been able to do so before.

For the first time since Essie was shot, Farrendel felt like, perhaps, everything would be all right after all.

CHAPTER
SIXTEEN

E ssie's head hurt. As did her shoulder. She groaned and squeezed her eyes even tighter shut against the pain.

"Essie?" Farrendel's voice came from nearby a moment before his gentle fingers brushed hair from her face. "It is all right, shynafir. I am here."

Had he said something like that to her before? She had hazy memories of pain and blood and sinking into Farrendel's arms.

She managed to peel her eyes open, blinking until his blurry image started to clear. Strangely, the woven branch and leafy ceiling of their treetop bedroom in Estyra came into focus behind him. When had they gone back to Estyra? Last thing she remembered, they had been in Escarland.

Bright sunlight streamed through the windows, causing even more pain to stab through her skull.

Stretching a hand toward him, she managed to get his name out of her dry, gummy mouth. "Farrendel."

She could not have said what she wanted. Just that she needed reassurance that he was close.

As if her saying his name broke something inside him, he leaned over her, cradling her head in both of his hands. Then he was kissing her, peppering her with light, barely restrained kisses to her mouth, her forehead, her cheeks, her neck, murmuring over and over between kisses, "You are alive."

She fisted her hands in his shirt, tugging him closer. All she wanted was to be held warm and safe in his arms. Some-place where pain and fear couldn't touch her.

But as he deepened the kiss with a relieved kind of desperation, another stab of pain flared through her head. She couldn't help her moan.

Farrendel was rolling off the bed and on his feet by the time she even got her eyes open. He paced back and forth beside the bed with stilted steps, his hands making random motions in the air. "Water. I should get you water."

He spun toward the cold cabinet with stumbling steps.

Essie grimaced and struggled to push herself into a sitting position. Pain lanced through her shoulder, and she sucked in a quick breath, trying not to cry out.

Farrendel whirled back toward her, reaching her side in a blink. "Sorry. Sorry. Should have helped you sit up first."

He fumbled with the pillows, getting in Essie's way as much as he was helping. But she wasn't going to push him away. He had clearly been frantic, and she knew what it was like to be in his place, waiting and fretting at a bedside. She had done it enough herself. He was unpracticed at it, now that their roles were reversed.

When she was sitting propped on pillows, Farrendel stood there for a moment, rocking back and forth as if unsure what to do. Then, he started. "The water. I was getting you water."

He was off again, rushing across the room. He fumbled through pouring a glass of water and returned to the bedside. When he held out the glass to her, his hand trembled so badly that water sloshed over the rim.

Essie quickly took the glass from him before he dumped it all over her. "Linshi."

"Is there anything else I can get for you?" Farrendel remained beside the bed, still shaking so much he appeared about ready to fall over. "Are you hungry? Miss Merrick made soup. It is very good soup. I should get you some."

Essie shook her head and sipped the water. The coolness soothed her dry mouth and eased some of the ache in her head. Before Farrendel could rush off again, she grabbed his sleeve. "No, don't leave. Not yet."

She needed him there with her. At least for a few more minutes.

Farrendel sat on the bed facing her, shifting as if sitting still for even a few seconds was difficult.

Essie managed another sip of water. Her stomach was still squirrely, but hopefully that would go away as she woke up. "What happened?"

"You were shot, and we had to go to Tarenhiel for a healer." Farrendel's gaze darted from her to his hands, up to the ceiling and down to the blanket on the bed. "You were shot in the shoulder and had a concussion from when you hit the cobblestones of the street. You are probably sore, yet. The magic is still healing you. It is best to go slow to heal head injuries, or so Rheva tells me."

He was talking in a rush, almost babbling the way she did. Essie took his hand, holding it between both of hers.

"Thank you for keeping me alive. My memories are kind of hazy on what happened, but I know that much. This must have been hard on you. How are you holding up?"

"I went to see Taranath. He gave me an extra strong dose of his medicine." Farrendel waved toward the door, his hand still visibly shaking. "But it is not about me. How are you feeling? Are you all right?"

"I'm sore, but you said that's normal." Essie grimaced and leaned her head against the pillows behind her. The headache was worse than the stiffness in her shoulder.

"Your arm will feel better if you keep moving it." Farrendel rolled his own shoulder, as if demonstrating what she should do.

Essie forced herself to lift her arm, then moved it back and forth. She didn't doubt his suggestion. He would know. He had healed from gunshots numerous times, after all.

Her stomach lurched, and she had to swallow back bile. "I'm a little nauseous, but that's probably to be expected since I haven't eaten in…how long has it been?"

The treetops were bright and green outside, but she couldn't make out the angle of the sun.

"About a day since you were shot." Farrendel shifted, pulling his legs onto the bed and sitting cross-legged.

She tugged aside the collar of her shirt until she could see the scar on her upper chest. She grimaced and dropped her shirt. "I have a scar. It's going to be visible whenever I wear a fancy dress."

Unless she only wore dresses with necklines all the way to her collarbone. That would be the only way to hide it.

"Essie." Farrendel's voice remained soft as he brushed his fingers against her cheek. "You know I don't mind your scar."

Those words were familiar, since Essie had said them to Farrendel often enough.

Here she was, complaining about a single scar, when Farrendel had that scar on his cheek, scars on his wrists and hands, scars from bullets and swords and stone lacing across his chest.

She reached out and took his hands, turning them over so that she could see the scars wrapping around his wrists from where the stone had pinned him to the floor. "You're right. I shouldn't fret about it. If anything, it makes us a matched set, doesn't it?"

The smile dropped from his face, and he tugged his hands free of hers. "You were shot because of me. The assassin shot you, knowing that keeping you alive in the heart bond would make me vulnerable. Once again, you were put in danger because of me."

He stared down at his hands, his shoulders hunched, his silver-blond hair falling to hide his face.

"It is not your fault." Essie eased from the pillows to rest her hand on his. "You are not responsible for the decisions of others, whether that is King Charvod of the trolls or Escarlish traitors or this new assassin."

"Still, your life would have been a lot safer if you had never married me." Farrendel wasn't looking at her, all tension and barely controlled panic.

True. Without Farrendel, she never would have been caught in that ambush near Lethorel, kidnapped by Escarlish spies, fought in a war to rescue him, killed both trolls and an Escarlish traitor, and now been shot while walking on the street of her home city of Aldon.

But without Farrendel, she wouldn't have a home here in

the treetop palace of Ellonahshinel. She wouldn't have gained his family or friends as her own.

Most of all, she wouldn't have him. She wouldn't have this love in her chest that was so deep it ached, nor would she know what it was like to experience such love in return.

Essie leaned forward and touched Farrendel's cheek, tipping his head so that he faced her. "I wouldn't trade you and what we have together for anything, especially not for something as fleeting as physical safety."

Farrendel still didn't meet her gaze, despite her hand cradling his cheek. "You did not know what danger you would face when you married me."

"I don't think anyone knows what they are getting into when they get married, even if they've known their soon-to-be spouse for longer than a few days." Essie traced the pad of her thumb over the scar on his face. "No, I didn't realize that simply marrying you would put a target on me the way it has. But I knew enough. I was not entirely blind to what it would mean to marry the infamous elf warrior Laesornysh."

Farrendel flinched when she said the title he'd earned, the one that meant *Death on the Wind*. "Because I am Laesornysh and because of my magic, we will never be safe. There will always be those who wish to see me dead, and they will target you to get to me." He paused for a moment, his gaze finally lifting to meet hers. "They will target our children."

That brought her up short. What could she say? It was one thing to bravely dismiss the danger to herself. She had knowingly, if a little naively, signed up for it when she married Farrendel.

But any children they might have would be born into the danger with no say on their part. If she and Farrendel had children, they would do so knowing that they would be targets. Both because of Farrendel and his magic, but also because of the magic they would inherit from him.

"I know." It was all she could say at that moment. She was too sore, tasting too much of the fear of the past twenty-four hours, to make life-changing decisions right now.

"It...we..." Farrendel pulled away from her hand. His mouth worked the way it did when he had too many words jumbled inside his head, unable to order them into speech. "I need to...I should tell you. Rheva found...when she...you..."

Essie's stomach lurched. What had Rheva found when she helped heal Essie? Was it serious?

But she couldn't panic now. She had to calm Farrendel down first.

She cradled his face with both hands, forcing him to look at her. "Deep breaths."

He sucked in several deep breaths, his tension easing.

"Now, what are you trying to tell me?" Essie held Farrendel's gaze, willing herself to remain calm for his sake.

Farrendel's silver-blue eyes met hers, and they didn't have the panic she expected to find. She couldn't say exactly what expression she saw there. "Our someday is today."

What was he talking about? Their someday was their dream for the future.

For children.

Essie gaped at Farrendel. Surely he didn't mean what she thought he meant. "Are we expecting? I'm pregnant?"

Farrendel nodded, still holding her gaze. Shouldn't he look more excited? Not this somber calm.

She gasped, wrapping her arms over her middle. "I nearly died. The baby? Is the baby all right?"

Was that why Farrendel looked so serious? Was something wrong?

Farrendel hunched farther in on himself. "Rheva says the baby is fine, as far as she can tell. She's been checking frequently. We should know for sure soon."

Essie blinked, a lump in her throat. That would explain why Farrendel looked so grim. He did not dare feel any excitement when their excitement could just as easily be turned to grief. "How..." She had to swallow and try again. "How far along am I?"

Her mind was whirling. She'd ignored certain things, thinking it was stress. Apparently not. But she couldn't be that many weeks along. Could Rheva tell with her magic?

"Not far, I do not think." Farrendel shrugged. "But you will have to ask Rheva. I did not hear much after she said *baby*."

She could understand that. She was having trouble absorbing it now, and she wasn't as prone to panic as Farrendel.

Then another thought struck her. "I used your magic. Could that have hurt the baby?"

Farrendel froze, his gaze swinging to the ceiling. "I do not know. I have never heard of an elven woman refraining from magic while in a family way. But it is also not a topic publicly discussed. Nor did any of them have magic like mine."

"I think I would worry less if the magic was mine. If that were the case, then my body would be immune to it, and I think that immunity would cover a child." Essie gripped the soft blanket in her fists. "But I'm only immune to your magic because of the heart bond. I have no physical, natural immunity to it that my body could use to shield a baby."

Farrendel shook his head, brow still furrowed. "Ask Rheva, but I think it would be best if you refrained from using my magic except in dire circumstances."

"Such as an assassin trying to kill me." Essie's chest tightened. "They haven't caught him yet, have they?"

"No." Farrendel's shoulders lifted in a shrug. "Your brothers are investigating, but they have yet to determine who was behind the attack and catch the assassin."

"Are we safe here?" Essie glanced toward the window, taking in the waving branches. As she stared, she took in the faint blue light glowing in the distance. She had never seen that before. "Should we go somewhere more secure? Like Lethorel or somewhere else?"

"You need to keep resting and should not travel. At least not until we are more certain the baby is well." Farrendel gestured toward the window. "We are well guarded, and I am maintaining a shield of magic around us. It is low-powered and simply warns me if someone crosses it, but an assassin cannot come close enough to target us here. Though, I am afraid there will be no trips into Estyra until the assassin is caught."

They were safe, but the two of them were basically under house arrest. Farrendel would survive hiding here well enough, but she was going to go stir crazy.

Essie stared out the window, not really taking in the view. A baby, who they didn't yet know would be all right. An assassin still out there trying to kill Farrendel and targeting Essie to do it.

She tried to smile, talking past the lump in her throat. "Should have known that your child would survive an assassination attempt before he or she was even born."

Even as she said it, she knew it wasn't funny. Her voice choked, then turned into a sob on the last word.

Farrendel was at her side in a moment, sitting next to her and drawing her into his arms.

She clung to him and pressed her face into his shoulder, trying to muffle her sobs against his shirt. "I don't even know why I'm crying." Her sobs drew out the last word as she cried harder.

This was all wrong. She and Farrendel were supposed to be excited at this news, not terrified. She was the one who was supposed to tell Farrendel, bursting with anticipation and coming up with a cute, fun way to tell him, not him tell her in the middle of talk of assassins. It was just so, so wrong.

By the time she sniffed her way to calm, Farrendel's shirt was soaked. Farrendel held her in his arms, her head cradled against his chest. She had her hands fisted in his shirt.

She was warm and safe. Loved. Right now, that was enough. Here, there was just Farrendel and her and their baby.

Perhaps she would stay here forever.

She heaved one last trembling sigh. "I don't think a couple is supposed to use the heart bond to keep each other alive quite as often as we do."

"No. We have made far too much use of the elishina. Let us hope this is the last time it is needed." Farrendel's arms tightened around her slightly, and he smoothed some of the sticky, tear-soaked strands of her hair from her face. "Your macha is here. She came along on the train when…"

When Essie was dying. Of course her mother would want to be with Essie at a time like that.

Farrendel's fingers rubbed Essie's shoulder, the stiff one

that had been wounded. "Rheva is giving her a tour of Ellon-ahshinel right now, but they will be back soon. I knew you would want to show her Estyra yourself, when it is safe to do so."

Essie nodded against Farrendel's chest, relaxing still further as his fingers eased the knots in her muscles. She had dreamed of having her mother here, but now with the assassin hunting Farrendel, she wasn't sure when she would have a chance to show her mother the city she had come to love as much as the one where she had grown up.

"I have not told her about...everything." Farrendel kept working at the stiffness in her muscles, easing the tension there until Essie felt as relaxed as a cat in the sun.

"We can tell her together." Essie smoothed her fingers against Farrendel's soft shirt.

Essie's stomach rumbled, giving another nauseous lurch. Perhaps they shouldn't wait too long to tell her. She was bound to notice if Essie started puking every morning. Her mother enjoyed having grandkids too much to overlook something that obvious.

"I can bring you food." Farrendel's voice rumbled in his chest beneath her ear. "There is soup. And fresh bread."

She tipped her face up so that she could look at Farrendel. "The bread sounds good. But you know what I would really love right now? A nice, warm bath. That tub was truly the best birthday present ever, you know."

He'd had a deep, copper tub grown in place with twisting, living branches. It was truly the most elegant bathtub she had ever seen. Between that and the handrails that finally made these elven rooms feel safe instead of precarious, she would never have a better birthday present.

Farrendel kissed her forehead. "I will start it running for you, then fetch some bread."

"Don't make it too hot." Essie reluctantly let him go as he eased from the bed. "You're the best."

As he left, she curled into the warmth of the blankets where he'd been. A baby. They were having a baby. For the first time, the expected thrill of excitement filled her chest, and she let herself dream of ways to tell her mother, her family, his family.

When Farrendel returned, he left the door to the water closet open, filling the bedroom with the comforting sound of water gushing into the bathtub. The soft smell of lavender wafted from the room as well, telling her he'd added the bath salts she liked so much.

Before Essie had the chance to do more than sit up, he scooped her up in his arms. Essie wrapped her arms around his neck, steadying herself as he carried her toward the water closet. "You're going to hover obnoxiously while I'm pregnant, aren't you?"

"Of course." Farrendel grinned, the somber look finally fading from his eyes. "I might even manage to be more suffocating about it than Weylind."

Essie laughed, then kept laughing because it felt so good. "You know, I think you might."

ESSIE'S MOTHER WAS, of course, excited beyond words for the two of them. Essie had a feeling that, as soon as the assassin was caught, she and her mother were going to take a shopping trip into Estyra for baby things.

It felt good to share excitement over the news. And, as

Essie had shown no symptoms of anything being wrong, she was starting to believe everything would be fine.

That evening, Essie and Farrendel sat on the porch that ringed their room, the new spindles in the railing blocking some of their view of the treetops.

Essie snuggled against Farrendel, his arm around her shoulders and a blanket warm over their legs. She closed her eyes and heaved a long breath. "This was a good day. Despite the assassin still out to get us."

Farrendel's arm tightened around her. "He will not get close enough to you to take a shot again."

"I am glad Iyrinder is well enough to join the patrols." Essie shivered, and Farrendel tucked the blanket over her shoulder. She hadn't found out until later that Iyrinder had been shot as well.

"He told me Miss Merrick took good care of him." Farrendel's voice held a note of puzzlement.

"Well of course she did." Essie cracked her eyes open and peered up at Farrendel. "They are sweet on each other."

"Ah." Farrendel's expression cleared, as if she had answered a mystery for him. "That explains why he turned down Weylind's promotion."

If it meant being separated from Farrendel's guard detail, and thus from Miss Merrick, of course Iyrinder had turned it down. Essie nodded against Farrendel's chest. "We will have to think of a different way to suitably reward him for saving you. Though if he just spent the last few days being cared for by Miss Merrick, he might count that as a reward in itself."

"Yes." Farrendel shifted, easing her head more onto his chest rather than his shoulder.

In the distance, the faint glimmer of his magic gave the leaves and trees a blue glow. Essie gestured to it. "Is it exhausting, holding up that magical shield around us? How do you even sleep?"

Farrendel's shoulder rose in a shrug. "I have enough strength to hold it in place for as long as it takes. I cannot sleep deeply, but that is a small sacrifice." His voice lowered, somber. "I doubt I would sleep much anyway."

Essie couldn't snuggle closer than she already was, but she tangled her fingers tighter in his shirt under the warmth of the blanket. He likely would have nightmares, after what they'd just been through. "I'm here for you. Watching me nearly die couldn't have been easy."

"No, it was not." Farrendel's arm tightened around her shoulders, and she sensed the way he tilted his head toward her by the way his breath brushed her hair. "You have been in battles before, but this is your first time being shot. That is not easy either."

Essie's chest tightened, her stomach giving a lurch that she didn't think was due to nausea. She was trying hard not to think too much about it, truth be told.

He pressed a soft kiss to her hair. "Do not be afraid to talk about it with someone if you need to. Even if it is not me, I am sure Rheva would be willing. Or we can set up an appointment with a counselor. There is no shame in needing help to process something, as you have told me often enough."

A lump formed in Essie's throat. This was Farrendel's care for her, that he would worry about how she was mentally handling this as well as physically healing. "I think I'm fine, right now. But I'll let you know." She tilted her head up, finding Farrendel's face only an inch from hers. She tugged herself up and kissed him gently. "Thank you."

His arm tightened on her, his other hand easing up her

back to cradle the her head. He kissed her again, deeper and longer. By the time he pulled back, Essie was melted inside, her thoughts nothing but mush.

Farrendel held her, tugging the blanket more securely over her shoulders. For long moments, they simply sat in silence, enjoying the night and the company. Tree frogs and night birds were starting to sing in the trees below and around them. Dusky gray filled the forest as night closed around them.

"A baby." Essie hugged Farrendel's waist, her head nestled against his chest. "I still can't quite believe it."

With her head resting over his heart, she could hear the way his heart beat harder, his breath hitching.

She patted his chest and looked up at his face. "Don't start worrying about everything now. That's the good thing about babies. You have months to get used to the idea and prepare. You aren't just handed a baby out of the blue with no warning."

While some of the edge of panic still lingered in his eyes, Farrendel's mouth twitched into a smile that was torn between humor and a bitter irony. "That is what happened to my father with me."

Essie paused, then gave a small laugh. "True. But that's not going to happen for you. Nope, we're going to spend months and months waiting and waiting. We'll talk about names. Fight over names. Get so many gifts we won't even know what to do with all of them while we are inundated with lots of well-meaning advice. And we are going to enjoy every step along the way."

"Even the nausea part?" Farrendel raised his eyebrows.

"Well, maybe not that part." Essie grimaced, her stomach giving another lurch just thinking about it. She wasn't looking forward to trying to navigate the tree branch pathways of Ellonahshinel and Estyra while hugely pregnant. While she wasn't clumsy, she wasn't as elegantly graceful as the elves.

Farrendel kissed her forehead. "I am ready. Or, I will be."

"I know." Essie tucked her hands against his warmth as the night grew darker and colder around them. Their lives were going to be rather busy for a while. Farrendel still had his classes at Hanford University, and she had her charities in both kingdoms. And now they would be parents on top of all that.

But they would handle it, like all the many generations of new parents before them.

As Farrendel's arms tightened around her, Essie closed her eyes. "You're going to be a great dacha. I'll be that crazy mother that manages to embarrass her children all the time. And this child—and any other children we might have—will always know he or she is loved."

CHAPTER
SEVENTEEN

"Why do you come to the library so late each night?" Elidyr sat across from Jalissa.

As they had been talking, he had given up on his pretense of keeping busy, much to Jalissa's pleasure. It was nice to simply sit and talk. She had never met anyone with whom she could talk the way she could with Elidyr.

Jalissa glanced out at the dark night. "I struggle to sleep when my brothers are gone. I fear…"

"You fear losing them." Elidyr stated it quietly, his shadowed eyes gazing at her with such compassion that it felt like a warm cloak settling around her.

"Yes." It was her greatest fear. Her father had gone to war, and he had never come home. Farrendel had gone to war, and he had never been the same since. Weylind had gone to war, and it had aged him and stolen his smiles. There were, after all, many ways to lose her family to war.

J alissa was freezing. She smelled like she had been sprayed by a skunk, rolled in animal dung, then rinsed off in a cesspool.

For three nights and days, she and Edmund had kept a watch on the *Times* building, only taking a few breaks to go back to the safe house and catch some sleep. She had met a few of the other men and women from the Intelligence Office, though *met* was a loose word for it. She had not been told their names. Occasionally, one of them would walk the street, pressing bread, soup, and a note into Edmund's hands. Sometimes, they would be at the safe house, and Jalissa found herself sharing a secretive meal with strangers and sleeping in the same bunk room with Escarlish women who did not introduce themselves.

And for three frustrating nights and days, they had learned nothing.

Jalissa settled deeper into her cloak and huddled against Edmund. She kept her whisper too quiet for anyone else to hear. "Is being a spy always this boring?"

Edmund's grin flashed, barely visible beneath the hood of his cloak. "The thing about being a spy is that, if things aren't boring, then you didn't do your job right."

"Makes sense, I guess." Jalissa sighed, her breath puffing in front of her face in the darkness of the early morning street. "How long do we sit here before deciding that this is a dead end?"

"I've waited months before catching a break before. Three days are nothing." At Jalissa's groan, his grin widened. "But in this case, you and I are going to stay here through today. If nothing happens by then, we'll pull out and the Intelligence Office will place different agents on duty here. We've nearly worn out our welcome in these disguises. If we hang around much longer, someone at the *Times* might grow suspicious."

Jalissa did not want to admit how welcome that news was. She had agreed to this. She had wanted to come, after all.

They lapsed into silence as they watched the first of the day shift of typesetters and press operators enter the building. A few minutes later, the workers on the night shift began leaving. As the sunrise tinged the sky pink, the editors began arriving, along with a few of the reporters, though Trent Bourdon had yet to show up for the day. Several boys of maybe ten or twelve darted in and out of the building, running errands and carrying messages.

Everything was like clockwork, the same clockwork Jalissa had watched for the past three mornings. Nothing out of place. Nothing unusual.

A boy, one with curly brown hair whom Jalissa had seen several times over the past few days, left the *Times* building, darting a glance around before he hurried down the street.

Jalissa was not sure what caught her eye this time. The furtive glance around could have simply been the natural caution of a young boy, alone, stepping onto a dangerous street. But something seemed off to her.

She nudged Edmund. "I think we should follow that boy."

The boy was still on the same street, but if they did not follow soon, they would lose him.

Jalissa had expected Edmund to ask for some explanation, but instead, he pushed to his feet, leaning onto his cane. He held his arm out to her. "Let's go."

She took his arm, hunching as he was to keep up her act

as an old Escarlish woman. Together, she and Edmund hobbled up the street, yet Edmund somehow managed to set a brisk pace despite his feigned feebleness.

Partway down the street, they passed Sarya in the guise of a drunken man staggering his way home. After a nod and a quick, whispered conversation, Sarya set off down one of the alleys to try to circle ahead of the boy.

The boy continued down the same street for several blocks, making it rather easy for Jalissa and Edmund to trail him.

At a larger cross street, he halted and glanced around, including behind him.

Jalissa tensed, ducking. The boy would see them. Would he recognize them as the same couple that had been sitting across from the *Times* building for the past few days?

But Edmund tightened his grip on her arm and dragged her forward. He whispered, "Never duck or halt or try to hide when a mark glances back. You'll draw attention to yourself. Pretend you are busy with your own business and take no notice of him."

Easier said than done.

Sure enough, the boy faced forward and kept on walking as if he had seen nothing amiss.

As soon as the boy was out of sight, Edmund straightened and pulled back his hood. He held the cane out to her. "He's seen us once. If he spots us still following after he turned that corner, he might grow suspicious. So we'll change our appearance in a few simple ways."

Jalissa eased to her full height, thankful to stand straight again since her back was aching from being hunched over. She pulled the hood off her head as well, revealing her grimy gray wig. Then she took the cane.

She and Edmund set off once again, this time with her using the cane to steady herself while Edmund was the helpful, elderly husband walking with his wife.

When they turned the corner, the boy was farther away, trotting along the sidewalk.

Edmund quickened their pace, and Jalissa was thankful that she had long enough legs to keep up with him without trotting in a way that would give away how much they were hurrying.

The boy took a few more turns, and each time she and Edmund changed their appearance. They ditched the cane and the cloaks. The gray wigs went next, tucked safely behind some trash barrels for someone to retrieve later. Jalissa's dark brown hair was pinned up in such a way that it looked like an Escarlish hairstyle, the style covering most of her ears. The grime on her face hid her slightly silvery skin tone. At another intersection, Sarya joined them so that they were walking three together instead of two.

Just when she was wondering what else they could ditch to change up their appearance, the boy raced up to another large brick building, opened the door, and disappeared inside. The clamor of printing presses—something that Jalissa had become very familiar with over the past few days —reverberated into the air.

"This is another newspaper office." Jalissa eyed it, though she didn't see any signs to denote the name of the paper.

Edmund frowned as he stared at it. "Not just any newspaper. The *Sentinel*."

"The paper that plagiarized your friend's article?" Jalissa eyed the innocuous brick building again. It looked like any other large, brick building in the city of Aldon, and this city happened to have a lot of big brick buildings.

"Yes. Not only that, but this paper has been a thorn in my family's side since they opened shop." Edmund scowled, rubbing a hand over the grime on his face. "They are known for their inflammatory tone. People read them looking for that, in fact. Even though no one could prove it, their articles were part of stirring up all those protests against the treaty."

The protests that were attended by people like Lord Bletchly and Mark Hadley, the leaders of a group of traitors who had betrayed Farrendel and Essie to the trolls.

Jalissa resisted the urge to gesture toward the building. "What does this mean?"

"That boy could simply be running errands for both papers. Errand boys aren't paid that well. He could have multiple jobs." Edmund sighed and shook his head. "But more likely, it means we have been looking at this the wrong way. I guessed that the person at the *Times* was the mastermind who stole the article and gave it to the *Sentinel* to further hurt Essie and Farrendel. But the mole is a mere boy."

"And that means the mastermind of the theft must be in there." Jalissa tipped her head in the direction of the building. "Someone must have told that boy what to look for. Probably anything to do with the royal family."

She should not feel so gratified at Edmund's nod. She was getting better at this spy thing.

"I should have seen it sooner." Edmund grimaced, shaking his head. "The *Sentinel* has been up to their elbows in whatever this is since the beginning. They plagiarized that article. They were the ones who broke the story about

Farrendel. I don't yet know how they are connected to the assassin, but there's something fishy here."

"Fishy?" Jalissa wrinkled her nose. She did not smell anything fishy, though it was hard to tell past the variety of stenches clinging to her.

"Not right." Edmund held his arm out to her. "We should keep moving. Someone might notice if we loiter in front of their building too long, especially since this is on a nicer street than the *Times*."

"Why is that?" Jalissa wrapped her hand around his arm in a manner that was growing increasingly comfortable. "Didn't the *Sentinel* start up only a few years ago?"

"Exactly." Edmund set off down the street. "The *Times* has been around for a hundred and fifty years. It was on a nice, safe street when it began, but the community has deteriorated around it. The *Sentinel* bought a building on a street that is currently in a safe, wealthier section of the city."

Sarya fell into step behind them, trailing far enough back that she would not appear as if she was a guard.

"Then why would the *Times* not move to a safer area?" Jalissa could not put her finger on it, but something felt off about this. "Surely it is detrimental for their business. Wealthy patrons will not want to visit to place advertisements. That is a big thing for your papers, I have gathered. Well educated editors and reporters, especially those from wealthier families, will not want to work in such a place."

"True. But it isn't so easy to just buy a large building in a good neighborhood." Edmund halted and looked at her.

"Yes, that is my thought." They were far enough away that Jalissa felt safe to gesture back at the *Sentinel*'s building. "If this is such an expensive neighborhood, then how could the *Sentinel* afford to buy a place here? And why here in particular? I assume there are other safe, though less expensive places in town."

"Most importantly of all, who funded them?" Edmund glanced back toward the *Sentinel* as well. "I think it's time we took a deeper look into the *Sentinel* and its finances. We have held off until now, since it would look bad if the Intelligence Office appeared to be hounding the *Sentinel* as revenge for their pieces about the royal family. They are not the only paper that publishes scandal sheets, after all."

Jalissa resisted the urge to snort. "Your Escarlish papers are much less polite than ours in Tarenhiel."

"Very much so." Edmund gave her a wry smile before he sobered. "We'll move most of the stakeout over to the *Sentinel*, leaving only a few people on the *Times*."

"Will we join that stakeout?" Jalissa could not help but grimace. Sure, this neighborhood was much cleaner than the last one. The disguises would likely involve better clothing and less odor than their current ones, but Jalissa was tired of sitting on the street doing nothing for days on end. She wanted to help Farrendel and Essie, but this seemed frustratingly fruitless so far.

"No. At least, not right away. I'd like to go through the paperwork myself first." Edmund's voice softened as they neared groups of other people strolling the streets at this time of morning. "I'd like to be prepared before we do any skulking around."

Skulking. Something he must be very good at, after all his practice while spying on Tarenhiel.

What would Weylind have done to him if Edmund had been caught? Would he have been sent back to Escarland? Or would he have been sentenced to death, executed in the forbidden grove? She shuddered, though she probably should not feel sick at the thought.

She shook herself. She did not want to dwell on Edmund's past spying activities.

Instead, she smiled, trying to put a light tone to her voice. "How do you plan to sneakily search the place since they have two shifts of workers and there are always people around?"

Edmund smirked. "An abundance of people can be as helpful as a lack. I'll see if I can go undercover as a worker. Since they are a place of business, it's even legal to do so."

"Maybe..." Jalissa trailed off. The thought was so impulsive that it was not like her at all. She had nearly blurted it out before she caught herself.

"Maybe what?" Edmund raised his eyebrows. The expression looked funny, with the grime matting his eyebrows and smearing his face.

Jalissa drew in a deep breath, then let it out slowly. If she wanted to be more than a decorative princess, then she had to start doing something *more*. And this spying thing with Edmund was not just something more, but it also turned being a decorative princess into an asset.

Facing Edmund, Jalissa lifted her chin and met his gaze. "Send me undercover. I will be less recognizable than an Escarlish prince in his own home city. You have female reporters, correct? Perhaps I can be one of those, looking for a job."

Edmund's gaze flicked over her face, studying her. "Female reporters do have a tough time of it. It would not be so odd that you would come begging to the *Sentinel* for a job. But..." Edmund shook his head. "You are a princess of a foreign kingdom. You don't have any legal jurisdiction to join the investigation. Any evidence you obtained wouldn't be admissible in an Escarlish court."

"Oh." She had not thought of that. She had gotten so caught up in all of this that she had forgotten that pesky detail. It was one thing to investigate with Edmund. It was another to have a go of it on her own.

"But it was a good idea." Edmund grinned and held out his arm to her again. "We'll make a spy out of you yet."

That should not have warmed her all the way to her still frozen toes. After this little jaunt in Escarland, she would finally pick an elf lord, marry him in a ceremony that was all pomp to hide the fact that there was no love, settle down with him in some estate deep within Tarenhiel, and never set foot anywhere near Escarland ever again. If she ever came to Escarland, it would be as an official ambassador who would never walk these grimy back streets.

Why did that future feel so...empty? It would not be as bleak as it seemed now. Surely she could simply choose to love whatever elf lord she picked and choose to fall out of love with Edmund. It would be fine.

Then why did her heart ache so much? Why did she feel far more alive now while wearing rags and smelling like a sewer than she had while dressed in silk in Ellonahshinel trying to pick her husband?

CHAPTER
EIGHTEEN

Edmund held his breath as Essie strode down the gangplank from the steamboat, the elven princess Jalissa behind her. Would Jalissa recognize him? Would she put everything together?

He smoothed a hand over his face, checking that the gritty feel of the cosmetics was gone. When he touched his ear, he felt only his human-shaped ear, no remnants of the fake points remaining. He had been rushed, rowing across the Hydalla during the night, getting cleaned up, catching the royal train at the nearest coal and water stop, then arriving at the outpost at dawn as if he had been in Aldon this entire time.

When Jalissa's gaze focused on him, no spark flared in her eyes. Her gaze remained cold, her expression hard and official. The mask of a princess sent as an ambassador and facing a prince she had never met before.

If he played his role right and didn't give away how familiar he was with elves and their customs, she would never realize that the loud Escarlish prince had been the shy, bookish elven servant she had once fallen for.

Still, he didn't think he could resist flirting with her. Just a little harmless flirting. Nothing more.

Edmund hunched over his desk in the Intelligence Office, papers spread over his desk.

Something was seriously off with the *Sentinel*. But the proof was turning out to be elusive.

The *Sentinel* sprang out of nowhere two and a half years ago with seemingly endless monetary resources. Overnight, they had turned themselves into competitors with the more well-established newspapers.

Yet, the tax office had done several audits back then and found nothing they deemed suspicious. The money had come from an anonymous grant, but all the proper paperwork had been filed. Too bad the *Sentinel* didn't have to disclose the source of the donation.

Edmund now had the tax reports from all the Escarlish nobility who had expressed dissatisfaction with the monarchy or the treaty with the elves over the past couple of years spread across his desk. Lord Bletchly's finances—particularly well-documented thanks to the investigation after he was revealed to be a traitor—lay on top.

General Bloam halted by Edmund's desk. "Any progress to report?"

Edmund tapped the paper in front of him. "I've found several small donations to the *Sentinel* in the tax records of many of these nobles, though there is no indication of who brokered the donations that were later consolidated to the large grant."

"I'll have it sent over to the tax office." General Bloam made a note on the clipboard he carried. "They can send their people out for interviews and audits. It will be less suspicious coming from them."

"The strange thing is that the donations don't add up to the full amount." Edmund grimaced and gestured at the piles of tax records. "I've gone over these multiple times, and every time I only get about half of the amount listed in the *Sentinel*'s file."

"There's another source of money not documented in these tax records." General Bloam sighed and made another note. "Any thoughts on where to look?"

"The *Sentinel* is owned by a group of their editors. Could they have each chipped in their personal fortunes to cover the difference?" Edmund glanced past General Bloam to where agents analyzed the public records of the owners and employees of the *Sentinel*.

"Not that we can tell. None of them are from noble families. They moved here from various small towns all across the kingdom around three years ago." General Bloam's voice had a peculiar note to it. Though, as was his way, he did not spell it out for Edmund, waiting for him to put the pieces together to make sure their hunches lined up.

Edmund stared off into space, turning that information over in his mind. "It's rather suspicious that a group of people from small towns so scattered that they couldn't possibly know each other would decide to move to Aldon around the same time to start a business together."

"Our thoughts exactly." General Bloam scowled down at his clipboard. "It's the kind of cover this office has set up too often not to recognize the tactics. We're trying to contact clerks in the towns to get confirmation that these people were citizens there in the past, but I don't hold out much hope."

Edmund stared down at the files on his desk. It was a common ploy in the spy game, to claim to be from a small town where it would be difficult to check someone's story unless an agent was physically sent there to question the local townsfolk. It obscured a spy simply popping into existence. "So who are they, really?"

"That's what we need to find out, and fast." General Bloam's mouth pressed into a thin line.

They didn't have enough information yet to start making educated guesses there. The tactics were those of spies, but were they foreign spies? If so, from where?

Or they could be Escarlish citizens who had gone underground like this for their own scheme. Perhaps anti-monarchists who were trying to undermine Averett. That was certainly the most likely scenario, given the stirrings of discontent last year. Perhaps they had even secretly been behind Lord Bletchly's and Mark Hadley's betrayal, encouraging them from the shadows while keeping their presence so secretive that they hadn't been uncovered during the investigation.

"We need to get a man inside." Edmund glanced back up to General Bloam, knowing the general would already have been working toward just that.

"I sent John this morning, but the *Sentinel* isn't hiring." General Bloam held Edmund's gaze. Not giving him an order. Not saying anything out loud.

But the message was there.

They needed a spy more than an investigator.

Edmund resisted the urge to grimace. He had enough guilt from some of the things he'd done in Tarenhiel. Illegally breaking into places was morally sketchy enough when he was a spy on foreign soil. But it was definitely crossing a line when he was a prince spying on his own people.

If he were caught, then it would be a political nightmare for Averett. And it would make prosecution trickier, if some of the evidence was obtained in a legal gray area. While the Intelligence Office tried to stick to a code of ethics when it came to certain things—like obtaining a warrant and searching in a legal manner—the laws didn't prevent them from taking other actions. There were those pressuring for more reform to the legal code, Averett included, but the laws hadn't made it through Parliament yet.

"I'll see what I can do." Edmund gathered the stacks of files, arranging the tax records with his notes on top so that the tax office could easily see what needed to be investigated.

If what he was going to do was already morally gray and politically dangerous, then adding a foreign princess into the mix wasn't going to help matters any.

But Jalissa was so determined to help in this investigation, and he couldn't bring himself to keep her out. He had been in her shoes, the younger sibling determined to find a way to help, even if it meant taking to the shadows.

They would simply have to avoid getting caught.

It took far too many rounds of pretending to gulp down his beer at a local tavern to finally drink one of the press operators from the *Sentinel* under the table. But, after two evenings of spying on the night-shift workers, Edmund had chosen this particular worker with good reason. Not only did Edmund vaguely resemble him, but the man was known by everyone to be a layabout. No one would think anything of it if he got passed-out drunk.

When the man finally slumped over the bar, Edmund helpfully aided the barkeep in carrying the man to a room to sleep it off, paying for the room himself.

As soon as the barkeep left, Edmund dressed in clothes identical to the worker's and checked that his wooden token embossed with the *Sentinel*'s logo looked passably identical to the one that the worker carried, which would gain him entry into the building for his shift. He added a few items to the hidden pockets inside his shirt. Some tricks of the trade to aid his mission, along with his weapons.

By the time Edmund slipped down the back staircase in the tavern and out the door into the alley, he was now Logan Porle, a nightshift press operator for the *Sentinel*.

Jalissa and her guard waited for him in the alley. While they currently both wore ragged cloaks, Jalissa was dressed as a middle class Escarlish woman in a clean calico dress and had her hair pinned up in such a way that it hid her ears. Cosmetics gave a pink glow to her skin, though her face was still a little on the thin side for a human. Sarya was dressed as a servant for a noble house in a black dress and white apron, a common enough sight in the area where the *Sentinel* operated.

"Are you both ready for this?" Edmund glanced between them.

Jalissa shrugged. "We are just standing watch."

Edmund waited until she met and held his gaze. "Don't sell standing watch short. It's an important job. It could be the difference between me getting in and out of there unde-tected or getting caught."

When Jalissa nodded, Edmund set off for the *Sentinel* building at a stroll, his hands in his pockets and his shoulders slightly slumped.

Jalissa and Sarya followed far enough back that no one would think they were with him. They would find places along the street outside of the *Sentinel* building to keep watch, moving around enough that people wouldn't accuse them of loitering. He had given them each a few coins to make purchases from some of the street vendors to aid in their disguise.

When he reached the line of workers waiting to enter the *Sentinel*, Edmund kept his head down. He looked enough like the worker he'd gotten drunk to pass at a glance, but these men worked with the real Logan Porle every night. They would spot him for a fraud in an instant if they got a good look at him.

At the door, a man waited with a clipboard. Each worker paused, showed his token, and told the guard his name. The guard checked the name off the list before nodding the man inside.

When it was Edmund's turn, he held up his token and slurred, "Logan Porle." While he hadn't imbibed, the smell of alcohol clung to him thanks to the copious amounts he'd spilled on himself while fake drinking.

"In your cups again, Logan?" The guard shook his head as he checked the name off his list. "You're going to get your hand caught in the press one of these days."

Edmund gave a sullen shrug, then trundled into the building at an ambling pace.

As soon as he stepped inside, the clacking of the presses slammed into him, along with the overpowering smell of ink and paper. The two large printing presses took up most of the space along one wall. Unlike the small, hand-powered presses of only a few decades ago, these had large gears attached to belts powered by a steam engine. The engine and boiler puffed on the far side of the room, blocked off from most of the room by a thick, brick wall. Only the open, double doors into the room gave Edmund a glimpse of the workers shoveling coal into the boiler to keep up the steam pressure.

Press operators bustled about, carrying paper, feeding it into the press, catching the printed papers as they left the press, and stacking them in order of the pages. Across from the press, typesetters organized the movable letters, already working on the next run of newspapers that would go out in the morning.

A loft, walled off from the rest of the room by brick and large windows overlooking the printing floor, contained the offices of the editors and reporters. At this time of night, only a few of the offices were still lit.

Edmund took his time, waiting while the other workers found their spot.

Finally, a glowering man standing next to the press gestured Edmund over. "Hey, Logan!" He then peppered a few choice expletives between orders for "Logan" to take his place at the press.

Edmund staggered his way over there, keeping his head down and hat pulled low.

The man's nose wrinkled, and he gave a few more curses under his breath. But he let Edmund take his place, walking away from the press without a glance back. Apparently, getting off his shift was more important to the man than making sure his fellow worker was alert enough to properly do his job.

Edmund studied the press for a moment, trying to figure out exactly what he was expected to do. One man fed paper into the press while someone else inked the plates. Another person caught and stacked the finished papers.

Yet, at this station, a canister of grease waited. Ah, so Edmund was the grease man, the low man in the pecking order who greased the moving parts, ran errands, and stuck his hand in the press to clear jams if necessary. In other words, one of the more dangerous jobs.

Tonight, at least, the printing press appeared to be running smoothly. Edmund quickly figured out his job, and any lapses were dismissed due to his supposed drunken state. He kept an eye on the windows and door, but he didn't see any signal from Jalissa to indicate that the real Logan had woken and was making his way to the *Sentinel* to take his shift.

Finally, one of the other press operators gestured from him toward the boiler room. "Fetch more paper."

Just the opening Edmund had been waiting for. With a nod, he set off toward the back room that contained the boiler. He hadn't seen any reams of paper or extra ink lying around the printing floor, so there must be a storage room somewhere. It seemed odd to store paper next to the boiler, but it was probably better than having it underfoot.

Yet when Edmund stepped into the boiler room, the stifling, muggy air almost instantly sticking his shirt to his skin, he spotted a staircase going down into a basement. Now that made more sense.

Light shone from the basement, so Edmund had no need of a lantern as he strolled down the stairs. When he reached the bottom, he found the basement well-lit by gas lamps, even though there were no windows, not even small ones set high in the wall at street-level like many of these buildings had.

Stacks upon stacks of paper reams filled most of the space, along with barrels of ink and stacks of blank engraving plates.

But the space wasn't as big as it should have been, given the size of the building above. Edmund wound his way through the clutter. As he neared the other side, he could make out a door set in an otherwise empty brick wall. Light shone around the door, though it was firmly closed.

Edmund dropped onto his stomach and peered through the inch gap at the bottom of the door.

The boots of two men were visible inside the room. One of them was moving about, but the other stood next to the legs of some machine.

Edmund twisted his head, trying to find an angle to see more.

That was a printing press. But it wasn't one of the massive, industrial steam-powered presses like the two in the room above. No, this was an older, hand-operated model. It worked in near silence, and any small clatter it made was covered by the noise of the other presses.

But what were these two men printing down here?

Edmund shifted, first to one side of the door, then the other, to see each side of the small room. The left side of the room appeared to hold more barrels of ink and reams of paper, though the paper wasn't the same color and texture as the reams of paper in the main part of the basement.

On the right side of the room were stacks upon stacks of what appeared to be the finished product. Edmund squinted at something at floor level, crumpled and forgotten in the corner by the wall.

An Escarlish banknote. He couldn't see the denomination, but he didn't have to.

These weren't spies. They were counterfeiters. That was where the rest of the money to fund the *Sentinel* had come from. They had used legitimate money to buy the items they would need, obscuring it among purchases for the newspaper, and then they had printed the rest.

And they must be very good. Edmund hadn't heard about counterfeit money turning up in Aldon, though he had been out of the kingdom more than he had been in it for the past four years. He knew more about what had been happening in Tarenhiel and Kostaria than in Escarland.

Carefully pushing to his feet, Edmund tiptoed away from the door and headed back the way he'd come. He couldn't linger too much longer, otherwise someone might come down looking for him.

On his way out, he grabbed as many reams of paper as he could carry, staggering up the stairs with them hiding his face.

When he re-entered the printing floor, he swept a glance across the room, taking in the bustle. Nothing appeared to have changed, except that the worker feeding the paper was down to his last ream and casting frequent glances over his shoulder.

Yet...there under the door, a tiny sprig of green waved frantically.

Time to get out of here.

When Edmund reached the press, he dropped the reams of paper at the worker's feet.

The worker jumped back, cursing.

Edmund hunched, mumbling and grunting. Dropping to his knees to hide his movement, he slipped a leather waterskin from his shirt, uncapping it. With a great show, he gagged, then heaved, squeezing the waterskin at the same time.

His own special blend of fake vomit splattered the floor, eliciting another round of curses.

A worker grabbed Edmund by the shoulders. "Out in the alley with you."

Edmund made a great show of staggering across the room, gagging and pretending to almost vomit one more time, before he left the building, faking vomit drooling down the front of his shirt.

He rushed down the stairs, hunching, as if intent on reaching the alley before losing more of the contents of his stomach. In the time he'd been inside, the sun had set, the streets now deep in shadow except for the places where the gas street lights cast a dim glow.

In the alley, he drew up short.

Jalissa and Sarya already stood in the alley, and they both had cloaks once again covering their clothes. At one side of the alley, a man lay squirming, bound in…were those vines?

Jalissa worried her lower lip, eyeing the mess on his shirt. "I am sorry to pull you out, but this man would not take no for an answer, and I was not sure what to do with him now that he has been subdued."

Edmund winced. This street was generally safe, but nowhere in a big city was truly safe at this time of night for a woman alone, even if Sarya had been lingering nearby. He'd hoped to be in and out of there a lot quicker than he was.

What were they going to do with the man now? If they simply let him go, he'd run off to the nearest tavern and start telling everyone how he was accosted by an elf near the

Sentinel. That was sure to get back to the counterfeiters and make them nervous.

They also couldn't turn him over to the nearest guard station either. They were bound to ask questions Edmund wasn't willing to answer. And he didn't yet know if he could trust the guards who patrolled this district. The counterfeiters could have paid off some of the local guards, which would explain why counterfeit money had yet to be reported.

That left only one option.

"We'll have to take him with us. I wouldn't mind questioning him on what he's seen, if he hangs around this street often." They wouldn't be able to hold him long at the palace, but long enough to deal with the counterfeiters. If the man knew anything, he would likely spill it if he thought it would save him from charges of assaulting an elven princess.

Edmund knelt next to the man and hefted him over a shoulder. The man squirmed a bit, making unintelligible sounds past the vine gagging his mouth, but he was too trussed up to fight back.

"This vine is rather handy." Edmund tugged at the plant binding the man's ankles. "I'd love to have a pocket full of these that I could use on missions."

Jalissa nodded, staring down at the man she and Sarya had captured. "I will have to consider how to make them portable…as long as those missions are not in Tarenhiel."

"If they were in Tarenhiel, plant ropes would do little good." Edmund grunted as he set out into the darkening streets with the man's weight across his back. "An elf with plant magic would simply turn the vines against me."

"True." Jalissa grinned as she easily kept pace with him,

her long stride a perfect match for his. "You would be bringing the means for your own capture in that case."

As they made their way back to the palace, Edmund stuck to the back alleys, avoiding streetlights, as he led Jalissa and Sarya back to the safe house. There, he left the man on the floor under Sarya and Jalissa's watchful gaze, while Edmund cleaned up and changed into something more befitting a prince.

When he returned to the main room, Jalissa glanced from him to the man on the floor. He could see her desperation to question him about what he'd seen inside the *Sentinel* building by the way she wrung her hands and rocked on her heels slightly.

"I'll tell you when we get back." He groaned as he picked up the man again. He had not reckoned on carrying a man across half of Aldon. His muscles and back would be sore tomorrow.

"I know." Jalissa's warm, brown eyes searched his face. "But you found something, right?"

"Yes." Though, he wasn't sure how it all fit together yet.

They hiked the rest of the way across Aldon. When they reached Winstead Palace, Edmund handed the man over to the gate guards and told them to alert General Bloam about the prisoner.

These guards were loyal to the royal family, so they didn't question Edmund's orders as the city guards might have. Instead, they let Edmund, Jalissa, and Sarya pass before some of them hustled the man off.

Jalissa stuck to Edmund's side as he hurried toward Winstead Palace, as if she feared being left out if she didn't keep up. She didn't even flinch when they stepped inside the stone palace. If anything, her jaw went harder, her eyes sharper.

Edmund went straight for Averett's study, breathing a sigh of relief when a light was still on inside. Good. For once he was glad his brother was up late working on paperwork instead of going to bed and sleeping as he ought.

He knocked, waited a moment until Averett's voice told him to enter, then pushed the door open, Jalissa at his side. Sarya waited outside, taking a place next to the door.

Averett glanced up from the explosion of papers strewn across his large, oak desk. The desk was so massively built that it could stop a bullet if need be. "Jalissa, Edmund, good. I invited that list of elven nobility that you provided, and almost all of them have said yes. Please tell me you have something. I'm going to be holding a press conference at that ball, and it would be nice to be able to announce that we've caught the assassin."

"I have something, but I'm not sure what it is yet." Edmund closed the door behind him, waiting until Jalissa claimed one of the chairs across from Averett's desk, before he pulled up a second one and sat. He leaned his elbows on the desk and faced his brother. "What do you know about counterfeit banknotes circulating in Aldon?"

"Counterfeiters." Averett gaped at him for a moment, blinked, then shook his head. "As far as I know, very little counterfeit money has turned up in Aldon recently. There have been reports of counterfeit money showing up in some of the other cities and towns across Escarland, but your Intelligence Office hasn't been able to track down the source."

Edmund nodded and leaned back in his chair. That would explain how they had gotten away with it. They had started the money off in places where there was less over-sight. By the time the money worked its way to a bigger city, its source would be hard to locate.

"How many of those towns were near places where that group of Escarlish traitors operated? What about towns near Lord Bletchly's holdings?" Edmund almost wished the man was still alive. He still had a lot to answer for.

But only almost. There was a poetic justice to the fact the man had been killed while betraying Farrendel and Essie to what he thought would be their deaths.

"I'm not sure. I'd have to look at the reports again." Averett shook his head before he met Edmund's gaze. "Are you telling me the *Sentinel* is really a counterfeiting operation?"

"Yes. They are operating a press in the basement." Edmund closed his eyes, seeing again the stacks and stacks of Escarlish bills just sitting in that room. "But I think they have printed far more than they have circulated so far. As if they are waiting for something."

"But what does this have to do with an assassination attempt on Farrendel?" Jalissa's voice was sharp, almost as if the question burst out of her despite her decorum.

Edmund opened his eyes and gave her what he hoped was a reassuring smile, though he really wanted to take her hand and hold it. "I'm not entirely sure. But this does seem to point toward our anarchist or, at the very least, anti-monarchist theory."

Averett nodded, leaning his elbows on his desk wearily. "Flooding the market with a whole bunch of counterfeit money all at once would cause distrust of Escarlish currency at best, inflation and a recession to our economy at worst. That by itself would put us in a bad position with neighboring kingdoms. But assassinating Farrendel on top of it…"

Jalissa caught her breath, eyes widening. "I see. It would disrupt the treaty between your kingdom and mine."

"Weylind and I have become friends. But I'm not sure that friendship could survive Farrendel getting assassinated on my watch. Especially not when this is the second time he has been hurt while in Escarland." Averett sighed and scrubbed a hand over his face. "I've already gotten a few stern messages from him. Only the fact that both Farrendel and Essie came out of this as unscathed as possible salvaged matters."

Edmund grimaced. He, Julien, and Averett had all but promised Weylind that they would never let an attack on Farrendel happen again on Escarlish soil. But here it was, less than a year later, and Essie and Iyrinder had been shot in an attempt to kill Farrendel.

Averett raised his head and speared first Jalissa, then Edmund with a look. "And I haven't even dared tell Weylind what you two have been up to. That's going to be your problem to face, if he finds out."

Edmund shifted, glancing at Jalissa.

She straightened her spine. "I can handle Weylind."

"That's what I was afraid of." Averett rubbed his temples again. "Just leave me out of it when you do, all right? I didn't find out until the morning after you'd left that first time. Do you think that gives me enough plausible deniability?"

Somehow, Edmund doubted it. Not when Weylind could out-do Averett when it came to big brother overprotectiveness. And that was saying something, considering Averett had sent Edmund to go spy on Essie and Farrendel. Granted,

Edmund had volunteered, so he wasn't immune to big brother impulses.

"Do you think ending the treaty is their goal?" Jalissa's tone turned formal as she eyed the two of them, as if hoping they would go along with her bringing the subject back to the matter at hand. "The anniversary of the treaty is a little over a week away. Not to mention that you, Weylind, and Rharreth are planning for that new bridge over the Hydalla River."

"The bridge isn't well publicized, and I don't know if anyone besides the engineers knows about the meeting with Rharreth and his stoneworkers that Weylind is hosting in Tarenhiel a few weeks from now." Lines creased Averett's face, as if he were far older than his late twenties. "But it is a distinct possibility, especially since the *Sentinel* has ties to the Escarlish traitors who betrayed Farrendel to King Charvod last year. The treaties we have with Tarenhiel and Kostaria have given Escarland power, and by extension, given the monarchy more power. There are many people who would like to see us sever such close ties with Tarenhiel and Kostaria."

Edmund nodded, but something still felt off. This was where things didn't add up. The *Sentinel* had started operations two and a half years ago. *Before* the treaty with Tarenhiel. Whatever their plan and motives, it had begun long before the treaty.

Had the treaty merely stepped up their plan? Were these anti-monarchist Escarlish citizens who were angry enough to kill an Escarlish princess right along with the elven prince?

Lord Bletchly and Mark Hadley had been willing to kill Essie since marrying an elf had tainted her in their eyes. Was this more of the same motivation, especially now that those at the *Sentinel* knew Farrendel was illegitimate? Maybe the assassination had been added to the plan after finding out that tidbit while filching information from the *Aldon Times*.

It still didn't sit right. Escarland's current economic boom was *because* of the trade with Tarenhiel and Kostaria, a trade that would only increase when the bridge over the Hydalla River was built. Escarland was the only source of troll and elven goods for the other human kingdoms.

Sure, there were those who didn't like Tarenhiel and Kostaria and advocated instead for closer ties with human kingdoms like Mongavaria with its booming seaports and rich overseas trade. The merchants who had gotten rich from trade with Mongavaria weren't happy with the change, though many of them had proved adaptable and switched their trade routes quickly.

On top of the trade, the defense treaty with the elves substantially increased the military might that Escarland could draw on. With Farrendel's magic fighting on their side, Escarland's army would be nearly invincible.

Months ago, the true benefits of the treaty with Tarenhiel hadn't been as apparent as they were now. Even many of its detractors had changed their tune since then, if only to associate with the popular side right now.

Killing Farrendel now along with flooding the market with counterfeit money would only weaken Escarland. Those were the actions of someone who hated Escarland—or was so blinded by thinking that their cause was right that they were willing to burn down the entire kingdom in the process.

"How do you want to handle it?" Edmund gestured to the door.

"Report to General Bloam and tell him I've authorized

keeping an even tighter watch on the *Sentinel* and all of its employees." Averett drummed his fingers on his desk, staring at the wall past Edmund's shoulder for a long moment, eyes unfocused. "We only have your word to go on right now. Not enough for arrests, but probably enough for a raid. The head editor and top reporters will all be here at Winstead Palace for the press conference in a few days. I would think that would be the best time to raid their building."

Edmund nodded. "I'll report to General Bloam. I'm sure he will brief you personally on any questions or concerns."

Even though it hadn't been by his choice, he had thought he was done with life in the shadows. But it turned out he had one more battle to fight, one more conspiracy to uproot. He wouldn't be forced to set aside the spy forever just yet.

F arrendel perched on the bench across the back wall
of his workshop. The research books for his homework spread across the surface, but he had yet to
write a sentence. His brain remained too weary, and it had
taken all his motivation just to get himself down here, much
less work on a paper.

He slumped against the wall and simply stared, as if
staring at the paper would make it write itself eventually.

A knock lightly rapped against the outer door.

He froze, staring at the door. He did not want company,
exactly. But he did not want to be alone either.

It might be Essie, coming to check on him after their
rough night. Or perhaps her mother, Weylind, or Rheva. He
did not want to see any of them right now, though hiding
was unlikely to make them go away.

Farrendel gathered enough energy to call out, "Come in."

The door opened, revealing the last person Farrendel
expected.

His sister Melantha stood there, shifting from foot to foot.

Her black hair remained short, arranged in some spiky style above the leather band around her forehead that served as a circlet. She wore a red shirt beneath a leather vest trimmed in white fur. Her skirt and boots were also made of fur. She looked more the warrior than he had ever seen her.

Melantha's gaze flicked to him, then back to her feet. "May I come in?"

He was not sure what to say. He had to work for several moments before he could get out, "Yes."

Melantha eased inside, leaving the door open behind her. On the other side of the open doorway, both Captain Merrick and Iyrinder took places near enough that they could step in if he called for them, but not so close that they would overhear if Farrendel and Melantha spoke at a normal volume. They were still being cautious with Melantha, treating her as if she would turn on him again.

"What are you doing here?" Farrendel winced. The words had come out harsher than he had intended, as if he were still suspicious of her.

Melantha halted in the center of the workshop, her hands in front of her as if to prove to him that she was unarmed. "Rharreth and Weylind are in a meeting, and I was told I would find you here."

"No, no." Farrendel shook his head, gesturing toward the open doorway. "What are you doing in Tarenhiel? Rharreth's meeting about the bridge is not for a few more weeks."

Melantha rolled her shoulders in a shrug, peering up at him with a hesitancy that he was not used to seeing from her. "We heard Elspetha had been shot, and we decided to come early. I wanted to make sure both of you were all right."

Farrendel squeezed his eyes shut. Melantha had

promised that if he were in trouble, she would come. And she had, even before he had a chance to ask for her help. "Linshi, isciena."

Melantha's shoulders eased from their tight posture. She gestured at the workshop. "This turned out well."

Farrendel nodded and pointed toward the cold cupboard that she and Rharreth had sent as their contribution. It was heavy, created of stone filled with magic ice. "I use your cold cupboard all the time. It works far better than any cold cupboard created by elves or humans."

"Trolls are good with the cold." Melantha's mouth twitched with the hint of a smile, but she remained in the center of the room, as if she did not dare approach.

Farrendel shoved aside a bunch of his books and papers, clearing a space on the workbench. "Feel free to sit. Or take one of the chairs."

Melantha glanced from the table and two chairs tucked into a corner to the space on the workbench beside Farrendel. After a moment, she crossed the room and lightly hopped onto the workbench, swinging her legs against the shelves below. She glanced at Farrendel, studying him. "Are you truly all right?"

Right now, he was weary and empty. His nightmares had been particularly vivid last night. Before, when he had dreamed about Essie being hurt, he could assure himself when he woke up that his dreams were a lie.

But now, she had been shot. His nightmares had real images of her hurt and dying with which to torture him.

It turned out that hot chocolate in the middle of the night caused Essie's stomach to churn. And her munching on soda crackers in the wee hours of the morning grated against

Farrendel's anxiety. All that added up to a very rough, tense night.

But he was not going to tell Melantha that. Besides, he was tired of everyone asking about *him* when it was *Essie* who had been hurt. "I am fine, isciena. I am not the one who was shot."

Melantha pressed her mouth into a tight line, as if she did not believe him. "I am concerned for Elspetha as well, shashon."

That eased Farrendel's ire, and he slumped back against the wall. "She is resting. It was a long night."

Melantha did not ask. She likely assumed it was merely the nightmares. She would not know it was nightmares plus pregnancy that had made the night especially long.

But enough about himself. He had spent all morning sitting here stewing.

He tilted his head to better face Melantha without moving from his slumped position against the wall. "How are you? Your letters indicated the trolls have become more accepting of you."

Melantha's smile lit her face this time. "Rharreth still has to challenge a troll to a fight in the training arena now and then. But it has been much better. Especially now that I have discovered I can defend myself with my healing magic." She raised her hand, showing him a glimmer of green magic around her fingertips. "It seems to elicit fear and awe that I can subdue even the strongest troll warrior with a mere touch. Even if I am simply sending them to sleep for a few minutes, they fear that I can make them so vulnerable."

"I can understand that." Farrendel drew up his knees so that he sat cross-legged on the workbench. He had been raised among the elven healers, knowing their capabilities and the ethical oaths of healing that bound them.

But it had been over a thousand years since the mountain elves—now called trolls—and the forest elves had split apart into two different peoples. The trolls no longer had experience with elven healers. It would be terrifying to know someone could send a warrior to sleep, where he could be killed with no chance to resist if Melantha and Rharreth so chose.

"In Kostaria, such strength is admired, even if it is also feared." Melantha shrugged. "We have gained the loyalty of the people and united Kostaria far more than I believed possible right at first. It means we can focus on more important things, rather than constantly fighting off challenges to Rharreth's reign."

"Good." While Farrendel did not necessarily like the thought of a stronger Kostaria, he was thankful that his sister would be far safer than she was when she first married Rharreth.

Melantha stared down at her hands in her lap for a long moment before she reached into a pocket and drew out a round stone. It had a hole in the top, through which a leather string had been threaded. Melantha fiddled with the stone, opening and closing her mouth as if she was trying to gather the courage to speak.

Finally, she turned to Farrendel. "I have something for you, but you can say no if you wish."

Farrendel shifted to better face her, but he did not interrupt her.

"The way you, Rharreth, Weylind, and I combined our power in the bridge over the Gulmorth inspired me to experiment in a way that would not have occurred to me before."

Melantha turned the stone over in her hands, looking at it rather than at Farrendel. "I took some stones from the section of mountain that has been seared with your magic, then Rharreth molded them while I infused them with my magic. I hope that they can provide a kind of constant protection against the effects of stone on an elf. But I am so far unsure if the stone is working or if I am simply healing myself by habit."

She held out the stone to Farrendel.

He hesitated, braced himself, and took it. The stone was too small to have caused him pain, even if it had been normal. But something warm and soothing washed over him when the stone touched his skin. "It feels…different."

"Good." Without the stone to fiddle with, Melantha instead twisted her fingers together in her lap. "I am hoping you will wear it and tell me if it works when you visit Winstead Palace."

Farrendel stared down at the tiny stone in his hand. While the connection between his magic and the elishina prevented him from being cut off from his magic, he still experienced headaches from stone. That made it difficult to join in some of the activities at Winstead Palace or enter the buildings at Hanford University. But this stone might eliminate even that mild discomfort and make all the difference for getting his degree.

"Linshi, isciena." Farrendel glanced up at Melantha, studying her face. "Rharreth is willing to give me this?"

Melantha nodded, holding his gaze. "Yes. From what I can tell, my magic only lasts a few months in the stone, so we will send you a new one as often as you need."

Farrendel held the tiny stone in his hand, not sure how to reply. It was a gift of reconciliation from Melantha, the sister who had betrayed him. But Rharreth was essentially erasing Farrendel's one weakness, even though Farrendel was still seen as the trolls' greatest enemy, despite the peace treaty between Tarenhiel and Kostaria.

"Linshi." The single *thank you* was not nearly enough, but Farrendel was not sure what else to say.

Melantha's smile turned wry. "To be honest, this is not entirely out of the goodness of my heart. I have personal reasons for this, and I need your help to experiment in ways I cannot. While the stone of Kostaria does not bother me since I can heal myself, there is a chance that my children could inherit the elven weakness to stone and yet not inherit healing magic. My child would suffer a difficult childhood, trying to grow up in Kostaria while susceptible to stone. I cannot let that happen."

Melantha's worries for her future children echoed his. Still, he forced a smile. "Are you trying to tell me something?"

She gave a returning smile, though it lacked the answering humor he had hoped for. "No. But I do not want to wait until it is a problem to figure out a solution. I even worry that all the stone might harm the child even while I am in a family way, if I cannot figure out how to heal him or her when I heal myself. It has been many centuries since an elf has been around so much stone while expecting."

Farrendel started, facing Melantha more fully. As if he did not have enough worries about his and Essie's baby right now. "Is that a concern? What about a child that Essie and I have? Would we have to worry about stone harming the baby?"

Melantha studied his face, her eyes softening. "You are not asking just hypothetically, are you?"

He probably should deny it. Only Essie's mother and Rheva knew. But he could not lie to his sister, nor was he skilled at hiding his worry. "Essie is expecting. We have not made the announcement yet."

Melantha reached out and gripped his shoulders in the elven version of a hug. "I am happy for you, shashon."

The tone of her voice was genuine, but there was a sad note to it that had Farrendel pulling out of Melantha's grip. Even after her betrayal, it still hurt that she was not entirely happy about this news. "Melantha, you do not have to pretend happiness."

He would rather she be honest than try to spare his feelings. He had suffered enough from her pretense over the years before the truth of her bitterness had come out during her betrayal.

Melantha reached out again with one hand, squeezing his shoulder. "No, no. I *am* happy for you and Elspetha." Her expression saddened, and she dropped her hand. "I am—I do not know—jealous, perhaps? Weylind and Rheva were married for many years before Ryfon was finally born, and I am much older than Weylind and Rheva were when they married. Rharreth and I have solidified our place on the throne, but if we cannot produce an heir, then the unrest will return. But it is not only that. I *want* children, and I know Rharreth does as well. And the thought that we might never...well, it hurts."

The tips of Farrendel's ears burned. Now he understood Melantha's sadness at hearing his and Essie's news. But this was something she should talk about with Essie or Rheva. Not him. This was a little *too* honest.

He cleared his throat as he stared down at the stone in his hands. "You have been married less than a year. Perhaps you will find that…you do not have to worry. Dacha and your macha had three children, after all."

"And dacha had a fourth."

When Farrendel risked a peek at Melantha, she had a hint of a smile back on her face. He matched her smile with one of his own. "A scandalously large family by elven standards." His existence was destined to cause a scandal even beyond his illegitimate birth.

"Perhaps I am worrying needlessly." The warmth was back in Melantha's voice and on her face.

"I can understand that. I worry needlessly all the time." Farrendel shrugged, then held up the stone. "I appreciate this."

"Here." Melantha pulled a leather string from around her neck, tugging another stone out from underneath her shirt. She slid the leather string over her head, then held it out. "Give this one to Essie. I can make another for myself when I return to Kostaria. If your child inherited your weakness for stone, it should protect him or her."

"I cannot thank you enough, isciena." Farrendel took the second stone, this one still warm from Melantha's skin. As he and Essie had no plans to return to Escarland any time soon, it would be a while before they could test if the stones worked. But he was grateful.

Melantha drew in a long breath, letting it out in a whoosh. "Well, now that we have gotten the delicate topics out of the way, there is something I have wanted to ask for a few months now."

Farrendel set aside the stone for Essie and pulled the other one over his head, tucking it beneath his shirt. "Yes?"

"Would you mind if I joined one of your practice sessions?" Melantha rubbed a thumb over calluses on her palm, calluses she had not had when she had lived here in Estyra. "Rharreth has been teaching me to fight with a quarterstaff and a knife. And…I would like to practice with you. If you would not mind."

For a moment, all Farrendel could do was stare at her. It had never occurred to him that Melantha would learn to fight. It just was not done for a healer to learn the art of war alongside the craft of healing.

But Melantha was living with the trolls now. Troll children learned to fight while they were still crawling.

Farrendel had enjoyed bonding with Weylind and Ryfon during their practices. Perhaps he and Melantha could continue healing their relationship over a practice bout.

For the first time that morning, Farrendel's lethargy bled away. He hopped to his feet. "I would like that. Did you bring your staff?"

"Yes." Melantha gestured to the door. "Your guards had me leave it outside."

Farrendel headed for the door, his steps lighter than they had been when he dragged himself down there this morning. Perhaps a good fight was exactly what he needed.

CHAPTER
TWENTY

Essie strolled down the stairs running along the outside of Farrendel's workshop from where the lift to their rooms had set down on its platform. Rharreth, king of the trolls and her newest brother-in-law, followed her, trailed by both elven and troll guards. She glanced at him, trying to read his expression in the hard lines of his face. "I am glad the meeting went well, despite the short notice."

"Yes." Rharreth's deep voice rumbled, like ice on a flowing river. "We will make more progress once your brother's engineers arrive. But we are on track to build the bridge in the next seven months or less."

"That's good. I can't wait until it's finished." Essie stepped off the stairs onto the spongy forest floor, thick with dense grass and forest plants. It would be much easier to go back and forth between their home in Aldon and their home in Estyra when a bridge over the Hydalla River connected the two kingdoms.

"It will be a boon for all of our kingdoms." Rharreth fell into step beside her. His gray skin stood out against the green of the forest while his white hair was bright in the late morning sunlight. He stood a good foot taller than Essie, his muscles so bulky that she felt tiny walking next to him. "Your people will see an example of what trolls can build out of stone. And the trade between our three kingdoms will flow more smoothly."

A bridge already spanned the Gulmorth Gorge between Kostaria and Tarenhiel, built by Farrendel, Rharreth, Weylind, and Melantha after the Dulraith secured Rharreth's throne. That bridge had given Averett and Weylind the idea for this one, though the one over the Hydalla was going to be built on a larger scale.

Essie knocked on the door to Farrendel's workshop, though the lack of guards around it seemed to indicate he and Melantha weren't inside. When she poked her head in, she confirmed that it was indeed empty. "They aren't here. I'm not sure where they went."

From deeper in the forest echoed a shriek, then laughter. Over the laugh came the sound of Farrendel's worried voice.

After sharing a glance with Rharreth, Essie set out into the forest in the direction of the noise. She made her way around several of the large trees, none as big as the tree palace of Ellonahshinel. As she turned the last corner, she halted, staring.

Melantha lay on her back on the forest floor, her legs propped up against a tree trunk. She shook with the heartiness of her laughter, gesturing toward the tree. "You make it look so easy."

"I do not know how to explain. I just...do it." Farrendel's forehead scrunched as he took a few running steps toward the next tree over, planted a foot on the bark, then launched himself into a back flip. He landed easily and shrugged. "You cannot hesitate."

Melantha huffed and sat up, rubbing her hip. She glanced over her shoulder at Rharreth and Essie, her mouth quirking. "At least the landing is softer than in Kostaria. I am not sure how I will practice flipping there without breaking my neck."

Rharreth strode closer, extending a hand to Melantha. "It's soft enough in the winter."

Melantha rolled her eyes, gripped his hand, and pulled herself to her feet. "In the winter, I am so bundled in layers I can barely waddle, much less perform feats of agility."

"I am attempting to teach her to fight like an elf." Farrendel crossed his arms and frowned at Rharreth. "You taught her to fight like a troll. She does not make enough use of her agility."

Rharreth met Farrendel's gaze with something that was part humor, part a challenge. "At least I taught her to fight. She keeps her feet on the ground like a proper warrior and doesn't leap about like a grasshopper."

"Grasshopper." Farrendel's voice turned flat.

Essie couldn't help it. She snorted, then burst into laughter. Everyone turned to look at her, and she waved to Farrendel. "A very deadly grasshopper."

Farrendel shook his head, but a smile broke across his face. The smile took on a sharper edge as he glanced at Rharreth. "Perhaps you want to test how deadly I am in a practice bout?"

Melantha huffed and met Essie's gaze with a shrug that said *Males, right?*

Essie grinned back.

Rharreth's hard face cracked with a smile of his own as he drew his sword. "It would be a pleasure to have a friendly bout with you while we are here, Laesornysh."

Farrendel drew his own short swords from where they were sheathed across his back. As Rharreth stepped toward him, Farrendel half-ran up a tree and launched himself into the air.

As the two of them clashed, Essie weaved around the space and settled onto the moss next to Melantha. "I think we might as well get comfortable. They are going to be a while."

"Yes." Melantha smiled, settling with her back to the tree next to Essie. "I hear congratulations are in order."

"He told you." Essie shook her head. "Why is this the one secret Farrendel has ever failed to keep? And to think I used to believe he never talked."

"He can talk rather nonstop when he is excited about something, though it has been years since I have seen him that enthusiastic about anything." Melantha held her gaze. "I am truly happy for you and Farrendel."

"Linshi." That meant a lot, coming from Melantha.

"If you need anything, let me know." Melantha shifted, her gaze lowering. "I know Rheva is taking good care of you, but I wanted to make the offer anyway. I was not a good sister to you when you married Farrendel, and I want you to know that I intend to make a better effort."

"Thank you." Essie wasn't sure what else to say. She was still working to build a relationship with Melantha after the whole betrayal. Things were getting better. After all, she had never chatted with Melantha like this before.

"I wanted to ask you…" Melantha fiddled with the edge

of her fur-lined vest, her focus on the practice battle in front of them rather than on Essie. "Is there any way to get another one of those mugs?"

In the trees before them, Farrendel crashed to the forest floor as Rharreth caught him midair. Before Rharreth could take advantage of the moment, Farrendel rolled and hopped to his feet, evading another blow.

Essie glanced between Melantha and the fight. "Those mugs? As in, the elf ear mug Weylind gifted you? You want another one?"

Essie couldn't imagine it. For some reason, the elves found the white ceramic mugs with elf ears molded onto the sides rather more ugly than quirky. Essie liked them, and Melantha seemed to have taken to it when Weylind had re-gifted one to her. But had she liked it enough to want another one?

"Yes. I keep my candy for my patients in it. Its quirkiness seems to set the children at ease. Though the warriors never say no to an Escarlish peppermint stick when I offer one to them." Melantha shrugged, turning to more fully face Essie. "Weylind said you would know where to order another one? If possible, I would like to have a gray one with white magic and pointed ears that would look like a troll. Then I could have both elves and trolls represented in my candy holders."

Using the small things in life for a political statement. Essie fully approved. "Yes, I can ask the artist to make a troll-themed mug. She is backordered now since the mugs have proven to be so popular. But if it gives her a chance to experiment with a new design, I'm sure she can work it into her schedule."

"Ask her to make a human-themed one too." Rharreth

grunted as he fended off Farrendel's attack. "That way the entire alliance can be represented."

Farrendel faltered in his attack, as if Rharreth's comment had surprised him.

Essie tried to imagine a mug with human ears sticking out of the sides, colored the same pale skin tone that the Escarlish royal family had. "That sounds…kind of awful."

"Not so quirky when it is your ears getting mocked, is it?" Farrendel glanced toward Essie, a hint of a smirk on his face. He had to quickly turn his attention back to Rharreth in time to block another sword swing.

"Maybe the artist could make the human one with flames or something, since fire is something human magicians can do with their magic." Essie could picture a white mug, human ears, and orange or red flames licking around it. That sounded far more acceptable.

"Excellent." Melantha smiled. "Rharreth and I are planning to visit Escarland after we spend some time here. Perhaps I could meet this artist in person?"

Melantha wasn't the sister-in-law Essie had guessed would ever ask to tour Aldon with her. But now, it sounded like fun.

If the assassin was captured and it was safe for Essie and Farrendel to return to Escarland by then. Hopefully that would happen sooner rather than later.

"I'd love to show you Aldon, if I can." Essie found herself grinning at her sister-in-law. "Maybe we could look through the different candy options. I've been sending things I thought your patients might like, but you and Rharreth might have a better idea of what Kostarians would enjoy."

"Yes, that would be lovely. With three mugs, it would be nice to have three different kinds of candy to offer patients."

Melantha grinned in return. "While I like the respect I have gained from my magic, I am not above bribing my patients if that is what it takes."

Essie couldn't help it. She laughed. If this kept up, she might even get to like Melantha before their visit was over.

CHAPTER
TWENTY-ONE

"My brothers returned home safely. The raids have been quelled, for now." Jalissa could not help her smile, the lightness to her steps, the joy in her voice.

Elidyr paused to look at her, stiffening. "Then I suppose I will not see you here in the library."

Jalissa shook her head, and she met his gaze, her heart more vulnerable and open than it had ever been. "No, I will still come. I do not come here every night because of worry for my brothers. Not anymore."

When he held her gaze with his shadowed green eyes, her breath caught. And, when he smiled that shy, soft smile of his, her heart sped up.

But it was his words that made her knees go weak. "Good. I would miss you."

J alissa waited in the entry of Buckmore Cottage. With Farrendel and Essie gone, the cottage felt empty, just her and her guard staying there.

Sarya stood in the corner, arms crossed. She wore her typical guard uniform of leather vest, leather bracers, and leather skirt over her trousers and tall boots. She wore a sword at her hip and a bow across her back, even though the bow was not a practical weapon for the ball. Still, it looked impressive, and that was probably the point.

A knock came from the door a moment before Edmund stepped inside. He wore a black Escarlish coat and trousers with a white shirt. With the slight curl to his brown hair, he cut a fine figure that had her thoughts fizzling to nothing.

Edmund, apparently, did not have that problem. His gaze softened, his smile wide. "You look beautiful, Jalissa."

Her face warmed, and she ducked her head, glancing down at herself. She wore a soft green dress that swirled around her in wispy layers. Silver embroidery decorated the bodice. "It is an improvement over the grime."

"Yes." Edmund's smile turned into a grin. "We both smell a lot better, too."

"Very true." Jalissa found her own smile widening. She preferred joking to sincere compliments. Sincere compliments made her heart think about love and forever, which was something she could never have with Edmund.

He held out his arm. "Ready to go?"

She drew in a deep breath, then wrapped her arm around his elbow in the human way.

Edmund reached over and adjusted her hand so that it rested on his arm instead. "I think we should enter like this tonight since so many of your people are here."

Jalissa nodded, her stomach clenching. She had been trying not to think about that too much. It was going to take all her skills as a serene elven princess to hide her jitters. It would be a busy night, pretending a relationship with Edmund, keeping an eye on the *Sentinel*'s head editor and reporters who were at Winstead Palace, and evaluating the elven lords who had come as potential marriage partners.

Honestly, it was that last one which churned Jalissa's stomach the most.

With her hand on Edmund's arm, Jalissa strolled next to him from Buckmore Cottage, down the path, and through the more extensive gardens outside of Winstead Palace. Sarya trailed after them, keeping watch.

At Winstead Palace, they wound through the hallways until they reached the main doors of the ballroom.

When they reached the doors, Edmund halted them, rested his hand over hers on his arm, and met her gaze. "Are you ready for this?"

Jalissa drew in a deep breath and checked that her expression was smooth. "Yes."

Edmund nodded to the footmen at the doors, and they swung them open.

Jalissa was blasted with the noise of the orchestra, dancing footsteps, and conversations. In front of them, dancing couples whirled in a blur of colors and glittering fabrics. Among the Escarlish nobles, elven nobility gracefully weaved through the other dancing couples. It was the most the two peoples had mingled since the war, and Jalissa paused for a moment, just taking in the sight.

This had been Elspetha's dream from the moment she had married Farrendel. She should be the one here to see this.

Next to her, Edmund stiffened, and Jalissa followed his gaze.

At the far side of the ballroom, editors and reporters clustered in a tight group, held back by green, velvet ropes. Occasionally, one of the reporters would lean over the ropes, shouting questions at the dancing couple passing by. When one of the elves passed close, a whole pack of reporters nearly fell over the ropes trying to get the elf to respond. Only the presence of the Escarlish guards kept the reporters from taking more drastic measures.

"Which ones are from the *Sentinel*?" Jalissa kept her voice low as she and Edmund moved away from the doors.

Edmund described each of them to her. Apparently the head editor and three reporters from the *Sentinel* were there, and Jalissa made a note to keep an eye on them. None of them seemed particularly nervous, which was good. Hopefully that meant they hadn't caught a whiff of the raid that was about to go down while they were here.

Across the room, King Averett, Queen Paige, and Prince Julien talked to a group of the head editors from all the newspapers that had been invited.

Edmund steered her to the punch table, handing her a glass before he took one for himself. "Who do you want to observe first?"

Jalissa resisted the urge to grimace. She would much rather focus on the *Sentinel* and spying.

But the reporters and editor were contained in the other side of the ballroom, doing nothing but harassing anyone who got close enough.

Jalissa sipped her glass of punch, using the motion to scan the elves and humans. Since Edmund wouldn't recognize the elves by name, she described them to him instead. "The male elf with the light blond hair and black tunic."

Edmund's gaze flicked over the bustle for a moment. "He would be all right, but he believes in the superiority of elves over humans. I don't think he would be willing to visit Escarland often."

Now that Jalissa studied him, she could see how his lip curled whenever one of the human nobles got too close. He stayed with a knot of other elves who had come for this event. One of the other young lords who had been on her list also remained in that group, not mingling. She would eliminate him as well.

Getting along with humans was a priority for whomever Jalissa married. Even if she never again served as an ambassador to Escarland—though she would not mind doing so if she could ever shake this lingering attraction to Edmund—Jalissa needed to know that her husband would treat Elspetha well.

"Why do you think he and the others came, if they do not like humans?" Jalissa swung her gaze back to Edmund so that none of her fellow elves caught her staring.

"Probably the politics." Edmund gave a slight shrug. "To get in your brother's good favor, they are making a show of working with humans."

That would make sense. Which was worse: the elves who had refused to come but were at least honest with their prejudice or the elves who were currently sneering at the humans but making a show of cooperation by coming?

None of them would make an acceptable marriage partner in either case. Jalissa mentally scratched all of them off her list.

She glanced around the ballroom again, trying to locate the next elf on her marriage partner list.

"How about the one with the dark hair? Dancing with the blonde-haired human woman?" Jalissa tilted her head in that direction. That one, at least, did not hate humans.

The dance ended, and the elf she had indicated bowed to the woman. He soon paired with another human woman as the next dance began.

Edmund held out his hand to her. "I think we need to get closer to observe."

Jalissa took Edmund's hand, her heart beating harder at his touch. When his hand rested on her waist, her knees went a little weak.

She should harden her heart. She was supposed to be trying to fall out of love with Edmund.

Instead, she swayed closer, as close as she dared in public like this. If only they were somewhere private. Then she would rest her head on his shoulder and lean into his strength while he held her in his arms the way he had when he comforted her in Kostaria.

Edmund's breath warmed her ear a moment before he whispered, "This is all for show, right? Our fake relationship?"

Jalissa caught herself leaning even closer, and she yanked herself back from Edmund. She opened her mouth, but she could not flippantly lie. Her ears and face were burning, and she was not sure what to tell him.

"Of course. How dare I presume that this would be anything but a pretense? I can see you working up to proper indignation." Edmund's grin was quick, his tone light. But he looked away from her, hiding what expression lingered in his eyes. "That elf with the black hair. He would be a decent match, though he seems a bit oblivious to the needs of his partners. Was he your top choice?"

Jalissa shook her head and tried to focus on the room past Edmund. After a few moments, she located Merellien Halmar dancing with an Escarlish woman. His light brown hair flowed down the back of his light blue tunic. She had to clear her throat before she tilted her head in that direction. "Brown hair, light blue tunic."

Edmund studied Merellien for several long moments, somehow still gliding through the dance steps without a stumble. He gave one nod. "He's all right."

Jalissa was not sure why, but her stomach dropped at those words. As if she had been hoping Edmund would tell her there was something wrong with Merellien so that she would have an excuse to take him off the list as well.

But that was foolish. If she eliminated all the elves on her list, it was not as if she would be free to marry Edmund.

The dance ended, and Edmund released her, leaving her cold.

He held his arm out to her, somehow still smiling as if his heart was not breaking the way hers was. "Then let's ensure he asks you for the next dance."

If she had been less of a princess, she might have dug in her heels. She should have been eager to dance with Merellien. If only he gave her the same feelings that she had when she was around Edmund.

But fluttering feelings were not everything. That was merely surface attraction. She could choose to ignore that and choose to love someone else. Right?

Edmund steered Jalissa through the crowd with the same seemingly unhurried, yet brisk pace he used when strolling down a street after a mark they were following. Almost before Jalissa was ready, they approached Merellien where he stood with a group of both elven and human nobles.

As Edmund and Jalissa reached the group, the human nobles greeted Edmund while the elven nobles turned to Jalissa. They then went through the expected round of introducing the elves to Edmund and the humans to her.

When the music for the next dance began, it was elven music for one of the simpler elven dances. Almost as if Edmund had planned it that way. Jalissa would not put it past him.

"Lord Merellien, would you look after your princess for me? I have promised this next dance to my sister-in-law Queen Paige." Edmund's smile gave nothing away as he nodded to Merellien.

Merellien bowed to Jalissa, a slight smile on his face. "It would be my pleasure, amirah. Would you be willing to join me for this next dance?"

His elvish almost sounded strange to Jalissa, after spending so much time the past week surrounded by Escarlish spoken by all tiers of Aldon's society.

Still, Jalissa nodded and lightly rested her hand on his arm. Together, they joined the dance floor again. A surprising number of humans were on the dance floor, though that could have been Elspetha and Farrendel's influence for the past few months.

For the elven dance, they did not touch each other at all as they progressed through the steps, though they wove through the patterns close enough to easily converse.

Jalissa drew in a deep breath and forced herself to face Merellien. "How are you enjoying this trip to Escarland?"

Merellien's deep blue eyes were focused on her, a smile

playing across his face. "It has been eye-opening, to say the least. I did not realize a human city had so many people."

Jalissa's smile widened. "That was my reaction as well, the first time I saw Aldon. If you have a chance, you should visit the Aldon Market or the main shopping district to experience the bustle for yourself."

"I shall do that." Merellien ducked his head as he and Jalissa twirled through the steps in unison. "Is there a place you would specifically recommend?"

"The Kingsley Gardens live up to their reputation." Jalissa resisted the urge to glance away from him.

Even though she had given him the perfect opportunity, Merellien did not ask to tour Aldon or the Gardens with her. Yes, she was still supposedly courting Prince Edmund. But it would have been natural to ask his princess to show him around the city where she had served as ambassador. She probably should not feel relieved that he had not.

Instead, the two of them lapsed into silence. Not the comfortable kind of silence, but the awkward absence of anything they wanted to say to each other.

Jalissa tried to find *something* to say. But there was just no draw to Merellien. Not the way there had been with Elidyr. Not like there was with Edmund. Instead, she was already bored, even though they had only exchanged a few sentences.

There was nothing wrong with Merellien. He was handsome. Honorable. A warrior who had fought nobly in the war. He was everything she should want in a husband. There was no reason why she should not marry him.

And yet, there was no attraction. Nothing.

Perhaps she should give it more time. Feelings could

develop through proximity eventually, right? Though, she had spent a great deal of time around Merellien the past few months while she tried to pick a spouse. That was far longer than it had taken with either Elidyr or Edmund for attraction to develop.

Was it shallow that she wanted to feel that draw to her spouse? Love was not all fluttery feelings. It was deeper and richer than that. Or, at least, that was what Machasheni Leyleira said.

Jalissa forced herself to focus on Merellien again. Was she really contemplating marrying someone simply because there was nothing wrong with him? What kind of reason was that?

She nearly stumbled over the next step as her mind whirled. Yes, fleeting attraction was not enough for a relationship. But emotion itself was not wrong. After all, the emotion of love was felt for more than just romance. The love for parents or siblings or friends was an emotion, but it was not fleeting.

What she felt for Edmund was not fleeting either. She was attracted to his physical appearance—his curling, brown hair, the way his face lit up when he smiled, the flutters she felt around him.

But it was more than that. She loved the way he looked at her and really saw her. Not just the proper princess, but the depth to her heart and soul. He pushed her to be more, yet he did not push her to be anyone else besides who she was.

And she was attracted to the depth she saw in him. On the surface, he was a laid-back, humorous prince. Yet, he had layers of secrets that he only showed to those he trusted.

She could see herself and Edmund, working together in

both courts as they watched for spies or traitors and navigated the intrigue of the nobles in a way that Farrendel and Essie could not. With Edmund, her life would never be boring and lonely.

Why had she been resisting? All because of one conversation with her sister, a conversation that Melantha herself later retracted as bad advice.

Sure, marrying Edmund would cause a scandal. But Jalissa had seen the way their two families would rally to protect their members through a scandal. They would survive.

Besides, Weylind had been right. The scandal of Jalissa marrying a human would go away the closer that Tarenhiel and Escarland became—something that would happen even more quickly if Jalissa married Edmund. Jalissa was not the heir. She was not even the spare. In a few years, the court would no longer care about her marriage whatsoever.

"Amirah?"

Jalissa started, blinking up at Merellien. Right. She was still in the middle of the dance with him. "I am sorry, did you say something?"

He shook his head. "You appear lost in thought. Is something troubling you?"

She smiled, and the expression felt far more genuine than it had a moment ago. "Not anymore. I apologize for my distraction."

Thankfully, the dance ended. Jalissa curtsied to Merellien, then turned and searched the ballroom. She had to find Edmund.

Would he even be willing to turn their relationship from fake to real? Had she pushed him away one too many times?

She did not know, but she had made her decision. If he

was willing, she would fight for this relationship harder than anything she had ever fought for before.

There. Edmund stood across the ballroom with both of his brothers.

Jalissa did not care if she appeared less than regal or proper. She strode across the room, ignoring the groups of both elves and humans. As she passed the roped off section, several of the reporters called out to her.

When she reached Edmund's side, he turned to her, holding out his arm without even breaking his conversation with his brother Prince Julien. As if having Jalissa at his side was the most natural thing in the world to him.

Though, Jalissa probably should not read too much into it. Perhaps it was just all their practice over the past week of pretending to be courting.

King Averett nodded to her. "Princess Jalissa, we appreciate that you have stayed to help smooth things over with the scandal in the papers and the assassination attempt."

"I am glad that Elspetha has recovered well." At least, that was what the messages they received from Estyra reported.

Both King Averett and Prince Julien studied Jalissa intently. They had been doing so ever since she and Edmund had started up their fake relationship. Of course his family would wonder what was going on.

But that would soon be over, one way or another. Either Edmund would tell her that he no longer felt the same way, or their fake relationship would become real.

"Edmund." She switched to elvish, knowing he was the only one of the three who understood it. "Is there somewhere we can talk?"

"Of course." Edmund rested his hand on hers on his arm,

nodded to his brothers, then led Jalissa a few feet away. "Is something wrong? Is it the reporters?" His gaze swung in that direction.

"No, I realized something a moment ago. I want to…" She trailed off, taking a deep breath.

But Edmund was frowning, not looking at her.

"What is it?" Jalissa turned to better face the velvet ropes and the pack of reporters.

"I don't see the head editor for the *Sentinel*."

Jalissa's chest tightened. Had the head editor realized what was going on? There was not much he could do about the raid, but it was concerning that he was no longer in the roped off area.

Edmund steered Jalissa back to King Averett and Prince Julien. When his brothers glanced at him, Edmund tilted his head the way they had come. "The head editor of the *Sentinel* is missing."

King Averett's mouth pressed into a tight line. Prince Julien, his expression mostly hidden beneath his red-brown beard, spun toward the door. "I'll check with the guards. Edmund, send for information on the raid."

Edmund gave a sharp nod, stepping away from Jalissa. "I'll be back shortly."

All Jalissa could do was nod, not trusting her voice. She had been about to blurt out her love to Edmund, and next thing she knew, they were in the middle of a crisis.

Yet, what else did she expect? This was the kind of life she would have if things worked out between her and Edmund.

As Edmund and Prince Julien strode away, King Averett held out an arm to Jalissa. "Let's join my wife. It's up to us to keep up appearances."

Jalissa pasted on her serene smile and rested her hand on King Averett's arm. "Of course." They could not alarm their guests or let anyone know something was going on.

That was the way of a court, no matter if it was a human court, elven court, or a court that was currently hosting nobles from both.

"You and my brother appear to be getting close again." King Averett was not looking at her as they walked along the wall, avoiding the clusters of people.

A day ago, she would have been more uncomfortable with that question, knowing their relationship was a mere pretense.

It was still fake for Edmund, but no longer for her. Perhaps not for him much longer either.

"Yes, we are." Jalissa's shoulders eased at the way the words felt right deep in her chest.

"You are aware of what he was." It was more a question than a statement, and King Averett still was not looking at her.

"I know he was"—Jalissa glanced around and lowered her voice—"a spy. In Tarenhiel. He has not shared details, of course."

She was not sure she ever wanted details. It was easier not knowing exactly what Edmund had done.

In the end, their kingdoms had not gone to war with each other, thanks to Elspetha and Farrendel. Whatever spying Edmund had done, it no longer mattered. Their kingdoms had shared so many of their secrets with each other when they had been allies during the war against Kostaria, and that had likely revealed more than Edmund's spying ever had.

"Good. I would not wish for that to stand between you."

King Averett glanced down to her, studying her for a moment in an overprotective, brotherly manner much like Weylind. No wonder her brother and King Averett got along so well. "He has been pretty morose the past few months. He made mistakes in Kostaria that were unlike him."

Jalissa had wondered if her rejection had played a role in his capture in Kostaria. She, too, had thought it seemed unlike him.

She could hear the gentle warning in King Averett's voice. He was worried about her breaking his brother's heart again.

Perhaps she would have been offended, but King Averett had reason to worry, after what had happened between her and Edmund months ago. Besides, her family had given Elspetha this same speech when she had first married Farrendel. It was only fair that Jalissa was given the same warning.

"I understand." Jalissa met King Averett's gaze without flinching. "It has been a lonely few months for me as well. But the past week has made me realize what is important and what is not."

King Averett nodded, sobering as well. "Something we have all realized."

Very true. They had been so worried about the public image of both royal families, and yet, in the end, that mattered very little. They could weather a scandal, as long as they had each other.

What mattered were their families. They had come so close to losing Elspetha and Farrendel, and they had yet to catch the assassin or find out why someone would try to kill them.

Jalissa glanced toward the door as they joined Queen Paige and the group of elven and human nobles with whom she was conversing. Would this raid provide answers? And where had that head editor gone?

CHAPTER
TWENTY-TWO

Edmund sipped at the glass of elven juice as he watched the elven warriors mingle. Across the room, Essie was butchering elvish as she talked with one of the warriors wounded during the wars. Farrendel remained at her side, giving her a warm, indulgent smile.

To everyone looking on, Edmund looked like one of the elven warriors, and he leaned on a cane and limped due to the stick he had taped to his leg underneath his trousers so that the knee no longer bent.

It was so tempting to walk across the room and talk to Essie. She had been here in Estyra for months now, and from all appearances, she and her new husband were getting along well. Yet it would be reassuring if he could talk to his sister.

But that was one unbreakable rule of spying. Never blow your cover by approaching someone you know.

E dmund paced in the entry hall as he waited for the intelligence officer to return with news on the raid.

Julien strode toward him, his mouth etched into a grim line. "Any news?"

"Not yet. Has the editor been located?" Edmund halted in his pacing to face Julien.

Julien shook his head, worry lines etching around his eyes. "No. And the guards stationed around the ropes don't recall him leaving."

A cold iciness spread through Edmund. That wasn't good. It would have been bad enough if the head editor had left, properly escorted out of the palace by the guards. But he had disappeared with the skill of a spy.

"Bertie? Finn?" Edmund took a step in the direction of the family wing, heart beating harder. What if the head editor was the assassin? Would he target Edmund's nephews?

"Additional guards have already been sent to secure the room." Julien rested a hand on the slim cavalry sword he had taken to carrying since starting his sword practices with Farrendel and his guards. "More guards are being brought in to secure the ballroom."

"Good." Edmund resisted the urge to reach for one of the knives he had hidden under his tail coat or the derringer up his sleeve. "We need to search the palace and locate him immediately."

"The guards are starting with the family wing, but it will be slow work with so many guarding Bertie and Finn and the ballroom." Julien grimaced. "One would almost think that was his plan all along."

There were even fewer guards since some had been sent

along with the raid being conducted by the Intelligence Office.

What was his target? Was he trying another assassination attempt? That did not make sense, trying to attack people in the sections of the palace that were the most well-guarded.

One of the castle pages raced into the room. He gave a hurried bow and waved a piece of paper. "I have a message for you, Prince Edmund."

Edmund took it, reading quickly. The raid had gone well, and the guards and intelligence officers were confiscating the press, the plates, and the counterfeit money. They had successfully surprised them while they had been in the process of moving the money. But a few of the junior editors remained unaccounted for.

"The raid is progressing well." Edmund passed the note to Julien and dismissed the page.

"Let's report to Averett. We're trying to keep this quiet for the sake of the guests." Julien tucked the note into a pocket.

Edmund nodded and followed. Once back in the ballroom, they rejoined Averett and Jalissa and reported to them in lowered voices. Paige had gone back to be with the boys to help ensure their safety.

Edmund found it harder than ever to pretend that nothing was happening. The search of the castle seemed to be taking forever, and he itched to join them instead of sitting here like a pampered prince. He had dealt with plenty of danger as a spy alone in a foreign kingdom. But here he was a prince who needed coddling.

A niggling started in the back of his mind. There was something that he should notice.

Jalissa was easing closer, saying his name. He held out

his arm, but his brain was too full to react more than that. He had to figure out what his spy instincts were telling him.

The head editor had used this party as an excuse to sneak into Winstead Palace. The remaining reporters, who had been quietly escorted away by guards, were not saying anything about where he had gone, but they were more confused than belligerent. Depending on when the editor sneaked out, he'd had plenty of time to try to kill his target, if assassination had been his plan.

If not assassination, then what? What else would he be here for?

Maybe something in Averett's study? Or the castle's records room?

Edmund stilled. Or the Intelligence Office. Whether by design or by accident, the head editor ended up here in the palace on the perfect night to search through the Intelligence Office. "I think I know what he's after."

Jalissa, Averett, and Julien turned to him, but he couldn't explain here. The bustle in the ballroom was dying down as nobles retired for the evening and the elves left for the temporary shelters they had grown in the trees of the parkland. But it was still too busy, and there was too much to explain.

Edmund simply turned and headed for the nearest door. He could hear the others on his heels, but he had to get to the Intelligence Office. As soon as he left the ballroom, he broke into a run.

He raced down the hallway, swerved around several corners, then took the staircase down to the lower levels of the executive wing, where all the administrative duties were performed. A group of guards bustled down the hallway, and he all but careened off the wall to get around them without slowing down.

At the large double doors, he had to skid to a halt in front of the soldiers guarding those doors and preventing the sensitive material gathered by the Intelligence Office from falling into the wrong hands.

"Has anyone else come through here?" Edmund rested his hands on his knees, gulping in deep breaths.

"A guard came through a little while ago. He said there is a possible assassin here in the castle. More guards are searching here." The guard waved back the way Edmund had come.

A single guard. The guards should have been searching in pairs at the very least.

Edmund hurried past the guards and entered the wing that held the Intelligence Office. He headed straight for the room where he worked and halted inside the door.

He recognized the two men and one woman who hunched over desks. Other than that, the room was empty.

Behind him, he could hear Averett talking to the guards, then the footsteps of multiple people coming closer.

He didn't wait for them to catch up. Instead, he wandered through the room, checking each of the desks to see if anything looked out of place.

Edmund halted next to one of the occupied desks. "The guard that was here looking for the assassin. What did he look at while he was here, and where did he go?"

Rick, one of the analysts for the Escarlish spies in Mongavaria, glanced up, then gestured in the direction of Edmund's desk. "He wandered about a bit, checking around each of the desks. He spent some time by your desk, I think. He left a while ago, heading for the records room."

Not good. Not good at all. "What did he look like?"

"Dark brown hair, long face. It was hard to tell much past his uniform cap." Rick shrugged. "I didn't get that good a look at him."

It was a vague description, but the hair color and face shape matched the head editor.

Edmund hurried to his desk. The papers on his desk were in the same stacks, but they were neater than when he had left them. Several of the drawers had been pushed all the way in when he had left them open just a crack.

The file on Mongavaria was on top. Something about it sparked a memory, and Edmund opened it, re-reading a few of the pages.

His gaze caught on one of the messages received at the Mongavarian palace from a military outpost high in the Whitehurst Mountains that separated Mongavaria from Escarland. The wording, the patterns in the writing, how had he not seen it before?

"Edmund." Jalissa's voice startled him, her tone scolding.

Only then he realized he was swearing out loud. In elvish.

"Sorry." Edmund drew in a deep breath, then frowned at her. She stood between Averett and Julien. "The guards allowed you back here?"

Averett shrugged. "I vouched for her. And Julien promised that he would make sure she avoided things she shouldn't see."

Edmund shook himself. It wasn't important right now. Even though she was a foreign princess, she was not the only, or worst, mistake the guards had made that day. "Averett, stay here with Jalissa. Julien, come with me."

Neither of his brothers argued with his orders. Edmund

strode out of the room and down the hall to the steel door that guarded the sealed room where the Intelligence Office kept all the files they had gathered over the years.

The door was locked, but when Edmund inspected it, faint scratches marred the edge of the keyhole. Signs that someone had attempted to pick—or successfully picked—the lock.

"He was here." Edmund drew his key from a pocket and inserted it. When he turned it, he felt the pressure of the lock unbolted. "Since this was locked, I don't think he's still inside. But stay alert."

Julien nodded, resting his hand on the hilt of his sword.

Edmund heaved the door open. Inside, rows upon rows of wooden cabinets lined the room, filled with tall, thin drawers labeled with paper slips tucked into brass holders.

With Julien trailing after him, Edmund walked down each of the rows, looking for signs that something had been disturbed.

In the section on Mongavaria, one of the drawers was not pushed back all the way, but Edmund couldn't find any other signs of tampering.

When he reached the section on Tarenhiel, he opened the drawer labeled with the dates when he had been a spy there.

The drawer was empty. Completely empty.

Edmund had to bite back more elvish curses.

"That drawer isn't supposed to be empty, is it?" Julien shuffled closer behind him.

"No." Edmund slammed the drawer closed and stalked from the room. How was he going to face Jalissa when he explained to Averett what was missing?

Edmund took the time to re-lock the room, then returned to the offices where Jalissa and Averett waited.

There was no way to sugarcoat it. Edmund faced Averett, unable to look at Jalissa. "The *Sentinel* is a front for a Mongavarian spy ring."

"What?" Averett's eyes widened. "Are you sure?"

Behind Averett, Rick and the other two analysts gaped. Edmund would have dismissed them, but this would effect the entire Escarlish spying operation in Mongavaria.

"Yes. They've been passing messages through the newspaper." Edmund reached over to tap the file on his desk.

"And the counterfeiting?" Averett crossed his arms, starting to pace. "Why draw attention to themselves with it?"

"Except that they were smart. They only circulated some of their money in cities away from Aldon, drawing our attention from their real source." Edmund scowled, staring down at the files on his desk. "I suspect that the counterfeiting was their initial plan to try to disrupt the Escarlish economy and force us to become more dependent on them. This spy ring began operating right around the time the Mongavarian prince first asked about a marriage alliance with Essie. With their spies sabotaging the Escarlish economy and their prince using Essie to get his fingers into Escarlish politics, Mongavaria would have been in a position to influence Escarland as they saw fit."

It was the kind of sway they had exerted over Nevaria, up until the recent annexation. To some degree, Escarland had, until recently, been dependent on Mongavaria. Escarland had needed Mongavaria's seaports. Much of their trade had come from Mongavaria. If Mongavaria had demanded higher prices at their seaports or forced merchants to pay higher tariffs, Escarland hadn't protested, since they were too busy worrying about a potential war with Tarenhiel.

"But our treaty with Tarenhiel changed all that. Instead of seeking increased trade and a marriage alliance with Mongavaria, we formed the alliance with Tarenhiel." Averett's posture stiffened further. "And Mongavaria lost the chance to secure Escarland under its sphere of influence."

Edmund nodded. How deep did the conspiracy go? Did Mongavaria simply want to affect Escarlish politics and keep them as dependent trade partners?

Or had it really been a long-term plot to set up a takeover of Escarland, as Mongavaria had just done to Nevaria? It was something that Edmund and the Intelligence Office would have to investigate further, once this current crisis was over.

Julien paced between the desks with a swift, long-legged stride. "Together with Tarenhiel, we now have the power to rival Mongavaria, militarily and economically."

"Is that why they tried to assassinate Farrendel?" Jalissa stood straight, her face smoothed of anything that would give away her thoughts.

Edmund braced himself against his desk. "Yes. The combined Escarlish-Tarenhieli armies are powerful, as we demonstrated by our swift actions in defeating Kostaria. But Farrendel is basically an army by himself. While he is alive, Mongavaria has no hope of defeating Tarenhiel and Escarland through war, if they should attack us."

"And if the defense treaty with Rharreth turns out like we hope, the combined might of Escarland, Tarenhiel, and Kostaria would be more than enough to not only turn back a Mongavarian attack, but also take over Mongavaria itself, if we had Farrendel fighting with us." Averett's jaw worked. "I have no ambitions for an Escarlish empire, but the Mongavarian king doesn't know that. He could see Escarland's growing power as a threat to their national security."

Perhaps the Mongavarian king feared Escarland was becoming too powerful. But Edmund didn't think it was merely that. Mongavaria's takeover of Nevaria and the accompanying name change seemed to indicate that other motives were at work in Mongavarian politics.

"They probably figure eliminating Essie is a bonus. Revenge for her turning down their prince for an elf." Julien scowled, knuckles going white from his tight grip on his sword's hilt. "I'm so glad we never let Parliament talk us into a marriage alliance between Essie and the Mongavarian crown prince."

So was Edmund. If it had all been a set up for a peaceful annexation, Mongavaria wasn't likely to be content to put those ambitions aside. Had their spies attacked Farrendel and broken into Winstead Palace as a prelude for a less-than-peaceful takeover of Escarland before the treaty with Kostaria could be signed?

"The *Sentinel* protested Essie's marriage." Averett rubbed a hand over his jaw. "Do you think this spy ring aided Lord Bletchly and Mark Hadley back then?"

"I found links between Lord Bletchly and the *Sentinel* in the tax records." If Edmund could go back, he would pursue that investigation differently. Would he have been able to save Farrendel and Essie from this second attempt on their lives here in Escarland if he had realized the *Sentinel* was more than just a gossip rag?

But he was the expert for Kostaria and Tarenhiel, not Mongavaria. Nor had the Mongavarian analysts looked too closely at what the agents specializing in internal affairs were doing. No one person had all the pieces to put the puzzle together, until now.

"But I can't say for sure. Likely, the spies at the *Sentinel* supported Lord Bletchly, knowing he would hurt Escarland in the end, and Lord Bletchly supported the *Sentinel*, thinking they were simply an Escarlish newspaper that shared his beliefs." Edmund faced Averett. "But their connection doesn't matter right now. The problem is what that Mongavarian spy took from the records."

Averett, Julien, and Jalissa stilled, staring at Edmund and waiting.

Edmund leaned even more heavily against the desk behind him. "They looked at the Mongavarian files. We'll need to warn our entire spy network there. And we'll want to alert our forts along the border, in case of an attack."

Rick, who had been gaping, turned back to his desk and started scribbling. Good. They would have everything ready to go as soon as General Bloam gave the official word to send the warning.

Averett gave a grim nod, the weary lines across his face deepening. "I'll order reinforcements to the border, just in case."

Edmund grimaced, unable to look at Jalissa. "Not only that, but they took the Tarenhieli files. All of them. All the safe houses from here to Estyra. All the established covers for the spies we had in Tarenhiel. And"—he had to take another deep breath to steady himself—"the doomsday plan."

Now it was Averett's turn to mutter under his breath. Julien stiffened, his hand falling from his sword.

"Doomsday plan?" Jalissa's voice was soft and low. Too gentle for the stab of pain it caused.

Edmund wasn't sure how his voice remained so calm when everything in him felt so shaken. "I came up with this plan long before our alliance while I was spying on Tarenhiel. If we went to war with Tarenhiel and if that war took a turn for the worst, this was the last-ditch plan to end the war quickly before we found ourselves overrun."

Jalissa's breath caught. "What was in this plan?" Her voice was tense, low. Far too calm, in that way he recognized as her anger.

Edmund opened his mouth, but his throat tightened too much to speak. This was his plan. At the time, he had thought this was the way to protect his family and his kingdom. When the alliance happened, this plan was put in the drawer, an idea that would never be needed.

Averett heaved a long sigh. "It was a plan to assassinate all the male members of the elven royal family."

Edmund finally managed to lift his gaze enough to glance at Jalissa. Her face had gone white, her lips pressed into a tight line. Her dark eyes flashed. "And you did not destroy this plan once the treaty was signed?"

"At first, we weren't sure how the alliance would go. And then, frankly, we forgot about it. It no longer mattered, and it was buried in the bottom of a drawer inside a locked vault." Averett shrugged, but it was a weary kind of shrug. "Before you get too offended, keep in mind that your brother has a similar doomsday plan for Escarland. And that plan likely involves Farrendel razing a good portion of the kingdom to the ground and performing a few assassinations of his own."

Jalissa snapped her mouth shut and looked away.

This was the reality of politics. Their families had become close since Farrendel and Essie's marriage, but their nations were still separate kingdoms that needed to have plans to protect themselves if need be, even against their closest allies.

"My version of the plan was designed to force peace." Edmund clenched his fists. "But these Mongavarian spies want to weaken Tarenhiel as a way to get at Escarland. I don't think they will stop at only male members. They might decide to kill your entire family."

For the first time, Jalissa's mask cracked. She turned away from them, her shoulders hunching.

Edmund hunched under the weight as well. This was why the Mongavarian spies hadn't moved to assassinate Farrendel and Essie earlier. The spies had been waiting and watching, gathering information as they tried to figure out how best to destroy Escarland's alliance with Tarenhiel.

When they had stumbled across the information about Farrendel's illegitimacy thanks to their spying on the *Times*, they had seen their chance. They had leaked the information that the truth was going to get out, knowing it would draw Farrendel and Essie to Escarland at a time of their choosing. They knew the scandal would cause Averett to call a press conference, giving their head editor—and most likely chief spy—the chance to raid the records of the Intelligence Office.

Mongavaria didn't have the information to pull off a mass assassination of the elven royalty. But Escarland's Intelligence Office did.

An assassination of the entire elven royal family was the only way to break the alliance to the point that Tarenhiel would stand aside while Mongavaria got its fingers into Escarland, one way or another. Perhaps, once Escarland was in its clutches, Mongavaria would turn its sights on Tarenhiel next, gobbling up one kingdom after another.

As to why Mongavaria seemed to intent on expanding their kingdom now, Edmund didn't know the answer to that. Not yet, anyway.

"We aren't going to let that happen." Averett straightened, the weariness dropping away. "Escarland caused this mess, and we'll stand by Tarenhiel while we fix it. Edmund, report to General Bloam and let him know what you discovered. Julien, rally the guards. I want every worker, reporter, and editor at the *Sentinel* arrested by morning. I'm going to warn Weylind."

"You'll want to check with General Bloam for the locations of the safe houses that I don't know about." Edmund slumped against his desk, his stomach churning as much as it had the moment Essie had been shot in front of him.

While Edmund could give Averett much of the information he would need to send to Weylind, he only knew about his own covers, his safe houses, and a few back up locations if his first one was compromised. He had learned more information since being desk-bound but nowhere near all of it.

No spy went into an enemy kingdom knowing everything. Edmund hadn't even known how many other Escarlish spies were in Tarenhiel at any given time, much less who all of them were. All he'd known was that he had been the one best placed to learn valuable information.

He had caused this. His plan—a plan that was never supposed to be implemented—was now in the hands of enemies of both Escarland and Tarenhiel.

And it was all Edmund's fault. He was a spy, and yet he had not managed to catch the spies in his own backyard.

"I'm going to track him down." Edmund met Averett's gaze, holding it. "After I report to General Bloam, I'm going to follow the spy to Tarenhiel. Weylind can prepare all he wants, but I know the plan. I know the locations of many of the safe houses. It will take a spy to catch this assassin before he kills anyone."

Weylind could send all the border patrol guards that he wanted to try to intercept the spy-assassin, but the elf warriors would struggle to find the safe houses based on directions given by telegraph. The Mongavarian spy had written directions and sketched maps to aid him.

Perhaps even Edmund wouldn't be able to find him, if the spy chose to use the safe houses, routes, and covers established by one of the handful of other Escarlish spies who had operated in Tarenhiel.

But he had to try. This was his mess, and he had to fix it, no matter what it took.

Averett gave a sharp nod. "Understood. I'll let Weylind know that help will be coming."

As Averett and Julien headed for the door, Jalissa turned hard eyes on Edmund. "I am coming with you."

Edmund shook his head. "No. I will move faster alone, and I'm trained for this."

Based on how easily this man pulled off a heist inside Winstead Palace, he was good. Very good.

Jalissa raised her chin. "I am coming. This is my family."

"I know." Edmund dragged his hand over his face. "But it will be dangerous, tracking him. I can't risk having someone inexperienced with me."

Jalissa crossed her arms, holding his gaze. "He will likely be watching for pursuit by a member of the Intelligence Office. But he will not be looking for a couple. I can be a part of your cover."

That was a good point. Something unexpected could be the difference between spooking the spy and catching him.

There was one other concern, however.

Edmund put on his light-hearted persona, and a smile eased onto his face. "If you spend that much time alone with me, you'd have to marry me."

Jalissa huffed and waved his words away. "Sarya will come too, of course."

Great. Another person who could slow him down.

Yet, both Jalissa and Sarya had caught on quickly over the past week. Jalissa had not been a hindrance, and her presence would make getting across the border into Taren-hiel easier, if they were stopped by any border guards.

Besides, he knew her deepest fears. If she stayed behind, she would struggle with the crushing worry for her family.

"Can you guarantee that your brother won't kill me when he finds out?"

"Which brother?"

"Weylind." Edmund shrugged. "I'm Farrendel's favorite brother-in-law."

A slight smile creased Jalissa's face. "I told you, I can handle Weylind."

He probably shouldn't agree. He would put her in danger. Both physical danger and the danger of scandal.

But a large part of him wanted her at his side. She had proven herself again and again. During the war. During this past week. While she was not a warrior, she was smart, observant, and tough in her own way.

"Very well." Edmund relaxed as he made the decision. "Be ready to leave in an hour."

Jalissa nodded as if unfazed by the time. It was already just past midnight, and they would be leaving in the early hours of the morning. He didn't want the spy's trail to go cold.

As Jalissa moved past him, she sent him one last smile, this one a bit more impertinent than he normally saw from her. "When you marry me, it will be because it is our choice, not because we were forced into marriage by a scandal."

Wait. Had he heard that right?

He caught her arm in a gentle grip. "You said *when*, not *if*."

Her smile didn't dim, but she peeked up at him. "I was going to tell you earlier tonight. I no longer want our courtship to be fake. If you are all right with that."

His heart beat harder, and he longed to pull her into his arms and hold her.

But they should talk about heart bonds and if Jalissa wanted to give up hundreds of years of her life for him. There were complications with their respective crowns and the scandals that could arise.

Yet they didn't have the time for all of that now.

He let his fingers trail down her arm until he briefly squeezed her hand before letting go. "Jalissa, my amirah, of course I want this to be real. But are you sure? Especially after I just told you about my doomsday plan?"

Jalissa gave a small flinch and glanced away from him. "I do not like it, but I understand. Your brother is correct that Weylind likely had a similar plan. Besides, you did not know me. You did not know my family. You were simply doing your job and protecting your kingdom."

It took all his self-control not to wince.

He had known Jalissa far too well when he'd made that plan. There was a reason he had argued for assassinations of only the male members, telling himself that he was at least protecting Jalissa, ignoring the twinge that told him that killing her family would still hurt her deeply.

Perhaps this was the other reason he had to take Jalissa along. Over the past week, he had shown Jalissa another layer of himself. She had caught a glimpse of Edmund the spy and not just Edmund the prince.

But this was his chance to peel back the final layer to reveal his last secret, lay his heart at Jalissa's feet, and see if she would still accept him once she knew everything he had done.

CHAPTER
TWENTY-THREE

Farrendel lay there, trying to figure out what had awakened him.

A person had crossed the boundary of his magical shield. An elf, based on the brush of elven magic. Likely not a threat, but it was never a good thing when someone approached his room in the middle of the night.

After easing out of bed without waking Essie, he grabbed his swords and quickly buckled them on over his loose shirt and trousers. He padded down the stairs to the main room, then tiptoed to the front window.

A guard Farrendel recognized hurried across the branch toward Farrendel and Essie's rooms.

Farrendel opened the door before the guard even had a chance to knock and stepped onto the porch, shutting the door behind him.

The guard jumped, then bowed. "Amir. Weylind Daresheni requested that I wake you, the amirah, and the amirah's mother and tell all of you to pack your bags. He will meet you at your workshop shortly."

"Did he say why?" Farrendel clamped down on his magic to keep it from flaring out of his control.

The guard shook his head. "No, amir."

Something bad was going down. Farrendel forced himself to take a deep breath, even as his chest squeezed tight.

The guard bowed one more time, then spun on his heel, placing his back to the door in a guard position.

Farrendel shut the door, bracing himself against it for a moment. Then, he ran back the way he had come, the steps cool beneath his bare feet.

Inside their room, Essie still slept, curled in a mound of blankets and snoring softly.

Farrendel gently shook her shoulder. "Essie, love."

She mumbled, groaning. When he shook her again, she lifted her head and blinked at him, her expression still hazy with sleep.

He brushed hair from her face. "I am sorry, but you need to wake up."

Essie rubbed at her face, her voice still slurred with sleep. "What's going on?"

"I do not know." Farrendel left her side and grabbed his travel bag from a hook. He shoved several shirts, tunics, trousers, and stockings into it. "Weylind sent a guard to wake us with orders to pack our bags."

Essie rolled out of bed, her eyes widening. Like him, she must know how bad this was if Weylind had given this order. "I'll wake my mother."

Within a few minutes, Farrendel, Essie, and Macha were dressed and packed. They piled into the lift, and Farrendel turned the crank to lower them to the roof of his workshop.

Essie gripped a tin of soda crackers and munched on one as they descended.

The sound of her munching grated against Farrendel's spiking anxiety, but he forced himself to take several deep, calming breaths. It would be worse if Essie did not eat and started vomiting over the side of the lift.

As the lift rested on the roof of the workshop, he sensed Weylind crossing his magical alert. But Weylind was not alone as Farrendel had expected. He felt the brush of several more elves, including Rheva, Ryfon, and Brina. Even more surprising was the cool taste of Rharreth's magic and his troll guards, along with Melantha. What was going on that Weylind had awakened the entire family?

Farrendel led the way down the stairs winding around the outside of his workshop. He let bolts of his magic dance around his fingertips, lighting their way, while his swords were a comfortable weight against his back.

He reached the forest floor as Iyrinder, Captain Merrick, and Miss Merrick approached out of the dark night, each of them carrying a bag. While Captain Merrick took up a guard position, Iyrinder nodded to Farrendel. "Weylind Daresheni ordered us to meet you here."

"He is on his way here. He crossed the boundary moments ago." Farrendel faced the direction from which Weylind would arrive. His magic gave off a faint blue light deep in the black forest, but it was not enough for Farrendel to see anyone coming.

"Farrendel, shashon." Weylind's voice called out a moment before he stepped from the forest, followed by Rheva, then Rharreth and Melantha. Both elf and troll guards fanned out, forming a protective half circle in front of the workshop as Ryfon and Brina stepped into the blue light from the magic Farrendel held in his hand.

Weylind halted in front of Farrendel, and unlike most of the others, he was not carrying a bag. "We received word from Escarland that Mongavarian spies infiltrated Winstead Palace and stole an assassination plan that Escarland had created back when it was feared our kingdoms would go to war."

"My kingdom had an assassination plan?" Essie wrapped her arms over her stomach.

Farrendel reached behind him with his free hand, and Essie took it, squeezing tightly.

Weylind rolled his shoulders in a faint shrug. "It was created long before the treaty last year. Your marriage saved both Escarland and Tarenhiel from implementing such plans."

Essie stepped closer to Farrendel and pressed her face against the back of his shoulder.

He would have pulled her into his arms, but his magic provided their only light. Nor did he want to relax his wary stance. "I am the target."

"We think we all are." Instead of the anger Farrendel would have expected at the news, Weylind's shoulders sagged, his face lined in weariness. "At least one—but likely more—Mongavarian spy-assassins are on their way here as we speak. I have sent several squads of guards to attempt to intercept them, but there are multiple places where they are likely to cross the river. Nor can I weaken defenses here to send more guards to aid the search. I have also given the order for the bulk of our army to reinforce the river border across from Mongavaria, in case this is a prelude to an attack."

Farrendel drew in a deep breath, his swords a heavy weight against his shoulders. This was his duty. If Tarenhiel went to war with Mongavaria, then Farrendel would fight it, no matter the cost to himself. "Where do you wish me to go?"

Would Weylind send him to guard the border with Mongavaria? Or search the border with Escarland for the spy-assassins?

"I am sending all of you to Lethorel. Since it is remote, it will be more defensible, and there is a chance the spies do not know its location." Weylind speared Farrendel with a hard look. "You will keep our family safe."

"But the border with Mongavaria..." Farrendel swallowed, trying to hide the relief at being sent to Lethorel instead of called into war just yet. "What if there is an attack?"

"Our army can hold off Mongavaria long enough to send for you, if that becomes necessary." Weylind's shoulders lifted in a shrug. "It is no easy feat for a human army to cross the Hydalla River, as Escarland discovered decades ago in their war with us. The human magicians are limited in the ways their magic can aid them, and their heavy armaments are difficult to transport. Unlike that war with Escarland, we are now at peace with Kostaria. I can send a much larger force to guard the river, and fighting alongside Escarland against Kostaria taught us much about the strengths and weaknesses of human weaponry. You will not be needed unless a full-scale war is indeed Mongavaria's intent."

Farrendel nodded. If this turned into a war, then Tarenhiel and Escarland would fight it together. And Farrendel would stand by both of his kingdoms, ready to unleash the full destructive power of his magic to defend them.

Until then, he would do as Weylind asked, keep their family safe, and hope this wasn't the start of yet another war.

Behind Weylind, Rheva put an arm around Brina's shoulders, holding her close. Rharreth's mouth pressed into a hard line while Melantha stood tall at his side, gripping her quarterstaff.

"Are you not coming to Lethorel with us?" Farrendel glanced around at their gathered family. "And Machasheni Leyleira?"

"Machasheni refused to come." Weylind scowled, the grooves around his mouth deepening. "I am not going either. I need to remain to run the kingdom, and I will attempt to keep up the appearance that nothing is wrong. Right now, we know the basics of the original plan. I do not want to push them into improvising. It will make them that much harder to catch before they hurt anyone."

Farrendel nodded, his chest so tight he could barely breathe at the conflicting duties tearing through him. He needed to keep Essie and their child safe, especially since she did not dare use his magic right now.

But to leave with Essie would mean abandoning his brother right when Tarenhiel might be on the brink of war.

Rheva released Brina and stepped to Weylind's side. She touched his arm, a gentle fire simmering in her eyes. "Then I am staying with you."

"No, dear heart." Weylind turned to cradle Rheva's face. It was a more affectionate gesture than Farrendel had ever seen them share in public. "Our children need you."

Farrendel looked away from the discussion that should be private, but that only brought Rharreth and Melantha into focus. They, too, were standing close and whispering to each other.

"Our children need me, but so do you." Rheva glanced from Weylind to Ryfon and Brina. "If something were to happen, you will need a healer. And you will need help to keep up the appearance of normality."

Farrendel's nephew and niece were shifting, looking even more uncomfortable than Farrendel felt.

"Rheva…" Weylind's voice lowered as he and Rheva whispered their conversation. Finally, Weylind sighed, shaking his head. "Farrendel and Essie need a healer with them."

Melantha stepped forward. "I will go with them. Not only am I a healer, but I have some defensive training." She glanced at Farrendel. "Besides, I owe them my protection."

Farrendel held her gaze a moment before he nodded. He would be grateful to have a healer along, if only to keep an eye on Essie and the baby. Strangely, he did feel better knowing Melantha would be there helping to guard his back. She was not yet a warrior, but she would provide a last line of defense if it were needed.

Rharreth joined Melantha, resting a hand on her lower back even as he faced Weylind. "I will stay here, if you will accept my help, elf king. We trolls are an element that this Escarlish plan would not anticipate. We could tip the balance in your favor."

Weylind held Rharreth's gaze for a long moment. Then he tilted his head in a nod. "Linshi, troll king. I will accept your aid as a gesture of the growing peace between our peoples."

"I'm glad you can see sense." Rharreth gave a brief,

savage smirk before he sobered and turned to Melantha. They spoke once again in lowered tones.

Weylind, Rheva, Ryfon, and Brina gathered in a group, exchanging embraces and tearful goodbyes.

Farrendel eased back a step and put an arm around Essie. Unlike his siblings, he did not have to say goodbye to a spouse or children. Instead, Weylind and Rheva were entrusting him with the lives of their children. Rharreth trusted him with Melantha's safety. The weight of those lives on top of the lives of Essie and his child settled onto his shoulders.

Essie gave him a hug, then stepped back. "Is there anything you need from the workshop?"

"I should take my homework." Farrendel grimaced. The last thing he wanted to do right now was homework. But he still had that paper to finish.

"I'll grab it for you. It's stacked on the workbench, right?"

"Yes." Farrendel glanced over his shoulder at the work-shop, searching it with his magical senses. It was empty. No lurking dangers.

Essie nodded and hurried toward the door. Her macha joined her, and together they disappeared inside. A single light turned on, brightening the space in front of the door.

Farrendel dropped the magic he had been holding in his hand, though he kept his magical alert boundary in place.

As Rheva clasped Ryfon and Brina in last hugs each, Weylind approached Farrendel.

"Stay safe, shashon." Farrendel gestured toward the blue glow deep in the forest. "You have seen the alert I have set up. I think you could put something like that in place with your magic. It should be even easier for you, since you can embed it into the forest itself in a way I cannot."

Farrendel had tried, when he first set it up. But his magic just killed the trees instead of lingering the way it did when he embedded it into stone.

"I will do that." For the first time that night, a smile tugged on Weylind's mouth. "It seems your study at the Escarlish university has already started to pay off."

"Yes." If things were not so dire, Farrendel might have felt more warmth at that.

He clasped Weylind's shoulders in an elven hug. If this was the last time he saw his brother, Farrendel wanted to have no regrets. And he would regret not telling Weylind before they left. "Essie and I…" Farrendel swallowed. "I am going to be a father."

For a moment, Weylind just stared at him. Then, he clasped his shoulders with a tight, almost frantic grip. "Then keep them safe, shashon. Keep both of our families safe. Burn the entire forest to the ground if that is what it takes."

Farrendel's stomach churned. That was not a light remark for an elf to make, especially not an elf with plant magic like Weylind. "I will."

Farrendel had gone into battles so many times at Weylind's side that it was strange to leave him behind to face this one alone. But Weylind was a great warrior in his own right. He could take care of himself. Surely a human spy-assassin would be no match for Weylind in his home palace, especially with Rharreth and several troll warriors at his side.

That did not make it easier to turn and walk away through the dark forest, leaving Weylind, Rheva, Leyleira, and Rharreth to face the coming danger.

CHAPTER
TWENTY-FOUR

Jalissa rested her hands on Elidyr's chest as he held her in his arms. When she tilted her face up, his green eyes were focused on her, his mouth only inches from hers.

She leaned into him, her heart pounding harder. Would he kiss her? Could he see how much she wanted him to kiss her?

He swayed closer to her, his breath brushing across her face.

She closed her eyes, waiting.

Then, he pulled away, releasing her.

Jalissa blinked, frowning. What was wrong?

"Jalissa, amirah…" Elidyr paced away from her. His use of her title stabbed her heart. He had not used her title in months. When he turned back to her, his face was solemn. "I cannot. We should not. I am sorry."

"Elidyr?" Jalissa tried to step closer, but he just backed away from her.

"I joined the army." His words were as good as a slap. "I leave for the border in the morning."

Jalissa sank into the nearest chair, staring at him. He was leaving for the war. Despite knowing how much she worried for her brothers, he was still leaving her to put himself in the same danger.

J alissa trailed behind Edmund as they left Winstead Palace and made their way through the semi-lit streets of Aldon. Sarya stayed behind Jalissa, and whenever Jalissa glanced back at her, Sarya had her hand on her sword.

They had left the palace an hour later than planned. But Edmund had gotten word that five of the suspected spies who ran the *Sentinel* had not been apprehended, including the head editor. Likely, they were on the trail of five spy-assassins instead of only one.

When they reached the tenant house, they tiptoed up the stairs to the top floor, not wanting to wake any of the actual tenants of the building.

At the top, Edmund held up a hand. "Wait here a moment. I'll scout the place first. If I'm not back in five minutes, assume the assassins got me."

"I do not think this is a joking matter." Jalissa frowned at him, but somehow she could not put any actual anger into the words.

"I'm not kidding. Not entirely." Edmund's grin quirked his mouth. "I would appreciate a rescue if I stumble across a pack of Mongavarian spies hiding in there."

"We might consider it." Jalissa attempted to look stern. "If you scream loud enough."

His grin widened. Then he turned back to the hallway, his expression sobering into his focused, spy look. He tiptoed down the hall until he reached the door. He pressed an ear to the door, then dropped to the floor and peered through the crack beneath. After another moment, he drew a knife and poked it under the door from one side to the other. He then used the tip of the knife to explore the crack where the door met the jamb.

Only then did he slowly turn the knob and disappeared inside.

Jalissa bit her lower lip and tried not to fidget as she waited. What if he got into trouble? Would she and Sarya hear anything? Or could those Mongavarian spies kill Edmund silently?

After what felt like hours but was probably only three minutes or less, Edmund appeared in the doorway and beckoned to Jalissa and Sarya.

Jalissa hurried down the hallway and entered the room, stepping to the side so that Sarya could walk in and shut the door.

A match flared, then Edmund lit one of the Escarlish gas lamps.

In the orange glow, Jalissa took in the mess that filled the room. The chairs were no longer neatly pushed into the table. Several of the cupboards stood open, cans and packages of food scattered as if someone had picked them over. Some of the costumes that had once been in the bedrooms lay on the table and the chairs.

"They were here." Jalissa grimaced at the mess.

"Yes. They were likely in a hurry to get to the train station by midnight." Edmund picked up several of the shirts and skirts. "That's when the last passenger train of the day leaves the Aldon station. The next train doesn't leave until six this morning."

Jalissa grimaced. That meant they had four hours to wait until they could leave, and they would be six hours behind the spies.

"If you are tired, you should get some rest. I'm going to clean up this mess and see if I can tell which costumes are missing." Edmund gathered more of the scattered items.

Jalissa's bones ached, and her eyes were gritty, but she was far too keyed up to sleep.

Instead, she picked up some of the items as well. "I will not be able to sleep yet. Sarya, please rest. That way you can keep watch on the train while Edmund and I sleep."

"Yes, amirah." Sarya strode past Jalissa and entered one of the bedrooms, leaving the door open.

For several minutes, Jalissa and Edmund worked in silence, picking up the main room. They set aside the items that belonged in the room where Sarya was resting, then carried everything else into the other room.

There, they had even more picking up to do. Edmund made notes on a small sheet of paper on the items that appeared to be missing.

After she straightened the last wig on its stand, Jalissa sat back on her heels and surveyed their handiwork. "That looks better."

"Yes." Edmund set aside his pencil and paper. When he met Jalissa's gaze, his eyes were a deep blue, though other colors swirled in their depths. "I am truly sorry that this plan of mine has placed your family at risk. It was never supposed to be used. Not like this."

Jalissa studied the costumes without really seeing them. It was easier to face the clothes than Edmund. "I know. And

I understand why you would have put such a plan together. But it is hard to think about you contemplating the best ways to kill each of my family members."

"It was my job." Edmund sighed, shifting his position on the floor where he sat. "Life as a spy is not glamour and adventure. Spying involves lying to everyone around you, including to your family back home. You can never tell the truth. Ever. You skulk in the shadows, stealing information, always knowing that if war comes, you could be asked to change from spy to assassin. When you live in the shadows, some of that darkness seeps into you."

His voice held a pain Jalissa had not heard from him before. On the surface, he always appeared to be a carefree prince, facing life with wit and humor.

But he had spent years as a spy in her kingdom. And it had left him far more scarred than even his family realized. It might not be the same kind of scars that Farrendel had, but they were still there.

Jalissa hesitated, then she set her hand on his where it rested on the floor. "I am sorry. It must be hard, keeping so many secrets from your family."

She knew all about that. She had not told a soul about her secret romance with Elidyr and, when he had died, she had mourned all alone with no answer for her family's questions about her change in mood.

"The secrets can be a burden...and a regret." Edmund pulled his hand out from under hers, then clasped her hand. His fingers were warm and strong, large against her slimmer, delicate ones. He picked up her hand and gently pressed a kiss to her knuckles. "I hope you still like me when I tell you all of them."

Jalissa's breath caught at the brush of his lips against her skin. Her face was heating, the tips of her ears burning, and she might just melt right where she sat. How could something as simple as a kiss on her knuckles turn her so weak around Edmund?

She did not care what other secrets Edmund still had. She would trust him to tell her when he was ready, and she would understand, even when they hurt. His secrets were the past. A darker past where Tarenhiel was torn between war with the trolls and near war with the humans. Things had been desperate, before Elspetha and Farrendel's marriage saved them all.

And, while Elspetha and Farrendel had been the beginning, perhaps Jalissa and Edmund could be the final link that bound their kingdoms together into an era of peace for both of their peoples.

Feeling bold, Jalissa leaned closer, her hand still clasped in Edmund's. "There is nothing you can tell me that will make me change my mind."

His gaze fell away from hers, and he released her hand. "I thought elves didn't make promises that they might not be able to keep. You don't know the secrets I have yet to confess."

"No, but I know what you were and what you did in my kingdom." Jalissa reached out and grabbed his hand in both of hers before he could pull away farther. "But now I also know that you will use those skills for the good of Escarland *and* Tarenhiel. You proved that in Kostaria, and you are proving it again now."

Edmund still did not look at her. Instead, he pulled his hand out of hers and stood. "We only have a couple more hours before the train leaves. We should pack our own costumes, change, and get to the train station."

Of course. Jalissa stood and brushed off her dress. Romance would have to wait. Right now, they needed to concentrate on tracking down these assassins and saving her family.

SEVERAL HOURS LATER, Jalissa boarded the Escarlish passenger train. She wore a sturdy Escarlish dress with her hair pinned up and under a kerchief to hide her ears. She clutched something Edmund had called a carpet bag that was stuffed with more clothes and spy gear.

Before her, the passenger car stretched long and crowded with rows of benches barely big enough to fit two people. Humans claimed several of the benches already, despite the early. More people shoved past Jalissa as she hesitated. Near the back, a mother wrangled a toddler while a baby screamed in her arms. Up front, a man puffed on a pipe, filling the train car with noxious smoke that seared Jalissa's nose and churned her stomach.

"I think I see a few open benches near the back, dearest." Edmund rested a hand on her back and gently nudged her forward. He wore generic Escarlish trousers and a worn shirt underneath suspenders and a coat with frayed sleeves that still hid his derringer. His light brown wig changed his appearance so much even Jalissa nearly started in surprise.

Behind him, Sarya wore a black dress, a hat, and a black veil, playing the role of Jalissa's recently widowed sister.

Jalissa worked her way down the aisle. There were so many people, she kept bumping into shoulders and elbows. Was this what the average Escarlish citizen experienced every day? Jalissa assumed conditions were not quite so noisy, crowded, or dirty on a Tarenhieli passenger train, but she had never personally experienced it so she could not say for sure.

"Let's sit here." Edmund gestured to two benches on the right-hand side of the train car.

The worn padding on one of the benches had a large hole while a dubious stain spread across the other. Grit ground beneath Jalissa's shoes while the pipe smoke was tickling her throat, along with a musty, unclean stench.

Gingerly, Jalissa slid onto the bench, holding the carpet bag on her lap. She did not know what else to do with it.

Edmund took the seat beside her while Sarya perched on the bench behind them. After a moment, a family claimed the seats across the aisle, and one of their girls sat next to Sarya, casting her wary looks.

"You can tuck your bag under the seat." Edmund leaned over and did exactly that with his carpet bag.

Jalissa wrinkled her nose. "The floor is filthy."

Edmund shrugged. "The carpet bags are sturdy and patterned so that they don't show the dirt."

How many other times had this bag been stuffed under seats like this? Jalissa hurriedly set it on the floor and nudged it under the seat, no longer wanting that bag touching her.

She brushed at her skirt, nearly jumping at the sight of the tiny, silver-colored band around her finger. It was all a part of their act, even if a part of her had shivered when Edmund slid that ring onto her finger. Would he someday do that for real? It was a human marriage custom, after all.

The train gave a piercing whistle, then a shudder vibrated through the wall, the bench, and the floor beneath

Jalissa's feet. The train chugged into motion, shaking and rattling in a way that felt like it would fall apart.

Edmund reached over and rested a hand over hers. Only then did she realize she had grabbed his arm and was currently clinging to him in a way that was probably painful.

"Sorry." She would have released him, but he kept his warm grip over her hand.

He grinned and slumped on the seat as if to get comfortable. "Feel free to sleep. It will be a while until our next stop."

Now that they were on the train, her weariness pressed down on her. By this point, she had been up for over twenty-four hours.

She squirmed on the bench, which might have been more comfortable without the poor excuse for a cushion that was lumpy in all the wrong places. The wall and tiny, soot-grimed window next to her were gritty with a layer of filth even on the inside. She did not care how tired she was. There was no way she was leaning against it.

Edmund pointed to his shoulder, his gaze soft. "You can lean on me."

Jalissa blinked, frozen as she processed that. She *could* lean on him. Not just as a pillow, though the freedom to snuggle with him for real and not just for show sent her head swirling with a giddy feeling. But he was safe and strong and someone she could trust with her heart.

She rested her head on Edmund's shoulder. He shifted and wrapped his arm around her shoulders, tugging her more firmly against his side. She tucked her fingers underneath his coat, warming her fingers against his shirt.

Her tension eased, and she let her eyes fall closed. As the

train rattled and whistled its way north toward Tarenhiel, she finally fell asleep, curled against Edmund.

TWENTY-FIVE

Edmund leaned on a cane and limped behind the elf nobleman he currently worked for as they navigated the branches of Ellonahshinel, headed for a meeting with King Weylind about the war effort. A meeting where Edmund would be studiously taking notes. And trying not to think of the elf princess he had to avoid.

Almost as if he had conjured her with his thoughts, he spotted Jalissa on the same branch, strolling toward them. His heart lurched at seeing her.

But he kept his head down, and she didn't even glance his way as they passed.

This was all he could ever be to her. The invisible clerk beneath her notice. He could never talk to her again, much less tell her the truth.

The train shuddered, and Edmund braced himself against the seat with his free hand. His other arm was wrapped around Jalissa.

Jalissa groaned and buried her face against his shoulder. "Please tell me this is our stop and not another pause for water and coal."

"This is our stop." Edmund couldn't help a relieved smile of his own. He shifted on the bench. His rear end had gone numb from the hard, lumpy cushion. His shoulder blades ached from the back of the bench.

He had forgotten how uncomfortable it was to travel across Escarland in the cheap seats on the passenger train. It had been nearly a year since he'd made this trip, sneaking from his spy station in Tarenhiel to Aldon to attend royal duties, and back again.

As uncomfortable as it had been, this trip had been pleasant due to Jalissa's company. Between napping, they had talked for hours, keeping their voices low so that no one would overhear Jalissa's Tarenhieli accent. Even after all that talking, he had not found her boring, and even their silences had been comfortable.

Behind them, Sarya had napped whenever they had been awake and had read an Escarlish novel she'd picked up on one of their stops when she was on guard duty. The novel must not have been that engrossing, since she had barely made a dent in it, despite hours of reading.

Jalissa sat up and stretched, groaning. "That was the most uncomfortable ride I have had the displeasure of experiencing."

Edmund chuckled and leaned forward to gather their bags. "This was always my least favorite part of the trip."

They joined the line of people flowing out of the train onto the platform. From the platform, a bustling street formed the town of Ayre, the end of the line for passenger trains along this section of the northern border. The Fyne River, the same river that flowed through Aldon, joined the Hydalla at this point, turning Ayre into a bustling center along the river trade routes.

Ayre's main street ended at the Hydalla River, where docks jutted into the river for steamboats to ply the waters, carrying passengers along the Escarlish shoreline and transporting goods all the way to the Tarenhieli and Mongavarian seaports at the mouth of the Hydalla where it dumped into the ocean. Riverboats from Aldon meandered up the Fyne to dock at Ayre, disgorging passengers who had enjoyed a more comfortable and leisurely trip than Edmund, Jalissa, and Sarya had.

Next to the docks, a tower built of stone rose high above the town. Escarlish soldiers walked along the top while steel plates covered openings where cannons could be run out, pointed across the river at Tarenhiel.

Beside the train platform, long lines formed outside of the outhouses that provided the latrine for the train station. Running water had yet to be installed here.

Jalissa glanced that way and grimaced, shifting.

Edmund led the way through the bustle. "I know a better place. This way."

On the east side of town, he led Jalissa and Sarya around the back of the one-room schoolhouse. This late in the day, it was empty of children. Edmund gestured to the outhouse. "I'll keep watch."

Jalissa's grimace deepened, but she didn't complain as she slipped inside. When she exited, she scrubbed her hands on her clothes, her mouth curled and her nose wrinkled. "That was disgusting."

"It was that or the forest." Edmund shrugged.

"I think I would have preferred the forest." Jalissa gave another shudder.

Sarya eyed the outhouse, then took a step back. "I will wait."

Edmund grinned and led the way out of the school yard and down the road toward the Hydalla River. Before they reached the river and the guard post, however, he turned onto a thin trail that led off into the scrub brush that bordered the river.

He, Jalissa, and Sarya hiked for nearly two miles before another stone structure rose above the short, scrubby trees. As they approached, a few crows cawed and flapped into the sky.

"What is this place?" Jalissa glanced around as they stepped through a stone archway.

The wall to their right was still standing, but it was nothing but a pile of rubble to their left. Before them, the collapsed remains of a castle keep loomed in a heap of stone, ivy, and trees growing up through what remained of the towers.

"This is an ancient elven castle." Edmund rested his hand on one of the stones. If he closed his eyes, he could imagine the ghosts of the people who had lived here hundreds and even thousands of years ago. "It was modified by the humans who founded Escarland, but it was eventually left in ruins after one of the many wars back then."

Jalissa also reached out but stopped short of touching it, her eyes considering.

Edmund studied the stones as well. What had it been

like, when elves ruled an empire that stretched over what was now Tarenhiel, Kostaria, Escarland, Mongavaria, and parts of several other kingdoms? The elves had ruled by the strength of their magic, back in a time when many elves had magic like Farrendel's. Would marriages like Essie and Farrendel's and Rharreth and Melantha's bring back some of that strong, wild magic of old?

No wonder kingdoms like Mongavaria were becoming worried. The decline of the elves had led to the rise of the human kingdoms, and Mongavaria, with its hundreds of miles of ocean coast, had an advantage over a nearly land-locked kingdom like Escarland.

Only the Hydalla provided Escarland access to the ocean, and even then, Escarland had to depend on the good graces of either Tarenhiel or Mongavaria to allow their steamboats to reach the ocean. Before the treaty with Tarenhiel, the power over the Escarlish ocean trade had rested solely with Mongavaria. Now, Escarland could bypass Mongavaria entirely if they so desired.

Edmund didn't move for a moment, giving Jalissa time to wander and absorb the sight of these ruins. As they had hiked, her kerchief had come undone and her glossy, dark brown hair had fallen from its pins, cascading down her back and revealing her pointed ears once again.

He loved her when she dressed in an Escarlish disguise, with dirt smudged on her face and smelling like a sewer. But here she was in her element. Graceful and serene as she explored the ancient ruins of her people.

She was as adaptable as he was, maneuvering through everything from the underbelly of Aldon to the court at Winstead Palace with little trouble.

When Jalissa returned to him, Edmund led the way

through the maze of the ruined castle. They entered the keep, clambering around fallen stones and undergrowth until they reached what looked like an old door with a rusted iron lock.

After checking it was safe, Edmund unlocked the door and swung it open, revealing a wooden floor and stone walls that were far sturdier and better maintained than the rest of the ruins.

On the floor were scattered wigs and clothing that Edmund recognized as some of the missing disguises that the Mongavarian spies had taken from Aldon.

It was galling, seeing them here. Edmund, and the Intelligence Office, had spent years setting up the safe houses and network in Tarenhiel. And here these Mongavarian spies were just cutting out all the hard work and stealing everything Edmund had built.

Sure, it was time this was dismantled, now that such an extensive spy operation was no longer needed in Tarenhiel. But he had not wanted it to end like this, stolen by their enemies and turned against both Tarenhiel and Escarland.

"It looks like the spies are sticking to my route into Tarenhiel so far." Edmund poked through the scattered disguises, noting which items were here and what was still missing.

There was no way to pass that information on to Weylind, now that Edmund and Jalissa were undercover. Nor would it make a difference if they could. The spies would be long gone by the time the information was sent up the chain of command to Weylind, back down to the border patrols, and a squad deployed in the correct area to set up an ambush.

"That will make it easier for us to catch them, correct?"

Jalissa peeked inside the small room, grimacing down at the scattered disguises.

"Yes." Edmund set down his and Jalissa's bags in the center of the small, stone room. "We can change into our sturdier clothes and leave the carpet bags here."

Jalissa stepped inside, then halted. Her nostrils flared slightly as she sniffed. "Do you smell that?"

Edmund drew in a deep breath, trying to sort through the smells. Damp earth. Musty stone. A hint of dust. "You have a better nose than I do. What is it?"

"There is a floral scent." Jalissa frowned. "I think it is the same scent I smelled in the apartment where the assassin set up his ambush."

Edmund turned around, scanning the costumes once again. There had been female costumes missing from the safe house in Aldon. He had thought the Mongavarian spies were planning to dress as women to obscure their trail.

But what if one of their number *was* a woman? Those costumes were for her.

"We're chasing six spies, not five." Edmund crossed his arms, still staring at the items scattered around the tiny room. "Five men and one woman."

The landlady had mentioned several female visitors, but what if it had been only one woman who changed her appearance each time? She would have been the one bringing messages back and forth between the assassin waiting in the tenant house and the rest of the spies at the *Sentinel*.

"Where did she come from?" Jalissa spun to face him. "She was not one of the editors or reporters at the *Sentinel*, was she?"

"No." Edmund shook his head. "All of them are

accounted for, except for the five we are chasing. Maybe she was posing as the wife or sister of one of them. I wish I could go back through the files and check for sure."

Jalissa nodded, biting her lower lip.

It was uncomfortable, not knowing where this mystery sixth spy had come from. But at this point, they had no choice but to go forward as best they could with the information they had.

"We should change and keep moving." He gestured toward the river. "The spies probably took the boat, so we might have to swim for it."

Jalissa huffed and shook her head, waving from her to Sarya. "We both have plant magic. We can make a boat."

"Right." Edmund grinned, though the expression felt weary. "I'm glad you came along. I wasn't looking forward to swimming the river again."

"Again?" Jalissa raised an eyebrow.

"Another story I'll have to tell you, when I show you my scar." Now his voice turned a little husky, and her ears reddened as he had expected. He stepped from the room. "If you'd like to change first, I'll keep watch."

Jalissa nodded, and each of them rotated through changing out of their basic Escarlish peasant disguises into elven tunics, trousers, and tall sturdy boots.

By the time Edmund finished and left the room, re-locking it, he found Jalissa and Sarya beside the river. A section of saplings had uprooted and formed themselves into a boat shape. Green magic glowed as the gaps filled in. Saplings jutted from the bottom and sides of the boat, forming paddles on their ends.

Before Edmund could drag the boat to the water, the

saplings around it bent, picked up the boat, and set it in the gently lapping pool at the edge of the river.

Spying was so much easier with magical help.

Jalissa straightened, surveyed her handiwork for a moment, then gave a sharp nod as if satisfied. She turned to Edmund, then frowned. "Aren't you going to disguise your-self as an elf?"

"Not yet." He gestured to the boat, then the far side. "All of my elf disguises are across the river. When I was by myself, I never knew when I'd have to swim for it or if I'd sweat through my disguise rowing myself across the Hydalla. It was easier to make the switch once I was across the border. As I was usually sneaking across in the cover of darkness, I rarely ran into problems."

Jalissa eyed him, probably picking up on his *rarely*. "You are fortunate you were never killed doing this."

"It was risky." Edmund shrugged, then walked down the bank toward the boat. "I'm counting on the two of you to get us free if we encounter troublesome border guards."

"I almost hope we run into trouble." Jalissa climbed into the boat she and Sarya had grown. "It would save us a lot of trouble if an alert border patrol arrested the Mongavarian spies for us."

"Somehow, I don't think it will be that easy." Edmund waited for Sarya to settle into the boat before he climbed in. He didn't even have to push off, since both Jalissa and Sarya pressed their hands to the boat and its paddles shoved them into the current.

Green magic glowed along the paddles, and they silently rowed the boat at a surprising speed.

Edmund rested his elbows on the sides, his legs sprawled

as much as he could in the small boat. Now this was the way to cross the Hydalla.

Yet, as they sped across the water, his gaze focused on Jalissa rather than the view of the brown river reflecting the tree-covered banks and the glowing sunset shining orange and gold to the west. The breeze tossed her hair while a smile lit her face in a way he had rarely seen.

Hers was such a practical magic. Not flashy or eye-catching, yet awe-inspiring all the same. Perfect for Jalissa.

As they neared the far side, he tore his gaze away from her and forced himself to scan the bank. Both for elven guards and for the Mongavarian spies. He didn't think they had caught up yet, but they must have gained some time. The Mongavarians were trying to find his hideouts based on his hand drawn sketches and instructions that had been a part of his file. That had to take them some time while he was leading Jalissa and Sarya straight to each location.

He spotted something in the weeds. "Veer more toward the east."

Jalissa nodded, and their boat turned with the current and paralleled the bank for a few yards before he directed them into an inlet.

There, pulled up in the weeds and draping branches of a weeping willow, was the rowboat that he normally kept stashed by the ruins.

Jalissa steered the boat to the bank next to the rowboat, and they all piled out. Jalissa touched the boat one last time, then it turned around and headed back the way it had come all by itself. At his look, she shrugged. "It will return to growing as saplings where they had come from."

It was such an elven mindset, to think of something like that.

Edmund led the way into the forest. They stayed quiet to avoid drawing the attention of anyone who might be wandering through this section of forest. It was a long, three-mile hike deep into the forest to reach the log cabin he had built in a hidden nook between two roots of a massive tree.

By the time they arrived, night had fallen over the forest, coming even earlier thanks to the thick tree cover far overhead. As they approached, Edmund didn't see any lights coming from the cabin.

"Wait here while I check if it's safe." Edmund drew a knife and tiptoed forward. At the door, he paused, listening. No sounds came from inside.

He dropped to the forest floor, pressed his hand to the door, and whispered the word to turn on the lights.

Lights flared, and Edmund squinted through the tiny crack at the base of the door. He couldn't see any explosives set to go off once he opened the door. Once again, he used his knife to probe around all the edges of the door before he lifted the latch.

When he heard nothing but the dull scrape of the latch, he eased the door open, peeking around the door before he cautiously stepped inside.

The cabin didn't appear disturbed, unlike the last two safe houses. The shelves of food items remained filled, the table empty, the chairs all pushed underneath in an orderly fashion. Through the partially open door to the back room, the bed and the costumes seemed to be in place.

Had the spies stopped here? Or had they stopped at one of the other Escarlish safe houses on this side of the border? Perhaps they had skipped the safe houses here in Tarenhiel entirely, knowing Weylind would have been warned of their locations and tried to set up ambushes for them.

No, they likely couldn't have bypassed all the safe houses, unless they had brought their own elven disguises. Humans were still rare enough in Tarenhiel that a pack of humans hopping the train and going to Estyra would draw too much attention. Whether they stopped at this cabin or one of the others, they would have had to get disguises somewhere.

Unease prickled against his senses. The Mongavarian spies had been following his route so far. Why change now? Not to mention, they had been so cavalier with the other two places. Why would they take the time to clean up after themselves here?

"Jalissa, Sarya? Could you both come here? Slowly." Edmund searched the cabin with his gaze, trying to pick out what was wrong.

The grassy forest floor was so springy that Edmund couldn't hear Jalissa and Sarya approach, but he caught a whiff of the faint floral scent of Jalissa's shampoo a moment before she joined him in the doorway.

"What is wrong?" Jalissa glanced around, but she didn't step inside.

"I'm not sure." Edmund gestured at the cabin. "Could you send your magic through the cabin and see if you can sense anything off?"

Jalissa nodded and pressed her hand to the cabin's wall. Green flowed from her fingertips. A few twigs and leaves sprouted from a few of the logs, as if the power of her magic was irresistible.

Sarya set her hand on the wall as well, her magic flowing along the other side of the wall.

After a moment, Jalissa's magic disappeared inside the bedroom in the back. She frowned, her forehead scrunching.

"There is something back there. Sarya, can you tell what it is?"

Sarya's magic rippled through the wall and into the bedroom as well. Her mouth pressed into a thin line. "There is an explosive. It is rigged to go off when the door is opened all the way."

As he had feared. The neatness of the front room was designed to lure anyone searching the cabin into a false sense of security.

A heat burned inside his chest as he took in the implications of a trap set here. The spies could have set up this explosive at any of the safe houses in Escarland to kill a pursuer sent by the Intelligence Office.

But, no. They had waited to set this trap in Tarenhiel where a searching border patrol was just as likely to stumble across it. Perhaps they were even hoping the elven guards would be the ones to trigger the explosion. The more elves who were killed due to Escarland's past spying activities and doomsday plan, then the more strain it would put on the defense treaty between the two kingdoms.

He glanced over his shoulder at Sarya. "Can you undo the wire that attaches it to the door?"

"I believe so." Sarya's frown deepened. "Perhaps we should move out of the doorway."

Edmund nodded and backed away. He shut the door, then the three of them moved to the side of the cabin with their backs to the giant root that stood taller than their heads.

The explosive probably wasn't that big, and they should be safe here.

Still, Jalissa placed hands on both the root and the cabin wall, until green power glowed in both. "I think that should shelter us."

Sarya nodded and pressed her hand to the cabin wall, her magic flowing into the cabin as well. She closed her eyes, forehead scrunching.

Edmund braced himself with his body between Jalissa and the door of the cabin. All he could do was hold his breath and wait. He couldn't see what was going on inside nor could he help in anyway.

Jalissa's breathing was going slightly ragged, and he didn't think it was because of holding her magic in place. Her face had whitened, her muscles stiff.

He stepped closer to her and gently rested his hands on her waist. Not pulling her closer nor crowding her if she wanted to pull away.

She leaned into him, though she didn't remove her hands from the cabin or root.

"I believe I have the wire free." Sarya didn't open her eyes. "I will remove the explosive from the cabin."

A root sprang from the ground outside of the cabin, opened the door, then slithered inside. After several long seconds, the root withdrew, wrapped around what looked like a grenade. The root dove back into the loam, taking the grenade with it.

Sarya pinched her hand, and the earth where the root disappeared glowed an even brighter green. A faint rumble vibrated through the forest floor, a tiny spray of dirt burping into the air.

Then Sarya slumped against the cabin wall. "It should be safe now."

Edmund relaxed and dropped his hands from Jalissa's waist.

She, too, released a long breath and dropped her magic.

Yet, instead of stepping back, she wrapped her arms around his neck and pressed her face tighter against his shoulder.

He rested his hands on her back, then rubbed up and down when she shuddered. "We're fine. You and Sarya were amazing. If I had been here by myself, I would still be trying to figure out how to disarm it without blowing myself up."

That just made Jalissa shudder again, her arms tightening around him. "Do not say that. I do not want to imagine you blowing up."

He snapped his mouth shut, not quite sure what to say since he had already said the wrong thing. He was so used to dealing with the danger, then moving on. If he dwelled on his close calls, then he would have curled into a corner in a quivering ball of fear by now.

But he didn't say that out loud, since it would sound like he was dismissing her fear. She had gone through plenty of dangerous situations before. It was to her credit that it had not numbed her the way Edmund's life had him.

After another moment, Jalissa drew in a deep breath, stopped shuddering, and stepped back. "I am all right. I just needed a moment."

Perhaps all he'd needed to do was stand there and hold her. He knew how to be a spy, but he had a lot to learn about being in a real relationship. Besides his family, every relationship he had was fake on some level.

That meant it was time to tell Jalissa the full truth.

A pang shot through him, sharper than anything he'd felt while Sarya disarmed the trap.

Jalissa had hugged him now, but would she still turn to him for comfort when she learned the truth?

Or would he lose her forever once she knew?

CHAPTER
TWENTY-SIX

Jalissa stood in front of the board where the list of those killed at the northern border was posted each week. She tugged the hood farther over her head, trying to hide the fact that she had been checking this board so frequently.

She scanned the names quickly, her heart aching to see so many deaths. So many taken from their families and friends because the trolls refused to end this war.

Then she saw it. His name. She read it several times, hoping beyond hope that she had read it wrong. That she was not seeing that particular name written in such black strokes against the ivory paper.

But there it was. Elidyr Ruven had been killed four days ago.

She pressed her hands over her mouth, even as a strangled sob escaped before she could stifle it.

He had joined the war to avoid her, and now he was dead.

J alissa sat on one of the chairs by the small table in this hidden cabin. She slumped against the back, yawning. She had not slept well on the train across Escarland, thanks to those benches that were more torture devices than suitable seating.

Sarya stood guard outside, with the outer door cracked open, keeping watch in case a border patrol swung by this cabin searching for the Mongavarian spies.

"You can rest, if you want. This is going to take me a while." Edmund spoke from the other room. Through the open door, she could only see his back and a slice of the mirror and table before him. The tabletop was covered with cosmetics and pastes and putties. He used the putty to smooth out the points he had added to his ears.

"No, I am fine." She sent her magic into the chair so that it curved in a more comfortable fashion around her. The Tarenhieli passenger train would be cozy for sleeping, and she could get several hours of rest that way.

Besides, she was fascinated by the way his steady hands smoothed putties and dabbed pastes across his face as he transformed himself into an elf. He had shaved the scruff that had grown after their day of traveling and now worked to use cosmetics to contour his face to give it an angular, elven appearance.

"Did you do this often?" Jalissa rested her head in her hand. She should not be impressed. This cabin, Edmund's skills, they were all for spying on her kingdom.

He smudged something along each of his cheeks. "Yes. It isn't easy for a human to pass as an elf. And I had to do a lot of traveling back and forth to attend to duties as prince of Escarland."

"What made you become a spy?" Jalissa stifled another yawn, blinking her gritty eyes. "It is an unusual choice for a prince."

"I was only seven when my father was killed in the war with Tarenhiel. I guess that started it." Edmund shrugged as he leaned closer to the mirror. "I was always observant, and when I was sixteen, I partially stopped an assassination attempt on my brother."

"Partially stopped?" Jalissa braced her head in both of her hands.

"Averett was still wounded, but I stopped the assassin from succeeding in killing him." Edmund opened a jar of powder and started dusting it on his face.

"Elspetha has never mentioned that."

"She doesn't know. She was hustled off, and then she stayed with Paige and her family. Paige's father was the general overseeing the castle guard at the time." Edmund tugged back the collar of his shirt and dusted the powder on his neck. "That's how Paige and Essie became such good friends."

Jalissa stretched, trying to keep herself awake. "How many secrets have you kept from Essie?"

He gave a wry chuckle as he dusted the back of his neck. "Too many, probably. She would have been much more prepared for her life in Tarenhiel if Averett and I had told her a few of the secrets we knew. But she was only five when our father died. I guess that made us a little overprotective of her. She's our baby sister. Don't tell me you've never kept secrets from Farrendel for the same reason."

It was almost as if Edmund knew she had kept secrets from her family.

But it was true. Her family worked hard to protect Farrendel. He was their little brother. The tiny baby who had come into their lives so suddenly and yet had become the glue that held them together through all their tragedies.

Edmund leaned closer to the mirror again, cutting off most of him from her view. He continued speaking, as if taking her silence for her answer. "Still, that incident brought me to the attention of the Intelligence Office. They initially started training me for work inside the palace, protecting Averett. But I had a gift for languages, and by the time I was nineteen, I was fluent in elvish. Tensions were escalating, and so few humans could speak elvish the way I could. The Intelligence Office was desperate enough that they agreed to let me spy in Tarenhiel."

Her chest tightened. Why was it so hard to picture Edmund as her kingdom's enemy, even now? "I can imagine that your brother was not in favor of that."

"No, he wasn't." Edmund reached over and picked up a long, blond wig. Its color sent a twinge through her, though Jalissa was not sure why. Edmund fitted the wig onto his head, the strands flowing down his back. "But kings have to be willing to sacrifice a great deal for their kingdoms, even their own brothers."

Jalissa understood that, even if she did not like it. Weylind had made that same tough decision over and over again, sending Farrendel into battle to save Tarenhiel.

She took a deep breath and asked a question that she was not sure he would answer. Nor was she sure that she wanted the answer. "Did you ever learn anything that hurt Tarenhiel?"

Edmund paused, then leaned on the tabletop, his shoulders hunched. "Yes. I knew enough to put together this assassination plan. I learned the locations of your family's rooms and your normal patterns of movement. I kept Averett apprised on your ongoing war with Kostaria. I gave Averett the information he needed to pressure your brother into that first diplomatic meeting."

Had she expected anything less? This was Edmund. Of course he had been an excellent spy.

"It..." She swallowed. "It is a good thing Tarenhiel and Escarland never went to war again."

"Yes." Beneath his fake hair and elven tunic, Edmund's shoulders shuddered. "I knew I was protecting my kingdom. I didn't want my brother to be killed in war the way my father was. But there was always this constant ache, knowing that the information I learned would harm those I had come to know in Tarenhiel. I came to love Tarenhiel, and it was my hope every day that, by spying, I could prevent a war and protect those on both sides of the border. I was a little surprised when the result was Essie's marriage. I can't say I'm too sad about that, even if I was horrified back then."

"I think we were all a little horrified at first." Jalissa smiled, thinking about that first moment when Farrendel introduced Elspetha to the family. "Except for Farrendel and Elspetha. And Machasheni Leyleira. She had a lot more confidence in them than the rest of us did."

"Yes." Edmund stood with his hands still braced against the tabletop. He paused for a moment, drawing in a deep breath. "Jalissa...I wasn't just a spy in Tarenhiel. I worked my way into Estyra. Into Ellonahshinel itself."

She froze, now wide awake. Something about the tone of his voice sent chills down her spine and squeezed her chest.

"Of all the things that I did while spying, what I regret

most is hurting you." His shoulders were so tense the tunic stretched taut over his shoulder blades. With his head down and the door partially blocking him from view, she could not see his face.

"What do you mean?" Her mouth had gone dry, her fingers numb. He sounded like he was talking about something specific, not just hurting her because he had hurt her kingdom.

Slowly, he straightened, though his shoulders remained the slightest bit hunched. Something about him *changed* in an indefinable way. His movements, his posture, the way he held his arms and his head.

He turned and faced her, his eyes down. His cheekbones appeared higher, his cheeks thinner, his skin tone silver. When he spoke, his voice was softer and slightly higher pitched as he spoke a greeting in elvish. "Elontiri, Jalissa Amirah."

No. It was not possible. Jalissa shot to her feet, pressing her hands over her mouth.

Elidyr Ruven stood before her. Everything about him was so achingly familiar, from the way he held himself, his eyes downcast, to that gentle, soft-spoken voice.

If she had not seen Edmund transform himself before her eyes, she would have said a completely different person stood before her.

"No. *No.* He died. You died." Jalissa squeezed her eyes shut, her legs going so weak that she had to grip the chair she had been sitting on to keep herself standing. This did not make sense. It was some kind of cruel joke. Had Edmund seen Elidyr and dressed like him to take his place? There was no way Edmund *was* Elidyr. "His eyes were green. I know his eyes were green. Yours are blue."

"My eyes are a muddy green-blue." Edmund still spoke in elvish—in Elidyr's voice. "I can change how they look by what color clothes I wear. If I wear green, my eyes look green. If I wear blue, black, or gray, my eyes look blue."

"A handy trait for a spy." Jalissa spat the words, her whole body shaking as she gripped the chair's back with white knuckles.

"It is." He peeked up at her in that hesitant way Elidyr used to. "Besides, it was always dark in the library. You rarely got a good look at my eyes or my face. I was only nineteen at the time. I had an easier time passing for an elf back then."

Jalissa flinched, staring down at her shaking hands clutching the chair.

Prince Edmund of Escarland never wore green. How had she never noticed that? He always wore black or blue-gray tones. But never green.

Elidyr only wore green. Not remarkable, especially for a servant at Ellonahshinel.

Elidyr, with his eyes shyly downcast. A servant facing his princess.

Edmund, with his eyes to the floor. A spy hiding his recognizable features from his mark.

Elidyr. A quiet elf servant who never raised his voice and rarely showed his wit.

Edmund. A boisterous human prince who laughed and talked loudly.

They were two such different people that Jalissa had never—would never—have realized they were the same person underneath the masks.

No wonder she and Edmund had seemed to share this instant connection. She had wondered how he could know her so well after only a few weeks. But it had not been mere weeks, had it? No, they had shared their hearts over those seven stolen months. While he had grown up and changed in the past few years, she was still essentially the same age and the same person.

She had to let go of the chair with one hand to wrap her arm around her churning middle. "Were you just using me the whole time? Did you make me…" She could not bring herself to say *love*. "Make me care for you as a way to get close to my family?"

She had thought she could take whatever he told her about his past as a spy. She told herself that she understood. Their kingdoms had been on the brink of war.

But she could not understand this. This was far too personal. Too real. Too painful.

"No." Even in the elvish, some of Edmund's normal voice cracked through his Elidyr mask. "I never used you. Not like that. It was an accident that I met you that day in the library. I was looking through the records stored there, gathering information. Honestly, I was terrified that you would see through my disguise. And maybe I did not leave when you kept seeking me out, thinking that you would be a good asset. But it did not stay that way. Our friendship was real."

"Not that real." Jalissa's shaking was subsiding as the churning shock moved into something hotter burning inside her chest. "You were lying to me the entire time. You were not even *you*. How could you pretend such sympathy for my worries for my brothers while you were plotting the best way to assassinate them?"

"Jalissa, I—"

"Do not try to justify yourself!" Jalissa snapped her head up and glared.

It was as if she could see Edmund, truly see him, for the first time. Those shoulders that were now too broad to be the Elidyr she remembered. The muddy-colored eyes that were as changeable as he was. The man who could put on and take off personalities the way most people changed outfits.

Could she ever know the real Edmund? Did he even know his real self at this point? Did his family?

She pushed away from the chair and stalked toward him. "You pretended to be my friend. You let me care for you, all while spying on my family and my kingdom. To think that I nearly *kissed* you." She shoved his chest, and it felt so good that she shoved him a second time for good measure, even if he only swayed a tiny step back. "And then you let me think you had died. And a part of me *died* that day. And I could not even share my grief since I had told no one about you."

"I never told anyone about you either." His words were nearly a whisper in a tone that was neither Edmund nor Elidyr but was somehow both.

She blinked up at him, the heat in her chest momentarily subsiding.

Edmund held her gaze, still not reaching for her. "I never told anyone about you. Not even Averett or my superiors at the Intelligence Office. Even though friendship with you would have been considered a great coup for a spy, I did not want to be ordered to use you to gain information. I could not do that to you. And then, when I realized I had let things go too far, I faked Elidyr's death to ensure that I would never be asked to use you against your family. I went back to spying, but I got a position with one of Weylind's advisors so I could get the same information without getting close to you again."

She refused to be swayed by such pretty logic. He had still *destroyed* her when she had thought he had died, and now the truth of who and what he had really been shattered her all over again.

Jalissa crossed her arms. "A few eloquent explanations do not make it better."

His eyes focused on her with such depth that it twisted something inside her. He did not reach for her, even as she stood this close. "I know. I handled things badly, especially back then. I was only nineteen, after all. But that is not an excuse for all the lies. I am sorry."

"No. Do *not* apologize." Jalissa pounded her fist into his chest this time. She was pain and fire and a flood of tears just begging to be released on a scream. "You have done too much for apologies."

Melantha had been just like that. After everything she had done to their family, she came back with profuse apologies, as if a few words could smooth over such deep damage. Jalissa had not been taken in by her, and she would not relent to Edmund now.

She spun away from him, marching toward the door. "You are disguised now. We should leave if we wish to board the next train."

Without waiting for his response, she left the little cabin before he could see her tears.

ON THE TRAIN, she and Sarya chose seats far in the back while Edmund sat in the front of the car. Compared to the dirty, smoky Escarlish train, the Tarenhieli train was a sanctuary. All clean and bright silver, with comfortable cushions on the benches and fellow passengers that remained quiet and subdued.

Jalissa leaned against the wall and tucked her head in the crook of her arm. The pins holding a wig on her head dug into her scalp, but the pain matched her mood. There, hidden by her arm, she finally let herself cry silent tears.

She had just decided she wanted to fight for a relationship with Edmund. But what was there left to fight for? A relationship needed truth as its foundation.

But how could she sort out the truth about who Edmund was from the many layers of lies and deceptions and masks?

"Are you all right, amirah?" Sarya kept her voice low, even as she glared at the back of Edmund's head. "What happened? Do I need to kill him?"

Jalissa mutely shook her head. She was not even sure what to tell Sarya. "You do not need to kill him. My brothers will do it for you."

Sarya made a noise in her throat. "That bad?"

"No. Yes." Jalissa sighed and let her head fall back to her arms. "I do not want to talk about it."

It was too much, on top of everything else that had happened in the past few weeks. No, in the past year. Past decades.

She was just so *exhausted* by all of it.

Was it too much to ask for a few happy years with no battles, no wars? Someone to love and who loved her in return the way she had always dreamed about?

She had thought that person was Elidyr, but he had died. Then he turned out not even to be real.

Then she had believed Edmund loved her. But he was nothing but layers of deceptions.

Perhaps she would just marry Merellien. Yes, she found him boring. But boring was good. Boring was safe. There was nothing wrong with Merellien.

Everything was wrong with Edmund. The fact that he was a human was the least of the things wrong with him.

Then why did her heart still hurt so much?

CHAPTER TWENTY-SEVEN

E ssie curled against Farrendel, pressed her face against his chest, and took deep breaths to try to control her churning stomach. In one hand, she clutched the collapsible bucket Farrendel had pulled out of his pack the first time she had puked over the side of the horse.

His horse had snorted, nostrils flaring, but it hadn't spooked, thankfully.

She had expected to be motion sick on the train. Which she had been. But who knew it was possible to be so nauseous while riding a horse?

Riding a horse while pregnant wasn't ideal, but it was the only way to reach Lethorel. There was a risk she would be thrown and land wrong. Especially since there had not been time to load their horses, including her mare Ashenifela, before they had left Estyra, so they had borrowed horses in the small town of Arorien.

In the end, she had decided to ride double with Farrendel. It slowed them down, but they were not moving fast with her pregnant and puking. He kept control of the horse, leaving her hands free for holding the puke bucket. And if they were thrown, she trusted that he would make sure she wasn't hurt.

Farrendel's arm tightened around her back. "We are almost there. I can see the glint of the lake through the trees."

"Good." She stifled a groan and a lurch of her stomach. Even the soda crackers and Melantha's magic weren't cutting all the nausea. "You are as relieved as I am, I'm sure."

"Yes." Farrendel's voice had a choked note to it. As she had learned, he didn't handle vomit well.

She drew in a deep breath and let it out slowly, attempting to swallow back the bile lingering at the back of her throat.

At least the ride was almost over. Everyone with them who hadn't yet known she was pregnant now knew. There had been no hiding it, after all. At least the news had cheered up Ryfon and Brina and distracted them from their worries for their parents.

"We are nearly there." Farrendel drew her from her thoughts, his breath brushing against her hair.

Essie raised her head. The lake at the base of Lethorel sparkled in the late afternoon sunlight, reflecting the perfect blue sky above and the leafy, spring trees along its edges.

At the far side of the lake, the large, sprawling tree of Lethorel held various treehouses tucked into its branches. Both the tree and the houses grown into it were smaller than Ellonahshinel, but that made it all the more quaint and charming.

Even though this was the site of her first battle, something inside her relaxed. Lethorel was a sanctuary. It was the place where Farrendel had spent most of his childhood, and he relaxed here as he rarely did anywhere else.

Her stomach gave a lurch, and she clutched the bucket tighter. If only her stomach would stay in place for a few more minutes. She squeezed her eyes shut and tried to breathe through it.

Finally, the horse halted, and Essie opened her eyes, bracing herself against the saddle's pommel.

Farrendel released her and swung down. He looked back up to her, studying her face. "Do you need help getting down?"

She glanced from the ground to the bucket. There was no way she could hold the bucket and safely scramble down from the horse. She held the bucket out to Farrendel. "I love you."

His nose wrinkled as he took the puke bucket, holding it well away from him.

While he set the bucket on the ground far from the horse, Essie swiveled so that she sat astride. Then she worked her foot into the stirrup, gripped the saddle, and swung down.

As she searched for the ground with her foot, Farrendel returned to her side and gripped her waist, gently lifting her the rest of the way to the forest floor. She turned and wrapped her arms around his neck, leaning into him while she worked to steady her stomach. "Linshi."

When she tilted her head up to look at him, his face was only inches from hers. But his mouth tilted, his nose still a little wrinkled in his disgusted face. "I love you, Essie, but I am not kissing you until after you brush your teeth."

"I don't blame you." She grimaced, becoming aware again of the gritty sourness inside her mouth now that he had reminded her. "Unless you need me for something, I'm going to go straight to our room."

She needed to brush her teeth. Maybe shower. Definitely curl up in bed and nap.

"Iyrinder is checking Lethorel now to make sure it is safe, then you can go in." Farrendel stepped back, his face hardening. "I need to place the alert shield and scout the forest."

Essie nodded and retreated to where he had placed her bucket. While Farrendel disappeared into the forest around Lethorel, Captain Merrick guarding his back, the rest of the elven and troll guards spread out in a semicircle. Ryfon and Brina gathered the horses, taking them toward the stables grown into the base of the tree.

Mother joined Essie and rested a hand on her arm. "How are you feeling?"

"I haven't had to empty out the puke bucket since our last stop." Essie picked it up. As icky as the thing was by now, she might still need it before she reached her room.

Melantha approached slowly, her gaze concerned, green surrounding her fingertips. "May I?"

"Please." Essie never would have made it this far without her sister-in-law's magic soothing her stomach as much as possible.

Melantha gently touched her fingers to the back of Essie's hand. Her magic flowed into Essie, easing the roiling in her stomach and the aching burn at the back of her throat from throwing up. While Rheva's healing magic was as soft and gentle as she was, Melantha's held a sharper, stronger edge to it. When Melantha drew her hand back, she held Essie's gaze. "You and the baby are both doing well."

"Linshi." Essie relaxed, glad when her stomach stayed

where it belonged. It was reassuring, having a healer along to check that the baby was fine.

"Come. Let's get you to bed." Mother steered her toward the stairs. Melantha followed them, carrying Essie's bag along with her own.

Since Lethorel was not as large as Ellonahshinel, it didn't take long to reach Essie and Farrendel's small suite, even if the rooms were on the fringe of the treetop summer palace. As soon as they entered, Essie collapsed onto one of the chairs. She needed to sit and gather energy before brushing her teeth and changing into comfy clothes for her nap.

Mother bustled about, unpacking Essie's bag. Melantha, of all people, took Essie's puke bucket and disappeared into the water closet, returning after several minutes with the bucket all clean.

Essie gathered enough energy to brush her teeth, wash her face from trail dust, and change into a soft shirt and trousers before she collapsed onto the bed.

WHEN SHE WOKE, she was cocooned in a comfortable warmth. Farrendel was at her back, a warm and secure presence. His arm wrapped around her waist, holding her to him.

"Feeling better?" His voice was a rumble against her back, his breath brushing her hair.

"Yes." She sighed, stretching, then curled back into the warm, comfortable spot where she'd been. "I needed that nap. It turns out traveling while pregnant is rough. But we got here. I'm fine, and the baby is well."

He rested his hand over the back of hers, threading their fingers together. "I will protect both of you."

"I know." Essie hugged their clasped hands to her, snuggling into the reassurance of his arms around her. "We've joked about pointed ears and red hair, but right now I just want this baby to be healthy."

Even if this baby wasn't healthy, they would still love him or her. They would have access to the best elven healers, and they would handle whatever would come.

He pressed a gentle kiss to her neck. "Yes."

This was far too serious. She didn't want to be somber right now. They had enough gnawing at them without borrowing more worries. "We're going to love this baby even if he or she is born with human ears and no hair."

"No hair?"

Essie shrugged. "A lot of times, babies are born bald."

Farrendel pushed onto his elbow, gaping down at her. His long silver-blond hair framed his face and brushed against Essie's shoulder and neck. "Human babies are born *bald*?"

Essie rolled to better face him, trying not to laugh at the way his forehead scrunched and nose wrinkled. "Yes. Aren't elves?"

"*No.*"

There was so much utter horror in his voice that she couldn't help a laugh. Of course elves would have a full head of luxurious hair at birth. Why had she expected anything different?

She squeezed Farrendel's hand. "Don't worry too much. Human babies get hair within a year or so."

Farrendel flopped onto his back on the bed next to her, staring at the ceiling for a long moment. Finally, he gave a nod, as if satisfied with the solution he had come to. "I see. I have a lot of in person classes I can take at the university if we stay in Escarland for a while."

For some reason, she found herself giggling. Apparently, they were going to hide in Escarland until their poor child had hair. She had the feeling Farrendel's "list" had gone from *healthy* to *healthy and has hair*.

When she finally wrangled her giggling under control, she glanced at the window. Sunlight still beamed inside, but it angled through the trees with a softer, more orange glow. Her stomach was at that uneasy state between rumbling and churning. "I slept through supper, didn't I?"

Farrendel rolled upright, then to his feet. "I saved some of the bread, cheese, and meat for you."

He pulled a plate out of the cold cupboard and returned to the bed, handing it to her.

Essie picked up the bread and took a bite as he sat next to her once again. When he was settled, she scooted closer so that she could lean on him while she ate. "I'm sorry I abandoned everyone for most of the afternoon."

"They understood." Farrendel put his arm around her, adjusting her against him. "I gave Macha a tour of Lethorel, then she retired shortly after supper."

Essie smiled as she ate. She could imagine her mother had coaxed Farrendel into telling stories of his childhood here while he'd showed her around.

"And while I was busy, Melantha had a long talk with Brina and Ryfon." Farrendel's shrug was more felt than seen with the way she rested against him. "They seem to have reconciled. When I left, Brina was still listening with rapt attention to Melantha's stories about life in Kostaria. And

Ryfon was getting fighting tips from one of the troll guards Melantha brought along."

"Good." Essie managed a few more bites of the bread, taking it slow to avoid setting off her stomach. The pain from Melantha's betrayal still ran deep in Farrendel's family. It wouldn't be erased overnight, but it was good to see the healing. "Does that mean we have the evening to ourselves?"

"Yes." Before she had a chance to ask, Farrendel released her, fetched a glass of water, and returned, handing it to her.

"Thanks." She waited to sip the water until he was settled back in place and stopped jostling her and the bed. From where she sat, she could see the bag stuffed with his homework sitting on the table.

There was one thing they had been putting off. She hated to ruin the moment, especially since Farrendel seemed to be having a good day, despite the worry about leaving part of his family behind in Estyra.

Yet, this wasn't something they could tackle on a day Farrendel was already struggling. And he felt particularly safe and relaxed here in Lethorel.

Essie set the glass of water on the window ledge next to their bed where it was grown into the wall. She stared down at her plate with its half-eaten slice of bread and untouched meat and cheese. "When I packed your homework last night, I also grabbed the files about your mother."

Farrendel stiffened, his arm tight around her shoulders.

"We don't have to. But I was wondering if this might be a good time for us to read them together." Essie picked up a slice of cheese, fiddling with it rather than eating it.

He remained frozen and silent, tension radiating from him into her. Had she made a mistake in bringing it up now?

If he wasn't ready, then she might have ruined their evening, and he would spend the late-night hours off by himself trying to work through the anxiety with physical exercise.

Finally, his sigh brushed her hair. "I think it is time."

Essie popped the cheese into her mouth, then set her plate aside. She could nibble on it as needed, but right now she had to focus on Farrendel. With their own child on the way, this felt like something she and Farrendel should tackle sooner rather than later.

After another moment of hesitation, Farrendel stood and crossed the room to the table. It took him a few moments to sort through the jumble she had made of his homework, and he arranged the books into neat stacks before he returned to the bed carrying the two large files.

When he joined her again, Essie rested her head on his shoulder as he laid the first file on his lap. She held his hand and waited, feeling his deep breaths and the way he was bracing himself before opening it.

Farrendel flipped open the front cover of the file folder.

As they read, the tragic story of his mother was revealed in every painful detail. She had grown up on the fringes of society, already in a difficult place in life from the moment she was born. But then she had only made her life harder by her decisions.

Essie couldn't help it. She cried. Several times.

She understood why Farrendel's father might have been drawn to this elf woman when he had been at his lowest. One hurting soul trying to find solace in another, only to leave each other even more burned and hurting.

Farrendel's father had come back from that. He'd had family and duty to give him a reason to stop the spiral and start living. But Farrendel's mother never had, even when given the chance to do so. Instead, she'd gone back to her low point until she was eventually killed.

There was nothing as tangible as a letter from her to provide closure for Farrendel. No record that she had ever contacted the royal family asking for information about her son. Just the story of a life that had been filled with pain and tragedy from its beginning to end.

But Essie had two things she hadn't had before.

A name. *Filauria.*

And a sketch of the elf woman, her eyes and expression hauntingly sad even in the black and white ink.

When Farrendel and Weylind stood side-by-side, there was enough resemblance that Essie could tell they were brothers, once it was pointed out. But Farrendel had gotten a great deal of his looks from his mother. The shape of his eyes, the tilt to his mouth, the set of his jaw and cheekbones. They were all mirrored on the paper before them.

"She was very beautiful." Essie rested a hand on Farrendel's chest and tipped her face up, waiting until he glanced down at her. "I know you'll always regret that you never had a chance to meet her. And it hurts, knowing that her life was one of such pain. But she gave you two of the greatest gifts that she could have. She gave you life, and she gave you a home by giving you up. When she knew she couldn't take care of you herself, she made the greatest sacrifice she could have in ensuring that you would be loved and cared for. It might not be the kind of mother's love that you wanted, but that doesn't mean it wasn't there."

Farrendel gave a nod, then pressed his face against Essie's hair. He was trembling, his breathing ragged and choked.

She held him tighter, giving him the silence he needed.

What would his life have been like if his mother hadn't made the sacrifice to give him to his father to raise? Would Filauria have gotten her life together enough to have been a good mother? Or would Farrendel have grown up on the streets, neglected? Would Filauria still have been murdered, leaving Farrendel all alone with no family and no friends at twenty years old, an age that was still a young child for an elf?

He still would have ended up in the elven army eventually, if simply to give himself a roof over his head and a few square meals a day. The Tarenhieli generals would have turned him into even more of a weapon than he had been, sending him into war without any concern for his mental state. If he had still been captured, would the army have launched a rescue attempt for a no-name elf, even if he was a warrior with great magic? Or would he have been left to be tortured, then killed at the hands of the trolls? Mourned for the loss of his magic, then forgotten.

Essie never would have married him. That much was for sure. There would have been no marriage alliance. No deepening ties with Tarenhiel. Nothing but war between Escarland and Tarenhiel, continuing war between Tarenhiel and Kostaria, until all three of their kingdoms had destroyed each other and Mongavaria swept up the shattered pieces.

It was such a bleak what-if to contemplate. Essie gave a shiver and gripped Farrendel's warm shirt tighter. In doing what was best for her child, Filauria had changed the course of history for three kingdoms.

When Farrendel's shaking calmed, Essie mumbled against his shirt, "Are you all right?"

His voice was still strained, but at least he was calm enough to talk. "I will be."

It was a start, at least. Essie touched the sketch still on top of the file in front of them. "Perhaps we can have this framed, and we can hang it in one of our homes."

She wasn't sure which would be more appropriate. Farrendel's family wasn't quite ready to see a picture of Filauria hanging in Essie's and Farrendel's main room in Estyra. Perhaps they could find a place on the wall in their bedroom.

Or they could hang it in Buckmore Cottage in Aldon. Though, it seemed a little strange to honor Filauria in the kingdom whose people had killed her.

Humans from Escarland had killed Farrendel's mother. Elves from Tarenhiel had killed Essie's father. Perhaps Essie should hang a picture of her father in Estyra, and the pictures could represent healing instead of mourning.

"I would like that." Farrendel shuddered one last time before he stilled. He pressed a kiss to the top of her head. "Linshi, my shynafir, for being here with me for this."

"Of course. I'm always here for you." Essie curled against his chest, not wanting to move from her comfortable spot. But she sighed, rolling enough to reach for the plate she had set aside. "Ugh. Even crying is making me nauseous now."

"Do I need to get the bucket?" Farrendel leaned away from her, as if worried she was about to vomit on his shirt.

"Not yet." She took a bite of what remained of the bread. It had gone a bit crusty while sitting out, but it was still edible. The meat was now hard and unappetizing, and the cheese had gotten that discolored, dry look to it. "But I think we might need to scrounge up some more leftovers."

Farrendel was shoving the files aside and on his feet in a heartbeat. "I can fetch something for you."

"No, I'll come along." Essie climbed out of bed, her legs

protesting after being curled up for so long. After spending so long in bed, she was on the verge of a headachy grogginess if she didn't get up and stretch. "Some fresh air will do me good. And if we hurry, we might even catch some of the sunset reflected in the lake."

The smile was back on Farrendel's face, even if it was still edged with a hint of weariness. "Yes."

"But first." Essie wrapped her arms around his neck and stood on her tiptoes to put her face nearly level with his. "You still owe me a kiss. I brushed my teeth. Then I ate some bread and cheese, but I haven't thrown up since then."

And then, even after that dubious statement, he kissed her. And Essie could think of nothing that spoke of love more than that.

CHAPTER
TWENTY-EIGHT

Edmund disembarked from the elven train, his boots sinking slightly in the spongy moss that covered the train station in Estyra. A breeze tossed the strands of his blond wig, as if to drive the dagger in deeper. He was returning to Estyra dressed as Elidyr for the first time since he had walked away from Jalissa years ago.

He had messed up. Not in telling Jalissa. No, he couldn't regret that, no matter how much it hurt to see her return to frostiness.

No, he had messed up back then. A nineteen-year-old who had foolishly ignored all his spy training as he let himself fall for the older, elven princess who had confided her heart to him on those dark, lonely nights. He had known better than to get close to a mark.

And then he had bungled it even worse in the way he had ended things by leaving, then killing off his cover.

Even now, he wasn't sure there had been a better way to handle that ending. He couldn't have told her the truth back then without risking war. The only way to have done things better would have been to never let their romance begin in the first place.

After leaving the platform, he waited in the shadows of a tree, trying to blend in with the bustle rather than appear to loiter. More elven guards than usual patrolled the platform, eyeing everyone getting off the train with added suspicion.

Good. That meant Weylind was taking precautions. But if the guards were still here, then the spy-assassins hadn't been caught when they had gotten off the earlier train.

Jalissa strode off the train with an abruptness to her steps that was unlike her usual, serene grace. With the light brown wig changing her hair color, the guards didn't give her a second glance, as they would have if they had recognized their princess stepping off the passenger train.

Sarya trailed after Jalissa, still looking a little too much like a guard to fully blend in. The two of them headed in Edmund's direction.

Jalissa halted in front of him, her face hardened into set lines. She spoke with a bite, her eyes flashing. "Well? Off to your next safe house?"

He resisted the urge to flinch. He deserved her anger, after all. "No. I never set up a permanent safe house here. It would have been too easily discovered. Besides, once I had gotten myself a job, first at the palace, then at the noble's home, I was provided a room."

"So glad my family could help you spy on us. That must have been so convenient." Jalissa crossed her arms, as if to better wall herself off from him.

He would not flinch. He had carried on after losing her twice before. No reason he couldn't do it a third time.

He gestured toward the dagger she wore tucked into her boot. The smile and the levity didn't match the disguise he wore, but he couldn't fully step back into the persona he had cast off so long ago. "Would it make you feel better to stab me?"

That just made her glare sharpen. "Maybe. But I will wait until after we have caught these assassins. You cannot find them if you are bleeding out."

"True." Edmund glanced around, noticing that the guards were starting to take notice of him, Jalissa, and Sarya still loitering. "Besides, you'd probably get arrested for assaulting some random elf here on the main street of Estyra. That might be a little awkward to explain when your brother has to come to verify who you are and bail you out."

Edmund started in the direction of the street, and thankfully Jalissa and Sarya kept pace with him without prompting. After a few seconds, the guards' attention swiveled away from them.

Jalissa waved her hand. "Both of my brothers would help with the stabbing if they found out the truth."

Edmund couldn't help a wince at that. Weylind's cold, disapproving gaze he could handle. It would be Farrendel's betrayed look that would hurt more than an actual dagger. His brother-in-law had experienced enough betrayal in his life without Edmund adding to it.

Would Jalissa tell them? Should Edmund? Weylind had formed friendships with all of them, especially Averett, during the war. And that friendship had led to deepening ties between their kingdoms. Would this secret not only shatter those ties, but the treaty along with it? The last thing Edmund wanted was for his spying during the almost war to cause an actual war.

He couldn't bring himself to look at Jalissa. "Perhaps it

would be better if they didn't find out. Or, at least, if Farrendel didn't."

"Fine. I will not tell them. But you need to promise me something in return." Jalissa stepped in front of him, forcing him to halt facing her. Her dark brown eyes had a steely look he had rarely seen in her. "I want you to promise that when this is over, you will leave Tarenhiel and never step foot in it again. I cannot force you to stay away from Farrendel while he is in Escarland, but I want you to stay away from my kingdom and my family. Understand?"

He caught his breath, his heart aching in a way that nearly had him hunching over. She was asking him to never return to the people and places in Tarenhiel that had come to mean so much to him while he had been a spy here. If Essie invited him to visit, he would have to find excuses to never come, ignoring the way his refusals would hurt her.

But if this was what Jalissa wanted, then it was the price he would have to pay. His life spent in the shadows had consequences. He forced himself to hold her gaze, no matter how it pained him. "If this is what you wish, then I promise to do as you ask once the spies are caught."

Jalissa nodded sharply, then spun on her heel to march down the street once again. "Good. Now, where do you suggest we start searching?"

Focus on the mission. He would mourn this loss when he was back in Escarland where he could throw himself into whatever work he could beg out of General Bloam.

Edmund forced himself into a casual stroll. "There are five places to rent rooms to stay in Estyra. I think we should start with the cheapest one tucked into one of the side streets. That's where I would get a room if I were them."

Assuming they didn't just camp in the forest somewhere

outside of Estyra. That was also a possibility, but it would be nearly impossible to find them if that were the case.

Jalissa's expression never wavered from that icy one. "Then lead the way."

He set out into the quiet bustle of Estyra, taking in the details with even more bittersweet longing than before. After this mission, he would never see this city again.

If that was what it took to help Jalissa move on, then he'd do it. He'd promised himself, when he'd proposed their fake relationship, that he would help heal Jalissa's broken heart and leave her better off than she was now.

But it seemed all he could do was break her heart yet again.

EDMUND SPEARED another bite of the mixed vegetables and meat piled onto a base of leafy greens on his plate. As he lifted the bite to his mouth, he sent a swift glance around the common room of the treetop hotel. Tables and chairs filled the room while a small countertop at one end provided a place for people to purchase a room and order a meal from the small kitchen at the base of the tree. The seating area spilled out onto an open-air deck space high above this back street of Estyra. It was nice, but not as large as some of the grander places to stay at the heart of the elven city.

At this time of the evening, twilight shrouded the forest, and the deck and tables outside were lit with elven lights strung through the leafy canopy overhead.

Jalissa and Sarya sat with him at the table. Jalissa was once again posing as his wife with Sarya as her sister. It had allowed them to get two rooms only one branch away from each other, and no one would notice if Jalissa bunked with Sarya rather than her supposed husband.

As he, Jalissa, and Sarya sat around a table near the center of the room, his back itched at being so exposed to the patrons clustered at the tables behind him. But the central table had given them the best view of the entire room, including the deck.

"Do you see anyone out of place?" He kept his voice low before he popped his bite into his mouth. He would miss elven food. They went for subtle flavors and textures over bold spices.

Jalissa started to shake her head, froze as she seemed to catch herself, then she dropped her gaze to her plate. "No. Everyone appears to be enjoying their evening meal."

Sarya kept eating her own food. As she didn't add anything, she must agree with Jalissa's assessment of the elves at the tables they could see.

He ate several more bites before he allowed himself another casual glance around the room. The elves at the various tables all remained the same from the last time he'd glanced around, caught up in their own conversations. One elf read a book while he ate, sitting at a table in the far corner. But he seemed to be enjoying the book far too much for it to be merely a front to spy on the room the way Edmund was doing.

But there by the front desk, a male elf had his back to Edmund as he appeared to be ordering food.

Something about that elf…Edmund focused on him more intently. Were his shoulders just a little bit too broad for the average elf? And was that hair color the same shade as one of the wigs that were missing from the cabin hideout? The elf taking his order had a scrunched expression, as if the male elf was not speaking very clearly...or he was bungling the elvish.

The male elf turned slightly, tapping his fingers on the countertop as he waited in a gesture that was just a little too human. No elf showed that much obvious impatience in a room filled with strangers. The front desk elf frowned even more, eyes narrowing.

Edmund forced himself to look back to his plate, lest the Mongavarian spy feel the intensity of eyes watching his back. "Do not turn around, but one of the spies is at the front desk, ordering food."

Jalissa's back stiffened, but other than that, she followed his instructions and didn't look up from her plate. "What do we do?"

"We can't spook him." Edmund forced himself to stab another bite of his food, even though his heart was starting to hammer in his chest, the buzzing rush of adrenaline beginning to spike through him. "When he gets his food and heads back to his room, I'll follow him. Wait a few minutes, then the two of you can follow me. But stay well back. If we can find out where they are staying, then we can grab them tonight."

Jalissa released a breath and gave the slightest of nods. Beside her, Sarya remained stiff and alert, a guard preparing for action.

Edmund risked another glance toward the spy at the front desk. He had stopped tapping his fingers and instead inspecting the food that had been delivered to him. Yet Edmund could tell he was using the action to cover the way he was studying the elf at the front desk.

The male elf running the front desk was shifting, doing a bad job of hiding his suspicions. Had an alert been sent to inns to watch for the spies? The elf began to reach for the curl of the communication root, the communication system that ran throughout Estyra and all Tarenhiel.

Don't do it, Edmund silently willed the elf. *Don't.*

The elf at the front desk didn't listen, of course. He began to tap on the root, sending a message.

The Mongavarian spy's hand blurred as he reached inside his tunic.

Spitting a curse in elvish, Edmund shoved away from the table, his chair falling backwards. But he was already too late. The sound of his chair hitting the floor was muffled by the thunderous crack of a handgun firing, splintering the serene silence of the elven city.

The elf behind the front desk fell, blood already soaking the front of his clothes. Even as he fell, the spy was already turning in Edmund's direction, cycling his revolver and leveling it at Edmund. For a split second their eyes met, and Edmund recognized the *Sentinel*'s head editor beneath the disguise.

Edmund tackled the elven woman that was between him and the spy, taking her to the ground as the gun went off again. His shoulder hit the ground while his back slammed into the center leg of the round table, sending the table toppling.

He had never heard elves scream in panic before. But their quiet city had never been disrupted by gunfire like this. More tables toppled. The pound of dozens of running feet filled the space.

Edmund peered around the edge of the table as he disentangled himself from the poor elven woman, who remained frozen on the floor in utter panic.

The spy was already gone, his food abandoned on the countertop.

Edmund bit back more curses as he pushed to his feet. He glanced around until he found Jalissa and Sarya.

Sarya hauled Jalissa back to her feet after shoving her to the ground when the gunfire started. Instead of panicking like the others running around the room, Jalissa's face was set. She, after all, had been shot at before, during the war.

He shoved his way between elves and around scattered chairs until he reached their side. "We need to get out of here."

"The desk clerk. We need to help him." Jalissa tugged at Sarya's grip, glancing in that direction.

Edmund joined Sarya in directing Jalissa toward the door. One elf vaulted the countertop, dropping behind it to kneel next to the fallen elf. "Neither of you are healers. There is nothing you can do. Right now, guards are on their way, and they are just as likely to arrest us as apprehend the spies."

Jalissa's jaw worked, but she stopped fighting them as they reached the door and elbowed their way outside, caught by the frantic tide of elves fleeing the inn.

When they stepped outside, Edmund glanced around. But as expected, he couldn't spot the spy. Not in the chaos.

Instead of giving chase, he led the way back to the forest floor, then down the no longer quiet street. Once he, Jalissa, and Sarya had found a sheltered spot beside a café that was in the process of closing for the evening, he halted to take a breath and assess their situation.

Jalissa turned to him, then frowned. "You are missing an ear."

He felt first one ear, then the other. One of his fake ear

tips must have been knocked off when he took the elven woman to the floor. His wig also felt slightly askew, and he did his best to adjust it without a mirror. "We can't check into another inn for the rest of the night. The guards are going to be searching all the inns tonight. They'll likely start turning this street upside down in a few minutes."

"Maybe we should head for Ellonahshinel." Jalissa shrugged, then tugged at her own wig, though she didn't yet remove it.

Edmund shared a glance with Sarya, and after a moment she gave a nod. Good. He and Jalissa's guard were in agreement. The last place they wanted Jalissa to go was Ellonahshinel. That would only add her to the spies' list of targets. If Edmund did nothing else, he could at least keep Jalissa from being assassinated.

But to Jalissa, he shook his head. "I'd still rather stick to the shadows. It will keep the spies looking over their shoulders, and perhaps they'll make another mistake in their jumpiness. After all, shooting that elf was already a big mistake. If the spy had kept his cool, he would have quietly walked away. He and his fellow spies had enough time before guards arrived to slip away without causing a fuss."

Spies were bad enough, but unprepared spies were worse. These Mongavarian spies were very skilled, he would give them that. But they had trained and prepared for a spying mission in Escarland. Their mission must have been unexpectedly changed in the past year since the treaty with Tarenhiel.

A year was far too short a time to properly prepare for a mission like this, especially while still maintaining their cover and spying in Escarland. They hadn't had time to perfect elvish or elven mannerisms. All of their information was stolen, not gained firsthand.

Edmund had managed a similar, quick change of spying location when he had joined the spying efforts on Kostaria. But he'd had access to the elves' established spying network, and Edmund only had to adapt to a dialect of a language he already knew. Even then, he had felt like he had been running blind, causing him to take risks that had ultimately led to his capture.

The Mongavarian spies had that same desperate edge to them. That desperation made them especially dangerous.

"So where do we go now, if we are not going to Ellon-ahshinel?" Jalissa glanced back the way they had come.

The bustle around the inn was increasing as a squad of elven guards arrived. Time for them to get moving.

"This way." Edmund led them farther up the street, then up the stairs to a small shop tucked into the branches of a maple tree. Even with the door shut, a myriad of floral and minty scents wafted from inside. A soft glow came from one of the windows toward the back, showing that someone was still awake and inside.

"This is Illyna's shop." Jalissa pointed at the door.

"Who better than one of Farrendel's friends to give us shelter?" Edmund raised his hand to knock.

"But how do you know where…" Jalissa shook her head. "Wait, never mind. I do not want to know."

She might not want to know, but Edmund figured it wouldn't hurt to tell her anyway. It wasn't like the pain between them could get any worse. "I'd tell you it was because I spied on Essie and Farrendel whenever they ventured into Estyra during the first three months of their marriage, but that wouldn't be entirely true. I knew Illyna before then, but she knows me as someone else."

"Of course you did, and she does." Jalissa huffed out a breath that was the elven equivalent of an eye roll. "Is there anyone you didn't spy on?"

"I avoided spying on your Machasheni Leyleira. She has a spy's instincts when it comes to observation."

"Oh, well that is comforting. At least you left my grandmother out of your nefarious activities." She gave another tilt of her head. "I can see why you do not want Farrendel and Essie to know everything. Your own sister might join the stabbing party."

He glanced over his shoulder at her, grinning despite the snap to her tone. "You do sarcasm very well. You should trot it out more often."

She made a frustrated growl in the back of her throat. "Just knock on the door already. If you keep standing there yapping, the guards are going to arrest us for looking suspicious."

Right. Edmund faced the door and knocked.

After a few long seconds, the door opened a crack. In the dark, Illyna was barely visible, her posture tensed, her long blonde hair falling around her shoulders. "Who are you and what do you want?"

Jalissa pushed onto the top of the stairs next to Edmund, taking off her wig as she did so. "Illyna, it is me. Jalissa."

Illyna straightened, letting the door swing open wider as she gave a slight bow. "Amirah."

"This is Elspetha's brother Edmund." Jalissa gestured to him. "Can we come in? We need shelter for the night."

Illyna's eyebrows shot up as she peered at him. Edmund could see why she was puzzled. He didn't look like he could be Essie's brother, with the blond wig, the fake pointed ear, and the cosmetics and putty giving him elven features.

But Illyna nudged the door all the way open with her foot. "Please. Come in."

As they trooped inside, Illyna sheathed the dagger she must have been holding out of sight. Her other arm ended in a stump just below the elbow. When they were all inside, she shoved the door closed with her forearm and drew the locking bolt.

When she turned back toward them, she glanced from Edmund to Jalissa to Sarya, then back to Jalissa. "Are the two of you…running away together?"

Jalissa stiffened, her whole body going rigid. "No, no. Of course not."

He should not feel hurt at her quick denial. Even if things weren't so strained, he would never run off with her. He would want to do things properly.

Or as properly as a human spy and an elven princess ever could.

"We'll explain, but could we go farther into the shop?" Edmund waved toward the back room. "We can't have the guards overhear multiple voices inside your shop. It would make it harder for you to deny that we're here."

Illyna's eyebrows shot up even farther. "If I did not trust Laesornysh and his princess so much, I would worry."

"You probably should be worried." Jalissa sighed and headed for the door at the back of the shop. "But you will be providing a great service for my family if you can help."

Edmund hoped that would be the case. If nothing else, he would quietly tell Illyna that she was protecting at least one of the members of the royal family from an assassination attempt.

If she would believe him, once he confessed to yet another of his secret identities.

After this mission, there would be no going back to the life of a spy. His cover was well and truly blown.

Yet, he no longer wanted that life the way he had even a few weeks ago. While he couldn't regret the way he had served his kingdom, he ached for the stain he would carry because of it.

It was time to walk away. He was done with always lying and pretending. From now on, he wanted a life that was real. With relationships that were true and honest. Or, at least, as much as he could as a prince stuck in a world of court intrigue and politics.

He wouldn't have Jalissa. He would live with regrets that would haunt him to his dying day, even as he hid them behind grins and banter.

But he would finally be free of the shadows once and for all.

TWENTY-NINE

Essie leaned against a comfortable tree—thankful that the elven forest was apparently filled with comfortable trees—as she watched Farrendel swing through the air on the rope swing, let go, execute a perfect flip in the air over the lake, and then tuck himself into a ball to create a gigantic splash the way her brothers had taught him.

On the tree branch, Ryfon was already leaning out to catch the rope as it swung back toward him. Brina scrambled out of the lake, water running off her clothes. They seemed to be having fun, even if there was a lot less shrieking and shouting than there would have been if it had been Essie and her brothers doing cannonballs into a lake.

"That looks cold." Next to Essie, Melantha gave a shiver before she returned to mixing her magic into a jar of juice.

"I would think you would be used to the cold." Essie tugged the blanket she had brought outside with her higher over her lap. The spring morning remained chilly, and she wasn't sure how Farrendel, Ryfon, and Brina could stand swimming in the frigid waters.

She rested her hand on Farrendel's swords, where they lay on the moss next to her. Farrendel had entrusted her with his swords, and she had the irrational fear that they would suddenly disappear on her if she wasn't watching closely enough. His boots, socks, and belt lay in a neat pile next to a towel.

Melantha gave another exaggerated shiver. "I doubt I will ever grow used to the cold. I think I only survived the winter thanks to the hot chocolate you and Farrendel sent to me."

There was a note to Melantha's voice that had Essie turning more fully to face her sister-in-law. "Is everything all right?"

Melantha tightened the lid on the jar, then set it aside. She leaned back against the tree next to Essie, staring up at the thick green leaves overhead. After several long seconds of silence, Melantha sighed. "I did not realize how intensely I would miss the sun. And trees. And green. How I missed *green*. Kostaria has forests of pine and spruce, but even those forests are not green the way Tarenhiel is green. I managed to get through this winter thanks to Rharreth's promise that we would visit Tarenhiel in the spring."

Essie wasn't sure what to say. She had missed Escarland during those first few months of her marriage, but not quite like that. Then again, she had only been away from her home and family for three months. Melantha had left Tarenhiel nearly nine months ago now.

Most surprising was the fact that Melantha was confiding this to her. The two of them had never been close, even before Melantha had betrayed Farrendel. And, while

Farrendel had worked hard to repair his relationship with Melantha and the two of them had kept up a steady stream of letters back and forth, Essie was still figuring out just what kind of sister-in-law Melantha would be.

Though, Melantha had washed her puke bucket for her the other day. It was hard to stay distrustful of someone willing to do that.

Melantha tore her gaze away from the leaves, facing Essie again. "Do not mistake me. I love Rharreth and Kostaria. I would not trade the life I have for one in Tarenhiel."

"Clearly." Essie forced a smile, waving from Melantha's short, spiky black hair to her leather clothing. "You look like a proper troll."

Melantha's mouth twisted into the start of a smile, even if it was still shadowed. "Yes. I am happy. It is just…"

"Even happiness can come with hard parts." Essie glanced back to the lake. Ryfon and Brina were both splashing Farrendel, all three of them laughing. Essie wouldn't trade Farrendel for anything, but choosing him meant choosing to love him through his dark days and nightmare-filled nights. It wasn't easy or glamorous or romantic. It was just…life. But it was still good. Still worth it each and every day.

"Yes." Melantha settled back against the tree. "Rharreth assures me that summer in Kostaria is very green and beautiful. Until then, I am going to soak up as much green as I can here in Tarenhiel until we return."

Perhaps it was a sign of how far Melantha had come that she was willing to talk about something that pained her rather than letting it smolder. This open, wiser Melantha was one Essie wouldn't mind getting to know better. "Are you still planning to visit Escarland to meet with my brother before returning to Kostaria?"

"Most likely. We have come this far south. We might as well go the rest of the way." Melantha shrugged, then quirked another of those tentative smiles. "Though I would not mind delaying, giving us another excuse to travel through Tarenhiel."

"My brother is eager to start work on the bridge between Tarenhiel and Escarland, as well as discuss more opportunities for trade. I'm sure he will give you plenty of excuses for travel if you wish." Essie paused, studying Melantha for a moment before she added, "I'm glad Kostaria has accepted you and Rharreth enough that you can travel more."

"So am I." Melantha's smile widened. "Though, we left Vriska in charge, so we cannot abandon Kostaria for too long. There is only so much Rharreth's shield band can do to keep the kingdom together until we get back."

With Rharreth's brother and cousin dead, he no longer had any family. He didn't have siblings who could watch over the kingdom the way Weylind or Averett did. Until Rharreth had an heir, Kostaria would be a little tense wondering what would happen to the line of succession if something happened to Rharreth.

That probably didn't help the pressure that Melantha was under as an elf ruling as queen of the trolls.

Before Essie could think of a reply, Farrendel walked up the pebbled beach and flopped onto his back on the forest floor next to her, his silver-blond hair a shade darker while wet, his loose shirt and trousers dripping.

"You look cold." Essie handed him the towel.

"I *am* cold." Farrendel swiped the towel over his face. "Is there any word from Estyra?"

"Not yet."

Farrendel grimaced and dropped the towel to the forest floor next to him.

It was uncomfortable, enjoying the peace and safety of Lethorel while also tensely awaiting word about those they had left behind.

"Weylind and Rheva will be all right." Essie rested a hand on Farrendel's shoulder, his shirt cold and wet. She glanced over her shoulder at Melantha. "And Rharreth. I'm sure they will keep each other safe."

Melantha's mouth twisted into a wry smile yet again. "If Rharreth and Weylind can stop glaring and posturing long enough to work together."

Essie could imagine Weylind's scowl and Rharreth's sharp glare. Good thing Rheva had stayed behind to play peacemaker between them, otherwise they might kill each other before the assassins got there. "Perhaps it will be good bonding time."

"After this past year, I think Weylind may have reached his limit of bonding time." Farrendel squeezed water from each of his sleeves.

"It is good for him." Melantha gathered her jars of juice and stood. "Is there anything you need, Elspetha?"

"No, I'm fine." Essie checked that her soda cracker tin was within reach, in case she needed something to nibble on.

Melantha nodded. "I will see if Brina and Ryfon need anything."

The two of them had climbed out of the water farther along the bank, sitting in a patch of sun as they dried off.

As Melantha strolled off, Farrendel placed his hands behind his head, wiggling as if to get more comfortable on the moss. He'd lain down in one of the rare patches of sunlight that pierced through the leaves overhead.

With his shirt still wet and sticking to itself, his movement exposed a line of skin along his stomach.

Essie flexed her fingers, telling herself she shouldn't poke him. Or tickle him. Farrendel trusted her because she didn't push his boundaries past what he could handle. And tickling would be crossing a line, tempting as it was.

Farrendel raised an eyebrow at her. "You are thinking juvenile thoughts."

She grinned, lowering her voice into an attempt at a husky tone. "How can you tell I'm not thinking romantic thoughts?"

He chuckled. "We have been married nearly a year. I can tell when you are thinking romance and when you are thinking teasing."

"Fine, fine. I'll save tickling and belly poking for a squishy little baby belly." She tugged on his shirt, straightening it somewhat. "Removing temptation. Because apparently you can read me like an open book."

He pushed onto an elbow and gently cupped her chin, tracing her mouth with his thumb. "It is all in your smile."

A year ago, he'd told her that her smile was the reason he had agreed to marry her. Her smile had given him hope that life could be more than darkness and battle.

Essie rested her hand over his. "To think, a year ago, it took convincing just to get you to hold my hand. And when you let me lean on your shoulder for the first time, it felt like a great victory."

"It was a great victory." Farrendel leaned his forehead against hers, his hand sliding from her cheek to gently cradle the back of her head. "We have come a long way in a year."

"Yes, we have." Her voice came out breathy and soft. Now she *was* thinking romance and how nice it would be to kiss him once his family wasn't looking.

Farrendel's gaze snapped to the forest, his hand falling away from her.

Essie tensed, glancing at the forest around them. "What is it?"

He sat up, then rolled to his feet. "Someone just crossed my magical alert." He paused, then the set to his jaw hardened as he reached for his swords. "Not an elf."

Essie scrambled to her feet, gathering her blanket, her tin of soda crackers, and his pile of boots, belt, and stockings.

"You need to get inside." Farrendel put a hand on her back and steered her toward the stairs to Lethorel. He dumped more magic into the heart bond, filling Essie's chest with a crackle, even as a wall of blue magic blazed to life between them and the forest.

Melantha, Ryfon, and Brina were still at the shoreline, but they jumped to their feet at the sight of Farrendel's shield.

While urging everyone inside, Farrendel tugged on his stockings and boots, then buckled his swords across his back. His hair and clothes were still wet, making him look ill-prepared for this battle.

The troll guards clustered around Melantha, but Captain Merrick and Iyrinder lingered next to Farrendel and Essie at the base of the stairs.

Iyrinder crossed his arms. "We are your guards, Laesornysh. We should stay at your back."

"I am going to flood this entire forest with my magic. It will be too dangerous for anyone but Essie to get close to me." Farrendel glanced from them to the forest, as if gauging how much time they had.

Essie also searched the forest. Was the assassin even now finding a perch in a tree and lining up his shot? Though, Farrendel's shield around them would keep them safe.

Farrendel turned back to Iyrinder, though his grip on Essie's hand tightened. "You will do me a greater service by guarding Essie."

Iyrinder frowned but nodded. Captain Merrick sighed and tilted his head in an acknowledgment of the order.

Farrendel drew Essie closer. "Use my magic if you have to. Melantha can make sure it does not harm the baby. But you need to protect yourself."

"I think, if you get a shield started, you can hand the magic off to me without problems. The magic is running through you in that case, rather than me. I'm just reaching out and keeping it going." Essie wrapped her arms around him and hugged him as tight as she could. No matter how many times she did it, she hated this moment, that pause before a battle where she had to let him go, knowing he was walking into danger.

She lifted her head to tell him that she loved him, but he cupped her face and kissed her before she had a chance.

Just as well. She didn't need to tell him, nor hear him say it in return. She knew his heart and felt it in their kiss.

Then Farrendel stepped back and turned away, facing the forest. Captain Merrick and Iyrinder hustled her up the stairs before Iyrinder used his magic to retract the stairs into the tree, making it difficult for anyone but an elf to scale Lethorel to reach them.

Essie sank to the floor next to the window, staring down at Farrendel's back as he strode alone into the clearing at the base of the tree. This was all too eerily like that day over nine months ago when she had huddled up here while Farrendel stood alone against the first wave of invading trolls.

A hand rested on her shoulder, and when Essie turned, she found Melantha standing there.

Melantha's dark eyes were grave as she clutched her staff in her other hand. "You should come away from the window."

Essie nodded, easing to the side so that she stood up next to the wall instead of in front of the window.

A dome of Farrendel's crackling magic sprang up around Lethorel, filling the view through the windows with blue lightning.

Essie reached through the heart bond, then paused and glanced at Melantha. "Farrendel and I have been unsure if my use of his magic would harm the baby. Could you make sure everything is fine?"

Melantha nodded, then rested her hand on the back of Essie's. Her cool, sharp healing magic flowed into her. "Actually, I think I can wrap a shield of my own around the baby. I protected Farrendel from the troll magic inside him. It should work the same way to protect the baby from Farrendel's magic."

Some of the tension in Essie's shoulders eased. "Linshi, isciena."

Melantha's magic settled deep inside Essie, a strange feeling that Essie had to ignore to keep from squirming.

With Melantha protecting the baby, Essie could concentrate on protecting the rest of them, leaving Farrendel free to fight the battle ahead of him.

Again, Essie reached through the heart bond. This time, she took control of Farrendel's magic from him. Since he had started the shield, the draw of magic was coming from him, even though she was now the one controlling it.

Essie tried to take slow steady breaths, squeezing her eyes shut as she concentrated on the magic she wielded.

Farrendel would be all right. He had to be all right. Surely he could take out one assassin.

If this assassin didn't shoot Farrendel first.

What would happen if Essie had to try to keep Farrendel alive through the heart bond? Keeping him alive was more strain on her body than keeping her alive had been on his. Would doing that harm the baby? What if she had to choose between Farrendel and their child?

E dmund pointed at the sketch of Ellonahshinel he had spread out on Illyna's worktable in her back room. Jalissa's eyebrows had risen as he'd sketched all the pathways of Ellonahshinel by memory.

Illyna, Fingol, Fingol's wife, and many of Farrendel's other friends crammed into Illyna's shop. Edmund might not have access to his own network, but Farrendel's friends and acquaintances were just as impressive of a group. They held great loyalty for their Laesornysh and his princess.

The pink light of dawn glowed through the one window behind him, casting shadows on the paper in front of him that were only partially dispelled by the elven lights glowing near the ceiling.

For the first time since leaving Aldon, Edmund was dressed simply as himself. Well, mostly. He still wore elven clothing, a blue shirt and black trousers he had borrowed from Fingol, since he didn't have any human-style clothes along. But he no longer wore the blond wig over his brown curls nor any cosmetics or putty to change the shape of his face and give him an elven complexion.

Edmund pointed at the center of the sketch, casting a black shadow from his finger over the location of the dining room near the center of Ellonahshinel's massive treetop palace. "The most logical time to attack would be during supper or right afterwards. It is the one time of the day when the elven royal family is guaranteed to be together at a predictable time."

He didn't say that it had been what he had suggested in his assassination plan. But across the table, Jalissa met his gaze and scowled. Even if no one else knew, she did.

"Would the king continue to keep such a rigid schedule, since he has been warned about the assassins?" Illyna glanced at Jalissa. Instead of the warm, friendly elf woman who ran a shampoo and conditioner shop, Illyna's harder edges showed in the set of her mouth and sharpness to her eyes. Here was the elf who had fought for her kingdom and lost a hand in the war.

Jalissa stared at the map a moment before she sighed. "He likely will, hoping to lure the assassins into attacking at a predictable time. If he changes his routine, the assassins will also change their plan."

They might anyway, since they likely knew Weylind had been warned and given the details of the assassination plan they had stolen. After all, if they hadn't guessed, the wary guards at the train station and the front desk elf at the inn had probably given it away.

But that plan was a place to start.

"If that is the king's strategy, then he will be well-guarded." Fingol shrugged and leaned more heavily on the table, taking the weight off the bad leg that gave him a permanent limp. "I want to help, but I am not sure what we can do that the king's guards cannot."

Edmund met the gazes of each of them gathered around the table. "The spies are looking for the guards and can avoid them, thanks to their uniforms. But you are invisible to elven society, and you will be invisible to the spies. You might see something that the guards won't."

Fingol nodded, as did a few of the others.

"Thanks to Farrendel, many of you are recognizable faces around the palace." Edmund tapped the sketch of Ellon-ahshinel. "If you can get into the palace on some pretext, then search the branches. You can divide up the palace among yourselves. Those of you who can't get in, search the forest and trees in the vicinity of Ellonahshinel. The assassins have at least one sharpshooter among them. He was able to target both Essie and Farrendel from a distance, so pay special attention to anywhere that has a clear line of sight to a section of Ellonahshinel where King Weylind normally goes."

The others nodded, including Jalissa.

"Search in pairs, though don't walk next to each other. This prevents one of you from being taken out by a spy without anyone else knowing. And if you do spot someone suspicious, one of you can linger and keep an eye on them while the other runs back to report to me." Edmund stared down at the sketched map rather than glance at the others. "I'm going to sneak into Farrendel's workshop, and you can report to me there if you find anything."

The workshop was at the outskirts of Ellonahshinel, making it a better headquarters than Illyna's shop.

Illyna straightened and faced the others. "I will lead those going into Ellonahshinel. We can get into Ellonahshinel by Laesornysh's lift. I know how to summon it in an emergency."

One of the other elves, a male with black hair and a scar across his face over a sightless eye, stepped forward. "I will lead those searching the trees surrounding Ellonahshinel."

Edmund stepped back, watching as the elves divided into two groups. With their warrior backgrounds, they followed orders efficiently, organizing into a command structure as if that was second nature to them.

Fingol stiffened, then turned toward the window. "Is that shouting?"

Everyone froze, listening.

Edmund cocked an ear. After a moment, even he heard it, despite his less acute human hearing.

Shouting. In Estyra. Never a good thing.

Illyna crossed the room and entered her shop, with Edmund, Jalissa, and several of the others following. When Illyna cracked open the front door, the sound of shouting blasted inside, along with a whiff of something sharp and acrid.

Jalissa stiffened. "Smoke."

Fire was one of the most feared things in Estyra. Their entire city and palace were created out of wood. Living wood, but it could still burn with a hot enough fire.

Several of the elves pushed toward the door, reacting on the elven instinct to rush to the fire to put it out.

The exact same thing that Weylind would do.

Edmund's stomach dropped. Forget waiting until evening. The assassins had figured out another way to take out Weylind. "Wait!"

The elves froze, then glanced over their shoulders at him.

"This is the work of the assassins. They are making their

move now. Stick to the plan, but hurry." Edmund layered steely command into his voice. He turned back to Jalissa and held out his hand. "The princess and I will find King Weylind and keep him safe."

No one argued, not even to point out that King Weylind already had plenty of guards protecting him. Jalissa and Edmund might make little difference.

But those guards would be just as distracted as Weylind, fighting this fire. And Jalissa and Edmund had seen many of these spies, at least while dressed in human clothing back in Escarland, although they had only seen one of them so far in elven disguise.

The gathered elves nodded, then Illyna and the other elf gave their orders, leading their respective groups from the shop.

Jalissa stepped forward and gripped Edmund's hand. He didn't think it was a sign that she forgave him. It was more a visceral instinct. A statement that they were in this together, at least until her family was safe.

Edmund hurried out of the shop on the heels of the last elf of Illyna's group. Jalissa kept up with him, their strides matching as if they had grown accustomed to running next to each other.

The shouting and smell of smoke came from the direction of Ellonahshinel. Even on this normally quiet side street, elves dashed from their homes and shops and raced toward the fire. Edmund and Jalissa joined the tide of elves racing toward the treetop palace.

As they reached the main street, it was as if all Estyra sprinted in that direction. Above their heads, tongues of flame leapt into the sky from the base of Ellonahshinel.

Jalissa gasped, her steps stumbling. Edmund tightened

his grip on her hand and kept them moving forward. He dodged around and between the other elves. In the chaos, none of the elves around them even seemed to notice his short hair and lack of pointed ears.

As they neared Ellonahshinel, they were halted by a thick, milling crowd, held back by a line of guards.

Jalissa hesitated, but Edmund shoved his way into the crowd, using his broad shoulders to his advantage. Jalissa trotted after him through the gap he created. She didn't protest his grip on her hand, even though he held it as a human would since it gave him a better grip so he wouldn't lose her in the chaos.

When they reached the line of guards, the elf warrior before them barred their way with his spear. "You cannot pass."

Edmund ignored the guard, taking in the scene at the base of Ellonahshinel. Fire licked up the side of one of the roots, the kitchen building entirely consumed in flames. Palace servants rushed about, throwing buckets of water on the fire. Those with plant growing magic layered roots over the building, trying to smother the flames.

Weylind wielded his magic along with the others. His raw, plant growing magic formed a green shield around the fire, preventing it from spreading to the rest of Ellonahshinel. He had his back to the crowd, fully focused on containing the fire.

Next to him, Rharreth also had his back to them as he blasted the fire inside of Weylind's bubble of power with his own ice magic. The fire burned the ice off nearly as quickly as Rharreth froze it, but the sizzling and hiss suggested that his efforts were slowly putting out the fire inch by inch.

Leyleira stood off to the side, directing the fire suppression efforts, while Rheva knelt by what looked like one of the kitchen servants. The servant coughed, red burns covering the back of his hand and flowing up his arms, both sleeves burned away.

All four of them were gathered here in front of Ellon-ahshinel. Perfect targets.

Edmund cast about, searching the nearby faces. Palace servants and guards rushed about, and it was hard to get a good look at anyone in the chaos.

The guard in front of him started, eyes widening. "You are a human!" He swung his spear toward Edmund's chest. "Halt! Surrender!"

Jalissa released Edmund's hand, stepping in front of him, pushing the spear aside as she did. "No, this is Prince Edmund of Escarland. He is not one of the humans you are looking for."

"Amirah!" The guard's jaw dropped, his spear going slack in his hands.

Edmund ignored the guard. The spies must be here somewhere. Was the sharpshooter perched in a tree even now, taking aim at Weylind's back?

Or would the spies commit this assassination close up despite the risk? With so much chaos, they could disappear into the crowd quickly. After failing to kill Essie and Farrendel, they would want to be extra sure of their targets this time.

There. A different wig, this one black. But the same too-human stride carrying the man toward Weylind's back. The same too-broad shoulders, now wearing an elven guard leather tunic emblazoned with a green tree. The same revolver now being pulled out from under the tunic where it had been concealed.

There wasn't time to call a warning. Just time to react.

Edmund shoved past the flabbergasted guard in front of him and Jalissa. He raced forward and tackled the Mongavarian spy before he had gotten the gun all the way up.

The two of them crashed to the spongy forest floor. With the landing so soft, it left neither of them stunned the way such a tackle would have on the streets of Aldon.

The spy rolled out of Edmund's grasp, coming up to his knees. As he raised the gun again, Edmund lunged between the man and Weylind. With one hand, he reached for the gun. He had to get a grip on it. He must keep it from firing or point it toward the ground.

With his other hand, he grasped his derringer and pulled it from its concealed holster along his forearm.

His fingers closed around the spy's wrist, even as the man's finger tightened on the trigger. As their eyes met, a gunshot boomed in the space between them.

Something punched into Edmund's stomach, and only his grip on the spy's wrist kept him from falling backwards. Gasping, he shoved the spy's arm toward the ground, trying to keep him from getting off a second shot.

As pain slammed through Edmund, so sharp he could barely breathe, he raised the derringer, pointing it at the spy's chest. "Drop your gun."

The spy's eyes widened. Instead of letting go, he reached his free hand toward Edmund's derringer.

Edmund squeezed the trigger. Even at point-blank range, his hand had wavered, and red bloomed at the spy's shoulder instead of his chest.

Still, it knocked the spy back, sending both of them to the ground again thanks to their shared grip on the revolver.

Edmund dropped the derringer, having used up its one shot, and clutched the revolver with both hands, preventing the cylinder from rotating and the hammer from cocking back. Blackness danced at the edges of his vision, but he hung onto the gun. If he let go, the spy would shoot again.

And that second shot might hit someone other than Edmund. He had to protect Jalissa and her family if it was the last thing he did.

JALISSA SCREAMED AS EDMUND COLLAPSED, red blood blossoming on both the front and back of his shirt.

Weylind was turning, his magic still holding back the fire. The guards were hurrying forward too, but they hesitated, most likely unsure if they should help the bleeding human or the elf wearing their uniform but wielding a gun.

Somehow, Edmund kept a grip on the spy's gun, even as the spy stood and tried to rip the gun free, one arm held stiffly at his side, blood staining his shirt.

No. He would not get in another shot.

Jalissa raced forward, drawing on her magic. She crashed to her knees next to Edmund and pressed her hands to the ground.

The grass lashed upward, wrapping around the spy. He let go of the gun to beat at the grass, giving a rather high-pitched squeal of fright as the grass caught his hands.

Another guard was rushing toward them. Yet there was something about him...Jalissa sent her magic toward him as well. Only when she had him bound did it register that he had reached into his tunic, as if for a gun, rather than toward his hip as an elven warrior would, looking for their sword or dagger. He also had a hint of scruff on his cheeks.

On the forest floor in front of her, Edmund groaned and dropped the gun, pressing his hands to his stomach. In seconds, blood coated his fingers.

He was bleeding from both the entry and exit wounds, a pool of red spreading over the moss around him.

Yet Jalissa did not have healing magic. She could not even press her hands to his wounds as she still held the two spies in the power of her magic.

Instead, she laced more of the grass with her magic and encouraged the plants to wrap around Edmund's middle. Would it be enough? Would he bleed out before a healer could tend him? "Rheva!"

"Jalissa?" Weylind's voice came from behind her, scratchy and deep from the smoke.

"There are four more assassins." Jalissa tightened her grip on the spies she held in her power. The men struggled against the grass, but they could not break her magically reinforced plants. "I need Rheva."

Even as she said it, a guard who had been approaching Rheva turned and bolted.

A root sprang from the ground and snagged the elf's foot, sending him crashing to the forest floor with such force that his wig went askew, revealing human ears. Behind Jalissa, Weylind gave a growl.

The spy rolled and muttered something under his breath, a moment before fire licked around his fingers. He grabbed the root holding him in place, burning it away.

That would explain why the fire had started so quickly and proved so difficult to put out. One of the spies was also a human magician.

He scrambled to his feet. Before he had gone more than a step, ice shot toward him, hitting him in the back and knocking him to the ground. More ice wrapped around him, holding him in place. The ice coating his hands steamed, but Rharreth held him tightly in the grip of his magic.

Guards converged on Rheva. Protecting her, yes, but also preventing her from getting to Jalissa and Edmund.

If only Jalissa had healing magic. She would even take healing magic with the same level of power that she currently had. It would be so much more useful than the modicum of growing magic she possessed.

Blood slicked the blades of grass she had wrapped around Edmund. She grew more, even as she knew they would not be enough. He had been gut shot from only inches away, the bullet tearing through him before exiting out his back.

Both Weylind and Rharreth were shouting orders. More guards, both elf and troll, rushed about. A few of them took control of the spies Jalissa captured, and she released the magic holding them.

From somewhere in the trees, the group of Farrendel's friends came forward, another human dressed as a guard bound and pushed in front of them. One of the warriors held the spy's wig in his hand.

A fourth spy. There could be two more, lurking about somewhere, including the female spy.

But right now, she did not care where they were. Someone else would have to track them down.

Jalissa kept one hand pressed to the ground, holding the magical grass that tried to staunch the bleeding. She rested her other hand on Edmund's shoulder. "Rheva!"

Edmund made a choking sound, curling even tighter

around his stomach. He spoke between gritted teeth, yet his tone was light. "You sound worried. Glad to hear you don't want me to die."

"Of course I do not want you to die." Jalissa gripped his shoulder tight enough it probably hurt. Not that her fingers digging into his muscle would hurt worse than what that bullet had done to him. "Now stop talking and save your strength. Rheva will be here soon."

"At least I have the good sense to get shot in Estyra with healers nearby."

How could he joke at a time like this? Jalissa wanted to scream again, this time in frustration. But that would not help him. "Rheva! I need a healer! Now!"

"Here." Rheva knelt next to Edmund across from Jalissa, her voice calm and soothing. Her magic coated her fingers as she pressed a hand to Edmund's forehead.

Edmund drew in a shuddering breath, some of the tightness in his face easing. Yet, his face remained gray and pale.

"Will he be all right?" Jalissa bit her lip and held her breath.

A slight frown crossed Rheva's face. "We need to get him inside. There is some of his shirt inside the wound that will need to be removed before I heal him all the way."

As she gestured to some of the guards and gave orders, Edmund rolled onto his back, reaching out to Jalissa with a bloody hand. "Warn Farrendel."

"What?" Jalissa gripped his hand, ignoring the squishy warmth of the blood.

"The other two…I think…" Edmund's eyes fluttered as he tried to focus on her, his voice weaker than it had been.

The guards lifted Edmund. He moaned and went limp in their grip.

Rheva kept her hand pressed to his forehead. Together, she and the guards headed in the direction of Ellonahshinel's stairs.

Jalissa pushed to her feet, hurrying after them.

"Jalissa." Weylind caught her arm, halting her.

She turned to face him, everything in her wanting to tug her arm free. "Edmund…"

"There is nothing you can do for him." Weylind's gaze was sharp, cutting through her. "I know why he is here. His brother said he would be coming. But what are *you* doing here? You were supposed to stay in Aldon where you would be safe."

She looked away from him, unable to hold his gaze. Behind Weylind, the kitchen was nothing but a shell of black rubble while char marks seared the trunk of Ellonahshinel's massive tree. But the fire itself was out, likely smothered by the combination of Weylind's shield of growing magic and Rharreth's ice.

They made it look easy, but it had taken great power on both their parts to hold such a shield against the heat of the growing conflagration and to put out the fire with ice. Who knew how far the magic-powered fire would have spread, if Weylind and Rharreth had not worked together to put it out?

"Jalissa." Weylind gripped her shoulders, his stern voice commanding her to look at him. "If something had happened to me and Rheva, you would have needed to stay alive to be there for Ryfon and act as his regent until he was a hundred years old. Unless you want that duty to fall onto Farrendel's shoulders?"

She flinched. She had not thought of that, when she had thrown herself into danger. She had only thought about protecting her family and fighting at Edmund's side, even if that fighting was from the shadows. Then he had shattered her trust with the truth of how deep those shadows went.

Yet even now, he was being carried to the infirmary, gut shot, after saving Weylind's life.

Everything in her chest was such a tangle. Anger for his betrayal. The choking bitterness over Melantha's earlier betrayal. That annoying weed of love that would not go away as much as she tried to kill it.

What had he been trying to tell her? Better to focus on that than on her feelings or Weylind's glare.

"I had to keep our family safe." Jalissa tore herself free of Weylind's grip, hands fisted at her sides. "Going with Edmund gave me the chance to help. We tracked the spies here, and as you can see, we were able to take them down. But there are still two spies out there somewhere."

Since neither of them had made an appearance yet, did that mean they had gone to Lethorel instead of Estyra? Was that what Edmund had been trying to tell her?

It would have been a simple thing for two of the spies to stay on the train and continue to Lethorel while the other four got off at Estyra.

Why those two spies in particular? One of them must be the sharpshooter who had targeted Farrendel before. A surprise shot from a distance was the only way to have a hope of killing him.

But why send the female spy? Would they think Farrendel was less likely to fight back against a female instead of a male? Which was likely true, but Farrendel could keep her well back if he was suspicious.

The first time Jalissa had smelled the female spy's

perfume had been in the apartment where the sharpshooter had waited for his chance.

Or was it *her* chance?

They had always assumed the man had been the sharpshooter, since he had rented the rooms.

But what if he had merely been the expendable one who had been assigned the boring job of watching both Winstead Palace and the main street, getting a feel for Farrendel and Elspetha's routine? Once he saw Elspetha leaving the palace alone and realized this was their chance, the woman sharpshooter was summoned from the *Sentinel* to take the shots.

The female spy had not worked at the *Sentinel* with the others. Maybe she had been sent from Mongavaria specifically for the mission to kill Farrendel. She was the trained assassin of the bunch.

Farrendel had been warned to look for a male sharpshooter. If he spotted both spies, he would focus on the man, thinking him the greater threat.

Weylind had kept speaking, giving her some lecture about being a princess and running off nearly alone, but she had tuned him out, the better to let him get out his grumpiness all at once.

But now she held up a hand, meeting his gaze again. "We need to warn Farrendel. The female Mongavarian spy is the sharpshooter. Or maybe both are sharpshooters, I do not know. But we need to warn Farrendel. I think the other two spies are headed for Lethorel."

That snapped Weylind's mouth shut. He gave a brisk nod. "I will send the message, though I will instruct my guards to continue to search for the last two spies here."

Of course. They could not assume anything at this point.

But Jalissa had a sinking feeling that the assassins were

not here and even now were on their way to finish what they had started back in Escarland.

She stared down at her hands, coated in blood yet again. Edmund's blood this time instead of Elspetha's, but still red and sticky and far too much of it. Had the spies already succeeded in killing Edmund?

F arrendel stepped into the quiet of the forest surrounding Lethorel, his skin prickling.

The assassin was here. He could sense it. Taste it on the air. Feel it through his magic.

He faced the forest where he had sensed the assassin cross the line of his magic. That had been a deliberate challenge. The man had to have seen the blue glow. He had to know it was there for a reason.

Farrendel released the shield of his magic around himself and stepped into the clearing next to the lake, making himself a perfect target.

It was time to end this.

"Assassin!" Farrendel shouted, flexing his fingers. "No more shooting at my wife to get at me. You have me now. So take your shot."

Farrendel waited. The forest remained silent around him.

There. His senses shot a warning down his spine. With a snap, he drew on his magic and blasted it out in a shield around himself.

Not a moment too soon. A bullet slammed into the magic, incinerated before it could go anywhere close to him, the echo of the gunshot coming a heartbeat later.

A savage grin crossed his face. Farrendel had allowed the assassin to take his shot.

But now he knew the assassin's location based on where the gunshot had come from. It was time to take him down.

Keeping the shield around himself, Farrendel knelt and pressed a hand to the ground. Always eager, his magic surged from him, racing along the forest floor and coating each of the trees.

Weylind had told him to burn the forest down if necessary, but Farrendel kept his magic in check, letting it flow over the trees without scorching so much as a leaf. No need to destroy this place that meant so much to him if he could help it.

He was not the young elfling with too much magic and too little control. Not anymore. He had the heart bond where he could dump any magic that grew too unstable for him to wield. He had Essie's steady presence, reminding him what he fought for. He had his training with Weylind and Ryfon and his magical studies at Hanford University.

A scrambling sound came from deep within the forest a moment before his magic pooled around a tree, then crawled up it. A shriek, and then Farrendel's magic was flowing up and over a warm, living body.

Even though Farrendel held his magic in such control that it did not even char the assassin's clothes, the man screamed like he was on fire. Through the magic, Farrendel could sense the way he was flailing, beating at the magic coating himself as if he could put it out with his hands. The man was going to fall from the tree and break his neck if he kept panicking like that.

As it was, he dropped his gun. It fell to the forest floor, and Farrendel's magic swallowed it. Still holding the rest of his magic in place, Farrendel let a few tendrils curl around the gun and do their worst, incinerating the gun where it lay. That gun had been used to hurt Essie. There would be nothing left to hurt anyone ever again.

The assassin was now curled on his branch, sobbing.

Farrendel flexed his fingers against the ground, his eyes still squeezed shut as he concentrated on his power.

This man had shot Essie. Had nearly killed Essie and their unborn child.

And now Farrendel held him in the grip of his magic, utterly helpless. All it would take would be a tightening of Farrendel's power, and this man would never be a threat to anyone ever again.

A hint of his anger shivered through his magic, burning away the assassin's frightened tears from his cheeks.

Farrendel forced himself to draw in a deep breath, then let it out slowly. Years ago, he had given in to his anger. Little more than a boy and devastated by his torture and the death of his father, he had crossed Kostaria, climbed Gror Grar's wall, and attacked the late troll king in his bed, killing him.

That assassination had stained his soul ever since.

He could not do that again. He was older. Wiser. It was one thing to kill a man in defense of himself or his kingdom. But right now, this Mongavarian spy was weaponless. Helpless.

Farrendel would have to drag the assassin back to Lethorel. They could keep the assassin captive until they received word it was safe to return to Estyra. Then he could hand the spy over to Weylind and Averett, and they could determine what to do with him from there.

That decided, Farrendel tightened the grip of his magic, nudging the man to climb down from the tree.

Instead of climbing, the man threw himself from the tree. As if he thought he still had a chance to run.

This far away, Farrendel did not hear him land, though he sensed the landing through the crackling bolts of his magic. He held his breath. Had the man died? Broken his neck?

A scream of pain rang out through the forest.

Nope, still alive then.

Farrendel released a long breath, letting all but the magic surrounding the fallen assassin dissipate.

It was over. He had captured the assassin who had tried to kill Essie. He straightened, taking a step toward where the man had fallen.

He was not even sure what alerted him. A prickling between his shoulder blades. An itching sense from his magic.

Even as he threw himself into a roll, something whipped past him, so close it sliced through a few strands of his hair.

He blasted a shield of magic around himself once again, even as he came up in a crouch, searching the trees that had been behind him.

There was a second sharpshooter. Someone who had waited until he had let the alert magic drop while he had been concentrating on the rest of his magic. Then, when he had released his magic entirely, thinking he had captured the threat, this second assassin had taken the shot. Only his instincts and quick reflexes had saved his life.

There, perched on a branch not far from Lethorel, crouched a woman with dark brown hair in a braid over one shoulder. She raised her gun again, aiming at him as if she thought she had a chance of getting to him through his magic.

Even as he held the magic around himself, he hesitated. He had fought woman warriors before. Yet it was one thing to stab a troll woman who was coming at him with an ax. For some reason, it felt different to lash out at a human woman who, with her braid and rifle, reminded him too much of Essie.

A blast of blue magic shot out, wrapping around the rifle and yanking it from the woman's hands.

The woman screamed as the magic touched her fingers. She let go of the gun and hunched over her hands, her fingers curled as if in pain.

For a moment, Farrendel just stared at the woman. That magic had not come from him. Then he dragged his gaze toward Lethorel.

Essie stood in the window, Melantha at her side. Essie's jaw was set and, when he met her gaze across the distance, she gave a single nod.

He had hesitated, but Essie had not.

This time, he sent a low-powered surge of magic through the forest, holding it as he scoured several miles around Lethorel until he was certain no more threats remained. All he could sense was a burst of elven magic coming through the root system toward Lethorel.

Hopefully it was a message that Weylind, Rheva, Rharreth, and Leyleira were all right. Then he could let go of the last of his worries and get back to the life he and Essie had fought so hard to live.

The room in the infirmary remained quiet this late at night. Jalissa shifted on the chair grown into the wall next to the bed. The door to the room stood open, and Sarya had stationed herself outside in the hallway.

Edmund lay, still and sleeping, with the blanket pulled over him. Rheva had assured Jalissa that Edmund would be fine, once he rested and the healing magic completed its work. It had to go slowly, patching such a grievous wound without overstraining his human body.

Jalissa watched his chest rise and fall, the motion reassuring. The blanket had fallen partway down his chest, giving her a view of his bare, muscular shoulders and just a few curls of dark chest hair peeking above the blanket.

She dragged her gaze away, her mouth a little dry. Apparently, she found chest hair appealing. Odd, since male elves did not have facial hair or chest hair.

"Keep staring at me like that, and I might get the wrong impression."

Jalissa jumped, snapping her gaze up to Edmund's face. Her ears burned as she gaped at him.

His eyes were half-open, lids droopy, while a sleepy grin quirked his mouth. He drew one hand from underneath the blanket and held it out to her as if expecting her to take it. "First you don't want me to die, now I find you waiting at my bedside. Keep this up, and I'll get the idea that you like me."

"I do not…" She choked the words out, her mind a buzzing, panicking mess. She was not even sure how she planned to end that sentence.

Edmund's grin faded, and he withdrew his hand, resting it over his stomach instead. "I know you don't. It's just as well that I will never return to Tarenhiel. It seems I can't help flirting with you even when I know better. I'm sorry. I shouldn't have."

She opened her mouth, but no words came. What was she doing here, anyway? He was right. Staying at his side like this was the action of someone who loved him.

But she was still angry with him.

Or was she?

She did not know anymore. That gunshot, the sight of him falling…it had torn through her as surely as the bullet had him.

He had been a spy. He had toyed with her affections and hurt her deeply all those years ago by faking Elidyr's death. He had come up with this assassination plot in the first place.

Yet he had told her the truth when he could have let the secret remain dead with Elidyr. He had thrown himself between a bullet and her brother, saving Weylind's life.

His gaze swung to the ceiling, giving a sigh. "You have

always been my weakness, you know. When I attempted to contact Melantha in Kostaria, I did it for you, even though it went against all sense to try to contact her instead of observing from a distance. But I knew you would be worried about her, even if you were still angry with her."

And he had gotten captured doing it. Jalissa had been there, when Rharreth had dragged Edmund across the border and thrown him at King Averett's feet like a piece of trash he had found littering his palace floor.

Jalissa stared at her hands in her lap, not sure what to say to that.

But Edmund went on in that sleepy tone even without a response from her. The healing magic must be making him more relaxed, more ready to talk than normal.

"I didn't even contact Essie after she married Farrendel, even though I was here. I barely got back to Escarland before all of you arrived." He was still staring at the ceiling, his eyelids drooping even lower. "With my sister, I stuck to my training. But for you, I threw it all away."

That should not warm her as much as it did. As if she found it endearing.

"I broke all the rules by falling for someone I was spying on. A princess of the elves confiding her heart to me and, instead of using you to get to your brothers, I broke it off. I couldn't let you be hurt any more than you already were. If I were discovered to be a spy, you would have been caught up in the middle of it. I had risked your reputation, your future. I couldn't keep doing it. That's why I left. That's why I faked my death so you wouldn't search for me and make yourself appear the fool before your court. It was all I could think to do to protect you."

Jalissa studied his profile, even as his words dug deep inside her chest.

She had blamed him, but he was not the only one at fault for their clandestine romance. She had been the one to keep seeking him out. She had bared her heart to him without his ever asking probing questions. And yet, even though she had foolishly met him alone at night again and again, he had never taken advantage of her, not even for information about her brothers. He had not so much as kissed her, showing far more wisdom than she had even though she had been older than him at that point.

If he had gained any information about the war effort, Weylind, or Farrendel, it had been because she had blurted it out to him before he had even asked for it.

When he had faked Elidyr's death, he had saved Jalissa from herself. That experience had made her grow up. Become a little wiser.

Yes, she wished there had been a way for him to handle it better. But he had been right. He could not have told her the truth that he was a spy without jeopardizing his kingdom or risking a war. Back then, he had been about the same age as Farrendel was now. Or, at least, equivalent to the age Farrendel had been when he married Essie before the heart bond caused him to age faster.

"I had to spend months re-establishing a new cover in a location that was not as well-placed as Ellonahshinel. I wrecked Escarland's spying activities in Tarenhiel for months because of you." Edmund tilted his head toward her again, a hint of a smile back on his face. "If I had still been spying in Ellonahshinel, I wouldn't have been late returning to report to Averett. He might not have agreed to the marriage between Essie and Farrendel. I was rather angry about that, you know. I would have gladly sacrificed myself to a marriage of alliance, knowing I would get to marry you."

Jalissa's breath caught, her mind whirling. What would have happened, if she had been the sibling Weylind had agreed to marry off instead of Farrendel? She would have found herself married to Edmund for the past year.

Even as her heart beat harder, she knew she and Edmund never could have done what Elspetha and Farrendel did. It had taken two people as forgiving as Elspetha and Farrendel to forge their love and bring their two peoples together.

But back then, Jalissa and Edmund had too many secrets between them. He would have eventually confessed, and she would have harbored anger and bitterness toward him, as she did now. The two of them would have destroyed the alliance, instead of building it the way Farrendel and Elspetha had.

His eyes sank all the way closed, as if talking had exhausted him. Still, he kept talking, as if determined to spill his thoughts before she cast him out of her life forever. "I wanted to fix what I had broken. That's why I asked for the fake relationship. We ended things badly twice. I thought if I could end things in a good way, for once, then maybe you would be all right. A foolish hope, it turns out. All I managed to do was hurt you even worse. I am so sorry."

"Edmund…" His name squeaked from her aching throat.

His eyes flicked open briefly as he glanced at her, reaching his hand out to her again as if he wanted to touch her but stopping short. "Even if it hasn't worked out between us, I'm glad I know you, Jalissa. I will treasure what we had, wherever we go from here."

He let her go with such a lack of bitterness that it jarred something inside her.

She did not even recognize or like herself anymore. She had been nursing bitterness for so long. First against Melantha, then Edmund. Almost without her realizing it, she had turned into everything she had despised about Melantha. Withdrawn. Bitter. Consumed with herself and with her own problems.

Could she forgive him? Forgive Melantha? Would that finally banish the pain that had squeezed her heart for the past several months?

Slowly, she reached out and took his hand. It remained limp in her grip, his chest rising and falling with his steady breaths. He had fallen back asleep. Rest was what his body needed, so she should not feel so disappointed.

Jalissa lifted their clasped hands and leaned her cheek against their fingers. She was tired of being bitter and alone behind her calm mask. Perhaps it was finally time to forgive and start healing.

SHE WOKE to a groan and a tugging against her hand. When she peeled her eyes open, she found that she had curled against the wall, her hand still gripping Edmund's.

He had propped himself up on an elbow as he tried to ease his fingers from her hold. When he glanced up, his gaze snagging on hers, he gave that quirked smile again. "Sorry I woke you. But this"—he held up their clasped hands—"is really going to give someone the wrong impression if you aren't careful."

Her heart lurched inside her chest, and she snatched her hand out of his, glancing toward the door.

Sarya lay across the doorway, sleeping. Or doing a very good job of pretending to be asleep. No one else seemed to be around, and the night outside the window remained inky black. Only a few hours had passed.

Edmund pushed himself all the way into a sitting position, hunching and giving another groan.

"No, do not get up. You need to rest." Jalissa rolled to her feet and reached to set a hand on his shoulder, intending to make him lie back down.

But she stopped short of touching him as she realized the blanket had slipped down to Edmund's waist when he had sat up. Lean muscles corded his shoulders, arms, and chest, while a bandage wrapped around his middle. That chest… and the little curls of dark hair…

She was not sure where to look. Or not to look. Her ears were on fire, her mouth so dry she could not even swallow.

"If it makes you uncomfortable, maybe you can find me a shirt?" Edmund made a noise in the back of his throat, as if he, too, were uncomfortable.

A shirt. Yes. That would help make him less…distracting.

Jalissa whirled and searched the far side of the room for several seconds, not really seeing it. Finally, she blinked and forced herself to focus.

Shelves filled the far wall. Most held bandages and some jars of juice to be used in medicine. But there on a bottom shelf rested a stack of plain green shirts and trousers.

She all but lunged across the room for them, kneeling before the shelves.

"Is there any word from Lethorel?" Edmund's voice came from behind her.

"Yes. Farrendel and Elspetha captured the last two spies, and no one was hurt. They are on their way back to Estyra even now." Jalissa picked up one of the shirts, trying to pretend her hand was not trembling. After a moment, she also grabbed a pair of trousers. She was not sure what was left of Edmund's after all the blood, and it would be better just to give it to him now rather than wait and have him awkwardly ask later.

"Good." Edmund stated that one word with the finality of someone who just had a decision confirmed as the right one.

Blindly, she crossed the room and thrust the clothes at him, trying not to look but catching a peek of his chest anyway before she stepped away and turned her back to him. "Do you wish for me to leave?"

"No. Just..." He made another muffled noise of pain. "Just give me a moment."

Perhaps she should stay, just to make sure he did not pass out trying to get dressed. "The healing magic is still working."

"I expected as much." More pained gasps and rustling came from behind her. "I've never had the pleasure of experiencing an elven healing before."

"You were never hurt while spying?" Jalissa kept her voice low as she faced the open door. Sarya had not awakened, even with all their talking. Her guard had been exhausted, but Jalissa would not put it past her to be pretending in order to give Jalissa this moment of semi-privacy.

"I was. But it wasn't like I could risk an elven healing." That hint of easy laughter was back in his voice. "They were sure to notice I was a human in elf's clothing.

The questions would have been a little awkward to answer."

"I can see that." Jalissa blinked down at her hands. If she had asked more questions back then, what would he have told her? How would she have reacted?

Maybe those were not the right questions, as her machasheni would say. The past was done. Neither of them could change it.

But she could control how she reacted now, and that would shape their future.

"You can turn around now."

When Jalissa turned, she found Edmund standing with one hand braced against the wall. He wore both the shirt and the trousers she had given him, the sleeves and ends of the trousers a few inches too long.

For the first time, Prince Edmund wore green.

Her gaze lifted to those eyes of his, the ones that now appeared more green than blue when surrounded by the deep greens of this place.

He took a step, one hand pressed over his healing wound and the other still braced against the wall. "Jalissa, I need to leave."

Her promise. The one she had all but extorted from him. She would have happily smacked her past self.

She did not want him to leave. Not anymore.

Almost before she realized it, she crossed the remaining space between them and rested a hand on his chest, halting him. "No. You do not have to leave. I do not wish to ban you from Tarenhiel."

He stilled. Then, slowly, he took his hand from the wall and rested it against Jalissa's waist. "Do you mean that?"

Jalissa nodded, staring at the green fabric of his shirt as

she forced the words past the lump in her throat. "I forgive you. I do not want to be bitter and angry all the time. We both made a lot of mistakes back then. You are not the only one who carries blame. I was just as free to walk away as you were, but you were the one with the strength to actually do the right thing and break it off before we hurt our kingdoms along with our hearts."

"Jalissa…" Edmund's other hand came up to cup her cheek. A layer of stubble darkened his jaw while shadows pooled beneath his eyes, the toll of the healing on him.

"You fight for Tarenhiel just as hard as you used to fight against us. First in Kostaria, and just now when you saved Weylind." She dug her fingers into the soft shirt, pulling him even closer. "Do you think we can try again? One more time?"

"The fourth time's the charm?" His mouth quirked in that grin she adored, his face only inches from hers. His thumb traced her cheek, sending shivers down her spine.

She swayed closer, their breaths mingling and heated between them. Would he finally kiss her? How she wanted him to kiss her.

Instead of erasing that last inch of space, he eased back, though he did not release her. His voice was low, his eyes strangely sad. "I still need to leave."

"What?" Jalissa tightened her grip on his shirt. No. He could not do this to her again. Nearly kiss her, then walk away.

"One more mission." Edmund's gaze held hers, as if willing her to understand. "I need to make sure Farrendel and Essie will stay safe, and to do that, I need to deliver a warning to the king of Mongavaria."

"I will go with you." The words burst from her before she

had even thought them through. But she did not regret them, nor did she wish to take them back. To choose Edmund would mean choosing to walk through this shadowy danger at his side.

Unlike before, he was not walking away with no explanation. He was trusting her by telling her of his mission. If his resolve to leave in the middle of the night was any indication, he did not intend to tell many other people.

"Not this time." That gentle touch of his thumb was back on her cheek, melting her knees until only her grip on his shirt kept her upright. "I will be traveling fast, sleeping in ditches and hitching rides on trains when I can. I'll stand a better chance of evading capture if I go alone."

She did not like it, but she nodded. Perhaps if they were married it would be different but dragging both her and Sarya across Mongavaria while trying to preserve her reputation would slow him down. If they had been discovered in Escarland or Tarenhiel, it would have been embarrassing but nothing more. Mongavaria would be a different story. If Edmund were captured, he would likely be shot as a spy. He needed all the advantages he could get.

Especially now that he could not even contact anyone from Escarland's established spy network in Mongavaria. There was a good chance the Mongavarian king might even now be arresting them, if Escarland had not managed to get a warning to them in time.

"I understand." Jalissa drew herself together. If she could not go with him, then she could help him before he left. "But allow me to gather some supplies for you before you leave. Rest while you can."

"Linshi, my amirah." Edmund's quiet elvish sent another shiver down her back. He had spoken those words to her as

Elidyr, but now he said them in his own tone of voice. He pulled her closer again. "This is my last mission. When I return, we'll talk about where we go from here. I want to do this right this time. No more secrets. No more fake courtships or lies."

That was why he had not kissed her. He was too honorable to kiss her now, when he was giving her more time to think about what she wanted before he returned.

Still, a farewell kiss would have been nice.

"I will be waiting." Feeling daring, Jalissa rested her hand against his cheek, his stubble scratchy beneath her palm. It took a great deal of willpower, but after a moment, she forced herself to drop her hand and step out of his arms. "Rest. I will return shortly with supplies."

He sank back onto the bed, a sigh escaping him as if he was more tired than he wished to admit even to himself.

Jalissa tiptoed from the room, stepping over Sarya where she still lay across the doorway.

As Jalissa started down the short hallway between the other private rooms in the infirmary, she heard the soft scrape of Sarya rising, then her footsteps following.

When Jalissa stepped outside onto the porch, she glanced over her shoulder at Sarya. "How much did you hear?"

Sarya's expression remained smooth, giving nothing away, though her eyes had a slight twinkle to them in the starlight. "Nothing, if you do not want me to, amirah."

Jalissa was not sure what she had done to earn such loyalty from Sarya, but she was grateful. Sarya had not complained, even as she was dragged through the back streets of Aldon, across Escarland on that uncomfortable train, then across Tarenhiel. "Linshi. I know this is not exactly what you signed up for when you volunteered as my guard."

A hint of a smile broke through Sarya's normally blank expression. "It has not been boring, amirah."

Sarya said it as if she considered that a good thing. That brought an answering smile from Jalissa. "It will be even less boring in the future, I think."

EDMUND SPRAWLED ON THE BED, eyes closed, as he waited for Jalissa to return. He probably should be planning out his next moves. After all, he would be going into Mongavaria blind. It was just the sort of unprepared, last-minute mission that caused a spy to make mistakes and get himself into trouble.

But all he could think about was Jalissa. The way he had woken to find her sleeping in the seating nook next to the bed. In sleep, she wore her serene expression, though it was even more gentle and peaceful. Her fingers had felt so small and delicate in his, yet her grip had been strong enough that he hadn't been able to ease his hand free without waking her.

And her forgiveness...he had not expected it. Had not dared to hope.

He had meant what he said. This time, he would treat her heart like the precious thing it was. He had wounded her far too many times already. This time, he would do things right.

Perhaps this was the reason they had never managed to make their romance work before. There had always been too much between them. They had needed to fail so many times to strip away his secrets.

That, and for him to grow up a little. He had been barely more than a boy, back when he had first fallen for her. While he was only a handful of years older, he was ages wiser. Heartbreak, years of spying, and a war had matured him into the man he was now.

Quiet footsteps padded into the infirmary and scuffled around the main room a moment before tiptoeing down the hall.

He opened his eyes and pushed back into a sitting position. Pain flared deep inside his stomach, lancing from his middle all the way to his back. He breathed through it, thankful when it faded after a moment. He was not as healed as he should be for a mission like this. But, hopefully, he would be fine by the time he had to cross the Hydalla River at the Tarenhieli border with Mongavaria.

Jalissa entered the room with a small pouch in her hands. Her skin seemed paler than it had been before, her hands a little shaky. Behind her, Sarya trailed after her, carrying a larger pack.

Edmund raised his eyebrows. That was the standard issue elven pack made of canvas and leather straps, including the green blanket tied to the top.

Sarya met his gaze, shrugged, and held it out to him. "I will not need it."

"Linshi." He took it, feeling its heft. It was full, but they had done well in not packing too heavily.

"Since the palace kitchen burned to the ground, we scrounged food from my cold cupboard, as well as some items from Elspetha and Farrendel's rooms. I did not think they would mind." Jalissa toyed with the pouch she held in her hands rather than look at him. "We also added some jars of juice laced with elven healing magic. They will not be powerful enough to heal you if you are near death, but they will help if you are injured."

"I'm sure they will be useful." Having elven magic on his side was convenient. He stood and shrugged into the pack, wincing as the movement tugged at his healing middle. If he were smart, he would wait until he was fully healed before leaving.

But he wasn't sure what Averett or Weylind would think of this mission. It was probably better if they had plausible deniability, if he were caught.

Besides, he didn't want to give the Mongavarian king time to regroup and come up with a new plan.

Jalissa's shoulders straightened, and she held out the pouch. "Here. I made these for you."

He opened the pouch and peered inside. What looked like five balls made from an ivy, glowing faintly green, filled the pouch. "What are these?"

"Do not touch them except with gloves." Jalissa bit her lower lip, her gaze flicking to him, then to the floor. "As soon as they touch skin, they will spring to life and immobilize whoever they are touching. They are strong enough to withstand knives or swords. But they will only last an hour. Then they will wither away into dust, leaving behind no trace. I am sorry I could not make more. My magic is not strong enough."

"Your magic is plenty strong. These are amazing." Edmund carefully closed the pouch and tied it to his belt, which he had found next to his boots and a pile of his weapons at the foot of the bed. He would have to use these sparingly, but they might solve his problem on how to get close enough to the Mongavarian king to deliver his threat.

He stepped closer to her again, resting a hand on her waist. "Linshi. Truly. These could save my life."

Behind Jalissa, Sarya silently stepped from the room. She halted outside the open door, giving them some semblance of privacy while also protecting Jalissa's reputation.

"I hope they help." Jalissa smoothed her hands down the leather straps of the pack he wore. "I want you to come back safe."

"I will." He probably shouldn't make such promises. But, if he made a promise, he would be even more determined to keep it.

How he wanted to kiss her. What if he were caught and killed? What if this was his last moment with her?

No, he would return. He refused to dwell on any other option. A spy who thought he might fail would make that reality come true. A spy only succeeded by having the supreme confidence that he could pull off his mission.

Still, he forced himself to stick to business rather than give in to the temptation. If he was going to do this right with Jalissa, then there would be no kissing until after they were properly and officially courting.

He laced his fingers with hers. "In the morning, tell Weylind where I have gone. He will pass the news on to my brother."

"All right." Despite the pain in her eyes, Jalissa held her back straight. There was steel in her, hidden beneath the serene exterior.

"I think Farrendel should do that thing with his magic that he did along the Tarenhieli-Kostarian border. The one that prevents the trolls from sending raiding parties into Tarenhiel anymore." Edmund dropped his gaze, shifting. "I don't think I'll start a war with my warning but it wouldn't hurt for the borders of both Escarland and Tarenhiel to be secured. Just in case."

"I will ask him once he and Elspetha arrive in Estyra." Jalissa's gaze focused on his shirt for a moment before she lifted her eyes to his. "How long will you be gone?"

"Three weeks. A month at the most." Unless he found himself walking all the way there and back, that should be more than enough time. If he didn't get back in a month, well, then he wasn't going to be coming back at all. "I'll be back before you know it."

She pressed her mouth into a tight line, blinking and staring down at the floor again.

He lifted their clasped hands and kissed her knuckles gently. "And when I return, I'll ask if I may court you. Properly, this time."

Gaze flying to his, she drew in a breath, opening her mouth as if to reply.

He quickly pressed his finger over her mouth, halting whatever she had been about to say, much as he wanted to press her for an answer now.

But he had made that mistake before, pressing for an answer when he should have been patient. There in the cold, Kostarian snow, she had turned him down. She had been right to do so, truthfully.

"No, don't give me your answer yet." He forced a smile as he dropped his hand. "Keep me in suspense a little longer. It gives me another reason to hurry back to you."

Right now, she was running on high emotion. She had been furious with him, then she had seen him nearly die, then she had forgiven him. She needed—no, deserved—time to process and be confident in her answer before she gave it.

Besides, they had plenty to talk about before they started

a courtship that, based on how serious they already were, would end in marriage. There were things like heart bonds and if she was willing to give up hundreds of years of her life for him.

This time, he wanted no regrets for either of them.

She nodded, but she gripped his hand again. "Do not hurry back too fast. I do not wish you to make mistakes because you were hasty. I am willing to wait longer, if it means that you will return safely."

"Of course." He thought about kissing her knuckles again but resisted. He had to walk away one last time. Releasing her hand, he stepped past her. "Don't worry. I'm a very good spy."

With that, he forced himself to walk out the door. In moments, he strode into the night without looking back.

THIRTY-THREE

Essie tottered from the Tarenhieli train and onto the platform in Estyra, still rubbing sleep from her eyes. If not for Farrendel's steadying hand on her elbow, she might have fallen flat on her face. "Ugh. I don't want to get on a train again. At least, not until I stop puking every time I'm on or in something moving."

"That may be difficult." Instead of Farrendel, it was Weylind answering her in a far-too-serious tone.

When she glanced up, she found Weylind waiting for them on the platform, arms crossed. Essie gave another groan and leaned into Farrendel. Of course Weylind would be standing right there and overhear.

She tried to surreptitiously glance down at her shirt and tunic, making sure she hadn't made a mess of herself while losing the contents of her stomach. Nope, she was still looking decent, even if she felt awful and icky.

"What is it, shashon?" Farrendel put his arm around her shoulders, holding her closer. "Are there more assassins?"

Jalissa stepped next to Weylind, her eyes a little red as if she had been crying. Still, she carried her head high, her movements graceful.

Essie blinked at her. Hadn't they left Jalissa back in Escarland? When had she arrived in Tarenhiel?

Jalissa's gaze swung to Essie, and her forehead furrowed. "Are you all right, isciena? You do not appear well."

Before Essie could do more than grip his shirt and turn toward him, Farrendel blurted out, "Trains do not agree with the baby."

"Baby?" Jalissa's eyes widened.

Essie groaned and let her head thunk onto Farrendel's shoulder. So far, he had managed to blurt it out to Melantha, Weylind, Brina, and Ryfon. The whole family was going to know at this rate. "You did it *again*."

He gave a wince. "Sorry."

"At least promise me I'll get to tell my brothers before you blab the news." She relaxed her grip on his shirt. He would know through the heart bond that she wasn't mad, not really.

With Farrendel's anxiety, she had wondered how he would react to the news of a child on the way. She would take *so excited he couldn't keep the secret for the life of him* over crushing panic attacks. There were still a few of those, but far less than there would have been had he not worked so hard to get to the healthier place he was now and kept up with the help that he needed to stay functional.

Essie's mother disembarked from the train behind them. She halted next to Essie. "You were able to tell me." Her smile swung to Farrendel. "But you can't help it if the father-to-be is too excited to keep the secret. Your father was always like that. It was such a struggle for him to keep the news to himself before we made the official announcement to the kingdom."

Essie didn't have many memories of her father, but she could picture her father's exuberance. It must have looked a little bit like the smile he'd had when picking her up and twirling her around until she couldn't stop giggling.

"Then Farrendel can be the one to make the official announcement in a press conference with all the reporters."

Next to her, he stiffened. "What?"

She grinned up at him. "Well, if you're going to go around blurting it to everyone, I might as well give you the joy of telling the entire kingdom."

He gave her a forehead-furrowing, tight-mouthed baleful look. "I am only telling friends and family in Tarenhiel. Escarland's people are all yours."

"I thought that threat might work." She patted his chest, then stepped back. They were probably making his family uncomfortable.

But instead of the shifting, looking-everywhere-but-at-them look she had expected, Weylind's mouth had a slight upward tilt.

Jalissa still gaped at them. "Baby," she repeated.

"Yes." Essie's grin was so wide it almost hurt. "Surprise."

Jalissa shook herself, laughed, and stepped forward to grip Farrendel's shoulders in an elven hug. "I am so happy for you, shashon."

"Linshi, isciena." Farrendel let go of Essie to return his sister's shoulder clasp.

When Jalissa turned to her, Essie didn't wait for Jalissa to give her a staid, elven shoulder clasp. It just wasn't enough for the joy of the moment. Instead, Essie pulled Jalissa in for a human hug.

Yet, Jalissa surprised her by giving her a hug back. "And I am happy for you, isciena."

And, when they stepped back, the smile on Jalissa's face held a depth of joy that had been missing in the past half a year or better.

What had happened while Essie and Farrendel and the others hid out at Lethorel? They had been gone less than a week.

While Jalissa had been congratulating them, Ryfon and Brina had disembarked from the train and were currently exchanging hugs with Weylind and Rheva. Their elven hugs, too, seemed a bit more emotional than elves normally got in public.

Melantha had left the train as well and was now embracing Rharreth. And…were they kissing? In public? Kostaria had really done a number on Melantha's elven sensibilities.

Machasheni Leyleira strolled forward and faced Essie and Farrendel. "You have my congratulations. This is indeed happy news that should be shared."

Wait, how did she find out? Essie gave herself a mental shake as she hugged Leyleira as well. One didn't question how Machasheni knew things. She had her sources, and they were impeccable.

Farrendel exchanged a shoulder clasp hug with his grandmother. "Linshi, machasheni."

Essie gave another exaggerated sigh. "Well, all of your family now knows. I guess I'll tell my brothers the next time I see them, whenever that is. Maybe by then I'll be able to plan a proper announcement."

Weylind faced them again, making a muffled, throat-clearing noise that was as undignified as he ever got whenever her brothers weren't around to make him loosen up. "Actually, we will be leaving as soon as the way is cleared to Escarland."

Essie moaned and buried her face into Farrendel's shoulder again. "Ugh. Not another train ride. My stomach is going to kill me."

"You do not have to come if you are not up to it, isciena." Weylind's tone had far too much sympathy in it, as if he hadn't picked up on the joke in her complaint. "We only need Farrendel."

"But he's going to see my brothers, isn't he?" Essie tilted her head so that she could glance at Weylind.

"Yes."

"Then I'd better go along. Otherwise Mr. I-can't-keep-this-one-secret will let it slip." Essie swallowed back her nausea. "Rheva or Melantha will come, right?"

"Rharreth has already agreed to come, so, yes, I believe Melantha will come as well." Weylind glanced over his shoulder at the two of them. They had stopped kissing, so they were able to nod as if they had been listening demurely to the whole conversation.

Rharreth shrugged, still holding Melantha's hand. "We planned to travel to Escarland anyway."

Farrendel wrapped an arm around Essie again, that wrinkle back in his forehead. "What is this about? Why do you need me? Has Mongavaria attacked Escarland?"

"No, but that is what we plan to prevent." Weylind gestured at the train behind them, as if everything had already been decided. Perhaps it had.

Essie shared a look with Farrendel and said loud enough for Weylind to hear, "Your brother is being cryptic again."

Weylind huffed. "I will explain on the train. There is no need to stand around here talking."

Farrendel raised his eyebrows at Essie. "He does have a point."

"You're just hoping you will no longer be the center of attention once we get back on the train. I see how it is."

"Can I come?" Ryfon's eager tone drew Essie's focus back to the others. Ryfon was facing Weylind, coming as close as an elf prince ever did to bouncing up and down in excitement. "Please? I never get to see Uncle Farrendel actually do amazing stuff with his magic. I just hear about it afterwards. It is not the same."

Weylind scowled, opening his mouth as if to refuse by habit.

Before he could, Brina joined Ryfon, her eyes big and brown and full-on puppy-dog pleading. She even had her hands clasped. "Please. You keep promising that I will be able to visit Escarland. All the assassins have been caught. It is safe now. Please."

Rheva rested a hand first on Ryfon's shoulder, then on Brina's, before she met Weylind's gaze with that soft but unbudging look of hers. "The anniversary of the treaty is next week. After everything that has happened, it would be good for us to show support for the treaty and for Elspetha and Farrendel by joining in the festivities on that side of the border."

Weylind blew out a breath that was so frustrated it even had a hint of a growl to it. "Fine, fine. A joint goodwill appearance with King Averett, King Rharreth, and myself would not be amiss, I suppose."

Rheva gave a small, satisfied smile. Essie had to hand it

to her. Her sister-in-law did not gainsay Weylind often, but when she did, she made it count.

Jalissa stepped forward, opening her mouth to speak.

Before she could get out a single word, Weylind turned on her. "No. Absolutely not. We will already have the entire royal family of Tarenhiel and Kostaria on a single train. We need at least one heir to stay behind in case there is still one angry Escarlish, Tarenhieli, Mongavarian, or Kostarian citizen who decides to go on a rampage and blow up the train. Which is not out of the realm of possibility, given the events of the past year. Granted, Farrendel can likely shield the train from such an explosion in that event, but you still need to remain here. No scurrying off this time, understood?"

Jalissa made something of a strangled noise in the back of her throat, starting to speak.

Weylind kept barreling right over her, as if he had weeks of pent-up scolding just waiting to be unleashed. "Besides, you just want to go along to stare across into Mongavaria with a lovestruck melancholy that I do not want to witness. He will not even be there or meet us at the border, so you might as well do your lovestruck staring while safe here in Estyra."

Wait, was that *he* referring to her brother Edmund? Essie glanced between Jalissa and Weylind. Was Edmund in Mongavaria? What was he doing there? Just what had gone down here in Estyra? All Weylind's message had said was that the spies had been caught and it was safe to return.

But Weylind continued his rant without giving Essie a chance to interrupt to ask. "You can keep your machasheni company, since she *will not be coming either*." At that last part, he turned his glare from Jalissa onto Leyleira.

"Of course not. Jalissa and I are due for a tea and a good long talk. Now are you quite finished, sasonsheni?" Leyleira's tone and eyebrow lift made it quite clear that Weylind was, indeed, finished, whether he wanted to be or not.

"Yes, machasheni." Weylind didn't exactly squirm beneath his grandmother's stare, but the suggestion of squirming was there in his voice.

Essie tried to keep a straight face. Even an elf king listened to his grandmother when she used that tone of voice.

For a moment, everyone just stood there in an awkward silence. Then Rheva stepped forward and rested a light hand on Weylind's arm. "My dear, worry is making you grumpy again."

Weylind reached to take her hand. It was such a rare, sweet moment to see between them, that Essie nearly turned away rather than interrupt.

But an awkward weight remained after Weylind's words, and someone needed to dispel it.

She dragged Farrendel forward. "I think Weylind needs a hug."

That had both Weylind and Farrendel stiffening. But before either of them could make a run for it, Essie gave Weylind a side hug, keeping a grip on Farrendel's hand so that he was somewhat dragged into the hug as well.

As the others gaped at her, Essie motioned. "Come on. Group hug."

Weylind made a kind of squawking sound at that, holding his arms out as if he wasn't sure what to do with them. Essie couldn't see his face, but she was pretty sure he was giving Farrendel one of those *Please call off your human* looks.

Rheva's smile widened, and she wrapped her arms around Weylind's waist in a tentative human-style hug. "I think a hug is an excellent idea."

Then, Ryfon grinned, sharing a look with Brina, before the two of them piled in, hugging Weylind, Rheva, and anyone else they could get their arms around. That had Melantha laughing before she joined in, squishing Farrendel between her and Essie. Jalissa shook her head, but hugged Rheva and Weylind. Even Leyleira delicately hugged Ryfon and Brina.

Weylind heaved a sigh and pointed to Rharreth, the only one who hadn't joined the group hug. "If I have to endure this, then you do too."

Rharreth smirked, his white hair and teeth flashing in the early morning sunlight, before he stepped in. With his large, burly arms, he gathered up a whole bunch of them and squeezed.

Now it was Essie's turn to give a groaning laugh. She hadn't thought this through all that well. She was now smashed between Weylind and Farrendel in the center of the group hug.

"Fine, fine. I am not grumpy." Weylind's tone had that fake scowling note he had when he was amused but didn't want to admit it.

Good. The last thing Essie wanted to do was be stuck on a train for hours with a glowering Weylind. Especially since she was likely going to feel miserable the entire way as it was. She didn't need him making it worse.

THIRTY-FOUR

J alissa stood on the platform, watching the train disappear into the green, leafy tunnel of trees that arched over the train tracks. All too soon, the silver train was nothing but flashes among the trunks until even that disappeared.

She understood why Weylind had wanted her to stay behind, even if he had been grumpily high-handed about it.

But for the first time in months, she did not want to cut herself off from her family while her heart was aching. This was the kind of ache that was soothed by being around people who were waiting for Edmund's return alongside her.

She drew her shoulders straight. Edmund would not want her to spend her time moping while he was gone.

"With Weylind gone, I should oversee the rebuilding of the kitchens." She was not sure who she was telling. Her machasheni was still there, but other than that, they were alone except for Sarya and the other remaining guards.

But now that Jalissa had said it out loud, the resolve filled

403

her. She might not be the strongest with her plant growing magic, but she could help. She had taken down two of the spy-assassins, and she had created those vines for Edmund to help him on his mission.

If anything, her magic was more suited for things like creating portable growing magic. Weylind's magic was so powerful that, like Farrendel, he had to expend great effort and concentration to keep it contained. But her magic was willing to be small, be patient, in order to fulfill its single purpose.

"Yes, we will both see to the rebuilding efforts." Machasheni Leyleira faced the direction of Ellonahshinel. "But first, tea."

"It is a little early for teatime." Jalissa fell into step with her grandmother's brisk strides.

"But never too early for tea," Machasheni said with that same finality that she had used on Weylind.

"The kitchens are in ruins. Can we even make tea?" Jalissa glanced ahead as they strolled the main street of Estyra. After all the excitement of the previous day and night, the street remained peaceful and subdued. A few people nodded as they passed, acknowledging their princess and former queen. At the far end of the street, the charred remains of the kitchens smeared black against the otherwise green and vibrant forest.

"Farrendel, the dear boy, gave me one of his heating devices." Machasheni Leyleira wore a contented smile, even as they faced the wreckage the Mongavarian spies had left behind. "I quite enjoy the convenience of being able to make tea whenever I wish, no matter the time of day or night."

"He is quite proud of those devices." He had offered her one, since he had a few extras after that sledding and

404

boarding event he and Elspetha had hosted during the winter. At the time, she had turned him down, not wishing to see anything that reminded her of humans—and of one human in particular.

Another person she had hurt while having her pity party. When she saw Farrendel again, she would have to ask if he still had one available. Or if he could make her one. Maybe he would even let her help. It sounded rather fascinating, how he melded human mechanics and elven magic.

"He will go far with his magic, I believe." Machasheni nodded, as if in approval of the future she was envisioning for Farrendel. "I have seen many centuries come and go. I have witnessed the humans and their innovations change our world again and again. Now, the humans are in a particularly inventive period. It will be to our people's benefit if we learn to make those inventions our own."

Jalissa nodded, thinking about the things she had seen in Aldon on her visits. There was great good in holding to traditions and history and old ways of doing things.

But her people tended to get stuck in the past, their world as nearly unchanging as their years. That kind of naivete would only get them swallowed up by some power-hungry, expanding human empire.

Like Mongavaria. Like Escarland could become, if they had a less honorable king.

Jalissa and Leyleira had to pass the ruins as they climbed the stairs, the acrid smell of smoke still lingering in the air.

Tarenhiel had already adopted some things, like trains. But, it had stalled there.

Elspetha and Farrendel had pushed Tarenhiel to look beyond its borders once again. His and Elspetha's child would further that end, a child of both kingdoms.

Jalissa and Edmund could work for that goal as well. Elspetha and Farrendel mostly stayed outside of the court. They were the prince and princess of the common people. Well-loved, but with little power among the nobility.

But Edmund was devious, and Jalissa was the perfect elven princess. Together, they could play—and win—the game of court intrigue and manipulation.

Edmund was a chameleon, adapting his outward personality to whatever was expected of him. But then again, so was she. It had felt so natural to her, conforming to expectations, that she had not even questioned it.

Someone else might try to change that trait of hers. They might dismiss her serene conformity as a weakness.

Edmund saw it as an asset. They could adapt together and, together, they would keep each other from losing the heart of who they were, even as they navigated through their masks.

Their families would help, of course. Their relationships kept them grounded, something Jalissa had lost by withdrawing in her hurt and pain.

Machasheni Leyleira led the way through the branching pathways of Ellonahshinel, and they arrived at her suite of rooms far too quickly.

Well, Jalissa was not going to put off this conversation with her grandmother any longer. But for the first time in a long while, Machasheni Leyleira's piercing gaze did not scare her. "If you are going to tell me that you told me so, I have already figured that out."

As she opened the door to her main room, Machasheni glanced at Jalissa, raising an eyebrow. "I believe it was your sister who told you so."

Jalissa winced. Yes, Melantha had tried to retract the bad

advice she had originally given. But Jalissa had not listened, far too stuck in her misery and anger. "I know. As soon as I can, I will talk with her."

She had hoped to have a chance on the train ride to Escarland, but Weylind had taken away that opportunity.

No matter. Melantha and Rharreth had to travel back through Tarenhiel to return to Kostaria when they finished with their business in Escarland. Jalissa would talk to Melantha then. Surely if Machasheni thought it a good idea, then she would ensure, in that no-nonsense way of hers, that Melantha did not leave Tarenhiel until the two of them had talked.

"Good. See that you do." Machasheni bustled inside. "Fill the kettle with water, senasheni."

Jalissa found the kettle next to one of Farrendel's heating devices and filled it with water from the tap. By the time she had figured out how to turn the heating device on, Machasheni Leyleira had set out two teacups, the china decorated with a delicate and elegant floral pattern, as well as the things for tea.

Machasheni Leyleira took a seat at the table while they waited for the water to heat. She gestured at the chair across from her. An order for Jalissa to sit as well.

After checking that the heating device appeared to be working, Jalissa reached for the indicated chair.

"And that young man of yours? Were you able to come to an understanding before he left?"

Jalissa's hand froze on the chair, the tips of her ears heating. It took all her self-control to pull out the chair without fumbling and gracefully slide onto it.

Her heart beating faster, harder, against her ribcage, she forced herself to meet her machasheni's gaze. "Yes, we were." How much did she dare tell Machasheni Leyleira? How much did her machasheni already know? "We still have a few things to discuss when he returns, but things are finally all right between us."

Better than all right, but she was not about to tell her machasheni that.

"Very good." Machasheni Leyleira regarded her across the table, those dark, piercing eyes searching hers. "You have learned a valuable lesson. Yes, it is perilous to follow the whims of your heart without listening to your head. But it can also be just as dangerous to listen entirely to your head without regarding the warnings and wisdom of the heart."

Jalissa dropped her gaze down to her empty teacup on the table before her. She had made both mistakes in recent years.

With Edmund, in his Elidyr disguise, she had followed her heart without heeding the warnings of her head.

Then she had gone the other way in the past few months by trying to force herself to simply pick someone to marry all on the cold logic of her head without regarding the promptings of her heart.

"Ask yourself. Is it right? Is it true? Is it honorable and good? If both your head and your heart can answer *yes* with honesty, then more than likely, that decision is the right one."

Jalissa nodded. When Machasheni spoke about the heart, she did not mean just the shallow, surface feelings. She meant the *heart*. The part of a person that knew right and wrong and felt the deep, moving emotions of love and sorrow and joy.

Perhaps Edmund had been wise, in giving her these weeks to ponder everything before she agreed to court him.

It was time she finally stopped to truly think about this decision.

Was courting Edmund right? Was it true, honorable, and good?

In their attempts before, when secrets and possible war had stood between them, she was not sure she could have said yes to all those questions.

But this time, she wanted to answer *yes*. She wanted their courtship to be based on what was right, true, good, and honorable.

She had three or more weeks to make sure that both her head and her heart were in the right place before she gave her answer to Edmund. Here, in an Ellonahshinel that was especially quiet without the rest of her family, she would have the peace for such soul-searching.

arrendel climbed down from the Escarlish train, nearly as thankful as Essie to finally stop traveling. She leaned against him, pale even with both Rheva and Melantha taking turns keeping her nausea at bay long enough for her to keep something down.

Above them, the Whitehurst Mountains loomed high into the brilliant blue sky. At this time of spring, the fields spreading out from the base of the mountains gleamed green while the green continued in ever darkening shades all the way to the forested peaks. Unlike the taller, craggier mountains of Kostaria, the Whitehurst Mountains were rolling, forested mountains, all green and earth instead of stone and ice.

Farrendel frowned at the mountains ahead of him. Would he even be able to embed a protective wall of his magic along this border? He had been able to do so along the Gulmorth Gorge since that was stone. These mountains had stone inside them, but it was deep beneath a layer of earth and loam. Nor would he have something as definite as a river to follow to find the border.

Around them, the army fort bustled with activity in the confines of an ancient stone fortress. The towers had been converted to hold large cannon facing toward the mountains while the men marching through the courtyard held guns instead of swords.

More of the human soldiers stumbled and gaped as Weylind, Rheva, Ryfon, Brina, Rharreth, Melantha, and Essie's mother climbed down from the train.

Both Weylind and Rharreth cast calculating looks at their surroundings, taking in Escarland's defenses along this section of border with the knowing eyes of experienced warriors.

For their part, Ryfon and Brina stared around at the castle with wide eyes. As neither of them had seen the encampments during the war, this was their first time seeing any part of the Escarlish army up close.

"Just wait until they see Aldon." Essie managed to smile up at Farrendel, despite the circles beneath her eyes after the rough couple of days.

"Yes."

The bustle of soldiers parted, emitting Essie's brothers Averett and Julien. Averett wore a circlet on his auburn hair. Behind him, Julien's expression remained slightly grim, framed by his beard.

"Glad you made it!" Averett's gaze swung from Weylind to Essie, and his smile faded. "Essie, are you all right?"

Before Farrendel could blink, Essie clapped a hand over his mouth and blurted in a rush, "I'm expecting."

Averett halted and blinked, forehead wrinkling. "Excuse me, did I hear that right?"

"Yes. Farrendel and I are expecting. It's early yet, but *someone* can't seem to keep it a secret." Essie fake-glared up at Farrendel as she removed the hand from his mouth.

"I was not going to tell them." He had spent most of the train ride rehearsing his vague answer to the *What is wrong with Essie?* question so that he would not get caught off guard and blurt out the truth again.

"This time." Essie held her pretend glare for another second before she grinned and stood on tiptoes to kiss his cheek. "I love you."

Farrendel did not have a chance to respond before Averett and Julien were on them.

"Congratulations!"

He endured a body-slam hug from Averett, followed by a hearty back slap. Julien gave Essie a bear hug that lifted her from her feet and made her squeal.

"So happy for the two of you!"

The back slap from Julien was hard enough to make Farrendel stagger a step. Averett exchanged a gentler, big brother hug with Essie as he said something to her in a whisper that Farrendel could not hear.

Farrendel should have dressed in his padded fighting leathers to protect himself from their exuberance. Next time, he was going to keep his mouth shut so that he and Essie could tell everyone all at once. Then he would only have to survive one round of congratulations instead of several.

Even worse, they still had to tell Essie's sister-in-law Paige, her nephews, and Edmund, once Edmund returned from his mysterious mission in Mongavaria.

Once all the congratulations were over, Averett gestured toward the mountains rising above them. "Now that everyone is here, we can head up to the border. The army has a narrow-rail train to the tower that guards the pass up there."

"Another train." Essie groaned.

"You do not have to come." Farrendel rested a hand on her back, then glanced at Averett. "I am sure you can stay here."

Averett nodded. "Paige came as well, but she is busy making sure the fort has accommodations ready for all of our guests, in case we spend the night here before returning to Aldon."

"Will you need me?" Essie searched Farrendel's face.

He drew in a deep breath, then let it out slowly. He always felt calmer when Essie was around, and that helped steady his magic.

But she would not be far away. And he would still have her steadiness in the heart bond, even if she wouldn't be right next to him.

"I will be fine." Farrendel put as much confidence as he could into his voice.

Even if he panicked and his control over his magic started to slip, he was not sure he wanted her stepping in to help him fix it. Melantha had shielded the baby when Essie had used his magic at Lethorel, but Melantha might be needed to use her magic elsewhere this time.

"Perfect. Then I'll stay here and share our news." The smile returned to Essie's face.

Beneath his hand, Farrendel could feel the way her muscles relaxed. It would be good for her to rest before they got back on another train. And she would enjoy celebrating their news with Paige, who had been a close friend of Essie's even before she had become her sister-in-law.

"I will stay here as well." Rheva stepped away from

Weylind. "I would like to greet Queen Paige. I have heard much about her."

Essie's mother hurried forward. "I'll show you the way." She strode deeper into the bustling fort, Essie and Rheva trailing behind, and began a story about the last time she had visited this fortress, back when Averett had been a baby and Essie's late father had been the crown prince on a good-will tour of the kingdom and army forts.

By some unspoken agreement, Captain Merrick along with some of Weylind's elven guards peeled away from the others and trailed after Essie and Rheva, ensuring that they would be more than safe here in the castle.

Some of the tension in Farrendel's chest eased. He would not have stopped Essie, if she had wanted to come with him all the way to the border. But he would not be quite as nervous if she and their unborn child remained safe, surrounded by Escarland's army and its fort.

Weylind eyed his children, as if he wanted to tell them to stay behind as well. But both Brina and Ryfon had crossed their arms. Brina's gaze was pleading, but Ryfon had a bit more defiance as he stared back at his father.

Finally, Weylind sighed and faced Farrendel. "Babies are easy. Remember that. It is when they start to think them-selves all grown up that parenting becomes difficult."

Behind Weylind, Ryfon and Brina shared a grin.

Farrendel did his best to solemnly nod. "I will keep that in mind, shashon."

By the time the tiny steam locomotive puffed its way to the mountain pass, Farrendel was even more glad Essie had not come. His teeth were about to be rattled right out of his mouth while every bone and joint ached from the jarring.

Only Rharreth appeared even remotely relaxed, as if rickety trains that felt about ready to fly off the tracks into the nearest river gorge were an everyday occurrence.

Melantha gripped Rharreth's arm the entire time, muttering something under her breath about how "it is not as bad as Kostaria's trains" the whole time, as if to reassure herself.

Farrendel had only heard about the terrifying experience of Kostaria's train through their mountains. He had no memories of it himself, since he had been unconscious when he had been a passenger in one.

When the train came to a shuddering, squealing halt, Farrendel tottered to the door and bailed out of the train car as quickly as possible.

The second train car disgorged an entire squad of Escarlish soldiers, as well as the troll and elven warriors that formed the guard details for both Rharreth and Weylind. Iyrinder came to stand behind Farrendel, guarding his back.

In the middle of their huddle, the Escarlish guards hauled not only four of the spies who had been captured in Tarenhiel, but also the rest of the spies at the *Sentinel* who had been arrested in Escarland.

The train had stopped on a broad shelf carved into the side of the mountain. The top of the ridge that formed this mountain pass was still a good hundred yards higher yet. At that point, a square, squat tower rose into the air, the trees cleared from its base to give it a clear view of both sides of the pass.

The rolling peaks of the mountains rose even higher all

around them, so dense with trees that Farrendel could not see far in any direction.

The crisp air wrapped around him, noticeably cooler than it had been down by the castle. Farrendel drew in a deep breath of it, both the coolness and the clean forest scent steadying him.

"The border is this way." Averett pointed, then hiked up the mountain trail headed in that direction. He had to halt for a moment as four of his guards jogged past him to lead the way.

As Farrendel hiked upward, he gazed at the untouched forest around him. Many of them were the same kinds of trees that were found in Tarenhiel, but the mountains gave them a different smell and feel than his homeland. Unlike the mountains of Kostaria, he might like to explore these. Perhaps he and Essie could come back someday. Surely there was a mountain retreat where they could stay.

A dream for the future. Essie would be so proud of him when he told her.

When they reached the top and halted next to the tower, the land flattened and spread away before them. Not quite as impressive a view as what they would have had if they had climbed all the way to the top of the peaks. But through the gap, Farrendel could still see miles of mountains rolling into a hazy blue distance on either side of them.

Directly in front of them, the pass in the mountains had been cleared of trees. It remained relatively flat for nearly half a mile. At the far side, another tower, this one round and flying the red and white Mongavarian flag, faced the Escarlish tower.

In the center of the grassy field between them, a large stone that appeared to be at least as tall as Farrendel had been placed too deliberately to be a natural feature of the landscape.

The door to the Escarlish tower opened, and a soldier peeked outside at them, bobbing a series of bows as he caught sight of Averett and Julien. The leader of the squad of Escarlish soldiers spoke to him in a lowered tone, likely explaining what was going on.

Averett gestured to the field. "That stone in the middle marks the border. Back when Escarland and Mongavaria divided the mountains between them, the kings agreed on the border and marked it with a stone like that every ten miles or so. This is where I'm hoping you will help, King Rharreth. With your magic, you should be able to find the stones marking the border from north to south. Farrendel can then use your magic to guide his power along the border."

Rharreth crossed his arms, eyed the stone, then faced Averett. "This is beyond the bounds of our current treaty."

"I know. And I would have proceeded with negotiating the new treaty first, if I thought Escarland had time to wait. But, thanks to those Mongavarian spies and my brother's current actions, I don't think we do." Averett faced Rharreth, just as calm and professional as Rharreth. "Consider this a goodwill gesture to open our treaty negotiations."

Rharreth's arms remained crossed, his blue eyes icy. "If I aid you in this, I will bring Kostaria into this little feud that Mongavaria has started with Escarland and Tarenhiel. My kingdom has finally come out of the grips of one war. I don't want to do anything that would drag it into another, especially one not of Kostaria's making."

Farrendel shifted, studying both the stone and the two kings. If Rharreth refused to help, would Farrendel be able to find those stones by himself? If the border ran in a straight line, it should be doable. Maybe. Though it would be a lot easier with Rharreth's magic to guide his and perhaps even help anchor his magic to the stone buried far beneath.

Weylind remained silent, watching the back and forth and not adding his opinion. Yet.

Melantha, too, stayed quiet at Rharreth's side. Though judging by the way she avoided glancing at Farrendel and Weylind, she likely knew what Rharreth was getting at and did not want to give it away with her expression.

Averett met Rharreth's stare without a hint of backing down. "I understand this is a lot to ask of you and your kingdom. But, if we sign the mutual defense treaty as we had previously discussed, your kingdom will be involved. It is my belief, however, that the combined strength of Tarenhiel, Escarland, and Kostaria will be enough to make Mongavaria back down without starting a war."

"You can't guarantee that."

"No, I can't." Averett's hard expression broke, giving a glimpse of the simmering worry and determination beneath. "But I must protect my kingdom and my brother-in-law Farrendel."

Farrendel started. What was Averett getting at?

"With the addition of Kostaria's warriors, our three kingdoms would be a match for Mongavaria even without Farrendel. It would eliminate Mongavaria's reason to target him specifically. It is my hope that Mongavaria will realize the futility of killing him and will leave him and Essie to live their lives in peace." Averett didn't turn his gaze away from Rharreth, his jaw firm.

But Farrendel shifted underneath the focus of the conversation anyway. Averett was using the might of kingdom politics to keep Farrendel and Essie safe. It was humbling, to see his Escarlish brothers stepping up to protect him like this.

Rharreth's jaw worked, his eyes softer than they had been before. As if the sentimental part of him wanted to agree, but the king in him could not just yet. "This is still a great commitment to ask of me and of Kostaria even before the treaty has been signed."

"I understand." For the first time, Averett glanced away from Rharreth. He shared a look with Julien, and Julien gave a single, solemn nod. Averett faced Rharreth again. "For that reason, I am prepared to offer my brother Julien in a marriage of alliance with Kostaria."

"What? No." Farrendel glanced between Averett and Julien. "No. Not for me."

Essie would never forgive Farrendel if the price of their safety was her brother's happiness. As much as Farrendel wanted peace and safety for Essie and their child, this price was too high. If anyone paid the cost, it should be him.

After all, that was why they were standing at the border right now. So that he could secure Escarland's safety with his magic. There was no need for a treaty or anything else.

Weylind huffed, his gaze swiveling to the sky as if searching for patience there. "Shashon, you are the last person who should argue against a marriage of alliance. Do you truly wish to argue that such a marriage is a bad idea and can never work?"

Farrendel opened his mouth, but Weylind had him there. His and Essie's arranged marriage had turned out just fine. As had Rharreth's and Melantha's.

But surely, after two successes, they were due for one to go horribly wrong. "But…"

"I have no intention of rushing things this time around." Averett's smile turned wry as he faced Farrendel. "I learned from last time. I'm not about to force Julien into a marriage with only a few days warning. Rharreth and I have the luxury of time to be more deliberate and thoughtful."

Farrendel could not argue with that either, much as he wanted to.

Weylind crossed his arms and raised his eyebrows. "Are you saying we made a mistake in how we handled Elspetha and Farrendel's marriage?"

Averett waved at him. "You were the one to argue for the wedding to occur in a mere two days, not me. But even you must admit, we were so desperate to avoid war and so distrustful of each other's motives, that we rushed things. We just lucked out that Essie and Farrendel are, well, Essie and Farrendel. Otherwise we could have had a disaster on our hands."

What did Averett mean? Farrendel shifted, not sure what to make of it.

Weylind gave a slight nod and shrug, as if to acknowledge Averett had a point.

Julien met Farrendel's gaze with those steady, brown eyes of his. "Avie and I have been discussing this option for a few months now. The proposed bridge over the Hydalla is just one example of what troll magic can offer Escarland. Right now, we have marriages linking Escarland to Tarenhiel, and Tarenhiel to Kostaria. But there is nothing directly linking Escarland and Kostaria. That needs to happen for the alliance between our three kingdoms to be complete and make us strong enough to stand up to kingdoms like Mongavaria in the future."

All good reasons, but not what Farrendel wanted to hear. "But are you sure?"

Julien's gaze did not waver. "Yes. I volunteered for this. Just like Essie did. Just like you did. If this is what it takes to keep you and Essie safe, then I'm willing to do it. Besides, I saw a glimpse into Kostaria's culture and kingdom when I fought in that Dulraith beside you and King Rharreth. I believe I can learn to respect their ways and love a wife from there."

Of Essie's three brothers, Julien had always been the most interested in hand-to-hand fighting techniques. And ever since that Dulraith, he had grown even more proficient in fighting with swords while practicing with Captain Merrick, Iyrinder, and Farrendel. Of anyone in Escarland, Julien was the most prepared to fit in with the trolls' warrior-oriented culture.

"All right." Farrendel sighed. Who was he to argue? Julien had clearly put more thought into this than Farrendel had when he had agreed to marry Essie. There was nothing Farrendel could do now but hope he knew what he was doing. "But the two of you have to tell Essie."

"Deal." For the first time, a grin crossed Julien's face, framed by his rugged beard.

"One problem." Rharreth cleared his throat, glancing between them before settling his gaze on Averett. "I don't have a sister. Or even a distant female cousin."

Melantha faced Rharreth, something almost like a smirk playing around her mouth, as she spoke in Escarlish. "You have a shield sister. As I have learned, your shield band is bound by blood, even if it is not the blood of family. I am sure Vriska would *love* to be considered for this marriage alliance."

Rharreth grimaced, sharing a look with Melantha.

Behind them, one of the male troll warriors who had come with Rharreth started, which meant he must have understood the Escarlish being spoken even if the rest did not. With wide eyes, the troll leaned closer to the warrior next to him and started whispering. Farrendel vaguely recognized them, though he did not recall their names.

Rharreth glanced over his shoulder at the two whispering troll warriors, an expression mirroring Melantha's smirk crossing his face. "Or some of the members of my shield band have sisters who could also be considered."

That made the troll who understood Escarlish choke, then cough, before he crossed his arms and glared at Rharreth.

"Exactly." Averett continued as if he had not noticed the discomfort of the trolls behind Rharreth. "The fact that you don't have a female blood relative gives us the freedom of options. My only requirements are that she comes from a family that proved their undying loyalty to you during the recent coup and that she is willing."

"And of the right age." Julien shrugged when Rharreth and Averett glanced at him. "I'm assuming someone of a compatible age is a given, but I thought I should add it, just to be sure."

"Yes, and that too." Averett's smile was genuine now. As if Julien's joking about this had been the last reassurance he had needed to know that his brother was willingly volunteering for this.

It had helped the twisting in Farrendel's chest. Surely if he and Essie could make things work, then Essie's good-natured brother definitely could.

Rharreth's slow nod turned more decided, as if he was

mulling over Averett's words and found them acceptable. "Yes, that could work. We can negotiate the exact wording in the treaty to allow for more choices, as well as time for them to meet and know each other before the marriage is required by the treaty. I have no desire to rush this any more than you do. If you are satisfied with that, then I am."

"I am as well." Averett held out his hand. When Rharreth just stared down at it, Averett waggled his fingers. "In Escarland, we shake hands to signify that a bargain has been struck. It proves that a man's word has been given and will be carried out as promised."

Rharreth took Averett's hand and shook once, firmly.

Farrendel eyed them. It really was a kind of all-purpose human gesture, meaning everything from greeting to a promise. Not very sanitary, but Rharreth seemed far less concerned about that than Farrendel had when he endured a handshake.

"Since that is settled, we can proceed with magically reinforcing the border." Averett waved toward the stone, glancing between Rharreth and Farrendel. "Do you have to go down there?"

Farrendel glanced at Rharreth, sharing a look with him. "I think it would be easiest if I could stand on the border, as I did in Kostaria."

Rharreth nodded. "I believe I will have to touch that stone to find the other ones and guide Laesornysh's magic."

"I was afraid of that." Averett grimaced as he pointed at the tower on the far side. "I don't know how the Mongavarians are going to react to a group of us walking over there, especially once you start wielding your powers. They may think they are under attack and decide to fight back. The cannon they have stationed there will reach the border."

"I will protect your backs." Weylind swept a critical eye across the space in front of them. "There are plenty of trees and vegetation for me to draw upon. I can hold back their small force for as long as you will need, if it comes to that."

"Thank you." Averett swept a glance over their group. "To all of you. Both allies and soon-to-be allies. I thank you for your willingness to use your magic to protect a kingdom that isn't your own."

Farrendel shrugged and reached for the crackle of his magic that simmered inside his chest. "I will gladly expend my magic like this if it means I do not have to expend it later fighting a war."

Weylind nodded, mouth set into a tight, grim line.

Rharreth glanced at the trolls guarding his back. "Some in my kingdom might disagree with me, but Kostaria has experienced enough war recently."

At a slight shift from Ryfon, Weylind turned to him and Brina. "The two of you will stay here."

Their faces fell, almost in unison.

Averett strode toward them, halting next to Ryfon. "I'm staying behind as well. Without magic, I would just be a hindrance. But we'll still have no problem seeing what is happening. If anything, we'll have a better view up here, since we will be able to see the whole landscape."

Their expressions brightened, as if they felt less left out now that the Escarlish king was also staying behind with them. Averett and Julien led the way off to the side before the four of them lined up like spectators waiting to watch a practice bout.

"We should keep our numbers as small as possible." Lines formed around Weylind's mouth as he regarded the stone set all by itself a quarter mile away. Now that Averett and Julien had stepped away, he had switched to elvish, something all the guards, both elf and troll, would understand. "It will be fewer people to have to protect and less chaotic if we should have to retreat quickly."

"Agreed. One guard each. The rest can wait here, ready to respond if needed." Rharreth turned to Melantha, still standing quiet and alert next to him.

She shrugged and flexed her grip on her wooden staff. "I know you do not like it, but you may need my magic, both to ensure that your magic and Farrendel's work together and to heal anyone if things go wrong."

Rharreth nodded, his mouth grim even as his gaze softened when he regarded Melantha. "You're right, of course. But if things do go wrong, Zavni will throw you over his shoulder and get you out of there."

The troll who understood Escarlish grinned and drew an ax from its place strapped to his back. "Of course, my king, my queen."

"I would expect nothing less." Melantha lifted her staff, a fierce light in her eyes.

She had found her place in Kostaria. Farrendel had few fond memories of that kingdom, but it was good to see his sister happy, as if in Kostaria she had finally found the place she belonged.

Rharreth faced the stretch of mountain highland before them. "Then enough chatter. Let's get this done."

CHAPTER

THIRTY-SIX

Farrendel had Weylind on one side, Melantha on the
other. Iyrinder provided a reassuring presence at
his back. The feeling of eyes upon him came not
just from those they had left behind, but also from the tower
far ahead of them, though he could not see any movement
yet.

Ahead of them, the squad of Escarlish soldiers escorted
the captured spies, approaching the border under a flag of
truce.

Farrendel and the others strode a little way behind them,
still shielded from view for the most part.

At the border, the squad halted. The commander said
something to the group of spies, then the Mongavarians
were pushed across the border. After a moment, once they
realized they were being set free, the Mongavarian spies ran
toward the tower, their hands still bound behind their backs,
as if they believed this was all a trick and the Escarlish
soldiers might yet fire on them while they fled.

Farrendel flexed his fingers, itching to draw his swords

as he watched the spies flee into their homeland. Averett and Weylind had made the decision to release most of the spies back to Mongavaria. Neither of them wanted to provoke Mongavaria through a mass execution, nor was keeping a whole pack of spies locked in a dungeon indefinitely worth the hassle. In the end, it had been decided to let them go to carry a message to their king that Tarenhiel, Escarland, and Kostaria would not stand for any of Mongavaria's meddling.

They had, however, kept back two of the spies to question them for more information on any lingering remnants of Mongavaria's spy network in Escarland.

The Escarlish squad of soldiers turned and marched back the way they had come, meeting Farrendel and the others only a few yards from the border.

The commander saluted Weylind and Rharreth, but, strangely, his gaze focused on Farrendel. "Are you sure you don't want us to stay to provide cover?"

Why was this commander looking to Farrendel for orders?

Farrendel glanced around. Right. He was the only one here with any connection to the Escarlish royalty. That must make him the ranking official in this commander's eyes.

He gave a stilted shake of his head. "No. Our magic will protect us. Protect your king. And be prepared to guard our retreat if necessary."

That last order would give this squad of soldiers something to feel useful, even if it would not be needed.

The commander nodded and barked orders. The squad parted, marching in two columns on either side of Farrendel, Rharreth, Melantha, Weylind, and their guards, before combining again to continue toward where Averett, Julien, Ryfon, and Brina waited at the base of the Escarlish tower.

Then, almost before Farrendel was ready, he and the others reached the single block of stone standing upright in the field. What looked like words had been carved into its face, but the stone was too weather-beaten and covered in moss for the writing to be legible.

The Mongavarians in the far tower had yet to react, likely too busy getting the reports from the returned spies.

Rharreth placed his hand on the stone and, next to him, Melantha did the same. Farrendel positioned himself next to Melantha, making sure she remained fully shielded behind the column of stone.

Melantha huffed and glared at him and Rharreth in turn, as if to show them that she knew exactly what they were doing. But she remained where she was at least.

Weylind halted on Farrendel's other side, the only one of the four of them who was fully exposed without the rock to shield him. Kneeling, Weylind tangled his fingers in the grass, though he did not reveal his magic yet. He kept his gaze focused on the tower.

The four guards also arranged themselves so that they had both a view of the tower but could also bodily shield their charges.

"Ready?" Rharreth met first Melantha's gaze, then Farrendel's.

Farrendel nodded and cautiously placed his hand on the stone as well.

A frosty dusting swirled around Rharreth's fingers a heartbeat before his magic burst into the stone, filling it with a chilly, immovable kind of power.

Farrendel braced himself for the spike of pain from touching a stone so laced with troll magic, but it did not come. After a moment, he reached with his free hand and touched where the stone Melantha had given him hung beneath his shirt against his skin. He had nearly forgotten about it, until now.

Beside him, Weylind flinched, grimacing as Rharreth's magic spread through the ground beneath their feet. In front of Farrendel, shielding him from the tower, Iyrinder rubbed at his temples, as if a headache was already forming.

Farrendel caught Melantha's gaze. "Your stone is working. I feel fine, even now."

Melantha flashed him a quick smile before she glanced past him at Weylind and Iyrinder. She darted out from the sheltering stone, pressed green-laced fingers to first Weylind's temple, then Iyrinder's. When they each relaxed, she flitted back into cover.

"There's some movement inside the tower now." The troll guard, Zavni, reported, his gaze focused intently in that direction. "Doesn't look like they are too stirred up just yet."

Rharreth's magic shot out in either direction, chilling Farrendel's toes even through his boots. "I can sense the bedrock beneath us and the next marking stones to either side of us. Laesornysh?"

Farrendel nodded and drew on his magic. If the Mongavarians had not been worried yet, they would be in a moment. With a deep breath, he poured his magic into the stone.

As soon as his magic clashed against Rharreth's, pain flared up Farrendel's arm and spiked in his head and chest.

Rharreth made a hissing sound between his teeth. "Melantha?"

Moments later, Melantha rested a hand on Farrendel's arm, then on Rharreth's.

As her magic flowed into him, the pain eased.

Farrendel squeezed his eyes shut, reached deep inside himself, and released his magic. It exploded from him into the stone, crackling high into the sky above them.

"Well, that got their attention," Zavni said with something almost like humor in his voice.

Weylind made a low growl in the back of his throat a moment before his magic flooded the ground beneath Farrendel's feet.

A groaning came from the forests on either side of them. Then, the trees almost seemed to *move*, closing the gap across the valley. Saplings sprang from the earth, growing rapidly into a wall.

A boom sounded. Seconds later, something crashed into the dirt well in front of them.

"A warning shot." Zavni's fingers flexed on the handle of his ax. "I don't think they'll shoot low a second time."

"Understood." Weylind's wall grew higher, strengthening from saplings to bigger trees.

Like a torrent, Farrendel's magic spilled to either side of him, racing alongside Rharreth's magic until it quickly caught up to its ends on either side. It churned at the edges, as if begging Rharreth's magic to go faster.

"Laesornysh," Rharreth growled between gritted teeth.

"Trying." Farrendel tightened his grip on his magic, concentrating on melding it with Rharreth's magic instead of fighting it.

As Rharreth pushed his magic farther, Farrendel channeled his power along it. He sensed the way trees and vegetation were incinerated along the border. But he reached past that, sending his magic deep into the ground to where Rharreth's magic had found the bedrock.

Another boom reverberated from the tower. Something

smashed into Weylind's wall with a shattering of wood and the groan of a forest in pain. The sharper cracks of rifle fire filled the air.

"Do you need me to shield us?" Farrendel was not sure how he would manage to hold a shield while also controlling the rest of his magic pouring along the border, but he would figure out a way if he had to.

"No." Weylind bit out his answer.

Good. Farrendel's magic was already fighting him. It wanted to surge, fully unleashed, but he had to keep it reined in and at the same pace as Rharreth's power.

"Can your magic go any faster?" Farrendel's fingers felt slick and burning with the power he was holding back.

"No." Rharreth's glare was piercing even though Farrendel was not looking at him. "My magic is steady as stone, not flighty."

"Like a grasshopper?" Farrendel let his magic blast into Rharreth's with just a little more power than necessary.

"Exactly." Rharreth grunted, his magic straining against Farrendel's.

"Are the two of you bantering at a time like this?" Weylind's tone conveyed that disapproving scowl of his. Another cannonball smashed into Weylind's trees, but his magic held back the splinters from flying into them.

"Essie's brothers would call this bonding." Farrendel spoke between gritted teeth. Despite Melantha's magic, his head was pounding, though he was not sure if it was from Rharreth's magic or from having to hold such a tide of his magic in tight control.

Through the heart bond, he sensed Essie reaching for him and the magic, asking if he needed her to take some of it.

No. He tried to tell her through the elishina, hoping she would get the sense of his words. *I have this. I can do this.*

He had been practicing with Weylind for just this reason, gaining finesse. If he could hold his magic steady over a swathe of forest without incinerating so much as a blade of grass or leafy twig, then surely he could handle this.

Two cannonballs thunked into Weylind's wall, and his brother muttered something under his breath.

Rharreth's magic crept farther and farther along the border in each direction, meticulously finding each marking stone.

Farrendel let his magic follow Rharreth's magic in spurts, holding it back for a minute or two at a time, then releasing it to catch up before he strained to contain it yet again.

Finally, the taste of muddy river came through the magic, first from the north, then from the south. Rharreth's magic had reached the two great rivers that formed the northern and southern borders of Escarland.

"Hold there to the south." Farrendel was shaking now under the building force of his magic that begged to be released. Sweat dribbled down his forehead and between his shoulder blades. "Follow the center of the Hydalla to the sea on the north."

It would do no good to reinforce this border if they left the crossing over the Hydalla from Mongavaria into Tarenhiel unprotected. Tarenhiel's sea coast would still be undefended, but it was rocky, with few harbors to provide a landing spot, especially for an army big enough to gain a foothold. Farrendel could create a magical barrier along that border—as well as along Escarland's southern and western borders—later.

Rharreth nodded, and his magic flowed through the bedrock beneath the river.

Weylind muttered under his breath again before saying, louder, "Hurry. Looks like they are mustering outside the tower, and they are wheeling one of their cannons to bring it closer."

"Oh, good. I'd love a good fight." A smacking sound of wood against a palm accompanied Zavni's words, as if he were hefting his ax.

"You cannot kill anyone." Melantha's tone held just as much command as Rharreth's. "Bloodshed would start the war we are trying to avoid."

"Yes, my queen."

Farrendel's magic coursed along Rharreth's beneath the river until, finally, Farrendel could sense the ocean, a mix of salt and power and unexplored darkness.

At last. He grasped a hold of that sense, letting his magic race ahead of Rharreth's until it fizzled against the crashing, roiling waves.

With a roaring in his ears, he unleashed the full force of his magic. Power tore along the pathways he and Rharreth had marked, rising high into the sky as far as anyone could see.

Farrendel snapped his eyes open and stared past the crackling wall of his magic. Past Weylind's tree barrier. To the hazy shape of the Mongavarian tower and the land spreading before them.

He remembered Essie, gasping and bleeding out in his arms. The way he had felt her through the heart bond, slipping away from him as death took her. The desperation to keep her alive. Finding out that the Mongavarian spy-assassin had nearly killed their unborn child as well as Essie.

433

He had not killed the assassin. He would not raze all of Mongavaria to the ground in revenge for what was nearly done.

But he would keep his family and his kingdoms safe.

He filled the magic with that determination, letting his love for Essie, his love for both Escarland and Tarenhiel, pour from him until the magic itself felt alive with it.

He was no longer shaking or sweating with the strain. His magic eagerly formed to his will, building and building like the mightiest of waves in the ocean.

"Ready?" Farrendel did not shout the word. He stood in the center calm of his magic's fury. Somewhere, distantly, the Mongavarians had begun firing rifles, such minuscule pops against the thunder in his ears. The bullets were nothing but pinpricks.

"Hold just a moment more," Weylind gasped between ragged breaths.

Then, Weylind yanked his magic back, slamming it into the maelstrom of Farrendel's power. Farrendel's power eagerly snapped it up as the threads of Melantha's magic helped twine the powers together.

Rharreth, too, poured another surge of his power through the line he had drawn.

Farrendel waited one heartbeat, two, sensing the magic building…

Then, he gathered it all in his mind and slammed it down, driving it deep into the earth where it was anchored by Rharreth's magic. The earth shook, giving a groan as if the mountains themselves were in pain from the magic Farrendel had stabbed into them. The magic flashed and imploded inside Farrendel's head.

He fell. He might have blacked out for a moment.

When he gathered his senses and peeled his eyes open, he found himself curled on the ground several feet away from the border stone, his face pressed to the dirt.

With shaking arms, he pushed himself into a sitting position, swiping his hair from his face.

Iyrinder lay near his feet, shaking his head as if his ears were ringing. Nearby, Weylind's guard was groaning while Weylind had pushed onto his elbows as he spat, as if he had gotten dirt in his mouth.

To Farrendel's left, Melantha rolled onto her back, rubbing at her temples. Rharreth reached for her, speaking urgently in a low tone. Most likely asking if she was all right.

The troll guard, Zavni, yanked his ax out of the ground where it had landed only a few inches from his ankle. "Warn us next time. I nearly cut off my own foot."

The other guard punched Zavni's shoulder. "Your own fault for waving your ax around when we weren't even engaged in battle yet."

Weylind spat one last time and grimaced. "That had better have worked."

A boom rang across the field. Then, a crackling blue wall shot from the ground, veined with streaks of both white and green, and incinerated the cannonball before it had a chance to cross the border.

On the other side, a squad of Mongavarian soldiers, who had been charging forward, skidded to a halt and gaped.

"I think it did." Rharreth regarded the swirling wall of combined magics, a grin curving his mouth.

Farrendel studied the magic as well. It seemed strong. Though, the section through the center of the river had not felt quite as stable as the land border, which claimed the bedrock of the mountains as an anchor.

It likely would not matter. Crossing the mountains with an army was treacherous, but crossing the Hydalla with an army would be even more difficult. At the very least, Farrendel's magic would provide a warning of any attempts, giving time to repulse an attack.

Farrendel pushed to his feet, brushing at the grass and dirt marring his clothes. He grimaced at the green smears of grass stains, already itching for a scalding shower to wash away the icky, dirty feeling crawling on his skin.

When he turned back toward the Escarlish tower, Averett and Julien were pumping their fists up and down, and the faint sounds of cheering carried on the breeze. Ryfon gave a whoop as well, then glanced about as if checking that no one had noticed a prince of the elves doing something so undignified.

Weylind's hand rested on Farrendel's shoulder. "Let us return. I believe you have your Escarlish home to show us."

Farrendel nodded, and together they strode toward Escarland. Toward the train that would take him back to Essie, then eventually on to Aldon and their cozy Buckmore Cottage.

If they had a nice weather, Farrendel would show Weylind, Rheva, Ryfon, and Brina the family camping spot in the forested parkland by Winstead Palace. He would love the see the look on Weylind's face as he tried to cook a marshmallow for the first time. It was a lot trickier than it appeared when Essie and her brothers did it. Ryfon and Brina especially would enjoy it.

Farrendel glanced over his shoulder where Rharreth and Melantha followed, now walking hand in hand. Perhaps he would invite them as well. They were family. There was something about sitting around a campfire cooking marsh-mallows that relaxed and bonded.

Behind Rharreth and Melantha, the blue magic retreated into the ground, leaving the border once again looking benign and peaceful. The Mongavarian soldiers still stood there, unmoving, and none of them raised a rifle to even attempt to take a shot at them.

THIRTY-SEVEN

The king of Mongavaria slept soundly in his massive four-poster bed, the silken sheets and finely woven blankets piled over him to ward off the damp chill of the ocean breeze seeping through the stones of the sprawling castle. The moonlight shone on the tufts of the man's white hair while shadows pooled in the lines of his well-worn face.

Edmund might have felt bad for what he was about to do to a man in his seventies. But this was the king who had ordered Essie and Farrendel's assassination, as well as the murders of the elven royal family.

Nor was this king a frail, elderly man. He was sharp-eyed and spry, the kind of man who would keep his heir waiting for the crown for many years yet.

Edmund had been there, hidden inside a dusty storage bench, while the Mongavarian spies had reported to their king. This man had raged about their failures.

Escarland might have shown them mercy. But Mongavaria had not. Even now, the shots of the firing squad seemed to echo into the night. Their blood stained the same stones where the three Escarlish spies who had not fled in time had also died.

A reminder of what would happen to Edmund if he were caught. Rharreth hadn't wanted to kill a prince of Escarland, but the king of Mongavaria had no such qualms.

Edmund stalked to the bed, reaching with one gloved hand into the pouch he'd tied to his belt. With one swift motion, he tossed back the covers, clapped a hand to the king's mouth, and pressed one of Jalissa's magical vines to the man's hand.

As the king's eyes snapped open, Edmund gripped a fistful of his nightshirt and hauled him from the bed, spinning him to face away from Edmund before he could get more than a brief glimpse of Edmund's silhouette in the moonlight.

The king started to claw at Edmund's hand, only to hesitate when Jalissa's vine sprang to life, twining up his arm with what had to be a constricting grip. With muffled yelling in the back of his throat, the king switched to yanking on the vine, only to have it catch his other hand and arm.

Edmund used the man's distraction to drag him across the room, well away from any weapons the king might have stashed in and around his bed. He forced the king to sit on a wooden chair next to a changing screen. The vine seemed to understand, wrapping around both the man and the chair within seconds, holding him fast.

Drawing his knife, Edmund pressed the edge to the king's throat and lowered the timbre of his voice. "Do not yell. It will do you no good. Your guards are as bound as you are."

Since they had only taken over their shift at the king's

door half an hour before, no one was likely to stumble across them before the hour provided by Jalissa's vines was up. The ivy had gagged and blindfolded them as well, rendering them helpless.

Too bad it was not poison ivy. That would have some long-lasting effects. Though, it might kill a man if stuffed down his throat, so it was probably just as well.

Edmund removed his hand from the king's mouth and instead gripped the man's fine, white hair, preventing him from turning his head.

"What do you want? Are you here to assassinate me?" Even now, the trussed-up king managed a belligerent tone, as if he still believed he could get the upper hand if he was only angry enough.

"No. Not this time." Edmund tightened his grip on the king's hair, yanking his head back in a way that would be painful. "But if you do not heed my warning, I will be back."

As tempting as it was to off him, a dead king would do Escarland and Tarenhiel little good. Mongavaria's heir was just as conniving as his father. It would only make things worse to put a younger man on the throne, providing him with the additional motivation of revenge. Not that the prince would mourn his father, exactly. But he would want revenge for an assassination inside Mongavaria's castle, something he would see as an affront to his power by a lesser kingdom.

And to think he was the heir that Escarland's Parliament had wanted Essie to marry.

No, better to leave the current king in power. The man was just frightened enough of death coming early that he would back off, even if he told no one why.

Edmund spoke near the king's ear in a way that would send chills down the man's back if he had any sense of self-preservation at all. "Stay away from Farrendel Laesornysh of Tarenhiel and Princess Elspeth of Escarland. Laesornysh is not the only power in the combined might of Escarland, Tarenhiel, and Kostaria. If they die, you die."

The king froze for a moment, as if the fear of that threat unnerved him. He would have heard reports of what Farrendel had done at the border. He must have even seen the horizon glowing blue.

When the Mongavarian king spoke again, his tone was even more defiant, an attempt to cover the lapse. "Who are you? Escarlish? One of those cursed elves from Tarenhiel? You are using their magic."

He wanted to know which kingdom had dared launch this attack on the very person of the Mongavarian king. It would give him a place to focus so he could divide and conquer.

But Edmund would leave him no clues to pinpoint which kingdom to target to avenge this deed. That was the point of making sure the king never got a good look at him. Jalissa's vines would disintegrate, leaving the king wondering if he had been captured by an elf or a human using something crafted beforehand. Neither of the guards had gotten a good look at him before the vines had blindfolded them.

"Maybe I am Escarlish." Up until then, he had spoken with his usual Escarlish accent, even if he had pitched his voice lower. He switched to an elven accent with the ease of long practice. "Or maybe I am an elven assassin. I might even be a troll from Kostaria."

That accent was rusty since Edmund had only practiced

it for a mere three months and had not spoken it since. But the Mongavarian king had likely heard very few trolls and wouldn't know the difference.

The king's throat bobbed, but his jaw hardened.

Edmund switched one last time. Mongavaria spoke a dialect of the same language as Escarland, much as Tarenhiel and Kostaria shared a root language before diverging. With Edmund's ear for languages, he had acquired a Mongavarian accent while traveling across their kingdom. "Maybe I am one of your citizens, fed up with talk of war and empire."

The king hesitated. Edmund's use of so many accents was sending him off balance, as Edmund had known it would.

Edmund traced the tip of his knife along the king's neck before drawing just a drop of blood. "I am the shadow who will haunt you to your dying day, and I am the wraith who will hasten that day if you move against Escarland, Tarenhiel, or Kostaria ever again."

Before the king had a chance to respond, Edmund released the king's hair and nudged the vine. As if sensing what he wanted, the ivy climbed up the king's chest and wrapped around his mouth and chin, gagging him.

Edmund sheathed his knife. Then, gripping the back of the chair, he spun the king to face the window and the glare of the moonlight, his back now to the door.

His mission complete, Edmund left the king's room as silently as he had entered, strolling past the wiggling, immobilized guards.

He still had two of Jalissa's vines. That should be just enough for the two guards at the postern gate he'd located earlier.

And then, he could turn toward home and the elf princess who awaited him.

.

THIRTY-EIGHT

F arrendel wrapped his arm around Essie's shoulders and adjusted the blanket as they perched on the bench next to the fire.

On the next bench over, Weylind glared at his sticky fingers, then glanced around as if desperately searching for a way to clean them. Rheva had delicately eaten a single marshmallow, and now kept up a steady conversation with Paige. Averett grinned as he leaned around Rheva and Paige to talk with Weylind.

Julien had joined Rharreth and Melantha, and they seemed to be discussing Kostaria and its customs. It might have been a serious topic, except that it turned out trolls *really* liked roasting marshmallows, and Rharreth was on his fourth or fifth one. His sugar high made him a bit more jovial than Farrendel had ever seen him.

Melantha delicately sipped at her hot chocolate, giving Rharreth a small, fond smile. She and Essie had already made plans to visit the local coffee shops for a hot chocolate taste-testing spree so that Melantha could pick out her favorites to take back with her to Kostaria.

Farrendel had not yet decided if he would join them. He would have to see if he was up for more people-time after the past few days. With nearly all of them together, minus Machasheni Leyleira, Jalissa, and Edmund, someone had been around nearly constantly since they had returned from the border, even when they split up into smaller groups to see and do separate things.

Just that morning, they had participated in a parade through the streets of Aldon to celebrate the signing of the new treaty between Kostaria and Escarland, a new alliance pact between the three kingdoms, and the one-year anniversary of the treaty that had started it all.

The Escarlish people had crowded the streets, cheering both the troll and elf kings as if they had never been at war with either kingdom. Though, Averett declaring the day a national holiday might have had something to do with it.

The crowds had even cheered for Farrendel and Essie. It turned out that announcing a baby on the way erased the recent scandals, at least for now. It would not last. Public opinion was a fickle thing even at the best of times. But at least Essie had gotten a chance to enjoy the festivities in Escarland for their anniversary without getting rotten fruit thrown at her, and that was all Farrendel could ask for.

On the last bench, Brina held Essie's nephew Finn in her arms, and the boy had nodded off to sleep some time ago. Ryfon helped Bertie roast another marshmallow, both of them thoroughly sticky at this point.

Essie snuggled closer to Farrendel's side, resting her head on his shoulder. "This is even better than anything I dreamed about back then. Can you believe it? We got married a whole year ago."

"It has been an eventful year." As Farrendel took in his family and hers gathered around this fire, he could not help but agree. Human, elf, troll. They sat together as one family. He certainly had never imagined this, a year ago. Back then, he had simply wanted a reprieve from war, even if it was only for a few years.

He had not expected his family would become closer and more whole than they had been in decades. Nor had he expected a new family that had embraced him so whole-heartedly that he could no longer imagine his life without them. Having Rharreth, the troll king, for a brother was a surprise.

But most of all, there was Essie. Their love, so much deeper and richer than anything he had known he could feel. The wonder of having a child on the way, knowing that he would be a father before another year was out.

"Uh-hmm." Essie's voice was quiet, sleepy.

"Ready for bed?" He could feel the way she was all but falling asleep against his shoulder.

When she made a mumbled noise that sounded like agreement, he stood, drawing her to her feet with him with his steadying arm around her shoulders. It took longer than he liked to say their goodnights to everyone, especially since Averett and Paige took the opportunity to declare it was time to get the boys to bed. Rharreth and Melantha decided that was their cue to return to Winstead Palace as well, followed by Julien, and it was long moments before Farrendel could finally duck away with Essie.

At least Weylind had decided that camping out in the forest with Rheva, Ryfon, and Brina sounded like a novel, family-bonding experience. Farrendel and Essie would have Buckmore Cottage to themselves tonight.

Farrendel heaved a deep breath as the fire and noise faded away behind him. Peace and quiet. Finally.

Essie yawned, still leaning against him as they walked. "I'm sorry we couldn't spend our anniversary at Lethorel as you had wanted."

"I do not mind. There is always next year. Or the year after that." Farrendel shrugged, keeping his pace slow for Essie's sake. He had the hope of many anniversaries to enjoy with Essie for hundreds of years to come, thanks to their heart bond. Spending this one surrounded by her kingdom and her family was not a trial as he might have once believed. "Today was about our kingdoms more than us."

"There is still tomorrow. We get to celebrate our anniversary all over again, this time for our elven wedding." Essie tangled her fingers in the front of his shirt. "Tomorrow will be just for us. No parades. No busyness. Just the two of us."

"Yes." That was fine by him. "As long as none of my professors track me down. I think I might owe a few of them some homework."

"No doing homework on our anniversary." Essie laughed, then stumbled over a root she likely had not seen in the darkness with her human eyesight.

Farrendel swept her up into his arms, glad for an excuse to hold her close.

She gave a tiny, surprised squeal before she wrapped one arm around his neck. As he started walking again, she rested her head on his shoulder.

Thinking about their weddings a year ago made him remember Averett's words at the Escarlish-Mongavarian border. He glanced down at Essie. "Do you regret how we married? We never properly courted, nor did I ask you to marry me in the traditions of either of our kingdoms. Both of our weddings were put together quickly with very little planning on your part."

Essie raised her head, searching his face as a wrinkle formed between her brows. "Do you regret any of that?"

"No." Yes, but only because he thought Essie deserved better than the rushed weddings and his awkward courtship afterwards.

For himself? No, he had no regrets.

Essie met his gaze, her smile soft and still touching something deep inside his chest just as it had the first time he had seen her. "No, I wouldn't change the past year. Well, I guess I would change your capture and torture if I could. I would never wish for you to have suffered that." She gently traced the scar along his collarbone, her touch so light and soft that it stirred thoughts of kissing her rather than the reaction to flinch. "But other than that, I wouldn't change a thing. Especially not our weddings."

He would gladly erase those weeks of torture as well, but he was at a place where he could appreciate the way it had pushed him to get to the better state he was in now and to continue what he needed to do to stay there, much as he was able. He would not wish the healing away, even if he still ached because of the brokenness.

"Good. I am thankful you have no regrets." He stepped into the back gardens of Buckmore Cottage. A single light glowed next to the door, but other than that, the cottage remained the cozy dark of an empty home waiting to enfold them again.

There, in the privacy of the shadowed garden, the tree frogs and night birds chorusing in the trees behind them, he halted, still cradling her to him. The moonlight shone against the red of Essie's hair and glittered in her eyes. Her moon-kissed skin still had a hint of the freckles scattered across her nose and cheeks.

Months from now, their lives would change again when their child was born. It would be a good change, but it was still a change, nonetheless. Until then, he wanted to savor each moment, each day.

He eased Essie back to her feet, though he kept one arm around her. He pulled the small jewelry box from his pocket, holding it in his hand for a moment where she could not see it.

Would she like it? Captain Merrick and Iyrinder had assured him it was a good design, but what did they know? Iyrinder and Miss Merrick were not even courting yet. What if Essie was disappointed?

"Farrendel?" Essie ran her fingers through his hair, causing the moonlight to shine along the silver-blond strands. "Is something wrong?"

He shook his head, then held out the jewelry box. "I got this. For you. For our anniversary. It is small, but we said we were going with small gifts and…" He trailed off, realizing that he was rambling.

Essie laughed and took the jewelry box from him. "Considering I haven't even had a chance to get a gift for you, due to the whole getting shot thing, then hunted by an assassin, then no energy thanks to being pregnant, you're doing better than me. You have nothing to worry about. I know I'll love it."

"You have not even opened it yet." Farrendel could not blame his churning stomach on her nausea this time.

Essie eased the box open, and her eyes widened, lit with moonlight. "It's beautiful."

He released a breath. He had thought so, but he had still worried she would not like the necklace and design he had picked out.

Essie eased the necklace from the box, and, after handing the box back to him, she put it on. The heart-shaped pendant was crafted out of silver and studded with small, tasteful diamonds. Where the two loops of the heart met, the silver swirled around an emerald and a blue diamond so that the two stones were tucked inside the heart. The pendant hung on a delicate silver chain. Its understated, flowing lines reminded him of an elven style, but the gemstones were Escarlish.

Essie touched the pendant before she smiled and wrapped her arms around him. "It's perfect. I love it. But I love you more."

He pressed a gentle kiss to her cheek, murmuring, "I love you, my shynafir."

Then he kissed her as he had wanted to do all night but could not with his family looking on.

He had no regrets for their past and every hope for their future. If he shared it with her, he would treasure every moment.

THIRTY-NINE

J alissa picked at her dessert, trying to pretend she was not restless. Around her, her entire family had gathered in Weylind and Rheva's main room, now that they had all returned from Escarland a few days ago. Even Rharreth and Melantha remained here, finishing up the last of their business before they returned to Kostaria.

Edmund had been gone for three weeks. She told herself that he was not yet late. But it was hard to sit there, knowing each day, each second, could be the one when he *finally* walked in the door.

Would he go to Escarland first to report to his brother? Or would he come straight here, knowing that she was waiting for him?

"Jalissa?"

She started, blinking, before turning to Melantha. By the look on her sister's face, it had not been the first time she had said Jalissa's name.

"Yes?" Jalissa set aside her plate. She was not going to

finish. Her appetite had not been what it should have been ever since Edmund had left.

Ugh. She truly was lovesick. She could not eat. Could not sleep. Could not think about anything or anyone besides him.

Melantha studied her with a sister's dark, knowing eyes. "I was wondering if we could talk?" She glanced around the room. "Maybe somewhere quieter?"

Jalissa had promised herself and Leyleira that she would talk with Melantha, but she had been putting it off. Not because she was still angry. No, she simply did not know what to say.

Her stomach churned, but she nodded and stood. Rheva glanced their way as she and Melantha headed for the door, as did Machasheni, who gave Jalissa a smile and nod. Other than that, everyone else seemed too caught up in their conversations to notice.

As Jalissa stepped onto the porch, the crisp night air curled around her, sending a shiver down her back. She hugged her arms to her middle as she strode around the porch until she and Melantha stood next to a wall without any windows or doors looking into the room.

When she turned to face her sister, Melantha halted in front of her. In the darkness, her fur clothing and spiky hair looked especially troll-like. She held Jalissa's gaze. "I am sorry. I am sorry for betraying Farrendel and for tearing our family apart. I was wrong to harbor such bitterness for so long. I—"

"I forgive you." The words came more easily than Jalissa had expected they would. These past few turbulent weeks with Edmund had taught her a thing or two about the pain of bitterness and the balm of forgiveness.

"You do?" Melantha paused. The night made it hard to read her expression, but some of the burdened hunch left her shoulders.

"Yes." Jalissa breathed easier as some of her own burden left her heart. "Yes, I forgive you. And I want to be sisters again. You have truly changed. It is not just an act. Honestly, you have been much more of a sister to everyone than I have in the past few months."

"Is everything all right?" Melantha tentatively reached out and clasped Jalissa's shoulders. The starlight reflected in the deep, compassionate look in her eyes.

It had been so long since her sister had looked at her with such genuine, sisterly concern that Jalissa's throat closed. She had to swallow several times before she could answer. "It will be."

Just as soon as a certain Escarlish spy prince returned.

"But it is a little better, now that I have my sister back." Jalissa clasped Melantha's shoulders. Yet, that did not seem like enough, not with the power of forgiveness and healing washing through her.

Maybe…did she dare…

She was going to court a human. Eventually marry him, more than likely. Adopting a few human gestures would not be amiss.

Jalissa let go of Melantha's shoulders and pulled her into a tight, human-style hug instead.

The old Melantha would have stiffened, sniffed, and said something condescending about humans.

This new Melantha embraced Jalissa in a surprisingly strong grip, making a noise somewhere between a sob and a laugh.

This was why forgiveness was so much better than

clinging to grudges and bitterness. No wonder Farrendel had chosen this rather than harbor anger, when he, more than anyone, deserved to hate Melantha for what she had done. Healing in the wake of forgiveness, restoration in the wake of true repentance, was a powerful, precious thing.

After a long moment, Melantha cleared her throat. "How long do we stand like this?"

Jalissa shrugged. "I do not know. Elspetha always seems to know just how long a hug should last, and I always follow her lead."

"So do I."

With a laugh, the two of them let go at the same time, stepping back.

Melantha leaned against the decorative railing with her back to it, facing Jalissa. "I know you just forgave me, and I am likely the last person in whom you want to confide. But if you want to talk, I am here for you. Well, I will be here for another three days. Then I will be there for you through letters."

Her normally refined and proper sister bit off her words with a muffled groan, as if embarrassed by her own awkwardness.

But the awkwardness was genuine, and that made all the difference.

Jalissa braced her hands on the railing next to Melantha, staring out into the night. Lights glittered among the branches, lighting the pathways and marking the sprawling rooms of the treetop palace. Even though Jalissa had grown closer to Elspetha, this was not something she could talk about with her, since Edmund was her brother.

"It is complicated." Jalissa stared down at her hands. How much should she tell Melantha?

"It is the Escarlish prince, is it not?" Melantha's voice was soft on the night breeze. "Do you still have feelings for him?"

"Yes." Jalissa sighed.

"And does he still have feelings for you?"

"Yes."

When Melantha did not reply, her silence seemed to ask, *Then what is the problem?*

Jalissa glanced at Melantha. "We have a *history*. And it is complicated. What if it is too complicated? What if we are not meant to be together, no matter what we feel about each other?"

"I can see why you would be concerned." Melantha stared off into the night, gaze thoughtful. "It is good that you are thinking it through rather than being carried away by feelings. But…"

"But that has been my problem, I know. Thinking too much these past few months and just making myself miserable when the answer was right in front of me all along." Jalissa flexed her fingers on the railing, trying to keep them warm in the chilly evening. "Yet what if that is just me wanting Edmund to be the answer when he is not? What if I am now deceiving myself?"

"You are making me glad I was not given the chance to overthink things." Melantha's mouth pressed into a line, as if she was trying not to laugh. At Jalissa's look, her expression sobered again. "Can you live without him?"

"No." She had tried. Several times, in fact. And she had been miserable every time.

All the elven lords she had considered in the past months had been those she could live with. But Edmund was the one she could not live without, no matter what name or disguise he wore.

"I see." Melantha rested a hand on Jalissa's arm. "Then I say give him a chance. It is not like he is going to ask you to marry him the minute he returns. Take your time courting him. While you are courting, you can always walk away if you are convicted deep in your heart that it is not the right thing to commit to marriage with him."

"But it will only hurt worse if I wait to break it off instead of just breaking it off now." Her throat squeezed with tears at just the thought of doing that.

Melantha huffed and patted her arm. "I hate to break it to you, isciena, but you cannot find love without risking heart-break. It takes a great deal of trust to hand your heart to someone else and, sometimes, you hand it to the wrong person and they break it."

Right. Melantha had been engaged to that elf...what had been his name? Jalissa had been about Ryfon's age back then, and she had never liked Melantha's betrothed all that much, so she had been relieved when they had broken it off.

"But when you give your heart to the right person, that makes it all worth it." Melantha's face softened into the mushiest, softest look Jalissa had ever seen on her.

"But how do you *know*?" Jalissa could not help the slight whine to her voice. It was just so frustrating, probably because there was no hard and fast way to tell. It was as Machasheni Leyleira said. She had to ask herself if it was right, good, honorable, and true, and then, if it was, trust that it was the right decision.

But trust was *hard*. And harder still with someone who had deceived her before. He was a spy. Deception for the good of his kingdom was a part of who he was, and she could not deceive herself by thinking that would change, even if he no longer played the role of spy.

Melantha gave a light, wry laugh. "I am not the right person to ask, I fear. I was already married to Rharreth, so he *had* to be the right one. We had already made the commitment to each other, so unless we wanted to be miserable, our only choice was to work hard to make the feelings match our duty. Same for Farrendel and Elspetha."

An arranged marriage was starting to sound better and better. At least then Jalissa would not have this crushing worry that she was making the wrong choice.

But, no. She needed to sort through this confusion. Besides, whenever she pictured an arranged marriage, she found herself picturing a wedding with Edmund, and that brought her right back to where she started.

Melantha searched her face again. "If you want better advice on knowing for sure before you marry someone, maybe you can ask Rheva. She agreed to marry Weylind. She must have seen something beneath all the grumpiness."

Jalissa could not help the laugh that burst from her. That was a good point. Though, Weylind used to be a lot less grumpy. Jalissa had been a toddler back then, but she remembered that much. Her only memory of Weylind and Rheva's wedding was that Rheva's dress had been pretty, but then she had fallen asleep during the ceremony, or so she had been told. "Maybe I will talk to her. She is always good at listening."

"Yes, she is." After a moment, Melantha turned to better face Jalissa, capturing her gaze with that piercing look that would turn out a lot like Leyleira's when Melantha was older. "But I know you, isciena. You already know what you want to do, and what you will do in the end. You have always been so scared of failing and making a wrong choice that you over-think something until you finally get your head to where your heart has been all along. I have seen you do it with everything from buying a new dress to forgiving me just now."

Jalissa froze. Did she really do that?

She had known that forgiving Melantha was the right thing to do and, truthfully, her heart had wanted to do it all along. But her head had taken a while to get there.

She had done it with Elspetha, too, when she had first joined the family. Even though Jalissa had wanted to see Elspetha as a sister from the start, she had pulled back from that initial impulse, her head and Melantha's attitude convincing her that she needed to be cautious and hold her at a distance. It had taken Farrendel's capture for Jalissa to finally turn to her as a sister.

Was she doing it again with Edmund? Had her heart already made the decision, back there in the snowy mountains of Kostaria even as she told him no when all she really wanted to say was yes?

Melantha smiled before she headed back the way they had come. "I look forward to your wedding, isciena. Whenever it is."

With that, she disappeared around the corner of the porch, most likely on her way to rejoin the others.

Jalissa slumped against the rail, shaking her head. After all this inner turmoil, could it really be that simple?

The good things in life usually were. Sharing moments with a sister. Pestering a brother about his grumpiness. Listening to her younger brother go on and on about mechanical jargon that she did not understand but enjoyed hearing just because it made him so happy to talk about it.

Sharing a squeal of happiness with the sister she had gained just over a year ago.

Seeing the twinkle of laughter in a pair of muddy, blue-green eyes. Feeling so loved and protected when she was with him, as if he truly saw the very depths of her in a way no one else had before.

Melantha had been right. Jalissa had made her choice, despite months of stewing and not admitting it to herself.

Bootsteps sounded from the other side of the porch near the door, out of sight from where Jalissa stood. The click of the door, then a flood of voices, louder than before, filled with greeting.

And was that…could it be…

Heart beating hard inside her, hardly daring to hope, Jalissa raced around the porch and shoved past the elf guard standing there, yanking the door out of his grip before he could shut it behind whoever had just entered.

She burst into the room, then skidded to a halt at the sight of the person standing only a few feet inside, the canvas pack at his feet.

Edmund. Whole and alive and here in Tarenhiel as he had promised.

He turned, his eyes—green while surrounded by all the greens of Tarenhiel—meeting hers. A part of her had expected him to be worn and haggard, with dark circles under his eyes and a bushy beard covering his face.

Instead, he looked good. Better than good. He was clean-shaven, the better for her to see the smile quirking his lips. He wore black trousers, black boots, and a deep green tunic of elven style, the cut too fine and fitted to be anything but made specially for him. And yet, the elven garb looked right, even with the very human curve of his ears and curl to his short brown hair.

She wanted to run to him. To throw her arms around him and say his name on a squeal of delight as he swung her around.

But her feet rooted to the spot, her body frozen. She could not even whisper his name as she took in the sight of him.

Instead, it was Elspetha who jumped to her feet, shouting her brother's name loudly enough to make the elves gathered in the room flinch, before she flung herself into his hug.

Edmund laughed, that human laugh that never worried about being too loud or too boisterous, as he lifted his sister off her feet and swung her around.

That was all right. Jalissa had waited this long for Edmund to come back to her. She could be content to wait until the right moment for a proper greeting.

He was hers. Her heart knew it. And now her head did too.

CHAPTER

FORTY

Edmund tried to ignore the shocked, wide-eyed expression on Jalissa's face as he swung Essie around. "Good to see you too, Essie."

She groaned, pressing her face into his shoulder. "Put me down unless you want me vomiting on your shirt."

"What?" Edmund hurriedly set her back down, keeping a hand on her arm, his mind racing.

She wasn't sick. If she had been, she would have been curled in her bed, Farrendel alternating between doting on her and anxiously disinfecting everything Essie had touched.

A quick glance from Essie to Farrendel confirmed Edmund's suspicion. They had the answer written all over their faces.

Essie opened her mouth, but Edmund cut her off by giving her another hug, making sure to leave her feet on the ground this time. "Congratulations! When is my niece or nephew due? Unless you're having twins? I always thought twins would be fun to have for nieces and nephews."

Behind Essie, Farrendel's face went white, as Edmund

had known it would. He probably shouldn't tease Farrendel, but it was just too easy sometimes.

It was going to be so much fun to watch Farrendel's face when he realized that he was *never* getting away from Edmund, no matter which family gathering he attended.

Essie rolled her eyes and pushed out of Edmund's hug, giving him a light smack on his arm for good measure. "Stop teasing. I'm pretty sure Melantha or Rheva would have mentioned if if we were having twins by now. Considering one or the other has checked on the baby every day for the past two weeks, I think one of them would have noticed if there were two of them in there."

She glanced past Edmund to where Melantha and Rheva were sitting, as if seeking confirmation.

"You are not having twins," Rheva said firmly.

"I can confirm. No twins," Melantha added.

Farrendel released a sigh and sank back against his seat, as if in utter relief that his introduction to fatherhood would happen one child at a time.

Essie returned to her seat next to Farrendel, whispering to him. Probably something mushy about how he was going to be a great father, since Farrendel's ears turned a little bit pink.

Edmund grinned, glad to see such happiness in their eyes. Another nephew. Or maybe a niece this time. Either way, he couldn't wait to play the role of fun uncle again. "Have you done the announcement ceremony yet?"

"Ceremony?" Essie's forehead wrinkled, and she glanced at Farrendel.

Oh, good. They hadn't. Edmund might have missed their wedding—both of their weddings—but he would be here for this.

"Children are rare for elves. Of course we have a traditional ceremony." Farrendel squirmed, as if he wasn't looking forward to it. "When we wish to officially make the announcement that we are expecting, we paint the rune meaning happiness in white paint on our foreheads, then visit our family, friends, and walk the streets of Estyra. Anyone who sees us will stop to offer their congratulations and advice, and sometimes a small gift if they have something on hand. We should have already done it to announce our news to my family."

"But *someone* couldn't help but blurt out the news every chance he got?" Essie fixed him with a look that had Farrendel squirming even more.

"Yes."

Edmund struggled to hide his smirk. The whole point of the ceremony was to tell the news to everyone without having to say the words *We are expecting* out loud. Because, of course, elves couldn't—or weren't supposed to—be that indelicate. But Farrendel was taking on more human mannerisms than even he probably realized.

Essie sighed. "Well, in that case, we should plan on tomorrow or the day after. We already made the formal announcement to Escarland. It wouldn't do to wait too long to officially announce it to Tarenhiel as well."

"Day after tomorrow would be best, I should think." Rheva shared a look with Leyleira, then Melantha.

Edmund recognized the look of someone plotting. It seemed Farrendel's family planned to make up for their lack of excitement for Essie and Farrendel's marriage by going overboard celebrating this happy news.

Weylind cleared his throat, the lines on his face warning that he was about to turn the conversation in a more serious direction. "Is the situation in Mongavaria resolved?"

His grin dropping from his face, Edmund met Weylind's hard, dark eyes and nodded. "It is. The Mongavarian king understands exactly what will happen to him if he tries to hurt Farrendel and Essie again."

Weylind gave one, sharp nod. "Good."

Out of the corner of his eye, Edmund could see Farrendel and Essie shifting, as if uncomfortable with how much it had taken to keep them safe.

Especially now that they knew about Julien's willingness to sacrifice himself to a marriage with a troll woman to secure that alliance. While Edmund hoped his brother would be happy with his choice, he couldn't help but be selfishly thankful Julien had been the one to volunteer for that duty. As Edmund's heart was already taken by a certain elf princess, this was one time he would have chosen his heart over his kingdom, if it had come down to it.

"Please have a seat, Prince Edmund." Rheva gestured to one of the empty cushions on the floor.

He did not move to take the offered seat. All he wanted to do was gather Jalissa into his arms and, finally, kiss her.

But he had to do this right. More than anything, when he at last kissed Jalissa, he wanted it to *be* right in a way it never had before. The benefit to his years of spying on Tarenhiel was that he was familiar with their customs and could follow them.

For that reason, he'd stopped at Winstead Palace before going on to Tarenhiel. He'd needed to report to Averett, gather the contents of the bag at his feet, and wash so that he didn't arrive on Jalissa's doorstep smelling of three weeks without bathing in anything other than a stream and wearing a bristly beard that he didn't know if she would like or not. They had yet to discuss her facial hair preferences.

Edmund squared his shoulders, faced Weylind, and spoke in elvish. "Weylind Daresheni, brother of Jalissa Amirah, I wish to ask to court her. I present these gifts to you and your family to prove to her and to you that my intentions are honorable."

Someone choked, then coughed, though Edmund didn't look to see who it was. He could hear Farrendel's faint *what?* followed by Essie's *I told you they had grown close during the war!*

But he kept his focus on Weylind, trying not to shift as the full force of the elf king's glower fell on him.

After several long, agonizing moments, Weylind snapped out a single word. "Proceed."

Not the most encouraging tone, but Edmund hadn't expected anything less from Weylind. He would play the part of disapproving older brother to the last, just to make sure Edmund was well and truly squirming.

Edmund picked up a wooden cane from where he had laid it on the floor next to his bag. He approached Leyleira, bowed, and presented her with it.

Leyleira raised her eyebrow, not reaching for the cane. "I am old, but I am not infirm."

"No, you are not. Nor is this a cane to aid a frail woman. It is the weapon of a former queen who carries it as a scepter of her wisdom." Edmund straightened and gestured to the cane. "It was carved by one of the finest woodworkers that Escarland's mountains have to offer. The top is shaped into a tree, representing Ellonahshinel, and it is formed out of solid oak, making it sturdy enough to knock on doors for entry or corral wayward grandchildren."

Almost despite herself, Leyleira's mouth twitched with a smile. Good. He was getting to her.

"And, if you press this hidden button here…" Edmund demonstrated. The top of the cane came off in his hand, and he pulled it out, drawing a slim blade the size of a dagger. "You now have a dagger suitable to dispatch any Mongavarian spies that might come calling again. It also works great to slice cakes at birthday parties." He slid the dagger back into the cane until it snapped into place once more. "All without carrying anything as garish as a leather sheath over your dress. You should never underestimate the value of a good cane. Do I need to go on?"

"No, I believe you have quite convinced me." Leyleira took the cane from him. After a moment, she tapped the head of the cane against his chest. "You have a rather questionable silver tongue, young man, but I believe you will do."

Some of the tension along his back eased. One family member and one blessing down.

As he turned to Weylind, the glower was still there, though tempered by a touch of humor. "I do not believe any of us will forgive you. Machasheni was already formidable, but now you have given her a weapon."

Leyleira made a tutting sound and tapped the cane on the floor. She tilted her head, as if discovering she liked the sound it made, and sharply rapped the cane on the floor again. Then, she rested her hands on it with a rather satisfied smile.

Now he was starting to feel a little rueful watching her. "I may live to regret that gift."

When he turned back to Weylind, the elf king had

crossed his arms, as if to warn Edmund that he would not be so easily won by a silver tongue.

Edmund reached into an inner pocket of his tunic and withdrew an envelope. He bowed and handed it to Weylind.

Frowning, Weylind opened the flap and pulled out the single sheet of paper. Perhaps sensing its import, he kept it tilted so that even Rheva next to him couldn't read it. The slightest widening of his eyes and lift to his brows gave away his surprise, and Edmund could see the moment Weylind spotted Averett's signature on the bottom, confirming that Averett had given permission for this.

After the Mongavarian spies had turned Escarland's Intelligence Office against Tarenhiel so neatly, Averett agreed that Weylind deserved to know this truth to clear the air between the two kings and two kingdoms. Under the table, of course. Only Averett, Weylind, and Edmund would know. Not even Edmund's superiors in the Intelligence Office would learn of this.

Edmund would tell Jalissa as well, though she already knew most of it. More than Averett, even.

After a long moment, Weylind slid the paper into the envelope, and he raised his gaze to meet Edmund's again. The hard elf king was still there, but the glower was gone. "Thank you for proving not only your honor, but your brother's honor as well. I will let you know when it is convenient for my schedule to discuss this."

Another knot loosened in Edmund's stomach. That was as good of a blessing as he would get from Weylind, especially since he was willing to give it even before their discussion.

Weylind folded the envelope in half, then half again,

until he had a tight square. He held it out to Farrendel. "Please destroy this."

Edmund breathed a sigh of relief. It had been a huge risk on Averett's part to put this offer in writing and sign it. A year ago, Weylind might have used such a letter as a weapon against him. But now, the two kings held a great deal of respect for each other. A friendship even, though Edmund wasn't sure Weylind would admit that out loud. And because of that friendship, Weylind was ensuring that this letter would never fall into the wrong hands.

And, perhaps, he was making one last jab at Edmund, showing him what *should* have been done with that doomsday plan after the treaty had been signed.

Brow furrowed, Farrendel took the folded envelope, pinching it between thumb and pointer finger. With a crackle, his magic flared bright, then vanished. Nothing, not even ash, remained of the envelope and letter.

By the way Essie was bouncing a little in her seat, Edmund could tell she was itching to ask what was in the note. Everyone in the room probably was.

But no one asked. They were royalty. They all knew that there were questions that could not be asked and answers that could not be given.

Now that the two hardest gifts were out of the way, Edmund set to work distributing the rest of the items. Ryfon received a book on the history of the castles of Aldon—one that Edmund had re-read to double-check that it was not disparaging of elves. Brina squealed, then clapped a hand over her mouth as if she couldn't believe she had done that, when he handed her a book on the history of Aldon. It was one of the quirkier history books, the kind with an easy-to-read narration that enjoyed pointing out the oddest facts the author could find.

For Rharreth, he had an Escarlish pistol with a matching derringer for Melantha. The weapons used the same ammunition since he figured that would make it easier for Rharreth to source. Weylind was still leery of providing the trolls with Escarlish weapons, but he didn't voice any objection to Edmund's gifts. A sign of the progress their three kingdoms had made.

Rheva had been more of a challenge, but he had finally decided on a fine linen tablecloth with intricate embroidery of flowers and birds around the edge. Rheva smiled, thanked him, and didn't even seem too surprised when it happened to be the perfect size for her tea table.

"And now, for my favorite brother-in-law." With a flourish, Edmund pulled out one of those elf ear mugs, the ones that an artist in Escarland had created. It was an interesting piece of ceramic, that was for sure, from its white color to the jagged blue lines running through it to the large elf-shaped ears sticking out from either side.

Farrendel frowned, his nose wrinkling. "I do not think you understand the purpose of this tradition. You are supposed to give thoughtful items that the recipients actually *like*. It is not the occasion for...humorous gifts." He did not look like he found this gift humorous, but he did not want to say anything more offensive out loud.

Far too easy. Edmund was really going to enjoy teasing Farrendel for many, many years to come.

Grinning, Edmund switched from presenting the mug to Farrendel to holding it out to Essie. "That's why this gift is Essie's. Or, part of her gift anyway. So that the two of you will have matching mugs in that new workshop of yours."

Essie laughed and snatched the mug, hugging it to her. "Yes! This is perfect!"

Farrendel kept frowning, as if he blamed the mug for the fact that he fell for the exact same joke a second time.

"Essie, the rest of your gift is a hand-carved mug rack, shaped like a tree. Fingol will be delivering it to Farrendel's workshop tomorrow, though you can put it wherever you want. It was too big to fit in my bag." Edmund reached out and tweaked her nose the way he had when she was little. "There are only spaces for twenty mugs, so choose wisely."

She laughed again, shaking her head. "You don't have to bribe me for my approval. You already had it."

"This is your gift, Farrendel." Edmund pulled out the second-to-last item in his bag and held it out. It was a pair of goggles like the ones the inventor Lance Marion wore.

This time, Farrendel's eyes widened, and he snatched it from Edmund's hand nearly as fast as Essie had claimed the elf ear mug. "This is the latest model. It has both magnifying and welding glasses attachments. I was hoping to get a pair the next time we were in Aldon."

"Well, there goes one idea for an anniversary gift." Essie gave an exaggerated sigh, touching the silver, heart-shaped necklace she wore.

Farrendel peeled his focus from the goggles with what looked like effort to share a smile with Essie. "You do not have to get me anything. You have already given me the best gift."

Edmund started to edge away. By the way Farrendel was looking at Essie, things were about to get disgustingly mushy.

Oh, well. He now had the perfect revenge. He would kiss

Farrendel's sister in front of him and see how he liked it then.

Essie patted Farrendel's shoulder. "Don't worry. I have other ideas. I was thinking maybe a pet cat. I've heard pets make great practice for parenting. I've always been more a dog person, but I think a cat might handle living in a tree-house far better than a dog. What do you think? Paige let me know that one of the cats in the stables at Winstead Palace had a litter a few days ago, if you want to pick one out. You aren't allergic to cats, are you? I've never noticed that elves struggle with allergies. Is that because elves don't have allergies or because your healers can help you manage them?"

Edmund caught only a glimpse of the semi-horrified, semi-intrigued look on Farrendel's face before he turned away. He had not officially received a blessing from Farrendel, but that was fine. Farrendel hadn't asked for Edmund's blessing before he married Essie, so now they were even.

Finally, Edmund faced the person he had wanted to see the most.

Jalissa still stood just inside the doorway, her hands pressed over her mouth. Her eyes glittered with a wet sheen, though no tears had yet spilled onto her face.

He halted in front of her, pulling out the last item from his bag. He had scoured every bookseller in Estyra until he had found an exact copy. And then, because he was senti-mental, he had sneaked into Ellonahshinel's library, stolen the book from the shelf, and replaced it with the copy. No one besides him and Jalissa would ever know the difference. Besides, she was Ellonahshinel's princess. The book already belonged to her, kind of.

He held out the elven book on Aldon's famous Kingsley Gardens, the same one she had been reading when they had met years ago on that quiet, lonely night. "I have presented my gifts to your family and to you for you to judge my honor and worthiness. Have I found favor in your eyes, my amirah? May I pay you court?"

With trembling fingers, she took the book, tracing its cover. A single tear trickled down her cheek. Yet, when her hand halted over a worn spot on the cover, she peeked up at him, sharing a smile that held the knowledge of the secret they held between them.

Sending a glance at her family, Jalissa grabbed Edmund's arm and dragged him toward the door with a surprisingly firm grip. She flung the door open with such force the poor guard wheezed a bit as it thunked into him.

Jalissa didn't halt until they were out of sight around the corner of the porch. Then she turned and flung herself into Edmund's arms so quickly he barely had time to wrap his arms around her. Her arms tightened around his neck, as if she feared he would walk away from her even now. The book he'd given her landed with a thump on the porch floor as she all but shouted, "Yes, yes, yes!"

He laughed, holding her tightly. She was a few inches taller than Essie, but he still managed to lift her off her feet. "Jalissa, darling, I only asked if I could court you. I haven't asked you to marry me. Not yet, anyway."

"And I will say yes with just as much excitement then." Jalissa tilted her face toward him, smiling with a wild abandon he had never seen from her. "I am so excited to finally have the freedom to say *yes* after so long of saying *no*."

It would be so easy to lean down and kiss her, but he resisted, smiling as he set her back on her feet, though he continued to hold her close. "Don't rush things. I plan to savor every moment of courting you properly."

She shook her head, giving him a fake stern glare. "Do not drag things out too long. You have already made me wait long enough. I do not have time to waste, you know."

"That is a very human attitude for you."

"I have decided to embrace a more human outlook on life, now that I will likely have a shorter lifespan than my fellow elves." Her smile didn't slip in the least, but Edmund's chest tightened at her words.

His smile faded as he searched her face. "Will you be all right with that? Giving up hundreds of years of your life to extend mine?"

"Yes." She answered without even a blink of hesitation. After a moment, her gaze dropped, and she toyed with the laces of his shirt. "I have experienced what it is like living without you, and that was only for a few months. It is worth it, if I never have to live without you again."

"If you keep saying sweet things like that, I might get distracted from these important conversations we need to have." Edmund gently tucked a strand of Jalissa's hair behind the tip of her pointed ear. "I want you to be sure. I know how you hate regrets."

She shrugged, her gaze swinging back to meet his. "I am sure. Besides, Farrendel will have a shorter lifespan due to his elishina. I suspect Melantha might not live as long as a normal elf either. And Weylind is so much older than me to begin with. Without an elishina with you, I would likely have to endure many long, lonely years of watching my siblings die before me. I do not mind giving that up to spend my years with you. But do you think we will? What if we do not?"

"We will." Edmund ran the back of his fingers over her cheek. "I know you. When you give your heart, you give it wholeheartedly. And I will never take that for granted again, no matter how long we live. You have all of me, Jalissa. Every name, every disguise, they are yours."

She melted against him, and he had to wrap an arm around her waist to steady her. Not that he minded holding her close like this.

Perhaps Jalissa had the right idea about a short courtship rather than a long one.

After a moment, she glanced back at him, worrying her lower lip. "I know I probably should not ask, but what was in that note you gave Weylind?"

"I promised no more secrets, and I meant it." He tightened his hold around her waist. "I gave Weylind one frank discussion where he could ask me anything about the Escarlish spying efforts in Tarenhiel—and my part in them—and I would answer honestly."

"Really?" Jalissa's eyes widened. "Does your brother know about this?"

"Yes. He included his own note to Weylind and signed it to prove that I have his permission to reveal Escarlish secrets to Weylind." Edmund owed Averett for that, even if it had been necessary for good relations between Escarland and Tarenhiel after the fiasco with the Mongavarian spies, regardless of Edmund's need to clear the air with his future in-laws. "Still, it is a bit under the table, so to speak. Besides that note, there will be nothing in writing. No one besides Weylind, Averett, me, and now you, will know."

"Ah. That explains why Weylind burned it." Jalissa nodded, her expression falling into that serene, elven princess look of hers, as if just thinking about politics made her put on her court mask. After a moment, her mask fell, revealing turmoil in her gaze. "Will you tell him *everything*?"

Edmund winced, but he kept his gaze locked on Jalissa. "What do you want me to tell him? It's your secret as much as mine."

Jalissa looked away from him, staring off into the night. "Weylind likes you right now. I would hate to see you endure months of his disapproving scowl, like Elspetha did after she married Farrendel. He might even rescind his blessing, if he learned…"

"How I dishonorably toyed with your affections?" Edmund grimaced just thinking about the way he had hurt Jalissa back then.

Jalissa's gaze snapped back to his, her chin lifting. "I was angry with you earlier, and I let you take the full blame. But let us be honest. I was a princess clandestinely meeting a person I thought was a lowly servant late at night, knowing the relationship had no hope of going anywhere. I toyed with your affections just as much as you did mine. I was lucky that you *are* honorable, otherwise I might have suffered much worse than a temporarily broken heart."

His stomach churned, just thinking about that. A less honorable man might have taken advantage of Jalissa, thinking to force a marriage and bag himself a princess. As lonely as Jalissa had been, waiting for her brothers to return from the war, it would have been too easy for someone to prey on her.

He and Jalissa had been carried away by their emotions, but they had at least held on to enough sense not to cross the line. He had not even kissed her, and nearly doing so had been what had shaken sense into him.

Edmund touched her cheek again, tilting her face toward

him. "I know it doesn't make everything all right, but I truly wanted to comfort you. I could tell you were hurting, and I wanted to help."

"I know." Jalissa reached up and traced her fingers over his cheek, her brow wrinkling as if she were marveling over having the freedom to do so.

Her gentle touch sent shivers down his spine, and it took all his self-control to stand still rather than sweep her into a passionate kiss. It was not yet time, and he forced himself to wait.

Her fingers fell from his jaw to rest lightly on his chest as she peeked up at him with those dark brown eyes, glittering in the starlight. "I think those nights in the library should remain our secret. We said no secrets, but that does not mean we cannot keep secrets from everyone else."

He gave a relieved laugh. This was the answer he had been hoping for, though he would have done whatever she had asked. "I agree. Then, in that case, all I will tell Weylind is that I impersonated a servant here at Ellonahshinel before I was forced to change my cover and spy elsewhere. No need to go into details."

If Weylind pressed, Edmund could truthfully tell him that it was too noticeable, for what appeared to be a young, able-bodied elf, not to join the army. When he'd reinvented himself, he'd chosen the role of a warrior crippled at the front, and that had made him much more invisible.

"Good." Jalissa smiled up at him. "It is our secret to treasure without my brother sticking his overly long, bossy nose into our business."

Edmund laughed, then gestured at the book she had dropped on the floor. "Yes. I can see how much you treasure that part of our past. And after I went through all the work of stealing it for you. I'm deeply hurt."

She shook her head, her mouth twisting as if she wanted to frown but couldn't. "I really should not find the fact that you stole my favorite book for me romantic instead of appalling."

"Don't fret. I replaced it with an identical copy so no one will even realize it's missing. If anything, the new copy is in much better shape than this one. Not quite as well loved."

"Even better. Then I will not feel guilty about keeping this gift." That wry smile remained on her face. "You are a bad influence."

"So I'm told." He rested a hand over hers on his chest. "I want you to be my co-conspirator in all of my plots and secrets from now on, as I'll be in yours."

"You are still planning to engage in plotting?" Jalissa raised one dark eyebrow at him, but her eyes still twinkled in the starlight.

"For the good of both of our kingdoms, yes." He shrugged, clasping her fingers with his against his shirt. "I'm not sure what it will look like yet. It will likely involve less undercover work and more spying while on official missions as ambassadors."

"I should not be surprised." Jalissa's smile took on a hint of a smirk. "You will always be my *ispamir*."

He caught his breath at her title for him, torn between the fact that he liked it and the instinctual fear of years of habit. "Spy prince? Isn't that a little…literal? A good spy doesn't go around announcing that he is a spy in his name."

"No, a good spy does not." Now she was definitely smirking. "But a great spy can. And you are about to tell my brother how you spied on his kingdom, only to eventually ask to marry his sister. Only the very best spy can pull that off."

He couldn't help it. He threw back his head and barked a laugh. "True. Edmund Ispamir. I like the sound of it."

"I thought you might."

"You are my perfectly sneaky princess."

He had not seen her smirk nearly enough. It was so adorable, all elven restraint with a dash of mischief. She cocked her head, that mischief still lingering in her expression. "What is our first mission?"

"A little bit of innocent plotting." Edmund lowered his tone, though there was no one close enough to overhear. "Fair warning, I intend to kiss you where Farrendel will happen to see. Just some harmless revenge for the fact that he married my little sister without so much as a by your leave."

Jalissa gave him a reproving look, still tinged with mirth. "It is not Farrendel's fault you were a little busy spying on Tarenhiel at the time."

"All the more reason he has no excuse. I was conveniently located so that he could swing by on his way to the border." Edmund attempted to sound huffy, but he wasn't sure he managed it. "Don't get me wrong. I like having Farrendel for a brother-in-law, and I can't imagine Essie with anyone else. But she's still my baby sister."

Jalissa was laughing at him. Not out loud, of course, but he could tell. She fought to keep a serene smile on her face, even as her eyes crinkled. "Very well. I will help with this plan. But it cannot be my first kiss. I do not want to experience that with my little brother as an audience."

"No, of course not." His laughter faded as he trailed his fingers through her hair again.

She swayed closer, their faces inches apart as she peered up at him with large, trusting eyes.

He felt that trust so deeply inside his heart. He did not deserve her trust, not after he had broken her heart so many times before.

Now, no more secrets stood between them. He had asked to court her properly, including proving his intentions to her and her family in the elven tradition. This moment was *right* when so many times it had been *wrong.*

"We don't have an audience now." His voice came out as a low whisper as he cradled her face, gazing into dark eyes shining bright in reflected starlight. "May I kiss you?"

Her answer was a tiny, shy nod against his fingers.

Despite the rushing of his blood through his veins, the heat in his chest, Edmund slowly, gently, kissed her.

SIX MONTHS LATER...

S tanding before the small mirror hung on a peg, Edmund straightened the elven tunic, studying the way the open neck dipped to a large V to expose a great deal of his chest. For how stuffy and proper elves were most times, they enjoyed living on the edge for their wedding ceremonies.

The commander of the outpost had graciously given up his quarters for Edmund's use today, as he had a year and a half ago for Essie for her wedding to Farrendel at this same army fort next to the Hydalla River. Edmund's wedding wasn't going to be held in the fort itself, but it was a convenient spot to get ready.

Somewhere across the river, Jalissa would also be readying herself, with her sisters gathered around her. His mother, Paige, and Essie, of course, were there as well, though they would return to the Escarlish side of the river before the ceremony started.

A knock sounded on the door, and Edmund hurried to answer it, expecting Averett or Julien coming to check on him. The two of them had been run ragged thanks to all the many, last minute organizational details that had to be dealt with thanks to a royal wedding and a bridge dedication happening all at once and involving guests from three different kingdoms.

Instead, when Edmund opened the door, he found Farrendel standing there, holding a silver bowl and carrying a leather sack slung over his shoulder. Edmund stepped aside to let him in. "Is this for the eshinelt?"

The eshinelt was the green paint used during the elven wedding ceremony. But, of course, there was a ceremony that accompanied the making of the eshinelt before the wedding. It was a tradition not without purpose, as it was thought to encourage the formation of an elven elishina.

Farrendel nodded, his ear tips a little pink, as he crept inside. He set the bowl on the commander's small, private dining table, staring down at it instead of looking at Edmund. "Machasheni Leyleira said I had to be the one to do it. She gave me the instructions again, to make sure I remembered them. But she would not come herself."

"She did not want to make the trek back and forth across the river. Understandable." Edmund halted at the table across from Farrendel.

"Well, yes. She claimed her old bones were not up to it."

"While thumping her cane on the floor in that way of hers. I am really beginning to regret that gift."

"Yes." Farrendel sighed and lifted his head just enough to glance at Edmund. "She is right, though. As usual. The making of the eshinelt should be done by father and son, or at least with a close relative. Right now, I am already your brother, thanks to my marriage with Essie. It has to be me."

Farrendel's mouth set in such a grim line that Edmund couldn't help but laugh. "Don't look so glum. Surely it can't be that bad."

That twitched the grim line into a hint of a smile. "No. But if something goes wrong with the eshinelt, do not blame me."

"With that attitude, something *will* go wrong." Edmund shook his head, then reached across the table to grip Farrendel's shoulders in the elven-style hug, waiting until his brother-in-law met his gaze. "I could wish for no one better to teach me to make the eshinelt." Before the moment could get too sappy, he added, "You are my favorite brother-in-law, after all."

Farrendel shook his head, but he was smiling now rather than anxious. "I have been your favorite because I have been your only one. But not for much longer." His smile faded, as if he was a little disappointed to be losing his favorite brother-in-law status.

Edmund grinned. He had been waiting for this to come up for months now. "That is where you are wrong. You will still be my favorite younger brother. My favorite first brother-in-law. And, most of all, you will be my brother-in-law squared."

"Squared?" Farrendel's nose wrinkled.

"Brother-in-law Squared. Brother-in-law Times Two. Double Brother. Whatever you want to call it." Edmund's grin grew as he watched the dawning realization—and slight horror—creep into Farrendel's expression. He turned his shoulder clasp into a good old-fashioned smack on the arm. "No matter which family gathering you attend, I'm going to be there. And as I fully intend to form an elishina with your sister, you won't even get a reprieve by having me die off early. You're stuck with me like a bit of mess clinging to the bottom of your boot that you can't seem to clean off."

"Is it too late for me to take back my blessing on this wedding?" Farrendel crossed his arms. With that attempt at a glower on his face, his resemblance to Weylind became more apparent.

"As I recall, you never officially gave it." Edmund waved a hand. "Not that I have any intention of asking for it, any more than you asked for my blessing before you married my sister."

Farrendel opened, then closed his mouth.

Edmund smirked. He had his brother-in-law there. He waited a moment, then decided it was best to take pity on him. "And look at how well that turned out."

The smile returned to Farrendel's face, there for just a moment, before fading. Farrendel's gaze dropped to the items on the table once again. "Essie has not said it out loud, but I can tell. She is relieved that you will likely have a heart bond of your own. She has mourned the fact that she was going to lose her entire family while living so long herself. I am thankful for her sake that one of you will live just as long as she will."

"And you? I know your family mourned that they would lose you early thanks to your heart bond. Do you feel that way about Jalissa?" Edmund wasn't sure he wanted to know the answer. Jalissa was willing to make the sacrifice, and that was all that mattered, in the end.

Farrendel shrugged, still not looking at him. "I am selfish. It will not feel early to me, since I will also age faster. I cannot help but be a little grateful that Jalissa will age with me. We will stay as we have always been."

Edmund nodded. Farrendel, understandably, feared being isolated from his family. Which might have happened, had he aged faster while Jalissa, his closest sibling, remained young for so much longer. This way, none of them would be alone.

"As for the others..." Farrendel gave another, smaller shrug. "Melantha is determined to be happy for Jalissa no matter what. And I believe Weylind has given up in weary resignation."

"Don't you mean grumpy resignation?"

"It does come across that way." Farrendel smiled again, and this time the smile stuck around. "He and Averett have turned it into another bonding experience, though Weylind will never admit it."

"Of course not. Now that we have gotten that out of the way..." Edmund gestured at the silver bowl and leather sack set on the table. "Where do we begin?"

Farrendel took the items from the leather bag, laying them out on the table in a precise order.

Edmund followed his directions to mash various of the herbs together, adding each ingredient in turn until the green paint formed in the bowl with the correct color and consistency.

"Is it ready?" Edmund gave the mixture one final stir.

"Yes." Farrendel hesitated, staring at the bowl.

Edmund sighed, something inside his chest squeezing. He did not feel inadequate, exactly. But it still ached a bit, knowing that there was one part of the elven tradition that he could not complete, and no cosmetics or fake elf ears could disguise it. In the end, he was not and never could be an elf. "This is the part where an elf husband-to-be would add his magic, isn't it?"

Farrendel nodded, but then he straightened his shoulders. "Essie does not have any magic either, and we have an elishina. I will bring this to Jalissa for her to add her magic. Her magic will be enough for both of you."

As Farrendel was not prone to optimism, he must really believe what he was saying.

"Linshi, shashon." Edmund smiled at the way the elvish felt just as natural as Escarlish.

Farrendel pulled a piece of leather from the bag, along with a small, green-glowing piece of vine. When he touched the vine to the leather, it twined around both leather and bowl, effectively sealing the eshinelt in place for the journey back across the river.

"Did Jalissa give that to you?" Edmund studied it. He didn't have magic of his own, and yet deep inside him, some instinct told him that magic hadn't been Jalissa's, even if it was in her style.

"No, Machasheni Leyleira. But she said she was inspired by Jalissa's creations." Farrendel picked up the bowl cautiously, as if still afraid he would manage to spill it despite the lid. "I was panicking at the thought of transporting this across the river."

Edmund held back his wince. When Farrendel said *panicking*, he meant that very literally. Edmund didn't like the thought that his wedding was causing his brother-in-law that much stress, but he kept his tone light. "How many trips across the river will this be today?"

485

"My fourth." Farrendel eased the pack's strap onto his shoulder, keeping his focus on the bowl. "And I still have two more trips to make when I escort Essie, Paige, and Macha back to this side and return to the Tarenhieli side myself for the ceremony." Only then did Farrendel look up, that teasing humor back in his gaze. "You and Jalissa just had to decide to make a big political statement by getting married moments *after* the bridge is completed in the sight of all your guests. You could not wait until tomorrow when I could have simply taken a train back and forth instead of the boat."

"Admit it. If the bridge had been here, you and Essie would have done the same thing."

"Essie and I are the reason the bridge exists."

"At least Jalissa and I are only having a single wedding. Not two weddings and double the work."

"Perhaps Essie and I were worth the extra hassle." With a smug smirk, as if gleeful that he had managed to give as good as he got in that round of banter, Farrendel spun and left the room, closing the door behind him.

Edmund shook his head, turning back to the mirror to check that he hadn't gotten any green paint on his clothes. He and his brothers were having too much of an influence on Farrendel. Next thing they knew, Farrendel was going to start pulling practical jokes on them.

Oh, well. Edmund could afford to let Farrendel have the last word in this round. He would have hundreds of years to get him back.

Edmund glanced at the clock. Only an hour left. He might have hundreds of years for this future, but that hour could not go by soon enough.

JALISSA HELD STILL as Melantha braided her hair, far gentler than Jalissa had been for Melantha's wedding. The mirror in front of her had been propped on a table that would soon be filled with communication equipment, once this building was turned into the main hub for transferring both messages and letters back and forth between the kingdoms.

As Melantha worked, she tucked some of the flowers Jalissa had grown into the strands. When she tied off some of the ends, Melantha held out her hand to Edmund's mother, where she and Queen Paige sat to one side of Jalissa. "I am ready for the tiara."

Edmund's macha picked up a wooden case and opened it. Inside, a slim, silver crest arched into a subtle pattern of flowers formed of pink, pale blue, and purple stones. Emerald leaves and stems twined together, and all of it was outlined with shimmering diamonds. "If I remember the family history correctly, Edmund's great-grandmother wore this at her wedding."

On the other side of Jalissa, Elspetha grinned and nodded. She sprawled in her chair with pillows stuffed around her to make the seat as comfortable as possible. At eight months pregnant, she was staying off her feet as much as possible before the ceremony.

No, not Elspetha. Essie. Jalissa was trying to remember to use her nickname, since it was what Essie preferred and a human custom that Jalissa could adopt.

"It is perfect. Linshi." Jalissa could have worn her elven crown, but she had asked Edmund's macha to bring an Escarlish tiara instead. Due to the nature of the elven part of the ceremony, both she and Edmund had to be dressed in an elven style. Since Escarland still needed to be represented somewhere, his crown and her tiara seemed a fitting place to do that.

Paige took the tiara from the box Macha held, stood, and joined Melantha behind Jalissa to settle the tiara in place. "I brought some dark thread to sew it into your hair. Do you want me to do it? Or your sister can?"

"Actually, I had a different idea." Jalissa reached up and touched one of the flowers that Melantha had fastened in place. With her magic, the flower sent out shoots to twine through both the tiara and Jalissa's braided hair, tiny leaves and flowers sprouting at intervals to complement the stone flowers in the crown. When she was finished, the tiara was held securely in place by a small, subtle crown of flowers.

Melantha brushed her fingers against the back of Jalissa's neck, a soothing tide of her magic flowing into her. "Just in case wearing stones on your head gives you a headache."

"Linshi." As Melantha stepped back, Jalissa half-turned in her seat and caught her sister's arm, halting her. "I mean it, isciena. Linshi. I am glad to have you here."

"I would not wish to be anywhere else." While Melantha still had a hard edge sharpening her eyes and her posture, that hint of iciness no longer felt like a wall to keep others out, but a strength to let people in. Dressed in leather and wearing her troll queen diadem, her bearing suited her more than ever.

Melantha had found where she belonged in the far northern mountains of Kostaria. And, today, Jalissa's place of belonging would change and grow with Edmund at her side. She wasn't sure what place they would find for themselves, but they would create it together.

A knock tapped on the door, and a moment later Rheva stuck her head in. "Melantha, are you able to step away? There seems to be some argument over where to put our troll guests, and I believe Weylind and Rharreth could use your help."

Melantha grimaced and hurried toward the door. "It must be serious if Rharreth cannot handle it by himself. Isciena, I will return when I can." Without waiting for Jalissa's answer, Melantha hurried after Rheva.

Before the door could swing all the way closed, Farrendel knocked on it, his eyes squeezed shut even though the door was only open a sliver. "May I come in?"

"Yes, everyone's decent!" Essie called back.

Jalissa indulged in a smile at that. How she loved having a human sister-in-law who would shout out what an elf would be too proper to say.

Farrendel peeked through the crack in the door, as if he was not positive he should enter, before he eased the door fully open. Crossing the room, he rested his hands on Essie's shoulders and kissed her cheek. "How are you?"

Essie laughed as she leaned her head against the back of the chair to look up at him. "Just fine. The same as I was an hour ago when you last asked." Essie glanced to Jalissa. "Seriously, I don't know what I'd do if he didn't have his classes at Hanford University to keep him distracted."

"You were warned that I would hover." His smile, though a tad sheepish, did not look at all repentant. After pressing another quick kiss to Essie's forehead, Farrendel turned to Jalissa. "You look beautiful, isciena."

"Linshi." Jalissa smoothed the skirt of her white dress. Another nod to Escarlish culture, since elves did not have such a tradition regarding the color of the bride's dress, though light green or blue were the most common colors. "With all the wedding preparations, I have not had a chance to ask. How are your classes going, shashon?"

Farrendel grimaced and glanced at Essie. "We survived."

Essie shook her head, sharing a look with Farrendel before turning back to Jalissa. "The first couple of weeks were rough, but Iyrinder's presence helped immensely. Though we all know why he has developed such an interest in human learning and culture. Isn't that right, Iyrinder?" At this last, Essie raised her voice.

Standing just outside the door, Farrendel's guard Iyrinder briefly glanced over his shoulder before he focused on the hall once again. "I have no comment, amirah."

Essie grinned, and Jalissa just shook her head. It was good to see more elf-human romances starting to flourish, and a part of her wanted to take credit for it. She and Edmund proved that Essie and Farrendel's romance was not just an anomaly.

"The eshinelt has been prepared, and Machasheni is waiting to finish it with you." Farrendel gestured to the room across the hall from where Jalissa, Essie, Paige, and Edmund's macha currently gathered.

Jalissa started to stand, then froze, turning to Essie. "I am so sorry we never gave you the eshinelt. You should have been allowed to at least complete the bride's part of the ceremony and stir it, even if you had no magic to add."

Essie shrugged, her hands resting on her rounded belly. "It's fine. Really. I don't have magic. There was nothing I could have added to it, unless I spat in it or something."

"Essie." Farrendel's nose wrinkled, his eyes widening in horror. "You do *not* spit in the eshinelt. That would be…would be…"

"Sacrilegious?" Essie gave that smirk that said she knew very well she was teasing Farrendel.

"Yes. And unsanitary." Farrendel grimaced. "That eshinelt was painted on my face."

"You shouldn't be so appalled. Your magic would have sanitized it." Essie waved her hand, as if brushing away his concerns.

Farrendel turned to Jalissa. "I do believe you spared me in keeping the eshinelt far from her."

Jalissa could have hugged them. It seemed Farrendel knew exactly what Essie was doing in teasing him, and that was make sure Jalissa did not spend her wedding burdened by guilt over how she had treated Essie back then.

"Still, I am sorry." Jalissa halted next to Essie and rested a hand on her shoulder. "I gave you such horrible advice before your elven wedding."

Even now, she cringed. Had she really told Essie not to fall in love with Farrendel? Ugh. She would gladly give herself a good shake for that one.

But Essie did not seem bothered by the memory. Instead, she patted Jalissa's hand, smiling at her. "I understood the sentiment, even if you could have worded it better. You wanted me to take care of your brother's heart. It is the same thing I want from you for my brother."

Farrendel shifted, looking away as if uncomfortable about the fact that he witnessed this conversation that was meant to be shared by sisters without one of the brothers in question lingering nearby.

Jalissa nodded to Essie. "I will." Then, she stepped past Farrendel, crossed the hallway, and entered the nearly identical room across the way.

Machasheni Leyleira glanced up as Jalissa entered, her

now ever-present cane at her side even if she was not leaning on it. "Senasheni. I see you are ready. Your young man is going to be quite convinced of how lucky he is to be marrying you, as he ought to be."

Jalissa approached the desk, where the silver bowl filled with eshinelt waited for her to stir in her magic. "You are rather fond of him."

"He has a wit after my own heart." Machasheni gestured toward the bowl. "I suggest you put in a little extra of your magic. You are providing the magic for two, after all."

"Is that what you told Farrendel when you taught him to make the eshinelt for his wedding?" Jalissa picked up the spoon but did not yet touch it to the paint.

Machasheni speared her with a sharp look. "It is none of your business what I told him. That was his wedding. This is yours."

"Yes, machasheni." Jalissa drew in a deep breath and called up her magic.

Yet, as she held the spoon in one hand, her magic glowing around the other, she hesitated, an ache throbbing in her heart.

Her mother had been gone for so long now—over a hundred years—that normally the pain was dull and faded. Her mother had not known Jalissa as an adult nor had Farrendel even existed back then.

But the ache was particularly painful today, a day when Jalissa should have had a mother at her side. This moment, the final stirring of the eshinelt, was supposed to be shared between a mother and daughter.

Weylind was the only one who had their parents at his wedding. He had made his eshinelt with their father at his side. Their mother had been there, proud to see her son grown up and getting married, even as she was kept busy trying to keep Jalissa presentable. Rheva's mother had still been alive back then, and Rheva would have treasured this moment with her. The two of them had enjoyed a wedding untainted by the ache of loss. It was hard not to be a little jealous at that.

Jalissa released a shuddering breath. Edmund had a similar pain today, missing his father. And his mother had spent much of the day here with Jalissa, filling the role of mother without trying to replace the mother Jalissa had lost.

It was the shared understanding of loss that had drawn Jalissa and Edmund together, during those quiet nights in Estyra's library. They had both been mourning the fathers they had lost, and both worried for the brothers they might yet lose.

Blinking away the burn of tears and swallowing the lump in her throat, Jalissa let her power flow into the eshinelt, pouring all those memories of Edmund into the magic. For a moment, the eshinelt glowed with a soft green light as Jalissa stirred, before the gleam faded.

"Well done, senasheni." Machasheni Leyleira claimed the bowl. "This will do very nicely, I should think."

Jalissa drew in a deep breath and nodded.

When Machasheni Leyleira left, taking charge of the eshinelt until it was time for the ceremony, Jalissa returned to the room across the way, only to find it empty. While she had finished with the eshinelt, Essie, Paige, and Edmund's macha must have left to return to the Escarlish side of the river. Rheva and Melantha had to still be busy sorting out the political problems involved in the guest list.

Jalissa sank onto the chair, thankful for a few moments of quiet to herself before the ceremony began.

If she were to have any doubts, this would be the time for them.

But, no. Even as she sat there, contemplating soon saying her vows to Edmund, the rightness of it echoed all the way from her head to the deepest reaches of her heart.

She belonged with Edmund, and he belonged with her. It had taken them several years of twists and turns to get to this moment, but they had needed that time to refine them into the people they were now.

EDMUND WAITED JUST to the Escarlish side of the center of the bridge, his family beside him. Behind him, the horses' hooves rattled against the cobbles as the drivers turned the carriages around after dropping them off. As symbolic as it would have been to walk from the Escarlish shore, the bridge was several miles long. Walking was not an option if they didn't want their guests to grow restless with the wait.

The new bridge arched in a graceful, stone curve over the broad Hydalla River. Linder Island, that once tiny rocky island in the middle of the Hydalla where that first diplomatic meeting had been held, no longer existed. It now formed the central supporting column of the span.

Graceful wooden posts with looping, sturdy roots already ran on either side of the bridge, and Edmund could barely pick out the two telegraph wires that had been artfully concealed by the elven creations. Those telegraph lines ended at the communication hub on the far side of the river, where elves would translate the messages sent on the elven root system and pass the notes on to the Escarlish telegraphers stationed there.

The muddy water of the Hydalla rippled out to either side of him, framed by the perfectly brilliant reds, oranges, and yellows of the fall leaves decorating the Tarenhieli bank.

To Edmund's left on the Escarlish shore, the new train yard sprawled alongside the river. All the steel rails ended there while elven root rails now extended down from the bridge to a terminal where cargo could be transferred from the elven trains to Escarlish ones.

From where he stood, he could not get a good look at the far side of the bridge or the guests gathered there. All he could see were the backs of the Escarlish guests, including members of both houses of Parliament, all the nobility since no one dared be left out of such an occasion, and Edmund's acquaintances in the Intelligence Office and elsewhere. Trent Bourdon sat near the back, already frantically scribbling notes on a pad of paper. There was one story in the press that Edmund could count on to be favorable, at least.

A section of trolls sat near the front. The troll guests had been divided in two, with half sitting on either side of the bridge. It had been quite the kerfuffle trying to get that arranged to everyone's satisfaction. But it had been important to have trolls represented on both sides, to signify that they were a strong member of this alliance.

Finally, the musicians began playing, the Escarlish orchestra near the front of the guests on this side of the border somehow managing to blend perfectly with the elven flutes and strings on the far side.

With a nod and grin at Edmund, Averett took his place at the front, Paige at his side, and led the way down the aisle between the Escarlish guests. Julien came next with his troll bride-to-be on his arm.

Essie followed, holding the hand of a nephew on either side. Bertie and Finn looked especially dapper in the black suits and white shirts that they had, amazingly, not smudged with dirt yet. The nanny was already waiting in the front row to take charge of them if they grew restless during the ceremony.

Edmund held his breath, watching in case Essie looked in need of help. But she seemed fine and, if she walked a little slower, that could be blamed just as much on keeping pace with the little boys as on being eight-months pregnant.

When he was sure Essie wouldn't need him to rush to her aid, Edmund turned to his mother. As she had spent most of the morning with Jalissa, he hadn't had a chance to talk with her yet.

Not that there was a need for words right now. He hugged her. And if he got a little lump in the back of his throat at her slightly teary hug and smile, well, it was his wedding. No one would blame him.

Then, she took his arm, and he walked up the cobbled, gentle slope of the bridge, past rows upon rows of guests, until he finally halted just shy of the center.

At the very middle of the bridge, a four-foot-wide section of the stone span was missing, though all the under girders, columns sunk into the river far below, and the wooden trestles overhead were all in place. Two large stone blocks, one on either side, waited to be used to finish the bridge.

Across the gap, Weylind and Rheva stood at the head of Jalissa's family, Rharreth and Melantha directly behind them. Edmund couldn't see Jalissa, screened as she was by her family. Behind them, rows upon rows of elven guests, with a knot of troll guests sitting together, filled the bridge.

Averett pulled Paige to one side, so that he could face the guests on both sides of the bridge as he spoke in a loud, carrying voice. "We are gathered here today to witness two unions. The marriage of my brother and King Weylind's sister, and the completion of this bridge that will join the shores of Escarland and Tarenhiel for generations to come."

When Averett paused, Weylind repeated the speech in elvish, then added, "From today forward, our three kingdoms will be linked by the bridges, both literal and figurative, that bind us together."

After Averett had repeated Weylind's words in Escarlish, Rharreth stepped forward, speaking first in the troll dialect that the elves would understand, then in Escarlish. "In the hope of many years of peace to come, I build this bridge."

He knelt and pressed his hand to the stone on his side. Weylind and Farrendel knelt too, hints of their magic curling around their fingers.

On the Escarlish side, Julien's betrothed knelt and rested her hand on the stone. She and Rharreth shared a nod. Then, their magic flowed into the bridge, cold and hard. Rharreth's side glowed white while her magic was a soft gray as she encouraged the stone block to flow into the gap, merging with the stone already laid down.

Weylind's magic coursed from him, and the elven train rails grew from the Tarenhieli side to join the roots already laid into the Escarlish side of the bridge, embedded securely into the flowing, forming rock.

Just before the bridge fully finished, Averett and Julien stepped forward, carrying the large, bronze dedication plaque between them. They set the plaque into the mushy, magic-filled stone at the very peak of the stone span, the metal settling as if into mortar instead of stone.

At the moment when everyone's magic was at its height, Farrendel's bolts of blue, raw magic flooded over the space. A few of the guests in the first few rows yelped and lifted their feet, as if afraid they would be burned.

But Farrendel had a tight control of his magic, his jaw set in determination. Even standing at the very edge of the gap with Farrendel's magic licking at his boots, Edmund didn't feel any pain nor were his boots damaged.

With a brilliant flash of magic and a boom that shuddered through the bridge beneath their feet, Farrendel slammed his magic into the stone, infusing the stone with the strength and protection of his power, just as he had along all of Tarenhiel's and Escarland's borders over the past few months.

A silence fell all along the bridge, as if both sets of guests were in shock. Then, most of the Escarlish guests jumped to their feet and clapped. A few even cheered.

As if taking that as their cue, the trolls stood and stomped and gave their deep-throated war cry cheers.

Not to be outdone, the elves finally cheered in their polite, subdued manner.

In the hubbub, Averett, Weylind, and Rharreth stood at the very center of the bridge and shook hands with each other. Then, all of them found their seats, including Farrendel who crossed to the Escarlish side to sit next to Essie.

And, finally, as Weylind took his place to the side of the bridge next to the Escarlish officiant and Leyleira halted next to him, holding the eshinelt in its silver bowl, Edmund finally saw Jalissa.

She wore a stunning white dress that flowed around her in an elven style, her shoulders left bare. Her dark brown hair cascaded down her back, the sides pulled away from her face in a pattern of interlocking braids. Yet nestled in the Tarenhieli hairstyle, was his great-grandmother's tiara, held in place with living flowers.

Rheva and Melantha took up the ends of Jalissa's train, and they sang the traditional elven wedding song as Jalissa slowly walked the last few yards toward him.

He strode to her, and they met in the center of the bridge, standing on top of the plaque his brothers had just laid. He held out his hands, and she slid hers into his. Together, they turned and faced her brother and the Escarlish officiant.

Weylind and the officiant smoothly went back and forth as they each completed the steps of both the elven and human wedding ceremonies.

Edmund slipped the ring on Jalissa's finger, one that matched the tiara she currently wore. The two of them exchanged the Escarlish wedding vows.

Then, Leyleira handed the eshinelt to Edmund. He held it out to Jalissa, and she dipped her finger into the paint.

Gently, she traced the runes on his forehead, then cheek, her touch sending shivers through him, and said the blessings with each. As she went to trace the rune on his chest, she froze, the tips of her ears going just a hint pink.

He smirked at her.

She wrinkled her nose back at him, drew in a breath, and traced the rune on his chest.

As she spoke the last word, Edmund caught his breath at the spark of *something* that pulsed into him. Essie had warned him that he might feel a hint of Jalissa's magic, but he had not expected it to be quite this strong. Like the magic had stabbed down into his very soul.

He blinked and handed the bowl to her. After dipping his finger into the paint, he traced the rune on her forehead, then on the soft skin of her cheek, and repeated the elven vows. When he traced the rune on her upper chest above the line of her gown, her ears went pink again, and his own face got a little hot. Farrendel was right. This was a weirdly intimate moment to have in front of such a large audience.

And then, as he spoke the final blessing, Jalissa sucked in a breath, her eyes widening and flashing up to meet his.

He smiled and gave her a tilt of his head to let her know that he had felt it too.

Leyleira stepped forward and claimed the eshinelt, a knowing twinkle to her eyes.

The Escarlish officiant cleared his throat. "Then by the power vested in me, I now declare you man and wife. You may kiss the bride."

Gasps came from the elven side of the bridge, as if a few of the stuffier nobles were so shocked that even they, with their overblown sense of decorum, could not hold back such a loud reaction.

Edmund took one of Jalissa's hands in his and cradled her face with the other, whispering, "Are you sure? We don't have to."

If the elven vows were a little intimate by human standards, then the human practice of a kiss at the end of the ceremony was just as much, if not more so, by elven ones. Jalissa had agreed to this part of the ceremony, but he would not pressure her if she changed her mind now that the moment had come.

But Jalissa smiled, stepping closer instead of back. "Yes.

Very sure. I want everyone in both our kingdoms to know without a doubt that I am your amirah and you are my ispamir."

Edmund was not about to argue with that. Ignoring their audience, he leaned down and kissed her. His elf princess. Her spy prince. For now and always.

EPILOGUE

FOUR MONTHS LATER...

E ssie followed the sounds of a baby's shrieking belly laugh and Farrendel's rumbling chuckle onto the porch that surrounded their bedroom in Estyra. For a moment, she simply stood in the doorway, drinking in the sight of Farrendel and their son.

Farrendel hung upside down from one of the rafters that held up the porch roof. He slowly curled his body upward, making faces at the baby held against his chest the whole time. Fieran's eyes widened, mouth in a round O, as if in anticipation. At the top, Farrendel held himself still for a heartbeat, as if doing upside down sit ups while hanging from the ceiling and holding a baby was no feat whatsoever.

Then, Farrendel dropped, swinging both himself and Fieran to hang upside down once again all in a rush that earned him another peal of baby giggles. Farrendel kept steadying hands on the baby's back and head, so the movement didn't jostle him.

Again, Farrendel curled upward. Again, Fieran stared wide-eyed as Farrendel made faces at him. Then they whooshed down once more in a rush of giggles and chuckles and Farrendel's long hair flying in an arc.

As the strands of silver-blond hair brushed the porch floor, their fluffy orange cat Mustache—named for the white line on his upper lip that gave him a permanent milk mustache—pounced from where he had been sunning himself and trapped a lock of Farrendel's hair beneath his paws, tugging on it.

Farrendel winced, then glared down at the cat. With his attention no longer so focused on their son, his gaze finally flicked to where Essie stood in the doorway. "Why did we get the cat again?"

Essie grinned and pushed away from the doorjamb. "To get us both used to messes and hair pulling."

"Then he has served his purpose very well." Farrendel cradled Fieran with one hand, curled until he could grab the roof branch with the other, then swung lightly to land on his feet.

Now that Farrendel was right side up, Essie crossed the porch, stepping around the cat, and kissed him. "Good morning. Thank you for letting me get more sleep."

Sometimes she fed Fieran and stayed awake, even though it was a ridiculously early hour that Farrendel, and now Fieran, apparently considered the normal time to rise. On those mornings, Farrendel would go off by himself for his usual exercise session. But some days, Farrendel would take Fieran while she went back to bed for more, well-appreciated sleep.

"I hope we did not wake you." Farrendel sat cross-legged

and laid Fieran on a soft blanket spread out near the railing, several of his toys scattered about.

Essie eased to the floor next to Farrendel and rested her head on his shoulder. "No. Besides, I love waking to the sound of baby giggles and your laughter."

Farrendel picked up first a round wooden disk, then a spruce tree made of stone that Melantha had given them. He offered both to Fieran, giving an extra waggle to the wooden toy.

Still, Fieran wrapped his fingers around the stone tree, immediately jamming part of it into his mouth and gumming it.

Farrendel gave a sigh, shaking his head as if he couldn't understand why his son preferred something made of stone over wood.

The stone tree was perfectly smooth, its branches rounded so that there were no sharp tips for Fieran to hurt himself. Even the top of the stone tree was extra pudgy, the whole thing looking like a dumpy, squat tree rather than a tall spindly thing, so that Fieran couldn't jam it into his mouth so far that he choked. The stone itself was laced with Melantha's magic so that it would not harm Fieran.

It was convenient that Fieran liked his stone toys. They had a small healing stone that they secured to his ankle whenever they entered Winstead Palace, just to be on the safe side. Instead of fighting them when they put it on, Fieran acted like it was some challenging game to twist around to put the stone at his ankle in his mouth.

Nose wrinkling, Farrendel plucked at his shirt, holding a large, damp section away from his skin. It smelled of sour milk, and had the clumpy, off-white look of baby spit up.

She could tell him that maybe Fieran wouldn't spit up so much on him if he didn't hang him upside down, but she didn't. Fieran enjoyed it too much, and he spit up on her while right side up just as much, so it likely didn't make a difference. "Do you need to go shower?"

While Farrendel was better at tolerating messes than he had been, his anxious need to be clean was still there. How long it took depended on how good a day he was having.

Farrendel released his shirt, lifting his head as if forcing himself to ignore it. "Not yet."

Fieran's eyes—a blue that was darker than the silver-blue of Farrendel's eyes—flicked between them at the sound of their voices. He continued industriously gumming the tree. Half of it was now thoroughly covered with slobber, and a glob of drool worked its way down Fieran's cheek.

Essie reached out and tickled Fieran's stomach, the fabric of his elven-style shirt and trousers soft and silken beneath her fingers. He smiled around the stone tree, kicking his tiny little legs.

Their son. She still couldn't get over his perfect little toes, tiny little fingers, and, most of all, his adorable little elf ears that even now were visible through the short strands of the red hair for which he had been named.

That red hair. It stuck up in several inches of the most untamable floof imaginable. No amount of water could get it to lie flat. Nope, her son was a little elf wild child.

Essie could feel Farrendel's growing tension in the muscles of his shoulder. She reached for his hand, squeezing his fingers. "What are you worrying about this morning?"

"His future." Farrendel held out his hand and released a cascade of gentle, magical sparks over Fieran.

Fieran dropped the tree and stretched for the sparks. He closed his fist around one, the spark fizzling out before he had even fully closed his fingers. Not deterred, Fieran stuffed his whole fist into his mouth.

"What about his future?" Essie tickled Fieran's toes as he reached for another spark, his whole face puckering as if in confusion that he couldn't seem to get the sparks into his mouth before they disappeared.

"I know how hard it was, being different. I had the taint of being illegitimate always hanging over me." Farrendel sighed, reaching out to brush his fingers over the top of Fieran's poof of red hair. "Fieran is half-elf, half-human. He will always be torn between two kingdoms, two peoples, and never fully fit in with either one of them. It will not be easy."

No, it wouldn't. And she didn't want to just tritely brush aside that concern. "I know. It will be up to us to prepare him as best we can and teach him about both sides of his heritage. We will provide him with an abundance of love so that he always knows he can find shelter and safety with family, even when everything else is hard. I know that there are things we won't be able to predict or prepare for. And we likely won't ever really understand what he goes through, being elf and human as he is. But we will love each other and love him, and that is the best thing we can do, in the end."

Farrendel nodded, though he didn't look at her. He pinched the stone tree at a yet unslobbered part and handed it back to Fieran.

Fieran's eyes widened, as if he had never seen that stone tree before in his life, and grabbed it, turning it over in his tiny fingers to study it, before stuffing the stone back into his mouth.

Essie turned to better face Farrendel, touching his cheek. "Besides, he will not be alone in facing that struggle, more than likely. If he does get any more cousins, all of them will either be elf and troll, human and troll, or human and elf. Only Ryfon, Brina, Bertie, and Finn are fully elf or fully human."

Finally, the hint of a smile creased Farrendel's face. "True. At least Fieran will not have the burden of inheriting a crown, as Rharreth's and Melantha's child will someday. He can be in the public eye as often or as little as he wishes."

"Exactly." Essie didn't mention that Fieran would also be titled and wealthy enough to never have to worry for anything a day in his life. She might be an optimist who saw the world through naïve, rose-colored glasses, but she was realistic enough to know that titles and riches would make Fieran's life much easier than that of a half-elf, half-human born to peasant parents, just as Farrendel's title had erased many of the barriers he would have normally faced due to the stigma of illegitimacy.

It was natural as a parent to worry. But Essie had to believe that Fieran would be all right. He would grow up well-loved and find his place, just as she and Farrendel had. Farrendel would be there for him, when he came into his magic and had to learn to handle the immense power. She would be there to smother him with hugs and kisses until she embarrassed him.

Fieran's face puckered again, and he waved his arms, giving the first sniffling cries that meant he was hungry. The stone tree flew from his slobber-slick hand, sailing far enough that it nearly hit Mustache. The cat scrambled away and raced the length of the porch before he jumped onto the railing, settling with huffy dignity into a patch of sunlight.

"Time to feed him again." Essie straightened, letting go of Farrendel's hand.

"Then I will shower." Farrendel jumped to his feet. After hesitating a moment, he peeled off his shirt, pinching it with two fingers and holding it away from him as if it was contaminated with a deadly substance.

But, instead of dashing away to wash away the baby spit, Farrendel leaned over, cupped Essie's face with his free hand, and kissed her, the strands of his long silver-blond hair falling around them.

Essie rested her hand on the bare skin of his chest, over the patchwork of scars and the fierce heart of a warrior that beat beneath, and kissed him back, trying to ignore the way Fieran's cries were building into a scream for just a moment longer.

Farrendel broke off their kiss with a wince, his head leaning sideways. Dropping his soiled shirt to the floor, he picked up Fieran, who had grabbed a fistful of Farrendel's hair and was tugging at it, alternating between stuffing the ends in his mouth and scream-crying.

Holding the baby out as far as he could with Fieran still clutching his hair, Farrendel gave him a pretend stern look. "You do not respect an elf warrior's hair as you ought. Thanks to you, I am thinking about chopping it off again."

Fieran's cries halted for just a moment, huge tears rolling down his face, before he went back to wailing, tugging even harder on Farrendel's hair.

"He's a baby. I don't think he's going to listen to you." Essie stifled a laugh as she pushed to her feet. Fieran's cries tugged at her heart, even though she knew he was perfectly fine.

"Worth a try. We are supposed to be teaching him about his heritage, after all." Farrendel held Fieran out to her, his head still tilted under Fieran's yanking. "Could you?"

She laughed and reached to disentangle their son's small, but surprisingly strong fingers from her husband's hair.

DON'T MISS THE NEXT ADVENTURE!

SHIELD BAND

Look for Julian's story in *Shield Band* (Elven Alliance Book 6), releasing in 2022!

FREE BOOK!

Thanks so much for reading *Pretense*! I know many of you have been waiting for Edmund and Jalissa's romance for several books now, and I hope it didn't disappoint! If you loved the book, please consider leaving a review on Amazon or Goodreads. Reviews help your fellow readers find books that they will love.

If you want to learn about all my upcoming releases, get great book recommendations, and see a behind-the-scenes glimpse into the writing process, follow my blog at www.taragrayce.com.

If you sign up for my newsletter, you'll receive a free novella, *Elf Prince* (*Elven Alliance* Book 1.5). This novella shows the beginning of *Fierce Heart* from Farrendel's point of view.

Farrendel Laesornysh, prince of the elves, never expected he would marry, much less that he would marry a human princess.

When a marriage alliance is the appeasement the humans of Escarland demand, this marriage is a price Farrendel is willing to pay, even if it is probably a trick by the humans for some devious purpose. It is either marriage or war, and Farrendel has already killed enough for a lifetime.

The human princess is probably a spy. Or an assassin sent to kill him on his wedding night. Yet if he can make this marriage work, as his grandmother seems to think, it might be the first breath of hope Farrendel has had in over a decade.

Sign up for my newsletter now

You will also receive the free novella *Steal a Swordmaiden's Heart*, which is set in the same world as *Stolen Midsummer Bride* and *Bluebeard and the Outlaw*!

Also by Tara Grayce

ELVEN ALLIANCE SERIES

Fierce Heart

War Bound

Death Wind

Troll Queen

Pretense

STOLEN BRIDES OF THE FAE

Stolen Midsummer Bride

A VILLAIN'S EVER AFTER

Bluebeard and the Outlaw

PRINCESS BY NIGHT

Lost in Averell

LIST OF CHARACTERS

Book 1 - Fierce Heart:

- Ashenifela – Essie's horse
- Averett – king of Escarland (humans)
- Brina – daughter of Weylind and Rheva. Princess of the elves. Younger sister to Ryfon
- Daesyn – human man from elf legends who formed a heart bond with the elven princess Inara
- Edmund – prince of Escarland. Brother to Averett, Julien, and Essie
- Ellarin – late king of Tarenhiel. Late husband of Leyleira. Father of Lorsan.
- Elspeth – princess of Escarland. Nickname: Essie. Younger sister of Averett, Julien, and Edmund
- Farrendel – prince of Tarenhiel. Younger brother to Weylind, Melantha, and Jalissa
- Illyna – a friend of Farrendel that he made during the war.
- Inara – elf princess from legends who formed a heart bond with the human Daesyn
- Jalissa – princess of Tarenhiel. Sister to Weylind, Melantha, and Farrendel
- Julien – prince of Escarland. Brother to Averett, Edmund, and Essie
- Leyleira – former queen of Tarenhiel.

Grandmother to Weylind, Melantha, Jalissa, and Farrendel. Great-grandmother of Ryfon and Brina

- Lorsan – late king of Tarenhiel. Father to Weylind, Melantha, Jalissa, and Farrendel. Son of Leyleira.
- Master Wendee – chief diplomat for Escarland (humans)
- Melantha – princess of Tarenhiel. Sister to Weylind, Melantha, and Farrendel
- Paige – queen of Escarland. Wife of Averett. Good friends with Essie.
- Rheva – queen of Tarenhiel and Weylind's wife
- Ryfon – son of Weylind and Rheva. Crown prince of Tarenhiel. Brother to Brina
- Vianola – late queen of Tarenhiel. Mother to Weylind, Melantha, and Jalissa.
- Weylind – king of Tarenhiel (elves)

Book 1.5 – Elf Prince

- Fingol – friend of Farrendel's from the war. Skilled with carving wood
- Iyrinder – bodyguard for Weylind.
- Sindrel – chief diplomat for the elves

Book 2 – War Bound

- Albert – Nickname: Bertie. Essie's oldest nephew. Son of Averett and Paige.
- Charles Hadley – owns the largest weapons manufacturing factory in Escarland. Father to Mark Hadley

- General Freilan – Escarland's top general/head of the armies
- Lance Marion – human inventor friend of Essie's and Farrendel's
- Lord Bletchly – one of the lords in Parliament
- Lord Crelford – one of the lords in Parliament
- Lord Fiskre – an elderly lord in Parliament
- Lord Kranshaw – one of the lords in Parliament who actively hates elves
- Mark Hadley – Son of Charles Hadley.
- Phineas – Nickname: Finn. Essie's youngest nephew. Son of Averett and Paige
- Thanfardil – elf in charge of the train system

Book 3 – Death Wind

- Charvod – king of the trolls. Older brother to Rharreth.
- Hatharal – Melantha's former betrothed
- Maxwell – head army surgeon for Escarland
- Nylian – head elf healer
- Rharreth – prince of the trolls. Younger brother of Charvod.
- Vorlec – late troll king whom Farrendel killed fifteen years before Fierce Heart

Book 4 – Troll Queen

- Brynjar - a male troll warrior who is a member of Rharreth's shield band
- Darvek - a male troll warrior who is a member of Rharreth's shield band.

- Doctors Harwell – husband and wife team of doctors specializing in trauma counseling
- Drurvas Regdrir – Rharreth's cousin and member of Rharreth's shield band
- Eugene Merrick – human captain assigned to guard Farrendel. Brother to Miss Merrick
- Eyvindur Gruilveth - a male troll warrior who is a member of Rharreth's shield band
- Ezrec – Zavni's father
- Inersha – troll woman who helps Rharreth and Melantha. Wife of Mymrar
- Leonard Harrington – magical engineering professor at Hanford University
- Lerrasah – Zavni's mother
- Miss Merrick – Essie and Farrendel's cook and housekeeper. Younger sister of Captain Merrick
- Mymrar – troll man who helps Rharreth and Melantha. Husband of Inersha
- Nirveeth - a male troll warrior who is a member of Rharreth's shield band.
- Taranath – Rheva's father and former head elf healer
- Vriska – a female troll warrior who is a member of Rharreth's shield band
- Zavni Rindrin – a male troll warrior who is a member of Rharreth's shield band

Book 5 – Pretense

- General Bloam – Edmund's boss in the Escarlish Intelligence Office

- Merellien Halmar – elf lord Jalissa thinks about marrying
- Sarya – Jalissa's loyal bodyguard
- Trent Bourdon – reporter at the *Aldon Times*. Acquaintance/friend of Edmund's

LIST OF ELVISH

- Amir – prince
- Amirah – princess
- Dacha – father (informal)
- Daresheni – Most honored king (or more literally, great king)
- Elishina – heart bond
- Ellonahshinel – heart of the forest
- Elontiri – welcome, greetings, hello
- Eshinelt - green paint used in elven wedding ceremonies
- Isciena – sister
- Laesornysh – death on the wind
- Linshi – thank you
- Macha – mother (informal)
- Machasheni – grandmother
- Sason – son
- Sasonsheni - grandson
- Sena – daughter
- Senasheni – granddaughter
- Shashon – brother
- Shynafir – fierce heart

ACKNOWLEDGMENTS

Thank you to everyone who made this release possible! To my writer friends, especially Molly, Morgan, and Addy for always being willing to fangirl over Essie and Farrendel with me! Thanks also to Savannah for the amazing cover and for the title, to Sierra for being my critique partner even when I start churning out books faster than you can read them, and to the entire Spinster Aunt gang for helping me to grow so much as an author. I would not be where I am without you guys! A special thanks to H.S.J. Williams for being my tortured elf partner in crime!

A special thanks to my dad and mom for encouraging me to follow my dreams, my sis-in-law Abby for inspiring so much of Essie, and my brothers for being even more amazing brothers than Essie's are. And to my twin-in-law Alyssa, for re-reading the Elven Alliance series even more times than I have. To my baby niece for inspiring Fieran's floofy hair and my nephews for being the best nephews an aunt could ask for! To Bri, Paula, and Jill for celebrating every release and milestone with me. To my proofreaders Tom, Mindy, and Deborah, thanks so much for tackling all my typos.

And, once again, thank you, Readers! Thank you for picking up each book and making this series successful! Thanks to you, I have been able to live my dream of writing full time! I love receiving all of your emails and messages that show just how excited you are about each book!

Made in United States
Orlando, FL
11 December 2021

11504515R00290